EVERY YESTERDAY

New South Wales, Australia: Three sisters reconnect and forge new lives. Coming home to attend her mother's funeral, Daisy Sheldon discovers fond memories at the childhood cottage she must now sell, and decides to settle in the nearby town of Inlet Creek. But can a passionate romance with an older man offer the future she wants? After a tragedy, Maddie is torn: should she stay and help her father run the family's sheep farm, or pursue a new relationship with a man of mystery? When he learns about her past, will she face rejection? And the death of a dear relative is the catalyst that gives Lilly the time and space to rethink her life — and the need for a fresh start, leaving England for Inlet Creek and the comforts of family and home.

Books by Noelene Jenkinson
Published by Ulverscroft:

OUTBACK TREASURE
HANNAH'S HOLIDAY
MAGGIE'S GARDEN

SPECIAL MESSAGE TO READERS

THE ULVERSCROFT FOUNDATION
(registered UK charity number 264873)

wa~~s established in 1972 to~~ provide funds for
resea

- re
  I
- at
  (
- d
  t   y,
  1
- p,
  ]
- rn
  (
- al
  ~

You   n
    I
Eve   l
  wc
    r(

T

Tel: (0116) 236 4325

website: ~www.foundation.ulverscrof~t.com

NOELENE JENKINSON

EVERY YESTERDAY

Complete and Unabridged

AURORA
Leicester

First published in 2019

First Aurora Edition
published 2020

A catalogue record for this book is available
from the British Library.

ISBN 978–1–78782–253–5

Published by
F. A. Thorpe (Publishing)
Anstey, Leicestershire

Set by Words & Graphics Ltd.
Anstey, Leicestershire
Printed and bound in Great Britain by
T. J. International Ltd., Padstow, Cornwall

This book is printed on acid-free paper

Dedication

'The love between sisters has been there for every yesterday'

These are the first lines of a poem by Carol Thomas in a book 'Sisterhood' given to me by my sister for a birthday some years ago.

I dedicate this book to my own sister of **every yesterday** — Valerie June.

You're in my heart.

PART I — DAISY

1

Still jetlagged after flying home from her freelance assignment in the Azores, Daisy Sheldon endured the lonely agony and deep sense of loss as her mother, Ailie's, warm-hued woodgrain coffin was lowered into the grave.

Alongside, gold lettering gleaming on shiny grey headstones, already sleeping for eternity, was her mother's quiet staunch sister, Aunt Mae, with dearly loved and sorely missed Granny Sheldon. Three strong and unconventional women who had raised Daisy, moulded her character and encouraged her dreams. Their inspirational spirits now the stars that would forever shine bright and guide her life.

Around her the sparse crowd gathered in respectful silence as the local minister's firm voice echoed on the breeze in the bush. The small number in attendance testament to the independent life her mother had lived. Never deliberately seeking friends, content in her own company, even after Granny and Mae died, happy and busy living alone on the small fifty acre farm.

But Daisy knew her mother would never have wanted nor chosen to be far from ex-husband, George Harwood.

This tiny country community lay secluded in unspoiled hinterland not half an hour from the spectacular southern coastline of New South

Wales, the region today blessed by a welcome burst of warm spring sun. Three generations of Sheldon women had instinctively sought this natural environment. Daisy was touched by a different kind of sadness than grief knowing she would not continue the tradition, and be the last. Over the years, as if to prepare her, she had warned her mother of the likelihood that her daughter would never live here but Ailie had seemed neither surprised nor disappointed.

Standing around the grave, the ceremony almost complete, Daisy allowed herself a moment of brief glances. Some local village faces she recognised, others not.

And then there was George, her mostly absentee father, hardworking and remote, rubbing shoulders beside her. At one point he almost caused her collapse when without a spoken word he gently squeezed her hand. The rare gesture touched her heart because he was not a demonstrative man. Despite being remarried, he was equally devastated over his first wife's passing.

He was here and only that mattered. His second daughter and her stepsister Maddie had accompanied him in from their outback sheep station west of Goulburn and filled Daisy's heart with an unexpected emotional lift.

At the sight of George upon arrival in the small stone church she had stifled her own emotions and the empty gaping hole inside her. Seeing the desolation on her father's face as she sat alongside him. The grinding jaw fighting his stoic outback male emotions. Suffering, too, she

4

supported him as his heart silently broke at having to farewell the love of his life.

'I'm so sorry, my dear,' he leaned over in the pew and whispered generously as he and Maddie had sat beside her in the front of the church.

'Me too. For you.'

He looked pale and ill. Understandable. But she worried for him. Because she travelled so much, she had rarely seen her father in recent years. Shocked, this time she realised the active outdoor man she remembered had severely aged. Or was it the haunting aftermath of Ailie's death?

The cold heartless bitch, Elizabeth, he had married after her own free spirited mother left him had dutifully given him two more daughters but, as far as Daisy knew, love had not accompanied that union. At least on Elizabeth's part. And perhaps impossible, too, for George when Ailie had always held his heart.

Elizabeth Harwood remained at home in her comfortable homestead inland, ever hateful of George's first wife and daughter. Although why Ailie and Daisy should have irritated her, Daisy could never fathom. They were hardly any threat, their lives so dissimilar as to be laughable.

Three daughters for sheep station owner George Harwood, no sign of the son and heir he must have craved, surely a hidden bittersweet pill of regret. None of his children showed any interest in running *Georgina Downs* alongside him. Not even Maddie who loved the outdoors so much and had to be prised from a horse.

George loved his daughters but a son would have been the ultimate hereditary prize. Maybe

5

there was yet hope in his only toddler grandson, Tommy, although that likelihood was still too far ahead to contemplate.

The graveside service ended, fellow mourners approached, murmured their condolences and left.

Although they shared rare childhood memories but never lived under the same roof and had not seen each other in years, Daisy's stepsister Maddie moved forward and gave her a warm meaningful hug. As if respectfully sensing their joint need for father and oldest daughter to have a moment alone, Maddie walked on, trailing the others leaving the cemetery while George lingered beside the offspring of his one true love.

'Staying for a cuppa?' she murmured.

George nodded. 'We should talk. Do you have time later?'

'Of course. Back at the cottage?' she suggested.

'As you want.'

'It won't be easy,' she warned, knowing that returning to Ailie's place, the scene of their past regular meetings, would tear his heart.

He scowled and mumbled, 'I know.'

'This past week was dreadful. The memories,' Daisy sighed. 'There's so much to go through but I can't focus long enough to start.'

She had learned after Granny Sheldon and Aunt Mae's deaths that you never fully recovered from a loved one's loss. And now Ailie. Her Mum. Daisy forced herself to remember only happy nostalgic memories and she clung to them with stubborn determination.

As Daisy pulled up a short time later in the dependable old farm ute, a cluster of cars was already parked in front of the church hall, its double cream painted timber doors flung wide welcoming the thin warmth of early spring sun.

There was no longer a town here. Only its remains. A single road meandered through. Iconic white posts stood either end of the football oval. The small stone church and attached timber hall, a necessity of larger families and greater populations in days past still thrived, both vital sporting and social outlets for the community. Old Ed's service station with its single fuel bowser survived, as did the weatherboard hotel, although long since closed and uninhabited. The handful of other derelict houses either rented now or beyond repair.

Locals shopped further afield at Nowra, half an hour north, or Inlet Creek the same distance away along winding roads down to the coast. The seaside village aroused its own memories.

Daisy coped with the gathering of locals, greetings, bottomless cuppas and generous afternoon tea provided by the district ladies but felt detached from it all. Her return visits to the farm in recent years were usually rare and fleeting before she flew off again on another assignment. Soon, with chats done, everyone gradually left, the hall grew silent and empty once more, the ladies cleaned up in the kitchen and the doors were shut.

Driving back to the farm cottage, Daisy sped ahead of George and Maddie in their big four wheel drive. They knew the way. The Sheldon farm was merely part of a rural district now tucked away in peaceful countryside shadowed by the stunning southern tablelands.

Lakes and rivers wound through the country-side, most finding their way to the sea, frothy white and pink blossom in orchards promising a feast of heavy fruit.

Turning in at the farm gate, Daisy was gripped by a pang of loneliness that she discovered assaulted her each time she returned home now. The humble fieldstone cottage was hidden behind barely visible rustic timber fencing and a prolific overgrown garden that both screened and pro-tected its setting. Every inch of well-turned and nurtured soil had always been planted with some-thing that flowered or produced food. Brick path paving wound between floral borders, climbing roses scrambled over fences and walls. Bees loved it all.

Further out beneath the fruit trees in the orchard paddock, native wildflowers including her namesake daisies spread their colour among the trunked feet of apples, apricots, mulberries and peaches.

Daisy stepped from the car to adore it all and daydream, inhaling every perfume, aware of the light breeze rustling through, backed by the sounds of honey eaters and lorikeets.

'It's been a while.' Maddie's voice jolted Daisy from reflection. Engrossed in visual thought, she had hardly heard them arrive. 'Still pretty much as I remember it though.' Maddie paused and her voice softened. 'Mother detested Lilly and I coming here occasionally with Dad but we so loved it.'

8

Daisy pulled a half smile. 'Lilly usually stayed inside but you either got lost or disappeared for ages when you came to visit.'

'There was so much to explore. It was exciting.' Maddie was smiling. Turning to Daisy, she added, 'Are you all right here?'

She nodded. 'Everything's in order actually. Mum lived simply. Her footprint on earth was light. It's just going to be hard sorting those possessions she treasured and actually kept, you know?' She slowly shook her head and rubbed her arms. 'I have no idea where I'm going next. Where my home or base might be.' When George appeared behind them, she glanced between both. 'Come in.'

'Actually, if you don't mind I'd love a wander,' Maddie said. 'Memory lane and all that. I shouldn't be too long. We have time don't we, Dad?'

'Of course. You're driving. We'll leave when you want,' he said with typical bluntness.

'Got your mobile in case you get lost?' Daisy teased.

Maddie grinned and Daisy watched her stepsister's sure-booted feet pick their way confidently around the cottage corner. Her long brunette hair swung about her shoulders, the bottom edges of her cardigan trailing over foliage as she walked away. Strange to see her in a dress instead of her usual jeans, shirt and jaunty black Akubra.

Indoors, Daisy flung the net curtains aside from the sitting room windows, letting light flood across the comfortable sofas and chairs, loaded with colourful cushions and draped with soft crocheted knee rugs. All Granny's work. Daisy sighed, trailing her fingers over them.

She guessed George had taken in enough cups of tea and would appreciate a nip of something stronger. She knew his favourite and Ailie always kept a bottle in the pantry for his visits. She found it and splashed a generous shot of the French brandy into two small cut glasses her mother had found at a jumble sale.

'Nothing will replace her,' George murmured bleakly as Daisy returned to see him holding a framed photograph of himself, Ailie and Daisy. The last one ever taken of them together some years before. He looked around as they clinked glasses and each sank into opposite seats.

Her father was still a handsome man and it was a rare treat to see the big outback man in a suit and tie. But although still physically strong, emotional loss perhaps had etched deeper lines into his suntanned face. Always short on conversation, Daisy wondered why George wanted to chat.

'I had the most glorious childhood here,' she said, as much to distract him as help her own sorrow. 'Despite few men about the house except for your visits, we were poor as church mice but always busy in a good way. There was poultry to be fed after school, Aunt Mae milked our few cows and ran a few sheep, and until Granny couldn't manage the garden any more, we had the most abundant crops of every vegetable from the garden and orchard. Such freedom.' She sighed.

'Until the coldest of bleak weather drove us inside, Granny and I spent most evenings out on the veranda, reading and chatting. She would challenge and question me on every topic and issue. Nothing was off limits. Mae would be in the kitchen making jam or bottling something and Mum cooked until she dropped. The pantry shelves and half cellar beneath the house always groaned with preserves.'

While George quietly sipped his drink, content to let someone else talk, she discovered it therapeutic to reminisce. At nights out here since returning, loneliness had become a burden. It was so nice to have company even though she knew her father and Maddie must leave soon. She cherished his company while she could. He was her only family now. But she wondered if her stepsisters might be in the background of her life, too. She had no one else. Elizabeth would surely have an opinion on that subject and discourage it.

'When Granny died I was heartbroken. She virtually raised me.' Daisy smiled in memory. No slur on Ailie who by mutual agreement became the breadwinner. 'Even when she was old, Granny ignored Ailie and Mae's protests and still puddled in the garden, sneaking seedlings or cuttings into any available space. She sometimes went missing but always returned brown and weary. When she was gardening she forgot time. In winter, unbelievably, the garden and Granny rested. She read all day. Stoked the fire. Baked. Made me stand beside her to watch and learn.'

'I wish that life had been lived with me,'

11

George muttered unkindly with savage regret.

With his drink all gone, Daisy assumed it was just the alcohol talking. Nothing anyone could do about it now. She leaned forward, rested a hand gently on his arm and took his glass, ignoring his bitter remark. 'Refill?'

'Why not? Maddie's driving,' he snapped.

Treading lightly, Daisy forced herself to speak of her mother, closely watching her father in case her nostalgia became too much for him.

'When she wasn't away working in pub kitchens or cooking on pastoral stations at shearing time, Ailie and I poured over an atlas and read about other countries. She didn't have the money to travel but encouraged me to higher education and opportunity.'

'She refused every penny I offered,' George pointed out with dented pride.

'I know. Pride.' Daisy paused. 'She wanted me to fly beyond the shores because she didn't. So I travelled abroad.' She chuckled. 'Growing up in a household of women who only drank tea leaves steeped in a pot, it seemed natural I became a travel writer specialising in the subject. I've seen most of the countries Ailie and I talked about, and where tea is grown.'

'Do you remember much of *Georgina Downs?*'

'Vaguely,' Daisy admitted with blunt honesty. 'Ailie always seemed to be in the garden and outdoors.'

With the station property being his sole focus above everything else, even family, perhaps it was important to George that she had childhood memories of it.

'Your mother designed the structure and planted the bones of the homestead garden,' he said, sounding his old positive self for the first time today. 'Thirty years later it's a beautiful haven in the outback that Elizabeth shows off at her garden parties for charity as though she created it herself,' he said harshly. 'That's how you got your nickname, of course. Outside romping about with your mother.' George stopped for a moment, clearly pained by reflections. 'Going off into the paddocks in spring making daisy chains with her.'

'I loved them. Still do. They're so hardy and colourful. Miles and miles of them. Ailie sat down with me while bees buzzed around us.'

'When she wanted to name you Harmony, I wasn't in favour but loved her so much I gave in.'

'The name didn't last long anyway. Few people know or use it.'

Daisy was heartened that George shared his own memories, too. Uniting in sadness was comforting.

His fond fatherly glance scrolled over her but Daisy wondered if her blonde olive-skinned likeness to Ailie hurt him. She never felt less in his eyes although others judged her in childhood because she was different in second hand or homemade clothes. Her forthright confidence had caused trouble in the classroom but boots were more practical on the farm than designer sneakers anyway. As long as her bare body was covered, she never cared much with what.

Daisy's height came from George. Growing up, she sensed the towering sun browned man as distant but protective. Ailie always smiling and breathless with excitement when he returned to the homestead whether he had been away for one day or many. Her parents had been openly loving and affectionate with each other and, for a few years at least, their family was secure and happy.

But even small, Daisy picked up on her mother's growing sadness. There were no raised voices, just anguished conversations, overheard by a child listening at the door.

You're never here. I need you. I must get away. I can't stay in one place.

And his returning deep voice. *You have Daisy here.* Silence, then *You'll break my heart.*

Then her mother's soft anguished reply. *This place is breaking my spirit.*

So Ailie and Daisy moved back onto the Sheldon farm with Granny and single Mae.

After a long silence, Daisy frowned. 'Ailie really hurt you, didn't she?'

'When you love deeply, it's a risk you take. But I needed you both in my life.'

'Did Elizabeth know?'

'Of course, but in true British tradition she said nothing. Just stayed cold and composed.'

'Is that why she travelled back to her family in England so much?'

'No. Our marriage was over and just window dressing for the public image so important to her.'

'I'm sorry.'

'Not your fault my dear. My own unfortunate choice.' Deserted by bohemian Ailie, George had remarried for social prestige. 'But Elizabeth gave me two more children.'

'Not sons.'

'No.' He winced and stared at the floor.

'I loved it when you brought Maddie and Lilly to visit so we all at least knew each other. It gave me a sense of belonging to you beyond this cottage.'

'I wanted Maddie and Lilly to see that all families were different.'

'And to see Ailie,' she teased, hesitating before blurting out, 'Did you only come to visit my mother for the sex?'

George glared at her and knocked back another swig of brandy. 'Absolutely not,' he muttered fiercely. 'I loved her with such passion. Love her still, even though she is gone.'

'I watched you both wandering off across the paddock holding hands,' Daisy added, not judging but giving him a moment. 'As I grew older, I guessed why but Maddie and Lilly were younger and I doubt they understood.'

Her heart equally lifted for him that he had known such a deep love but also wrenched for him that he had been unfaithful, accepting such a tenuous passionate relationship with her mother yet, in contrast, enduring such bitter unhappiness with Elizabeth.

In the past before George's visits here after the divorce, Ailie beamed with such happiness. 'Daddy's coming,' she would say, filled with excitement.

As she grew older, Daisy asked, 'Why doesn't he live with us?'

15

'Because he lives on his sheep station,' was the usual reply.

Once, Daisy pushed it. 'But don't married people live together?'

'We're not married.'

'Why not?'

'Honestly,' Ailie had sighed, fighting a smile, trying to be serious, 'that grandmother of yours has much to answer. She's far too liberal.' Then paused a moment to reflect and explain. 'Because some people love each other but can't live together,' she bluntly explained.

Obviously George's visits had sustained Ailie. She left Daisy behind, often for weeks, with Granny and Aunt Mae, to travel the countryside doing what she loved. Cooking and catering on vast outback pastoral stations and anywhere she was needed, the breadwinner for the all-female family.

Aunt Mae and Ailie were illegitimate daughters of Granny and the only man she had apparently ever spoken of, Fred Sheldon, an itinerant labourer. A man Daisy had only ever seen in an old sepia photograph but never knew. Apparently Granny and Fred eventually married but he always disappeared again. Before Daisy was born, they had received word of his accidental death somewhere out in isolated country where he had been working.

In time, Ailie had married George. Disastrously but with great passion. Private resourceful Mae never socialised much and kept to herself. She had neither loved nor married. She scaled ladders, pruned trees, picked fruit and weeded everything

16

Granny couldn't. Each woman had ignored convention and followed their own path in life.

Guiding her thoughts back to more recent times, Daisy raised another matter. 'Does anyone else know about the beach shack?'

George scowled and shook his head. 'Only you, me and Ailie.' He put down his empty glass and rose, adding gruffly, 'Best keep it a secret.'

'Keep what a secret?'

Engrossed in their conversation, neither had heard Maddie walk in, flushed from her walk. George cleared his throat, briefly stumped. Daisy and her father exchanged an uncertain glance. She wasn't helping him out of this hole of his own making.

'We were just talking about our visits to Daisy and her mother here,' he lied.

'But Mother knew about them.' Maddie crossed her arms, frowning with reservation.

'Yes but it was against her wishes and you know she's touchy about any mention of my first marriage.'

'Of course but it shouldn't come up again. Now Ailie's gone,' Maddie added quietly with compassion, still clearly unconvinced by the explanation.

With the moment salvaged, George hugged Daisy tightly before they left but lingered. 'If you need anything,' he muttered.

Public affection didn't come easily to George but she knew he would always be there for her. 'I know.'

'Daisy.' Maddie hugged her too. 'We should keep in touch.'

'Sure.'

Daisy felt the offer was genuine but wondered how Elizabeth would take that news since the second Mrs. Harwood jealously guarded Maddie, her husband Aaron and their son Tommy who all lived together in the station homestead. Her youngest, Lilly, worked in the fashion industry and lived in England.

As the dusty four wheel drive backed out and drove away, Daisy wondered when she would see them again. With Ailie no longer here, there was no reason. But the bond between George and herself was enough that she believed they would maintain contact.

He was a good strong man, tough but fair. He inherited the pastoral estate from his own father and her grandfather, old Mac Harwood, and built it up by sheer hard work and ambition.

As an adult, Daisy realised she had never told crusty George, despite the separation of distance, he was not only her father but also idolised. The want born of a little girl who had always lived in Ailie's shadow. She simply hungered for some sign of his love and acceptance. Yes, he had done the right thing and attended Ailie's funeral, but for himself. Not so much for his oldest daughter. He had been bleak and distracted all day.

The knowledge and disappointment stung. She had a good mind to tell her stepsisters what she knew. But she wouldn't. It simply wasn't her nature to be spiteful and betray her father's promise.

Even though he had been unfaithful to his second wife. She sighed, excusing his actions on the premise that you couldn't help who you fell in love with and his second marriage was an unhappy disaster. Could you blame the man for seeking comfort elsewhere?

★ ★ ★

In the following weeks, Daisy worked room by room tidying and cleaning the farm cottage ready for sale. Leafed through Ailie's dog-eared and handwritten fat recipe books, baking as an escape to cope with her daily and sometimes overwhelming grief. Those precious volumes, more valuable than gold, she would never relinquish.

She was unprepared for her other work of handling and sorting her mother's few personal possessions. Deciding what to keep and wondering where on earth she would store it all. Touching and folding Ailie's clothes, remembering when she wore them and pressing them to her face to inhale her smell.

With Ailie's death and a jumble of memories still raw in her heart, Daisy felt lost and the need to stay close to family. Couldn't bring herself to even entertain the thought of leaving and heading out into the world again. Not yet.

Instead, she regularly visited, brought wildflowers from the farm garden and tended the three women's graves in the small country cemetery where she had so recently laid her mother to rest. Wandered the rows of high ornate headstones denoting the deeply Christian or wealthy and those of simpler folk like Granny,

Mae and Ailie whom she loved so much.

As to Daisy's future plans, the farm held so many memories but there was no question she must sell because she wasn't a farmer and held no interest in the property anyway. A tribute to her mother's stamina that she operated it alone even as she aged. Besides, there was lots to sort and do before any sale.

One thing she knew, this unassuming little property was valuable. Purely from curiosity, she had phoned one real estate agent in Inlet Creek and almost collapsed, speechless, when he started talking seven figures. But the farm's worth extended far beyond its material value.

What on earth would she do with that kind of money? Invest and sit on it as a nest egg to secure her future when she tired of travelling? But she didn't know what she wanted that to be just yet.

Needing more social interaction, Daisy knew she would be too lonely living out here and, although her childhood had been free and bucolic, the property also held bittersweet memories. Everywhere she looked, each room she entered, reminded her of the three awesome females in her life all now missing. Only images on photographs or memories in her mind.

Daisy had made some friendships through her travels and work in Australia and abroad but few remained close. There were no ties leading her anywhere else in particular so, assuming the true Sheldon approach, she trusted fate would step in to guide her.

And waited. To see where life led her next.

2

For weeks Daisy hardly saw another soul. No locals, probably barely remembering her, came to visit and there had been no word from George or Maddie since Ailie's funeral, not that she particularly expected it. She had only ever been on the edges of their lives. Besides at this time of year, the Harwood pastoral station would be busy shearing thousands of sheep.

Meanwhile she had methodically worked through the cottage. All the cupboards were virtually empty now, the interior looking rather chaotic, increasingly bare and sad, the pantry and cellar preserves boxed or crated to go somewhere. But where? The whole time Daisy sorted and packed up, she had mulled more than anguished about her future. Sheldon women didn't anguish. They sorted stuff out.

In the back of an old timber cupboard, she had been delighted to find all of Granny's tea sets neatly stacked together. Dozens of pieces of gorgeous floral collectible china the Sheldon women had used all their lives. Ailie had never believed in possessions, worked hard and lived simply but these keepsakes belonging to her mother she had treasured and carefully stored. Daisy's inheritance to be equally cherished.

Which only raised yet again the eternally recurring question. Where would she store it all once she sold the farm?

Since returning home, such as the cottage was to her now, Daisy had lived off the garden's bounty, in her sorrow feeling no particular need of people. Like her mother, embracing travel and new experiences but, for the moment anyway, content enough in her own company. Yet the restless feet she had always heeded were telling her that right about now she needed a change of scenery. If nothing else, to blow away the cobwebs of memories that hung heavily about her since Ailie's funeral and isolation of living on the farm.

So Daisy decided to take a day off. Or two.

Inevitably, the pull and connection to Inlet Creek since talking to George after the funeral had reopened memories, tempting her down to the coast to revisit the seaside village of her childhood.

Locking up the cottage and packing an overnight bag in case she stayed in town, she turned the ute out of the farm gate and headed for the sea. The scenic half hour drive to Jervis Bay wound through lush countryside before joining the highway. Further on, eucalypt forest and a bracken understory hugged the road as she turned east for the run across to the coast. And that first tantalising glimpse of the South Pacific Ocean from the rise above town.

Daisy had not actually returned here for years. In the past whenever she came home between travels, it was usually only for a matter of days on the farm to spend precious time with Granny, Ailie and Aunt Mae. One by one now all gone. A wave of aching loss rolled through her chest and she choked back a sob, practising her steady breathing to help ease the yearning until it passed.

Intuitively as she entered the outskirts of town, she slowed down to fully absorb and reacquaint herself with the busy village. Inlet Creek had grown to become quite the little seaside hub. It was positively humming. Yet it was still early spring and not even tourist season when a chill wind could still whip in off the sea, deterring all but the locals and hardiest travellers.

Grey nomads hauled caravans behind powerful four wheel drives or SUVs, or drove motorhomes. Couples strolled hand in hand, children skipped around their parents as they strolled the narrow main street opposite the beach.

So many quaint shops and she was surprised to see one or two premises vacant. But no big stores she was pleased to note, allowing the village to retain its peaceful carefree charm. With no traffic lights and only the occasional roundabout, its lazy unhurried atmosphere survived.

Daisy manually wound down her window letting in a light salty breeze. She slowly cruised the length of the main street, turned and did it again. The Portside Hotel still thrived for cold beers and roast lunches, as did a small number of takeaways and eateries. The historic Seaview Hotel looked as though it had undergone a complete renovation and been transformed from its former shabby self.

She noticed the old boatshed, as she recalled

once drunkenly derelict and leaning into the sea, had been restored and painted as white as the beach sands that stretched for miles along the coast. The old shaky foundations must have taken some work. Denim blue windows, shutters and doors allowed it to blend into its surroundings and water's edge setting, its signage announcing its new life. The Boatshed Restaurant. Of course.

Inlet Creek now projected an air of fresh life without being overrun. Daisy felt relieved and heartened that the village progress had not destroyed its unique ambience of old.

Before going for a wander about the town itself, out of a driving need and curiosity, Daisy decided to investigate the Harwood family beach shack. If she hadn't forgotten the way. It was only accessed via an old rickety wooden bridge across the shallow stream where the town's namesake, Inlet Creek, met the sea. Mangroves hung over the water along its banks but at the river mouth, levels ebbed and flowed, creating warm shallow pools and tidal sandbars between stretches of soft white sand. Ideal for children and sheltered sunbathing with a park and picnic area beneath the trees.

Daisy filled with a sense of familiarity as she rattled over the bridge. A short time later, watching out for it, she turned into the concealed gravelled driveway amid low scrub that led to the shack.

She pulled up, turned off the engine and just sat awhile in the ute staring at it. Shack was misleading. It was anything but. This was no flimsy second class building but a substantial pale blue timber holiday house. All was quiet here at the rear, the dwelling's white shutters closed at every window.

Images flooded across Daisy's mind of winter days as a child here. They had been rare and perfect times taken for granted, now imprinted in her memory never to be forgotten. If she needed comfort, she only had to close her eyes or leaf through the small but precious bundle of old photos recently found at the cottage stuffed at the back of one of Ailie's cupboard drawers.

On a nostalgic sigh, Daisy turned the ute around and headed back into town. She glanced to her right and the bush block behind the beach house. Judging by the thin trail of smoke, old Harry still lived in his hut amid the native eucalypt bush. George used to go and visit him, two old blokes who seemed to know each other having a chat.

Back in town, Daisy found a space in the beach carpark, eased her long limbs from the ute and stretched, pushing on a pair of sunglasses against the day's sunny glare off the water.

Scanning every direction, her attention was captured by a nearby French boulangerie. Unusual of itself because it was one of few waterfront buildings along with the Surf Club and a beachside caravan park and camping complex further down, the beachfront reserved mostly for parks and playgrounds.

Outside the bakery, a traditional French ornate wrought iron street lamp with a light inside the glass lantern at the top gave the street-front extra character together with a simple black sign with gold lettering hanging underneath.

The enticing yeasty aroma of freshly baked breads wafting from inside the boulangerie and long queue extending to the front door told its own story so she joined it. Daisy had learnt years ago there was always a good reason why a Frenchman would stand in line to buy a baguette.

Inside, Daisy's baking eye and travels in France revealed this establishment as authentic. Shelves of traditional French breads revealed long crusty baguettes in cane baskets, egg and butter-rich brioche, rustic country loaves, the round wholemeal pain complet, plaited breads sprinkled with seeds and small rolls.

Also ready-made sandwiches, quiches and mini pizza together with eclairs and fruit tarts, all beautifully presented in small display cases on the counter.

To keep the customer line moving, two young girls and a slightly older guy wearing a white hat and apron, the baker himself perhaps, of a similar age to Daisy, moved with brisk efficiency serving and packaging orders into labelled brown paper bags.

Clearly the man's patrons didn't mind the wait as he flashed a slow easy smile in their direction. From beneath his hat, a few strands of dark wavy hair curled over his forehead, lightly beaded with perspiration. Now she had moved closer, she listened, charmed, to the sound of his rounded flowing French accent and received a cheeky sexy grin. He'd get on.

When he approached, her younger self might have melted into the floor. But she had been exposed to her share of charismatic Frenchmen. This man's casual banter was for everyone, not Daisy alone, so she thought nothing of it.

'Madamoiselle?'

Regardless, his quick flashing gaze took in every inch of her leggings, long stretchy top hugging her body almost to her knees, over which she wore a short denim jacket. Then his keen eye rose again to her wild blonde hair, extra messy because she had driven with the ute window down. Resisting his flirty attention, from habit Daisy automatically responded in his native language.

'Fougasse, s'il vous plait.' She allowed herself the indulgence of the savoury bread loaded with olives, sundried tomatoes, anchovies and herbs.

'Bien sûr,' he said softly, and with a swift controlled movements packaged her bread. 'Do you wish for something more?' he reverted to accented English.

'A mug of tea for takeaway, please.'

'Je suis désolé,' he grinned, with an accompanying shrug of his shoulders, not sorry at all. 'We sell only coffee.'

Continuing his teasing game, Daisy rolled her eyes playfully as though appalled before she grabbed a bottle of sparkling water from a nearby cold drinks cabinet and said, 'That's all. Merci.'

'Mangez bien,' he murmured as she left.

Once outside without turning around, she

sensed the Frenchman watch her leave. Her mood lifted from their brief exchange because the appealing baker had evoked memories of France and her extensive world travels, times of freedom and excitement. The sometimes hectic schedules between assignments. The nomadic life she had always known and loved.

It wasn't that she craved that life again just yet. It was just that Daisy realised for the first time in weeks she hadn't felt this happy over anything at all. Even such a simple light hearted exchange.

Which, sadly, only emphasized her solitary state when she took a seat on a bench overlooking the beach and glittering blue waters of the ocean rolling in low waves onto the sand before rushing out again.

She pulled apart her bread, eating reflectively, aware of the movement of life and people around her but the activity and noise were unnoticed as she sank into her own deep thoughts. Yes, she ate alone, but somehow the village hum felt familiar and reassuring. A comforting sensation that took her by surprise. She had needed this life around her again and was glad she came.

Still craving a hot cup of tea, she wandered across the street to a café. Seeing every table full and customers two and three deep at the counter, Daisy patiently waited to be served. She was in no hurry.

When her order was eventually taken, the flustered waitress apologised. 'Sorry. Really busy since the caf down the street closed last winter. Bill and Marj retired and no one's taken up the lease.'

Daisy smiled. 'I'm in no hurry.'

A few minutes later, sipping her refreshing mug of green tea, she strolled the single main street, impressed by the neat paving and landscaping along its length. On a whim, she peered in at the real estate agent's window. You never knew. Maybe a place would capture her eye. Then she shook herself back to reality because she had no idea where she wanted to be after she sold the farm. The agency also took accommodation bookings, she noted, so she decided to return later and find a bed for the night.

The squeaky white beach sands beckoned so she removed her shoes, dangling them from one hand with her hot drink in the other. The wind off the water whipped her long blonde hair about and, although chilled, Daisy felt invigorated. The air was so much fresher by the sea. Some equally brave souls, mostly excited chattering children, paddled or played in the shallows. Their sand-castles and channels, she noted with a wrinkled brow of amusement, had been built much too close to the water's edge and would be washed away with the incoming tide.

She decided to stride out on the damp sand above the waves to the rocky outcrop at the other end where Inlet Creek estuary joined the ocean. When she reached it, to her amazement she saw one hardy soul had stripped off, left a heap of clothes and a towel strewn over rocks, and was stroking out in a strong swim parallel to the beach. She was cheeky enough to peep closer. Jocks as well? Was the man swimming nude?

On a wicked impulse, she sat on the beach and hugged her knees. Be interesting to see his reaction when he emerged. Clearly this location was chosen for its seclusion. And judging by his slightly silvering grey hair, the swimmer wasn't young. Daisy wondered that it would have been safer swimming closer to town and not so far away from help should he need it. Must be invigorating on a fresh day this early in the season though.

Eventually the brave swimmer turned and swam for the beach. When he stood up in waist-high water and waded toward shore through the waves, he suddenly halted when he caught sight of Daisy on the beach. His shocked stare and raised eyebrows only lasted for a moment though, replaced with the hint of a grin. His firm muscles flexed as he brushed water back off his hair, his body graced by a light tan. Maybe in his fifties but certainly in good shape.

He raised an arm and called out. 'Don't want to alarm you but I'm in my birthday suit. I won't come out until you leave, all right?'

He held himself too proudly to be self-conscious. Intrigued, Daisy understood he was being a gentleman.

'Liberating, isn't it? I've done it myself.' Daisy pushed herself to her feet. 'Cold?'

'Not once you get in,' he chuckled deeply with a foxy smile.

When he waded closer and his hips grew visible, Daisy took it as a signal to leave and walked away toward town. She was sorely tempted to look back because he was a rather stunning physique for an older man, but resisted. If the bottom half was as enticing as the top it might have been worth risking a quick glance.

He reminded her of ageless older movie stars like Richard Gere, Kevin Costner and George Clooney. They still oozed loads of sex appeal. There was just something about them.

She sighed and grinned to herself. Another happy experience for the day. It had certainly been the right decision leaving the farm for a break.

Although it was growing late in the afternoon, before finding a bed for the night Daisy wandered out along the pier. A few fisherman sat on its edges waiting patiently for a tug on the line. Small fishing fleets, motor boats and yachts of every size were moored in the clear turquoise waters, larger commercial fishing trawlers anchored further out.

The bakery on the beachfront she noticed was already closed. He undoubtedly rose in the middle of the night as all bakers did and retired early. Her wrong assumption was soon disproved.

As she reached the end of the pier, she spied the appealing Frenchman tying up a small motor boat alongside. Somehow he deftly climbed the steps to the top while swinging a respectable catch from his fingers, his dark hair windswept, the relaxed look on his face one of contentment.

Idly, she wondered how he would cook the fish and what masterpiece he would create for dinner tonight. French chefs were well known for their culinary skills. The baker's talents surely extended into his own kitchen.

Observing her approach, his eyebrows raised in acknowledgement. He smiled easily and half raised an arm in greeting. 'Bonsoir.'

'Bravo,' she grinned as he passed, feeling a tug of disappointment that he had not at least paused to chat. But then they did not know each other and she had merely been just another customer in his bakery today.

Returning to the street and before heading to the real estate agent's office, Daisy stopped to stock up on a few extra supplies to cook her own dinner from the village produce market selling fresh seasonal foods to buy or swap, and a selection of baked goods. Almost as good as her own, Daisy thought cheekily, grinning to herself.

Moving on, she hesitated at the estate agent's window to scan the properties for sale and rent before going inside. She whistled softly to herself at the steep prices for vacant blocks of land and homes. A small new housing development and a holiday apartment complex were underway, and it appeared a new retirement village had opened recently, too.

Inside the office, Daisy had no trouble in the off season before summer finding a small timber cottage B&B on the edge of town for her overnight stay. Totally distracted by one particular advertisement and a wild possibility, her brain fired up with a crazy idea and she enquired about it.

At the B&B that night, she sat out on the veranda surveying the gentle but restless movement of the ocean as the sun sank into the horizon in a blaze of orange. The water's ebb and flow rather mirrored her own feelings at the moment.

Giving in to an unusual impatience, she grabbed some cottage notepaper from a small desk indoors. Rare for Daisy or indeed any Sheldon woman really to write out ideas for a plan. Having been raised that way, she normally winged it but this notion needed more serious thought. She was potentially playing with her future.

While waiting for her green tea leaves to brew in the cast iron Japanese teapot she had packed and brought along from the farm, she alternated between daydreaming and frowning and tapping her pen on the paper. Probably all wishful thinking. She would sleep on it.

Next morning, she remained pestered by the same thoughts that simply would not go away all night. Was this a sign? Was there something to it, after all? One way to find out. She would go and take a look. Why not? A quick investigation couldn't hurt.

So she didn't fight her instinct but meditated first on the front deck before she packed up the ute and ventured back to the estate agent. With a hand on the door knob, she took a deep breath and plunged inside. Emerging ten minutes later with a bunch of keys in her hand.

Daisy's heart pounded as shaky fingers pushed a key into the lock of the former café up for lease. Nice double French doors for entry. She stood still and whipped a glance around the entire premises in one sweep. Looked modern enough and structurally sound. Could do with a coat of paint, new tables and chairs to create the ambience she sought to achieve. But basically all the storage, refrigeration and facilities she needed were already there. And joy of joys, across the corner was an open brick fireplace. Its flames would throw out a blast of welcoming warmth in winter. If she made it that far.

Her mind spun with baking and food. There were enough cafes in town already serving coffee but she did not intend to be their competition. Estate agent Murray had told her that Bill and Marj had run a busy café seven days a week.

But while there were plenty of up market restaurants and bistros in town, including the Boatshed and the Portside pub, apparently, surprisingly, there was a lack of smaller establishments serving quick and healthy quality lighter sit down meals and fare. Daisy speculated why some enterprising person hadn't already snapped up the opportunity. So she was pleased to hear of the shortage and a gap in the town's hospitality market.

All the Sheldon women had simply loved tea. It had been a ritual. An event. With all of Granny's tea sets and her love and knowledge of baking passed down to the third generation, Daisy envisaged cakes, biscuits, muffins, light lunches, soup and damper. Maybe even stock some French boulangerie croissants and additional treats from across the street. Depending on the baker's agreement, of course. Maybe one or two specialty items exclusively for her that he didn't sell in the shop.

But it wasn't just the ground level shop premises and its possibilities that had captured Daisy's interest. At the back of the shop, a short staircase led to an upstairs flat.

She took the steps two at a time and gasped. What a gem! This was gorgeous. And it all came with the property. A decent well-equipped kitchen-dining area across the rear, cosy sitting room beyond at the front that looked out over the street and the sea. To the side was a modern laundry-cum-bathroom and a huge double bedroom. All looking like it had just been freshly renovated.

Thank you Bill and Marj, Daisy sent up a silent prayer. She must remember to ask if they still lived in the area and invite them to her grand opening.

Less than an hour later, she stood in the street in front of the estate agent's offices again in a daze, her head reeling from the decision just made. She had signed the lease papers, paid her deposit and held the same bunch of keys, now her own. Daisy Sheldon, what have you done?

3

Brimming with a sense of excitement and new purpose as she returned to the ute, Daisy mentally ran through a mind full of positive reasons to open her tearooms.

Apart from simply *why not?* she had a cupboard full of tea and china, truckloads of knowledge, plus she had learnt to bake from the best. Daisy had no qualms about her abilities. Yes, she would need help, a small staff, but she intended to give it a decent try for the next year. It would keep her busy, less time to sink into self-pity and grief in the coming months over the busy summer tourist season.

Her only concern was being unable to settle in one place. If her itchy feet resurfaced she might be in a spot of bother. After all, she had been travelling for ten years. No, somehow this decision felt right. At least for now. She needed to stand still for a while. Despite estate agent Murray's cautious warning, if the tearoom didn't work, she could resell.

Who knew? Maybe she would be a huge success.

And stay.

Daisy barely remembered driving back to the farm from Inlet Creek. Her mind flooded with ideas. In the coming days she packed during the day and poured over the Sheldon family recipes by night, baking and testing. Tweaking ingredients.

Suddenly her life had changed pace and become a whirlwind. And she wouldn't have had it any other way, now driven by an inner excitement and passion. But with the weather warming up she needed to get her shop premises ready, her own possessions and furniture into the upstairs flat, and her business concept in order as soon as possible.

Two days later when she returned to town with what she knew would be the first load of many on the farm to seaside run, she carried out a bittersweet decision and placed the farm on the market for sale. When the agent, Murray, came out to the farm to investigate, he raved with enthusiasm. Especially since it was a prime season to sell, the property rampant with abundant spring and looking glorious.

In a moment of panic and unable to bear the thought of the Sheldon farm being wrenched from family hands after three generations, she almost changed her mind and removed its listing. Everything seemed to be happening all at once. So she tried not to dwell on her feelings of guilt because that only bred a sense of liability and regret, neither of which was justified.

So she hauled a covered rented trailer behind the farm ute and began the final move from farm to sea. All the valuable family and stepsister photos came with her. The precious boxes of preserves, cooking gear and as much furniture as she knew she would use or need in the shop and flat. She would leave the rest on the roadside as freebies or have a garage sale.

Because the *Shop for Lease* sign on Inlet

Creek's main street no longer applied to her newly-leased premises and had been removed, and Daisy buzzed in and out through the open double French doors unloading every day now, people stopped out front. Some to ask questions and chat or merely watch. Word would spread. She simply had to trust her conflicting idea of ignoring the current trend that these days everyone wanted coffee for dedicated tearooms instead.

She would stock and serve every variety of foreign loose leaf teas she could acquire from specialist importers. There would be no teabags in this shop.

When she grew too tired to return to the farm, once her dismantled bed and mattress had been lugged upstairs and rebuilt, she stayed in the flat.

Late into the night, Daisy sat cross legged on the bed with her laptop sourcing appropriate supplies including tea signs to decorate the walls. Like *You're my cup of tea. Tea is a hug in a mug*. Or in her case, cup. *Keep calm and drink tea. It's always teatime*.

She ordered the same sayings for exclusive tea towels, mugs and other tea-inspired giftware to sell in the shop.

She bought tins of white paint for the walls and the biggest rollers they sold from the hardware store. Then splashed it about like a mad person and stood back to admire her efforts.

Daisy loved that every business in town was small and locally owned.

The only furniture store ordered in the rustic

white scrubbed wooden tables and chairs she chose, plump taupe cushions for the seats and crisp white cloths which would showcase her floral tea sets to perfection. She sought to achieve a light seaside cottage feel by introducing small bursts of pastel blue and green in the décor elsewhere.

She already had a box full of small glass vases from the farm which she planned to use for fresh flowers on each table daily and organised to be supplied by the only florist in town, an eager young start up like herself named Molly. Who would also conveniently supply lush green plants and potted seasonal floral colour for the tearoom as well.

Molly suggested two young locals, Tara and Susie, trained in hospitality and looking for work over the summer holiday break from university. Daisy had already contacted them and arranged interviews.

With painting done, the warm toned slate floor washed, huge front picture windows scrubbed until they gleamed, all fittings installed, supplies sorted and decorations done, Daisy figured she was pretty much set. And had already made the decision to simply call her tearoom *Daisy's*.

After ten days of starting before dawn and working until midnight, Daisy was on the cusp of opening. Spending every rare spare moment baking to perfect her recipes, so there remained only one more detail to organise.

She waited until just before the boulangerie closed in the late afternoon, then walked across the street to introduce herself to the baker and hopefully do business. The front door sign was turned to CLOSED but when she tried the knob, it opened.

The staff had already gone for the day. Presumably the baker was somewhere out the back because Daisy could hear humming above what sounded like traditional French accordion music followed by a haunting saxophone.

'Halloo,' Daisy called out through an open door behind the counter toward the rear of the shop.

The humming stopped and soft footsteps approached. The baker appeared wiping his hands on his apron. '*Mademoiselle*,' he acknowledged quietly. 'We are closed.'

'Of course. Um,' she waved a hand in the air behind her, 'I'm opening tearooms across the street very soon.'

'So I see.' He grinned and extended a hand in offering. '*ALors*? How can I help you?'

Nothing ventured so she plunged right in. 'As well as my own menu of baked foods and light lunches, I would love to make it even more special and, perhaps,' she hesitated, suddenly anxious, 'stock some of your pâtisseries?'

'Aha.' He smiled. 'Then perhaps we should introduce ourselves and . . . chat? Daisy.' He said her name with a low chuckle.

He had seen her new tearoom sign then. 'Love to.' She extended a hand. 'Sheldon. And you are?'

'Jacques Landry.'

He pronounced his name like shark laundry.

His accent was quite beautiful and reminded her of Paris and French countryside travels with such strong nostalgia she could not resist smiling.

'Jack?' she queried, knowing his French name might be James.

He nodded. 'Please, come through to the terrace.' He indicated she should move ahead of him.

As they passed through an enviable giant bakery and kitchen area that took up the remainder of the downstairs area, Daisy drooled. A vast commercial kitchen like this, fully equipped, must be a dream. But then she remembered the cosy kitchen of her childhood and brief return visits home to the farm where she and Granny or Mae, or with Ailie alone in recent years, had been so cramped for room as to rub elbows with each other as they chatted and laughed and baked in the tiny cottage.

She sighed. Big was not necessarily better for her. She preferred intimate and trusted locals and tourists alike received and supported its originality and difference.

Jack stepped ahead of her to open a back door, revealing a rear walled garden terrace. Beneath the first fresh green leaves unfurling from a grapevine above, sat pots of sorrel, chervil and tarragon, sending out their strong herbal scents as they brushed past to sit in comfortable chairs. A timber table was pushed to one side.

'What brought you all the way here to a small seaside village in Australia from France?' Daisy asked.

Jack's olive skinned face clouded but only for a moment. 'My mother, Adele, is Australian. My family have always been bakers and she met my father Bruno while travelling. We live in Talmont on the Atlantic coast. A place of much beauty with an estuary like Inlet Creek. But also a dune system, salt marshes and meadows, fish ponds and oyster beds.'

'Do you plan to return?'

'Not just yet,' he murmured. 'I have travelled to see my mother's country. I backpacked and worked in Queensland for a year until I followed the coastline south and discovered,' he waved an arm, 'all this. It almost felt like home,' his brows furrowed, 'so for now I stay. And you?'

'I've been working as a journalist abroad for about ten years.' With a pinch of nostalgia, she reflected a moment on her family. 'My grand-mother, aunt and mother lived on a small farm in the hinterland, about half an hour away.'

'Lived? Are they no longer there?' he prompted softly.

'Granny and Mae died some years ago. My mother just recently.'

He leant forward and took her hands in his own. '*Je suis désolé*, Daisy.' The gentle intimate gesture brought tears to her eyes. 'You are all right?'

She nodded, unable to speak. That a stranger should care enough to ask touched her deeply.

'And you have returned to stay?'

She took a long steady breath. 'Not sure. My father lives on a sheep station out west. He has always been around but doesn't figure largely in my life. While I make up my mind, I've decided to open the tearooms.'

'Then we are two of a kind. I wish you well. So, how can I help you?' Jack offered, finally releasing her hand and leaning back in his chair again to listen.

Still recovering from her moment of sadness, Daisy was grateful that Jack moved on to talk business. 'I noticed you sell your own boulangerie specialties but I was hoping you might be prepared to make one or two delicacies especially for my tearooms?'

She held her breath, hoping he would agree and that the extra work it would create was not too much to ask, especially ahead of the busy summer season.

He tented his fingers in thought. 'For tearooms. No coffee?' he teased.

She shook her head and laughed. 'Absolutely not. If you knew my family you wouldn't even ask.' She paused. 'Can you do it?'

He shrugged easily. 'Of course. But perhaps every other day?'

Daisy beamed. 'Whatever works for you. Suggestions?'

'We have much choice in France, no? Canelé?'

At the mention of the small cylindrical pastries of rum and vanilla with a soft custard centre and dark caramelised crust, Daisy whispered, almost pleading, 'Could you?'

'For you, of course. And then maybe friands with raspberries, almonds and a snowy dust of icing sugar?'

'Bliss!' While she was on a roll and Jack so

agreeable, she pushed her luck, smiled sweetly and asked, 'I hate making them myself but I don't suppose — macarons?'

'Why do you dislike to make them?' he growled, frowning.

'They're too fussy. I prefer simple and traditional.'

He heaved an overstated sigh. 'But only if you display them on a tower or carousel? *Oui?*'

Daisy clapped her hands and laughed, rising to her feet. 'Do I need to sign something? Do we need a contract or agreement?'

'What for?' he shrugged. 'Are we not friends?' He rose, placed his hands on her shoulders and, as the French do, kissed her on both cheeks. 'That will be enough for us I think.'

Daisy clasped her hands together tightly, so grateful for Jack's easy agreement and co-operation. 'Thank you so much for this.'

While he was a most handsome and appealing Frenchman, Daisy sensed a reserve in him. They were both in business. To be friends and neighbours was perfect.

'I shall make your samples and bring them across to your tearooms tomorrow.'

★   ★   ★

Next morning Daisy was fussing and pricing everything on the countdown to opening, so absorbed in her work that she jumped when a voice sounded behind her.

'You are much too cheap.'

She spun around to see Jack standing in the

middle of her tearoom carrying a huge tray of luscious pâtisseries.

She was torn between what he held and what he had just said. 'I beg your pardon?'

'Your prices.' He indicated some of the labels already written. 'You should double them. People in the city pay twice what you're asking.'

Daisy sank with relief. For a moment there . . . 'Well we're not in the city, thank heavens. And I don't want to take advantage of my customers. I want them to return.'

'Fair enough but this is also a business, no? You need to make a living.'

'I certainly hope so.' She shook her head and took the tray from him, setting it on the counter. 'These are stunning.'

She took his remark on board and was prepared to rethink her costing but life as a Sheldon woman was never about the money. Jack had made no comment about her tearoom yet so she held her breath when he cast his gaze about with a keen eye. He walked between tables, hands sunk deep into his white apron pockets. Somehow she knew she could accept and appreciate whatever comments or criticisms he made. They would be honest.

Finally he turned and tossed his disarming easy grin at her from across the room. '*Très spécial*, Daisy. Pity you will not be serving coffee though, hmm?' he teased.

'Cheeky. Do you have an invoice for these?' Daisy began transferring the pastries from his tray into her glass counter.

'My gift for you.'

'I thought you said we were both in business to make money.'

'Next time, *oui*?'

'I'm opening this weekend.'

'One more day. Bonne chance.'

'Merci.'

And with that, Jack left.

★ ★ ★

Opening day in *Daisy's*, even with her two young casual staff, Susie and Tara, was a wonderfully mad rush. Where he found the time, Daisy had no idea but Jack brought flowers, kissed her on both cheeks then disappeared. She was moved.

The vegetable soup with damper and Jack's pastries ran out, cakes were devoured with all manner of teas, there were a few groans about the coffee but Daisy steered them toward other suggestions and most seemed satisfied. Hopefully teased enough by the difference to return.

Daisy had always considered that when she sat down for a pot of tea and some quiet time, music was an intrusion. So her tearoom patrons only heard the tinkle of china and low hum of conversation.

Mid-afternoon when Tara was wiping down and resetting a newly-available table, Daisy looked up in shock from brewing a pot of Australian lemon myrtle tea, to be served with Granny's Royal Albert Lady Carlyle for a grey nomad couple, to see a familiar face and torso. This time fully dressed. And how good did he look. He settled in the only vacant table and

46

began reading the menu.

'If you can take this to table five, I'll serve the gentleman who just came in,' she whispered to Tara, grabbing an order pad and heading in his direction. She couldn't resist. Her journalistic curiosity surfaced and she itched to know more about him.

He glanced up as she approached and she became the recipient of his charming smile. 'Daisy.'

'You have me at a disadvantage.'

'As you had me the other morning. I guess we should formally introduce ourselves.' He rose and extended a hand. 'Charles Richmond, grazier.'

He sounded important and his diction was polished. The Australian equivalent of landed gentry? She accepted his warm suntanned hand. 'Daisy Sheldon, journalist and tea lady.'

Whoever he was, Charles Richmond was one distinguished sexy older guy. His damp greying hair settled into natural waves.

'Looks like you've been out again?'

'Every day at the Point.'

'Well then,' Daisy grinned, 'I might wander down there just to watch you get in and out of the water.'

He chuckled. 'You're a very forthright young lady.'

'I was blessed with some awesome and positive female influence. My father's a sheep man. Runs a pastoral station west of Goulburn.'

'I live a bit closer in the other side of the Southern Tablelands on a sheep property, too. *Lowlands*. I come down here to the coast from time to time for a break.'

Daisy felt charmed and attracted by this refined man of the previous generation but still young at heart despite his clearly superior social class. She didn't personally believe in that sort of pointless distinction but the practice certainly existed and thrived.

'I hope you like tea.'

'Absolutely. That's why I'm here.'

'What would you like?'

Charles flashed her a loaded glance. 'What do you have?'

Talk about a James Bond moment. Charles Richmond was chatting her up!

'Most teas from around the world, served as they should be and the food to go with it.'

'What would you recommend?'

'Well, you could work your way through each of them.' Daisy considered him a moment. She could recommend a Twinings classic but she decided to delve deeper. 'You've travelled?' He nodded. 'Favourite place?'

'I did rather enjoy the north African countries. The colour and buzz of it all. So different to my life here at home.'

He almost sounded regretful at the thought. 'How about a Moroccan mint tea, then? Gunpowder green tea steeped in boiling water with lots of fresh spearmint and sugar.'

'Sounds sweet.'

'You didn't try it while you were there?' He shook his head. 'It is sweet but very fragrant and refreshing. And it's served in tea glasses from a silver teapot.'

'Does it come with food?'

Daisy nodded. 'A bowl of sticky sweets, almond-filled tea biscuits and intricate pastries steeped in honey and sprinkled with sesame seeds. The tea you will find is like a minty tingle in the mouth.'

'Then that is exactly what I shall try.' His gaze travelled to her lips as he spoke.

When she turned away to go and prepare his order Daisy smiled to herself. Charles Richmond was quite the lady's man and she was fascinated by him in a way she couldn't explain. More than a little shocked by the extent of her own feelings toward him. Which took her by surprise because, although he was devilishly charismatic, his flirting contradicted one of the first things she had noticed. That he wore a wedding ring.

Where was Mrs. Richmond?

She had never crossed that line before and didn't intend to start now.

4

Evenings became busy baking times for Daisy. Over the coming days, boosted by the initial success of her tearooms, she settled into a routine. Rising early to prep or do last minute decorations on the day's specials, then striding out for an early morning walk along the beach.

Passing Jack's boulangerie, lights blazed from every downstairs window. As promised, but as yet still operating on a verbal understanding, every other day before he opened, her appealing French baker brought over her tray of gorgeous French pastries. He stayed only briefly while Daisy transferred the treats into her chilled display cabinet before flashing her his cheeky winning smile and departing with his usual *bonne journée*.

Which in amusement she repeated, in French, wishing him a good day, too.

Granny Sheldon had always woken with the dawn, if not before, and sipped a cuppa from one of her tea sets sitting in her favourite chair on the farm cottage veranda watching the sun rise. Hot, cold, rain or shine it was her morning ritual. As Daisy grew older she joined her and they sat in silence together. In later years it became a habit in her own life even when she was far from her home roots and Daisy used it as a meditative start to the day.

Daisy convinced herself the beach walk was

for the fresh air and exercise since she would have no chance to escape outdoors for the rest of the day. It certainly wasn't to see Charles. But of course it was inevitable she met him once she reached the rocky point at the far end of the beach. And deep down she knew it was what she wanted.

By mutual instinct, their meetings evolved into Daisy sitting on her usual rock. Alone at first, waiting for him. Disappointed if he didn't show. When Charles realised how early she arrived, his appearances soon grew more reliable. Which delighted Daisy who shamelessly watched him as he stripped off then ran, every toned muscle flexing, as he dived into the incoming waves with youthful energy, or stroked out in his easy swimmer's crawl parallel with the beach. Either way, no matter how long Charles swam, Daisy postponed leaving until he emerged again.

It became their daily earthy and very private dance.

And she wouldn't see Charles again until he arrived at the tearooms in the late afternoon. His timing deliberate and impeccable because by then her patrons had thinned. She only served him sometimes so her interest didn't become too obvious.

Inevitably, Charles lingered. The girls finished up and left, allowing Daisy the delight of sitting down at his table to chat. Their topics proved as stimulating as they were varied. Daisy talked with passion about the teas of the world, and both shared their travelling challenges and experiences to countless countries around the globe.

Daisy hugged these precious absorbing hours. Hit by unexpected waves of grief and desperately lonely despite her busy days among people, Charles' older company became vital to her day. He listened with sensitive patience to her ramblings and they both learned about each other.

'My wife Miriam died some years ago after a long illness,' Charles told her. 'Cancer. I nursed her through it. We have married sons in Sydney and overseas,' he added.

Daisy appreciated his confidence of family news but grew alarmed because it meant Charles was free to pursue a romantic opportunity without restriction. He already knew she was single and unattached. Her nomadic lifestyle dictated it. Quite simply, she and Charles had clicked from day one's first spark. And with his available situation coming to light, surely there was no harm in it?

But with that first fizz of attraction for Charles also grew an awareness of the age difference and possible stigma. Daisy battled to ignore all potential obstacles, refusing to feel awkward. Charles seemed untroubled by any of it which also leant her courage. He made her feel so alive.

But as yet, and Daisy smarted with disappointment over it, Charles had made no other moves toward her. Touching was gentle and brief but nothing else eventuated. Not even so much as a kiss on the cheek. No invitation for a date or meeting beyond the beach or tearoom. Ever the gentleman. Which, being a healthy woman not lacking in the odd experience in the past, became the cause of Daisy's deep frustration. And just when her whole body sang in response to their mutual blossoming attraction, Charles made an unwelcome announcement.

'I must return home to my country property tomorrow.'

Her heart skipped a beat of disappointment before she could respond. 'Holiday over? Work calls?'

Daisy tried not to show her private shock over the bombshell. She knew he had another life. Is that why he had remained detached, knowing he must leave? His attraction was genuine, of that she was sure. Or was he just being blasted well honourable again and giving them both time apart to reconsider before jumping into anything more?

'Something like that,' he said softly, taking up her hands in his own. 'I'll be back.'

And with that simple reassurance, she had to be satisfied.

As days passed, she missed him. When Jack finished at the bakery late one afternoon and came across the street to her tearoom for her following day's order, he glanced around the empty shop.

'I haven't seen your Charles around lately.'

Daisy bristled and raised her guard. 'He's not my Charles and he's gone back home. Holidays don't last forever do they?' she laughed, trying to hide the hurt inside.

'He must get lonely out there.'

'I doubt it. He's not fully retired and still accepts an occasional architectural contract.

Lowlands is a working sheep station but he has a manager for the property, a housekeeper, and gardening staff apparently.'

To stop talking about Charles and distract her mind away from him, Daisy changed topic. 'The eclairs are becoming popular. Perhaps we could have more? And we've sold out of those little fruit tartlets with the vanilla cream so I'll have them again. And a slab of opera cake. That chocolate and coffee combination is proving irresistible. I'm finding my customers rather like small delicacies with their tea. One lady claimed it went with the experience.'

Jack smiled and nodded, watching her as though she was a fascinating specimen of some kind. Daisy turned away from his gaze, blushing with embarrassment, unnecessarily fussing behind the counter.

'So,' he drawled, leaning on the counter, 'are you okay, *mon ami*?'

Jack's query jolted Daisy's thoughts and she frowned. 'Of course. Why do you ask?'

'You must miss your mother?'

At mention of Ailie, a pulse of surprise shot through her, followed by a wash of grief that settled in Daisy's chest at the mention of her name. She nodded. 'I miss all of them,' she found herself confessing with a sigh of nostalgia, 'and everything they were to me. Mae was the quiet one but Granny and I were really close. She died just before I was heading off to university. She left the farm equally to her daughters, Mae and Ailie, but all her cash savings came to me.' Daisy choked up with gratitude as much as emotion. 'I was shocked actually.'

'Why?'

'Because I hadn't expected anything and I didn't feel worthy of her generosity. I know why she did it though. Granny had poor eyesight but loved stories. I went through two or three books a week reading to her of an evening for hours. She was so interested in the world, she inspired and encouraged me to travel, go out into the world and see it all and come back and tell her all about it.

'Plus with Ailie coming and going to work on stations and in pubs, I guess by association I understood that a person didn't have to stay put in the one place all their lives as Granny and Mae had. By a quiet word here and there over the years, I knew Ailie didn't want me to feel limited in what I did with my life and impressed on me the importance of doing whatever I loved the most.

'So I completed a degree in geography which explored the relationships between people, places and environments. When I finished university, it was a no brainer really. I always knew the next phase of my life would be travelling and discovery.'

Jack sent a side glance in her direction as he settled into a stool at the counter. 'Do you miss travelling?'

Daisy considered his question, finished tidying up and leaning against the counter. 'You know I really haven't had the time. At first it was the trek just to get back home and the funeral. Then it was going through the cottage and visiting

Inlet Creek which led to all this.' She grinned, waving an arm about her tearoom. 'I was on Sao Miguel Island in the middle of the north Atlantic Ocean when the lawyer phoned me with news of Ailie's death. I learned later that she had become unwell in the months after I left.' The agony of that knowledge still haunted Daisy when she allowed herself to dwell on it. 'But Mum didn't contact me because she didn't want me to worry.'

'What were you doing in the Azores?' he asked gently, when it became obvious Daisy struggled with her emotions.

'Researching tea,' she laughed through watery eyes. 'What else? You know I don't have coffee but do you want a cool drink? A beer? Wine?'

'Rouge?'

Daisy nodded and slid off the stool. 'Just for you. I prefer white myself but I'll join you with a peppermint tea.'

She opened and poured a hearty Bordeaux red for Jack knowing his preference from a casual remark he had made once, and sourcing it from a surprisingly well stocked local outlet.

'Ah, *magnifique*,' he admitted wistfully after his first taste of the wine. 'This takes me home. So, the Azores?'

Daisy's fresh peppermint leaves had steeped in the pot so she poured herself a cup, taking a sip while it was still almost too hot to drink. 'I discovered Sao Miguel Island is the oldest and only remaining tea plantation in Europe. How could I not go and investigate?'

'Indeed.' Jack glanced across at her over the

rim of the wine glass he swirled in his hand.

'It's a rather quaint and unique enterprise actually. I knew nothing about it before I went and was amazed by what I found. The island itself is gorgeous. The estate is lush green and stunning. You reach it by unsealed roads through pine forests. The tea is grown in hill slopes above the sea with sweeping ocean views and breezes that drift over the plantation. Then you can wander through the buildings following all the steps in the process. Old machinery is worked by hand and they use hydroelectricity in the manufacturing from a stream that runs through the property.' Daisy sipped her tea again and lowered her voice. 'Of course I brought back lots of tea packets.'

'It must have been a desolate journey flying home,' Jack observed quietly, taking a long appreciative swallow of his wine.

'I think I did it all on autopilot.' She groaned and pulled a tight apologetic grin. 'Excuse the pun. The island belongs to Portugal so it was over a two hour flight just to get back to Lisbon, then almost another gruelling 24 hours with just the one stop in Dubai before Sydney. Before I left, the news came as a shock to me, naturally, but I was so focused on organising my trip home, Ailie's death didn't really hit me until I walked into the cottage again and knew she would never be there again.'

'So, do you think you will stay here in Inlet Creek?'

'Too early to say but I'm making friends and business is thriving. Visitor numbers are increasing daily. There seem to be more travellers than locals in the tearooms now. At this stage, I believe I will honour my lease for the full year. How about you?

Jack shrugged and grinned. 'Like you, I am settled. For now.'

Idly, Daisy wondered where their future paths would each lead them. 'Been fishing lately?'

He shrugged, his gaze drifting elsewhere. 'Now and then.'

Jack's business, like Daisy's tearooms, kept him busy but she noticed him escape occasionally in his boat out to sea or motor along the inlet fishing. At sea, she saw he always took a mate but along the creek seemed to venture out alone. Usually late afternoon. His sales girls remained in the bakery selling the last of his luscious addictive food for the day before locking the doors and turning the sign to CLOSED while Jack grabbed some quiet time and drowned worms.

'So, you are not lonely with Charles away?'

His random question caught her by surprise and she mentally stumbled before responding. 'Charles is a friend like you.'

It wasn't a complete lie but their friendship was platonic. Although, if she was honest, she knew in her heart she wanted it to be more. In the light of Jack's comment, clearly she and Charles hadn't been as careful as she imagined. Perhaps infatuation had made her lazy.

Still feeling a sense of annoyance that Jack had quizzed the depth of her relationship with Charles, Daisy added defensively, 'It's not wrong to have an older man as a friend. Do you have older women friends?'

'One or two. In the past.' Jack shrugged, that easy roll of his shoulders that spoke volumes yet actually revealed little or nothing and left a person wondering.

'It's not unusual for a woman to notice older men, actors for example, with an indefinable appeal. The camera loves them. Charles is like that. A suave sort of man.'

'And this is the kind of man you like?'

'Not usually.' Daisy was forced to admit.

A scowl crossed Jack's face and he finished the last of his wine. 'Ah, a female thing, then?'

'Exactly. And why not?' Daisy reasoned. 'It's all right for older men to scrutinize younger women and young men can be drawn to mature women. Who's to say why any person is attracted to another? From afar or not?' she challenged.

'Why indeed?' Jack's voice and dark gaze grazed her softly.

Because it was growing late, Daisy had baking to do and Jack was needing sleep for another early morning start, he kissed her on both cheeks and left soon after. Leaving her with the remembered feel of his warm lips on her skin and the lingering sweet aroma from his wine when he had pulled her close.

Because she was short of time the following morning, Daisy almost shortened her usual walk along the length of the beach. But fate stepped in and her feet carried her mechanically toward the Point. As her gaze drifted idly out to see, she frowned. A swimmer? No! Charles had been away less than two weeks. It must be someone else.

All the same, she was anxious to know and her walk broke into a run.

Daisy gasped with schoolgirl excitement. She couldn't explain it and maybe it was a silly infatuation but her feelings would not go away. She stood in the shallows with waves washing over her feet and ankles, madly waving her arms to get his attention. Her effort worked because Charles noticed her, stopped and stood up, his beautiful broad smile just for her.

She ran into the sea, leaping over waves to greet him, laughing. 'You're back.'

He walked out to meet her, unashamedly exposing every inch of his muscled body. 'You sound surprised. You shouldn't be.'

'It hasn't been long since your last holiday.' It took all of her concentration to focus on his face and not lower down but even her one brief glance proved remarkable.

'You can never have too many holidays.' He grew serious and moaned, 'I missed you, Daisy.'

Then pulled her against him and into his arms for their first and deeply passionate kiss. Finally releasing their built up tension. To Daisy, he tasted salty and luscious and she was in heaven. With Charles' wet body pressed against her, the dampness soaked Daisy's own clothes, so that she felt every moulded curve and bulge as they pressed together. She breathed heavily and tingled with sensual heat. She slid her arms around his neck and combed her fingers up into the back of his hair.

'My God, woman,' he chuckled when they broke apart, 'you're shameless.'

'Only with you.'

Which was true. She was no puritan. There had been men in her life, rare casual lovers who had filled mutual desires at the time. She saw nothing wrong in expressing the freedom to make love. But none had left her with this lightning attraction, this sense of worship where she felt almost a desperation to be not just needed but special to the other person. Daisy was on such a high she didn't analyse or question why. Just let her feelings free.

As Charles strode nearby to the rocks and began retrieving his clothes to dress, Daisy asked, 'See you at the shop later?'

As he zipped up his fitted cargoes, chest still bare, he murmured, 'I was thinking of somewhere more . . . private.'

Daisy's heart swelled with devotion at the promise. 'Dinner this evening? In my flat above the shop?'

'Eight?'

She nodded. Because she couldn't resist, Daisy strode over to him and grabbed the luxury of one more slow kiss before she could tear herself away to walk back to town.

Dripping wet. Hoping she didn't meet anyone she knew and needing to explain. *I had this mad urge to run into the ocean fully clothed.*

5

Daisy's brain went into total melt down for the rest of the day. Charles was back. She counted down the hours and then the minutes, shoved Susie and Tara out of the tearooms early and cleaned up herself instead.

Daisy decided to keep the dinner simple tonight because she wasn't even sure they would bother to eat. The menu would be fresh caught local fish and a crunchy Asian salad with boiled baby potatoes smothered in lashings of butter and herbs. If they proceeded as far as a sweet course, she would grab slices from one of her stunning dessert cakes from downstairs in the tearoom fridge.

This minimal preparation then allowed her time to soak in a heavily scented bath and dress with leisure and care. She combed through a spritz of detangler to tame her wild blonde waves and pulled on a vibrant boho tunic that floated about her knees. She had found the cheeky short dress in an op shop but couldn't remember where, and slid her feet into a pair of embroidered black babouch, bought on her last trip to Morocco. Easy to kick off later, she thought, smiling to herself.

Then her guest of honour arrived. At least, Daisy heard his footsteps on the outside staircase that gave direct access to her flat. So far, Jack was the only other person who had used it. The fleeting reflection briefly stalled her thoughts.

She opened the door before Charles reached the top. The body she hoped to explore tonight was hugged with fitted trousers and a white open necked shirt. Looking very debonair and trendy. And he carried flowers and wine.

They smiled at each other, neither saying a word until after one long stirring kiss. She dipped her nose into the perfumed petals of the posy when he offered it and led him into her flat. This evening there was only token lighting and one white fat candle flickering on the small dining table.

Charles scanned the soft blue and white beachy décor as he stepped inside. 'Very nice.'

He liked it. Daisy was ridiculously pleased over his approval.

Their reunion was so not about the food. They only made an attempt at small talk, the air in the room humming with underlying tension. They nibbled a few mouthfuls, eyed each other a lot and drained the rather pleasant bottle of what Daisy guessed was a very classy chardonnay that Charles had brought.

It compared more than favourably against what she usually drank. Drinking such an obviously superior wine as Charles had given made Daisy feel special but with an awareness of the vast difference in his tastes compared to her own.

Glimpses flashed back of Italy and home grown brews, trodden by foot and served in a large carafe dumped in the centre of the table to be constantly refilled. It generally meant a long noisy night and a possible hangover but she had learnt to pace herself and survive.

Daisy stowed the leftovers in the fridge, soaked their dishes in the sink and they retired to the comfy sofa in her compact living area. Charles' arm immediately went around her and he drew her close. Kissing took over, conversation ceased and it was all about touching, feeling and exploring.

When he made no move to leave later, Daisy hinted, 'Do you need to find your way home?'

'You're not sending me away?'

Daisy chuckled. 'Not if you don't want to go.'

With one hand discovering her body beneath the dress, he murmured, 'You're not afraid of what's happening between us?' His warm lips pressed tender erotic kisses over her shoulder and neck.

Daisy groaned. 'No.'

'Good. In my gross lack of experience with women in recent times I feared I may have misread your interest.'

'Never,' Daisy breathed and shook her head, holding her breath. Suddenly his weight lifted from the sofa and he stood up, drawing her up too so they stood facing each other. He took her hands.

'Daisy, I don't want to assume . . . anything but I'd love to keep seeing you. Privately.'

His old fashioned hesitation and mindset was sweet, and she smiled to herself. 'You mean like dating?' she chuckled, teasing, then noted his serious expression.

'You're unsure?' he asked earnestly.

The moment had arrived yet Daisy paused. Deep down she wanted to leap in with both hands and feet. Her attraction to Charles was fierce but what next? Would tonight be it or become an affair? In Charles' presence she felt special and, right now, although she had tried to fight the constant sense of emptiness that came with grief, she wanted to be loved. By this man. She needed the safety he promised.

She tingled all over when he watched her talk. Not that they had done much of it tonight. His gleaming hazel eyes washed over her with reverence making her burn with warmth. Despite his reserve and her own momentary brooding lapse, Charles had taken the lead and made the first move. There was no question Daisy knew in her heart she would willingly follow.

'I'm flattered by your interest,' she whispered, 'and staggered to feel so strongly about you.'

'Then I'm pleased. Would you prefer to be discreet . . . elsewhere?'

'I don't give a damn really,' she growled, chuckling.

'I may not want to leave.'

'Then don't. I have until nine in the morning when the shop opens.'

With that admission, Charles moved in and drew her against him, kissing her with such powerful tenderness she might have mistaken it for caution. Until his urgent roving hands caressing her curves with such considerate expertise told another story.

When they broke apart, Daisy took Charles' hand and began leading him away. 'Would you like to see my room?' she whispered.

'I'm so pleased you asked.'

Regardless of their momentary hiccup of confusion, they both knew where their cravings would lead and both eagerly anticipated the destination. With care, they undressed each other in the dark, Charles ever gentle and respectful. Groaning with need when they settled on the bed together, Daisy gave everything of herself to him.

With slow and tender care, he pleasured her to heights she hadn't experienced in far too long.

'Oh, Charlie,' she gasped.

★ ★ ★

Daisy woke early as usual to the sound of the alarm on her mobile phone. As she stirred and stretched, she found she was alone. She sank back onto her pillow with disappointment because Charlie hadn't woken her to say goodbye before leaving.

Craving each other so badly meant there was no doubt she would see him again. All the same, to love her and run seemed out of character. He could at least have left a note. Not to do so was more the action one of her younger one-night stands might have taken. An acknowledgement of mutual need and nothing more.

She stretched, quickly refreshed under a shower and sipped her morning cup of tea while she put finishing touches to her cakes and took them downstairs to the chilled display case in the tearoom. She debated whether to have breakfast or go for her beach walk. The latter meant she may see Charlie again. Too soon? Did she want to?

Somehow, because he was such a gentleman, Daisy wanted and expected Charlie to contact her first. She had never chased men and didn't plan to start now. But a nagging instinct cautioned her to hold back and wait.

So, smiling to herself because Granny would be critical she didn't cook it from scratch, Daisy ripped open a sachet of instant oats and made porridge in the microwave.

As she ate, her reflections naturally centred on how last night had been the most reverent lovemaking she had ever known. She adored that Charlie cherished her so much but his approach had been almost controlled. Daisy felt bad for being so critical of a man she worshipped like a god but with his physique, she expected he would be lusty and playful. Charlie had seemed surprised by her abandon.

Out of nowhere amid her sensual reflections, Daisy's thoughts flashed to Jack, almost with a sense of betrayal and was appalled. What was that about? She kicked it away like she might a pebble or shell on the beach.

Jack Landry was a gorgeous man and a good friend. That was all. A confidant. Someone to share the highs and lows of her days. Someone to tease without fear and have fun.

Perhaps being a foreigner in this country and stranger to town he seemed to enjoy and appreciate her company too. So why this sudden concern for his opinion and why was he even on her mind?

Right about now, Daisy longed for another female to share her budding feelings. Her three strong Sheldon women had always been the backbone of her life. Instead, being her only, if distant, family, her thoughts flew to her stepsisters. Lilly was in England but being the youngest they had never been particularly close. Maddie was nearer in age and only a phone call away. Could she?

Daisy wandered through her small front sitting room sipping a pungent green tea she was reminded of a teahouse in Japan where she had once stayed. It overlooked the water, too, except it had been a lake and she had been wrapped in a kimono.

Idly she considered Jack. He was a bloke but easy to talk to. Although the subject might be a bit sensitive. Talking about her feelings for one man to another. Daisy stared out the window across the street to the beach. And recognised the object of her thoughts.

Daisy frowned. Why was Jack fishing at this hour of the day and not in the bakery? She sighed and shook her head. A sign? Talk about fate. Granny and Ailie had both held strong beliefs in karma. Those tiny ESP moments in life where you channelled a connection to another.

Whatever he was doing down there, his presence was too hard to resist and her decision was made. She snagged her denim jacket from its peg by the door to the outside stairs because she would need it against the fresh early morning chill.

With purposeful strides, she crossed the street and walked along the pier to where Jack sat juggling a line in the water, a cane tackle basket beside him.

'This is new.' She sat and dangled her legs over

the side, the smell of briny air drifting into her senses on the light wind.

Their shoulders brushed and he glanced at her, unsmiling.

Into the silence because she couldn't curb her happiness she blurted out, 'Charlie's back.'

'I noticed.'

His comment was said so quietly Daisy thought she may have misheard and swung a glance sideways to ask, 'You've seen him this morning?'

Scowling out across the water, the hint of a grin threatening his lips, Jack nudged her with his elbow. 'I saw him coming down the outside stairs when I started work early this morning.'

'Oh.'

Daisy took a moment and worked it out. That meant Charles had not stayed long with her at all. Had he been ashamed? Disappointed?

'Are you in love?'

Daisy slowly shook her head, bouncing her messy curls. 'But I adore him. I can't seem to help myself.' She paused. 'Am I foolish?'

'That you must decide for yourself.'

'You don't approve because he's probably twenty years older than me!'

'It is not for me to judge.'

'But you are. I can tell by the tone of your voice you disapprove. Why do you care?' And to hurt him just a fraction, she provoked. 'Don't French people love freely and aren't married couples open to affairs?'

'Flirting is a harmless way to have fun. To gaze on another with appreciation.'

'Charlie and I are both single free adults.' Daisy grew annoyed that she felt the need to explain.

'True. Then why have you come?'

Why indeed? Daisy wasn't altogether sure herself.

While she hesitated, he asked, 'To seek my opinion?'

Daisy knew a sense of niggling hurt that Jack didn't seem to realise this discussion and confidence was just about having a chat. Sharing. 'You're a sexy Frenchman, I thought you would understand. You must know what love is all about.'

After a while, he said smoothly, 'I have loved. Yes.'

Daisy caught the edge of sorrow in his voice but a frown still creased his forehead. He was looking out to sea a lot and not the usual cheerful Jack. An alarm rang in her mind. She had been so blind. 'And lost?'

'*Oui.*'

'Recently?'

He shrugged. 'More or less.'

'Oh God, I'm so sorry, Jack.' She laid a hand on his arm. 'Is that why you left?'

'Part of the reason only. I did want to see the country of my mother's birth, so when my fiancé Juliette was disloyal to me and went to another man, it seemed the ideal time to leave.'

Daisy realised she had been so absorbed in the newness of moving to Inlet Creek, and the excitement of meeting Charles, she hadn't taken the time to find out about Jack. She knew nothing about him, hadn't bothered to ask and

70

was stunned by his revelation. Feeling deeply regretful over her selfish ignorance, she scolded herself. She had not been a good friend.

Jack's failed engagement would have hit him hard if they had planned to marry. His emotions would still be raw or at least always on his mind. Apart from speaking fondly about his family back in France, was this the reason why he seemed remote and wary? If Juliette had been the love of his life, of course.

Daisy's heart went out to Jack and she determined to be a better friend. Difficult when the man kept to himself but maybe in time he would feel he could trust her and open up more.

As Jack scrambled to his feet and reeled in his line, Daisy rose, too, glancing northward to the furthest end of the beach. Was Charlie up there for his usual morning swim?

She waved to Jack as she walked away back down the length of the pier, realising she still didn't know why he had oddly gone fishing this morning. He hadn't explained when she arrived and commented on the fact. Distracted by their frank conversation, she hadn't thought to ask again and he hadn't offered.

★ ★ ★

For Daisy, as spring advanced, her life also blossomed in every way. The tearoom trade rose steeply and remained constant. Even with her young energetic staff, Tara and Susie, proving efficient, the shop became demanding but rewarding. Her whole body sagged with weariness by day's end, especially after the frantic school holidays peak period, her first experience of daily pressure.

Because she loved what she did with a passion, Daisy coped.

But at the back of her mind and in her personal life, however, was an increasing source of frustration. Disappointment was creeping into the Charlie relationship thing causing Daisy to pull back and think that perhaps as a couple, and even longer term, they mightn't survive.

Their magnetism was still strong and Charlie made regular visits to Inlet Creek for a few days or week before returning to his property inland again. For Daisy, her time with Charlie felt inadequate and like a table tennis match, with all his travelling back and forth.

But during his absence, she discovered a fact that came as a surprising revelation. She welcomed someone special in her life. Someone more permanent. A steady partner. Was it because she'd never had one? Maybe it came from knowing she would be living in Inlet Creek for a year in complete contrast to her recent globetrotting life. But Daisy began to sense an unfulfilled longing. Apart from her pockets of more powerful grieving over Ailie's death, there was a strange inner development, an underlying loneliness that without warning had stolen into her psyche.

So despite the undeniable heat always simmering with Charlie, she began to wonder if he was the right choice. Would their affair peter out like a flame that flares and dies? Was it only ever meant to be temporary or would it last?

More to the point, did she want it to?

The lives of Daisy Sheldon and Charles Richmond were on entirely different levels. A no brainer to work that one out up front. Daisy didn't worry about it so much as allow niggling thoughts to sometimes drift into mind over their imbalance. Whether it happened when they were together or upon reflection later when Charlie had gone home again, Daisy began to notice potential future unrest.

Charlie gave no indication of anything amiss between them. Ironically, to Daisy's annoyance, this unease bothered her. Needing him so badly, she feared losing what they were building before it had barely started.

Daisy gained the impression that Charlie was just a really private person or being cautious. He never readily volunteered information about himself and his life. Once Daisy had nudged him and asked where he stayed when he came into town. She had no idea, since they always met in her flat or drove up or down the coast to a restaurant that Charlie inevitably knew.

She learnt he roomed in the Seaview Hotel, an historic establishment with accommodation, newly renovated, and which had impressed her the day of her first visit to town. Apparently with a private dining room for guests alone — Charlie would appreciate that — removed from the drinkers on stools at the bar counter and the throngs of locals and tourists eating in the popular hotel bistro.

All the same, their relationship had become steady and comfortable, if predictable. Rather than being bored, Daisy learnt it brought her a previously unknown peace of mind. She missed him when they were apart and loved him with passion when they weren't.

Added to working a busy tearoom and bothered by unwanted concerns over her private life, there developed the first whispers of gossip. Inevitable perhaps in a small town but for Daisy, unwelcome. In the past, boyfriends were fleeting, affections grabbed when you could while living a life on the move.

Locals had obviously put two and two together. Perhaps Charlie had been seen coming up to her flat. Yes they were a couple. Never raised to care much for the adverse opinions of others, Daisy bore it with patience. If anyone pushed with questions, she merely told them Charlie was a very dear friend.

When Charlie came into the tearoom now, he openly kissed her on the cheek. They smiled at each other and touched, reassuring her that she was respected and loved and not some sordid affair. Clearly, Daisy Sheldon and Charles Richmond had a thing going on.

Whether it was the fact that Charlie was a silver haired widowed catch decades older than Ailie Sheldon's daughter or that his new love interest was a rather attractive bohemian blonde, both with district connections to Inlet Creek, they would never know.

But some people simply could not hold their tongue and delighted in pointing it out. To Daisy. In person. In public. In the tearoom.

As she served customers, Daisy managed to

slide their loaded comments aside, keeping her calm and dignity as best she could. It was no one's business how she lived her life.

Her daily regulars, Doreen and Rose, proved the worst. Daisy suspected because they had nothing else to do and liked to be amid gossip central in cafés, her tearoom or anywhere else people gathered in town.

They challenged her ' . . . *the age difference, dear* . . . ' until Daisy grew emotionally exhausted.

Somehow amid everything happening in her life at the moment, she managed to hold it all together. So she longed for the days when Charlie returned and she could melt into his arms, be so reverently loved and forget the world outside. He was due back any day now.

6

Next morning, Daisy received a phone call from Murray at the real estate agency. He had an offer for the farm!

Leaving the girls in charge of the tearoom soon after it opened and about to hit the morning tea rush, she strode to his office to discuss the proposition. Almost her asking price and vacant settlement within thirty days. Stunned at the frightening speed of the contract and imminent handing over, on Murray's recommendation and her own intuition, Daisy agreed to both, signed the papers and left.

Walking back along the main street, Daisy felt desolate, second guessing her decision. Had she done the right thing? That nasty little sense of betrayal and abandonment of the farm reared its ugly head again after decades of the property being in the Sheldon name. But she brushed it aside. Instead of feeling bad, she should be celebrating except, given the sentimental situation, the thought of popping the cork on a bottle of bubbly hardly seemed right.

Knowing Charlie was due to return and that she had to clear out the farm and cottage as soon as possible and she still had the tearooms to run, Daisy explained her predicament to the girls.

Tara made a lifesaving suggestion. 'Why don't you ask Marj and Bill to come back now and help out? They're in here almost every day anyway.'

'They'd probably work for nothing if you gave them free tea and cake,' Susie piped in, laughing.

So Daisy phoned them and the former owners fell over themselves to oblige.

'Retirement isn't all it's cracked up to be,' Marj admitted, gushing on the other end of the phone. 'A body needs to keep busy and there's only so much gardening a person can do.'

Within an hour, Marj and Bill arrived just in time for the lunch crowd so Daisy raced upstairs to change from her waitress gear and apron into leggings, a long Asian-style tunic and light sneakers. Then she refuelled the old ute, piled into it and headed back out to the farm to rescue any last belongings she wanted to keep from the cottage. Surprisingly relaxed in her mind about leaving the tearoom in capable hands.

Once out at the farm alone, Daisy wandered around the empty cottage, seeing images of Granny, Ailie and Mae in her mind, remembering Granny sitting over there in her favourite chair. Ailie or Mae with their sleeves rolled up in the kitchen and wonderful aromas wafting through the house. Almost hearing their voices echoing around the bare rooms, recalling snatches of conversation, the sound of laughter. The simple life and happiness they had all shared here together.

Outdoors she strode around, stopping to weed where necessary, sweeping paths, checking the garden shed which still contained all Granny and Mae's treasured tools. They were of no current use to Daisy and would be sold with the property. Then she strolled further out into the orchard, the blossom long gone and tree boughs leafy green now, beginning to set fruit.

Daisy knew the new owners were a young couple with a toddler seeking a tree change from the city. She smiled to herself. The youngster was going to have a beautiful childhood growing up here. Daisy sighed, leaning on the boundary fence, looking out to the hills beyond and trees defining watercourses in the valley, cattle grazing and the sting of the midday spring sun already promising summer. Another family and future generations would build their own memories here now.

And though she believed she would never have been ready to leave and sell this amazing place, she was realistic to know it was time to move on. Life was all about cycles and changes. Who knew what lay ahead for anyone?

'There you are!'

Daisy spun around at the sound of a female voice to see Maddie striding through the grass and wildflowers toward her, swinging a hamper in one hand and a six pack of beer in the other.

'You're a hard woman to find,' Maddie teased. 'I've been looking all over.'

Daisy almost wept with gratitude. If ever she needed family, and especially a stepsister, it was today. And wearing her usual outdoor gear of jeans, a rugged checked work shirt and black Akubra pulled low over her forehead, Maddie looked entirely sexy.

Her sister dropped her belongings onto the grass and they hugged.

Daisy glanced over her sister's shoulder back toward the cottage. 'You're alone?'

She nodded. 'Disappointed?'

'No. Absolutely not. This looks perfect. And promising.'

'Tommy's home with Mother. Which means our Nanny,' she chuckled. 'Mother is simply not into grandchildren. And Dad is out supervising the wool bales being loaded and trucked to market. I went to Inlet Creek first to see you and take a look at your tearooms but they said you were out here. *Daisy's* is gorgeous.'

'Thank you. Oddly, after all my globetrotting these past years, I feel quite settled in Inlet Creek.'

'You don't mind I've intruded?

'No, just reminiscing. I would never send you away. You're my only family now along with George and Lilly.' She frowned. 'Why did you come?'

'You know it was the damndest thing. I just got this sense that I hadn't come to see you and I should.'

'Well your arrival is perfect timing. I need a friend.'

'I've been out on horseback rounding up flocks and bringing them into the shed for weeks. Tommy misses us this time of year because Aaron's a shearer so he's on the boards all day grappling with heavy woolly sheep. Shearing's done now though but that's no excuse I know. I apologise for not visiting sooner. Tara told me you've sold this place now.' Maddie set her hands on her hips and did a scan of their surroundings. 'Bet that wasn't easy, huh?'

She glanced back to Daisy who slowly shook her head.

Maddie wrapped an arm about Daisy's shoulder in comfort. 'Well we have supplies,' she announced with a wiggle of her eyebrows. 'Kirra prepared the food and I snagged the chilled beer from the hotel drive-through in town. Kirra was sad though to hear that you were leaving your *country*.'

Daisy had heard George mention Kirra previously. A local aboriginal woman, a descendant of the few remaining of the Gandangara people. From what Daisy had learned previously, apparently Kirra had been employed as a qualified and experienced cook at Georgina Station for decades. Sadly, Daisy didn't remember her.

But Daisy did know that the *country* Kirra referred to as all Indigenous Australians called it, or the place where you were born, was their cultural connection to the land and all living things. Their way of belonging and believing.

Daisy chuckled at Kirra's concerns. 'I was born on Georgina Station but I haven't gone far. I'm still at Inlet Creek.'

'Let's crack open these bottles and take a break.'

They sat down on the grass beneath the welcome deep shade of an old peach tree and backed up side by side against its thick trunk. Over the years, Mae had always pruned across the top so the branches spread wide, and the fruit was lower and easier for them to pick.

Maddie opened the hamper and snapped the

tops off two beers, cold and dripping with condensation. Daisy accepted hers and they clinked bottles.

'Here's to happy days to come?' Maddie suggested.

Daisy nodded. 'And fond memories.'

From the hamper, the sisters pulled apart chunks of savoury damper to eat with crisp cold salads and thin tender slices of roast lamb.

'Oh my God, good country cooking,' Daisy said with a mouthful, washing it down with a slug of beer. 'Love it.'

'So, you need a hand here or are you pretty much done today?' Maddie asked.

'I have the old ute packed with the last few things. I held a garage sale some weeks back and managed to offload everything for a song.' Daisy turned to her stepsister. 'It's so good to see you again, Maddie.'

'You, too. It's great you're back for a while. Lilly's in England indefinitely, living and working. She has this toff of a new boyfriend. Not sure he sounds her type but with her being away in recent years, it's great to have you around now. There's only so much a girl can stand from Mother and just being around mainly blokes on the station.'

'What about you?' Daisy asked. 'With shearing done for another year and summer coming, it will soon be too hot for much, especially out west on *Georgina*. You could always come across to the coast,' she hinted.

'I might just take up that suggestion. Tommy loves the beach house although we don't come across to it often enough,' Maddie laughed then grew serious. 'Aaron wouldn't be interested though. He's preparing for an outback rally. Working on a hotted up old classic Holden Monaro. Sporty two door thing. So he's spending all his time at the moment in the workshop with another guy from the station. Sponsor decals all over the car. Aaron drives and his mate, Nobby, is the navigator. They've teamed up before. Aaron's all about speed and adventure, being out there chewing up the dirt. Basically raising hell and dust.'

'Those rallies are usually in a great charity cause though, aren't they?'

'For sure.' Maddie didn't sound too enthusiastic.

'But, as you said, he's competed before?'

Maddie nodded, frowning and reflective. 'Most years.'

Daisy read Maddie's reservations in her reflective gaze beyond the orchard to the bottom paddock. 'You mind though.'

As they talked, they nibbled on the contents of the chiller box; diced pineapple, strawberries, blueberries, plus orange and apple quarters.

Maddie's hesitation before responding spoke volumes. 'It's bothered me some in recent years now we have Tommy. What with all the challenges and thrills, creek crossings, tricky roads and rugged desert. Aaron's so competitive. I try not to but I still worry.'

Daisy recognised this as quite an admission from Maddie, usually carefree and relaxed, taking everything in her stride. At least that was what Daisy remembered from the times George brought her stepsisters out to the Sheldon farm as all three girls grew up. Maddie was the positive outgoing one but Lilly much more restrained.

'Well,' Daisy said, attempting to play down Maddie's fears and any potential dangers, 'sounds like he's had plenty of experience. I'm sure he'll have a ball and be just fine.'

'You're right. Aaron takes risks but he's a natural behind the wheel and skilful. I forget to give him credit. He's always been a daredevil. Pushes boundaries, you know?'

'And I'll bet that's half his attraction.'

'Yeah. Aaron West is sure sexy and wild. We've been married five years but country chicks still give him the eye even when I'm around.' She turned to Daisy. 'Any man in your life?'

Daisy pulled a wry smile. 'Funny you should ask.'

Maddie raised her dark eyebrows. 'Spill.'

'The situation is a bit random actually which shouldn't be an issue since I was pretty much raised without too many boundaries and to be open-minded.'

'Half your luck,' Maddie chimed in. 'Father was always casual and encouraging us to be outdoors and active on the station. But Mother can be a tyrant. To her, going riding means a nice leisurely trot or canter across an English field not galloping out in the bush, so she had other ideas for her daughters. She had a fit when I met Aaron and we married within months.'

'But you were over twenty-one?'

'Didn't matter to Mother. Rules and etiquette.

Go on about this new guy of yours. What's so odd? I'm curious.'

'I have this instinct. Like something's not right or about to happen. Maybe it's his age?'

'You cougar!' Maddie chuckled.

'The other way around, actually,' Daisy corrected.

'A silver fox huh? You mean like Dad's age?'

'Almost I guess. But he's trim and fit.'

'And between the sheets?'

Daisy swung a slow glance to Maddie and grinned. 'A smooth operator.'

'No tiger?'

'Not exactly.'

'So is it like a casual thing or more serious?'

'Honestly?' Daisy sighed. 'I'm crazy for the guy. Smitten.'

'But?'

'He's so classy. Not the type I'm usually drawn to.'

'Mother would say classy is good,' Maddie quipped. 'Why the doubt? It can't come from your own lack of self-respect and confidence. You've always had bags of that.'

'True.' Daisy shrugged, hugging her knees and frowning a distant glance across the dappled orchard shade. 'Just a feeling. Probably nothing. I'm just not sure yet what we're meant to be. I've never been in one place long enough to indulge in a long term relationship so I guess we'll see what happens.'

'Well, if he's special, I hope it works out for you.'

Somehow later they managed to squeeze in a

square of chocolate cake each and a thin wedge of melt-in-the-mouth apple pie with the lightest crispy crust and hints of cinnamon and cloves in the fruit.

'Do you think Kirra would give me the recipe for this?' Daisy asked as she licked her fingers. 'It's different to Granny's recipe. Go down a treat in the tearoom.'

Maddie chuckled. 'I'm sure she would. She remembers you.'

Daisy's heart filled with warmth to think that she was still in Kirra's mind from all those years ago. 'She does?'

'Of course. You were only tiny when you left but Kirra's a part of the furniture. Been there forever. The homestead wouldn't run without her.' Maddie paused. 'Would you ever be interested to come out to Georgina again?'

'To be honest I've never given it any thought. I've been travelling and George never asked. Not that we ever expected him to once he remarried.'

'I live out there, too. I can invite who I like. I know Dad wouldn't mind but we might have to leave it until Mother's away. Think about it?'

'Might prove tricky and more trouble than it's worth. But thanks for the offer.'

By late afternoon, Maddie made a move to leave and Daisy was keen to return to Inlet Creek before dark so she could unload the ute. They hugged warmly, exchanged mobile numbers and parted, promising to keep in touch more often. She had no doubt they would because, today, a new connection had been forged between them.

Back in town again, Daisy arrived just as the tearoom was closing. The girls, Marj and Bill all offered to clean up so she took the opportunity to unpack the last few of her farm keepsakes from the ute. Somehow she found places for them in the flat. She showered and slipped into a silky kimono wrap, a souvenir of her Japanese travels, deciding what she felt like eating for dinner, not that she was hungry after her feast with Maddie out at the farm.

When her mobile rang, she noted the caller and was delighted. 'Charlie!'

'I wanted to give you time to finish in the tearoom before I called.'

Just the sound of his deep calming voice made Daisy feel that everything would be okay. 'You're very thoughtful.'

Missing him as always and feeling reckless, Daisy wished Charlie was more spontaneous and had just shown up and been lying naked on her bed in the flat when she arrived home. They could have showered together and done all manner of wonderful things. She sighed. Charlie was a beautiful person, the ultimate gentleman and she knew she was more than fond of him.

'Day after tomorrow I'm coming to town on business.' He discreetly cleared his throat. 'I wondered if you might like to return with me to *LowLands* overnight?'

Daisy's heart leapt with joy. Was this the beginning of a turnaround with Charlie?

She hated to gush but her response was swift. 'I'd love to get out there and see your home. It's been frantic in the tearoom as always and now

86

I've sold the farm I'm finishing that up and my head's spinning from it all. A night away would be bliss. I've been getting Marj and Bill back in occasionally. I'm sure they'd jump over themselves to close the shop for me and open up again next day. Plus Tara and Susie are so capable and reliable, they've become my right and left arm.'

She knew she babbled. Silence on the line a moment followed her outburst until Charlie said with a hint of humour in his voice. 'So that's a yes, then?'

'Did you expect I would refuse?'

'I was hoping not.'

To explain away her absence and lessen the chance of further gossip, Daisy decided to tell the shop girls she still had a few more things to collect from the farm and would be staying in the cottage overnight to save travelling back in again.

When Tara queried no furniture in the cottage, Daisy replied happily, 'Sleeping bag on the floor. I'll be fine.'

In actual fact, she had arranged for Charlie to pick her up out there. Which meant for the next two evenings in the flat, she would madly need to bake extra supplies for the tearoom and store it all in the shop chiller. And stay up into the early hours each night to accomplish it.

Because of her change of routine, Daisy felt obliged to tell Jack. Purely out of courtesy. He was a business partner and it might be embarrassing if he called into the shop to find her missing — not that he would seek her out — but he deserved the consideration to be told she would be away. She had been gone on her regular daily trips lately but this was for longer and she didn't want him to worry. From an occasional comment he made, she suspected he was keeping an eye on her. That it would involve Charlie's movements, too, from time to time bothered her only slightly. They were all grown adults living their own lives.

★　★　★

Jack was packing up the few remaining loaves and leftovers which he donated to a local food charity when Daisy entered the shop. The days had lengthened with late spring but despite it still being light outside, the boulangerie lights blazed.

'*Bonsoir*, Daisy. This is an unexpected surprise.'

'Hi.' Trying to sound casual and upbeat, she explained her situation. 'So basically, while I'm away, if they run short over there and need to place another order with you, can you just improvise and bake whatever you please? The girls know what's popular with customers, but feel free to choose.'

'Of course.' Jack watched her steadily for a moment. 'Are you all right?'

'Fine. Why?'

'You're only going out to the farm but you seem restless. That's not like you.'

Those perceptive flashing eyes were way too sharp. Sometimes she gained the impression that Jack was becoming a big protective brother watching out for her and perhaps felt more responsible for her than he should. She appreciated his caring but it wasn't necessary.

'Lots happening at the mo, that's all.'

He shrugged those broad shoulders of his. 'If you need help with anything, you have only to ask.'

'Of course. Thanks.'

Daisy escaped before Jack fathomed her deception. Those dark eyes of his were all-seeing. And she grew annoyed with herself for feeling discomfort at her cover up as she walked back across the street, rubbing her arms against the early evening chill whipping in off the sea. When had she ever felt the need to hide the truth from anyone? Especially those she cared about.

She told herself it was to avoid any more unnecessary natter but in reality it was largely to consider Jack's feelings. Why, she had no idea. He didn't love her like Charlie did. They both understood they were just good friends with business dealings. So why her concern and Jack's increased sense of protection?

7

The following week, Daisy's reunion with Charlie when he met her out at the farm was as enthusiastic and loving as usual. He greeted her with a broad smile and a deep kiss creating a sense of possession that she belonged only to him.

'Finished my business in town. I consulted with a new client for a stunning beach house build further along the coast.'

'Great. Do I get to see the plans?'

'If you want.'

'I want you,' she murmured and kissed him again.

Daisy grew pensive and excited as they drove the further two hours to Charlie's *LowLands* pastoral property.

For all their unity and strong attraction, she felt uncomfortable that they had met in secret and the familiar churning in her stomach that had started up recently happened again. A sense of unease that hit her from time to time. That something would come between them and this magical time would end. She couldn't see why because neither wanted it to.

She must have dozed off for a while because she was jolted back to reality as the car rumbled over a cattle grid and sped up the long gravelled driveway lined with towering gum trees. Wow, quite an entrance.

And then she spotted the house. A grand historic homestead for which she was totally unprepared. Acres of rooftops, verandas and chimneys and while it was nothing short of impressive, its image only highlighted the disparity between Charlie's life and her own. Daisy realised she was struggling with how to manage this contrast, the issue of their ages and lifestyles, if only in her thoughts, and a private deeper concern.

Pulling up beside the ornate square portico, she whispered, 'Holy shit, Charlie, you're a dark horse. This is a mansion.'

He reached across and laid a hand gently on her knee. 'It's home.'

Charlie accepted such grandeur as normal in his life. She didn't so much feel out of place here as knowing in her heart that, in complete contrast, she had been raised with simplicity and still preferred it today. The Sheldon farm cottage had been compact but homely and a place of idyllic happiness. This substantial building looked too grand to be classed as a home. So formal, where the Harwood property, Georgina Station, although equally rambling was more comfortable and relaxed. She frowned as she fought to recall vague impressions from her childhood of that other big homestead.

As they emerged from the car, Daisy spun around to take in the view of huge old trees dotted like parkland across the sweeping lawns running away from the house to a charming lake.

As she gazed, captivated by it all, Charlie slid an arm about her waist. 'Shall we go in?'

Loving and attentive as always, Charlie made her welcome yet Daisy felt like a visitor. And they hadn't even stepped inside. Regardless, she determined to enjoy and appreciate her stay, learning more about Charlie in the process. She could only believe his invitation meant their relationship was growing stronger.

'Do you live here alone?' she asked as they climbed the shallow broad steps to the wide veranda and he opened the front door.

'My housekeeper, Margaret, and her gardener husband, John, look after me and tend the place. They live in a cottage on the property.'

'In a house this big you must entertain and have heaps of visitors.'

'No.'

'Really? What about your sons and grandchildren?'

He shrugged. 'They seldom visit.'

Perhaps like her they didn't consider it all that warm and inviting or the distance out here too great to be bothered. The younger generations seemed drawn to cities.

'That's sad,' was all she could say, sensing a deep loneliness here in this magnificent house, and hoping Charlie's attraction to her was not in an effort to fill it. She believed, despite her niggling reservations, they had potential for so much more.

'Yes, it rather can be at times I must admit.' He allowed her a tender glance. 'But now I have you,' he said softly.

His endearing confession made Daisy's heart burst and she linked her arm firmly through his.

As he led her down hallways as spacious as a single room in her flat, Daisy was equally charmed and gobsmacked. Archways, ornate cornices, drapes hugging bay windows with generous sideboards showcasing what looked to be extremely precious pieces of china, collectibles, antiques and gently ticking mantel clocks.

Having passed a formal sitting room and dining room, they sauntered into the huge light-filled country kitchen. The baking she could get done here with all this space and appliances.

Daisy gasped with delight when she saw a bespoke cupboard of china. 'You have tea sets. Please tell me you use them.'

From the regretful look on his face and similar tone in his voice, she knew Charlie's answer before he gave it. 'Not these days now Miriam's gone and there's no lady to organise such social niceties. We used to host garden parties and family gatherings but that all ended when she died, I'm afraid.'

So far, Charlie hadn't spoken much of his late wife so Daisy considered this a breakthrough of trust to confide in her. 'That's a pity. You have so much room here,' she said tactfully, choosing not to dwell on his loss. Daisy walked across the kitchen to the picture windows. 'Look at that view.' After a moment, she turned back to him. 'What else should I know?'

He grinned, hands sunk into his pockets, admiring her. 'Hasn't the village told you everything about me yet?'

'I've never indulged or listened to gossip and never likely to. I don't fit the mould. Besides when I'm working in the tearoom I'm too busy focusing on fulfilling orders. My head is elsewhere.'

A rare silence fell between them as they gazed at each other across the central island bench. For something to say to fill it, she asked. 'How many rooms?'

Charlie shrugged. 'Overall, not sure but eight bedroom suites I believe.'

Daisy gasped and chuckled. 'You could house the homeless. In the farm cottage, we only had two bedrooms. Mum and Granny shared so Mae and I always bunked together. But we all rubbed along well enough. All gone now.' Daisy sighed. 'Well, I'm chattering and you're listening. You've been most polite and patient. You're probably bored but you did invite me out here.'

'I love you and your company,' he murmured. 'You revive me.'

Daisy picked up on the L word he had just said and was gripped by a moment of heart stopping alarm. 'Don't your sons come home? Not even for Christmas?'

Charlie shook his head. 'As I said, rarely. Two live in Sydney and one is overseas. They have their own lives and families.'

'That's bloody unforgiveable. And selfish. Pity they don't at least bring your grandchildren. Granny always said I was the sunshine of her life. Made me feel special. She was the dearest soul,' Daisy ended wistfully.

'I must admit since Miriam's death, I do feel the need to see more of my family,' Charlie admitted. 'Your blunt thoughts are probably close to my own but I've never actually voiced them to my sons.'

'You should. Get it out of your system.'

All this talk of another adult family brought to the fore the fact that, in contrast to her own, Charlie already had another marriage, had lost his wife and already lived a larger part of his life.

'So, what now?'

'Margaret will have left a meal. Up for lunch?'

'Absolutely.'

Charlie rescued a platter of chilled lamb salad from the fridge which they shared out on plates together, cosily working together in the kitchen. He produced and poured a white wine with a classy label and they settled to eat at the end of the vast kitchen seated at the round dining table in a bay window overlooking the homestead grounds.

Daisy reflected on her picnic beneath an orchard tree out at the farm with Maddie recently and this more formal setting. Charlie really did spoil her and she appreciated it but sometimes she wished he would be more unrestrained with her. His nude swimming promised hidden depths to his character just itching to be free. Maybe she was the woman to help him shake them loose?

'So, talk to me, Charlie. If you don't socialise much, what do you do out here on your own?'

He smiled at her indulgently. 'I have my architectural commissions and regular consults with the property manager about our sheep and cattle breeding programmes. The general running of the property. That sort of thing.'

'Have you had other female . . . friendships?' Daisy ventured.

He glanced across at her with amusement but

readily replied. 'No, actually.'

'So I'm special, then?' she teased, not probing for compliments nor expecting an answer but seeking to find out why he had not sought out women in his life, even for companionship. Maybe, like their first encounter that day at the end of the beach, he waited for them to come to him.

After lunch, when they had found and demolished chocolate mousse desserts and lingered over a refreshing pot of peppermint tea that Charlie considerately brewed especially for her, using two of the tea sets from the china cabinet, he made a suggestion.

'There's something I would like to show you in the library.'

Daisy shrugged, intrigued, thinking it would be his new beach house commission design. 'All right. Whenever you're ready.' She waved a hand over the table. 'Should we clear up first?'

He shook his head and grinned. 'Margaret will do it tomorrow.'

So, there would be no one else out here. Just the two of them in this great big house. Daisy's heart beat a touch faster with anticipation.

Charlie rose, pulled back her chair and took her hand, leading her into a fabulous room, filled on every wall where there wasn't a window or door with bespoke shelving of every imaginable book. By one window was a slightly angled table littered with papers where he obviously did his architectural work.

But he didn't usher her across there. Instead, he strode straight to a particular shelf and tugged out a number of books, clearly knowing exactly what he wanted. Daisy had no idea what they might be but could see the author was a C.L. Wetherill and they were some kind of books with art illustrations and paintings.

'You asked earlier about other . . . relationships.'

Coming out of the blue, Daisy wondered where this change of conversation was going. Suddenly they had moved from his work to his personal life.

As Charlie leafed through one particular volume, seemingly lost in thought, he commented idly, 'I know this author actually.'

'Really? How exciting.'

'Her name is Clare.' His hand gently brushed across the book cover. 'She probably lives somewhere in Europe.'

With that single fond gesture, Daisy suspected it was a former lover and her own current relationship with him became muddied waters. 'How did you meet?'

'University of Sydney. A stunning place to study architecture with such eminent and historic Gothic sandstone buildings. The jacarandas were magnificent when they bloomed in the central quadrangle.'

'Lucky you. So what did Clare study? Was she literati?'

'Oh, my Clare was never posh.' Daisy noted the warm possessive manner and how his whole face brightened as he spoke about her. 'Anything but. She did fine arts, the books came later.'

'An artistic soul.'

'Yes.'

'A close friend?'

Charles hesitated and glanced at her knowingly. 'Very. Once.'

Daisy raised her eyebrows. 'Tell me,' she persisted, reaching out to lay an encouraging hand on his arm. And feeling just a teeny bit envious that he spoke so fondly of another woman. Then she noticed a rising blush spreading over his face. Charles Richmond bashful?

'You'll think I'm just a foolish sentimental old man.'

'Never.' Daisy scoffed. 'You should know I don't judge. And fifty is not old.'

'It's perhaps inappropriate,' he hedged.

'Why?'

'It should be obvious. I don't want to offend you, my love.'

There was that word again. On the one hand her heart leapt with joy to hear him say it, on the other it sank with misgiving and the reality that there had been others equally special in his life. And that awkward premonition resurfaced that she was just the current attraction, although Charlie so graciously made her feel like she was the centre of his life.

'I'm a big girl, Charlie,' she assured him generously. 'You won't.'

'It was all a long time ago.'

'Yet it's stayed with you all these years,' she challenged.

'Honestly, I'd rather not talk about it.'

'Then why raise it? We all need or like reminiscing in our lives, no matter our age. God, Granny was always talking about the past. It gave

98

her great pleasure and I loved listening.'

'It won't serve any purpose.'

'Does it have to?'

She could see he had gone so far but no further, as though unable to finish what he started. Whatever it was came with deep emotion. Daisy could see he was growing uncomfortable. Whatever his history with this Clare woman, she had been important to him.

'Why do you find it so difficult to talk about? I'm happy to share my past experiences.'

'I don't want to upset you.'

'You mean, like, jealous?'

Charles shrugged. 'You mean a great deal to me, Daisy.'

'You and Clare were lovers, right?' She came right out and said it.

After a long pause when she had begun to believe he wouldn't answer, he finally admitted, 'Yes. And in love, actually.'

Daisy's mood sank. Yes, Charlie might have begun to love her, just a little, but this woman had drawn out a depth of emotions revealing what she suspected. That no matter what women came into Charlie's life, Clare Wetherill would always hold his heart. But what about Miriam then? Had she been second best?

'That serious, huh?'

Daisy tried to sound unaffected, pushing aside her own feelings to draw Charlie out more. She understood it was an important moment for him. Perhaps he'd never even spoken of it to anyone else ever, otherwise it might have been easier for him.

'We were so young. After university, Clare headed for Europe to explore her creative self and, of course, I sought to build my professional career. So we parted ways.' He paused and frowned. 'A decision I shall forever regret.'

Daisy choked up with heartache for him as he went on and a heavy sense of dread for their own evolving relationship.

'I'd like to believe Clare is still alive. She may have married, too, but we each moved on.'

Ah but not willingly, Daisy knew.

'A beautiful woman like her would have had any number of admirers over the years.' He rambled with nostalgia. 'She had such a depth of charisma yet was completely oblivious of her own power. Men were drawn to her, as was I.'

Although he minimised the friendship with Clare, Daisy could see its effects were still with him. Like her parents George and Ailie, they parted but ached living without each other. In her parents' case they kept in touch but, for Charlie, how much harder and more painful never to see each other again.

Daisy slid her arms about Charlie's waist, tilting her face to his. 'Love me?' she whispered, knowing that right now, they both needed each other for different reasons.

He claimed her mouth in a crushing kiss of longing and need, his hands roaming in all her familiar places. After a while, he draw apart and led her upstairs, their footsteps silent on the carpet underfoot. At the top landing, Daisy removed her shoes to feel her feet sink into the plush pile.

'Left or right?' she murmured.

In the plush bedroom with luxurious comfort and privacy, Charlie did something entirely unexpected. He moved away from her to a cabinet which he opened, pressed a few buttons and soon gentle rhythmic music filtered out into the bedroom.

In his arms, they shuffled and swayed and kissed as they tried to dance. Every few moments, one or the other removed another piece of clothing until they stood naked, bodies pressed together, and stumbled toward the bed. Falling back onto it with the laughter of lightness and forthcoming pleasure, Daisy knew this attraction was heavily tilted toward lust. She was a sensual woman and Charlie's hooded glances as they began to make love, told her he knew it.

'Daisy, you're lovely,' he groaned. 'You're a breath of fresh air in my life.'

And there she had her reason, yet adored him still. 'And you're very welcome in mine,' she whispered.

Hours later after much dozing and much more lovemaking, Daisy and Charlie moved themselves downstairs, wrapped in silken robes to drink wine and rummage for snacks. Charlie lit a fire so they could snuggle together before it on an elegant yet comfortable sofa. But desire overtook them again and they made love on the floor.

Returning upstairs to the bedroom, the night became one endless succession of lovemaking, driven by lust. Mostly it seemed all about the sex which both equally craved but Daisy was now honest enough to realise that they also satisfied a void in each other at this time in their lives, although for vastly different reasons.

Daisy now understood she had craved stability after loss and, clearly, Charlie's life was empty of companionship. They had both acted on their initial chemical attraction and sought the other for their separate needs.

Next morning, after a late breakfast, Daisy tossed her few belongings back into her overnight bag and Charlie carried it downstairs. The long drive back to the coast became a time of contemplation.

Halfway back to Inlet Creek and the sea, Charlie asked, 'Are you all right?'

She nodded, smiling. 'Reliving memories I shall have for life,' she chuckled. 'Thank you for last night. You're amazing.'

Which was true but sadly the overnight rendezvous only confirmed she would never be comfortable in his world. She adored this beautiful man and had clung to him when she needed an anchor. But when the sex faded, that something deeper she now desperately craved would be missing.

Until now, Daisy had not identified that she hungered for what George and Ailie had. Even now, with her mother gone, George yearned for his first wife with a love that extended beyond death. Daisy had never experienced it herself, even with her cherished Charlie, and would not know it until she felt it, that much was clear.

So for whatever reason, born of a crazy romantic longing buried deep inside her until now, she believed in *the one*, and knew she would wait until he entered her life.

Charlie was the dearest man but he had already found the love of his life, even if he didn't know it. He belonged to Clare. She turned away to glance from the car window as her eyes misted, choking up with sentiment.

When they reached the farm and parted, Daisy clung to Charlie with a desperation borne of the knowledge that their time together was passing. He gave no sign that he felt it, too, speaking of seeing her again and Christmas, so her heart ached all the more for what had to be done.

That night after she returned to the coast, Daisy wept. For Charlie and then for herself and her recent loss. The evolution of her grief for Ailie finally breaking, too, leaving her exhausted and desolate.

But next morning, as the early summer sun streamed through her curtains, floating them away from the windowsill at the whim of a salty sea breeze, as much as she adored Charlie, Daisy knew he needed to be set free to go where he belonged. He deserved a second chance and the love of his life.

Didn't everyone.

Which gave her a brilliant idea for his Christmas present. But she would need Jack's help.

8

Daisy waited until the tearooms were closed for the day before taking a deep breath, combing fingers through her tangled mass of sun bleached hair, spreading a coat of clear gloss over her lips and sauntering across the main street toward the boulangerie.

Crazy but she always felt this need to see Jack, especially after visits with Charlie, almost like feeling obliged to account for her movements. Jack was just always around and there for her but, today of all days, she needed him even more. To ask his advice and thoughts on her idea.

By this time of day, Jack was free, too, so she pushed the front door of his bakery — always open even though the sign said CLOSED — allowing her senses to indulge in the aromas of baked bread as she walked through and out the back. As always she saw him in the vine-covered courtyard seated in an old cane chair with an open bottle of Bordeaux cab sav for company beside him on a small table.

Jack glanced up at her approach. 'I thought I saw you return in your ute this morning.'

Daisy smiled to herself. He didn't miss much and it was almost reassuring. He held up the bottle of red. She sighed, preferring white, which he knew but he constantly teased her about it, trying to change her mind.

She nodded. 'If I must.'

He offered her the plate of olives, cheeses and broken crusty baguette with a small dish of olive oil on the side.

She had indulged in great gulps, bearing the thick strong flavour compared to a lighter white, until it was almost gone before she said much. Attuned to her reflective mood, Jack remained silent. Sometimes they didn't talk much at all when she spontaneously called in like this. Eventually they made conversation. It was like the draining of the day's workloads for them both, a time of unwinding.

When she couldn't hold it in any more she blurted out, 'I think it's over for me with Charlie.'

Through the haze of her almost finished first glass of wine, Daisy observed Jack quietly. He was such an attractive man with his curly black hair and olive skin. But even such a good friend would have limits and she wondered if he thought poorly of her for discussing her lover with him.

So when he turned sharply, almost knocking over his glass of wine, she thought he was angry. But Jack was never angry. Instead his compassionate gaze almost made her weep again but she had done enough of that last night. Like a true friend, in this moment when she needed it, he ignored any private opinion, his empathy for her distress paramount.

His voice softened. 'Are you all right?'

'I'm fine. You never approved, did you?'

'It is not for me to say.'

'I've been a fool, haven't I?' She felt sheepish and drained the last drops of lustrous red in her glass.

With a philosophical shrug, Jack said, 'Being a fool sometimes does not make one a fool all the time.'

Knowing Jack personally doubted the wisdom of her affair with Charlie, evident in dark gazes and frowns whenever she spoke about it, his mild positive reaction surprised her.

He didn't ask what happened but Daisy didn't allow him the opportunity because a flood of explanations followed including pretty much everything that she and Charlie had done and said, and her thoughts. Except the sex. It would be tacky to mention that. He would have guessed. Daisy sighed over the awesome memories that would be no more. She just needed to gather the courage to tell Charlie.

'Does he know all this?' Jack quizzed her seriously with concern.

'We both know where we stand.'

'You might but does he?'

Daisy frowned. 'Of course.'

'Are you sure?'

'Well we've not put it into so many words.' She paused. 'I don't believe I'm wrong in thinking you doubted the wisdom of my relationship with Charlie,' she said quietly. 'I questioned it myself. But he is an admirable person and true gentleman so I want to do something for him.' She explained her idea and why she considered Jack the best choice. 'Will you help me?'

Jack scowled at her with amazement. 'This is what you want?'

Daisy nodded and they began.

★　★　★

Most nights over the following week, Daisy and Jack either sat cross legged on her living room floor, heads together huddled over her laptop, Googling, or sat at Jack's tiny table in his upstairs kitchen above the bakery eating some awesome meal he had prepared. The tiled floor was cool on their feet after a warm day and the French doors flung wide to welcome in the lovely evening breezes that carried in off the ocean. Along with an occasional seagull that perched on the balcony railing.

Then they continued with more research, gradually slotting together each piece of their Christmas puzzle as they found it.

Then one night they were rewarded.

'Bingo!' Jack and Daisy high-fived each other. 'Too easy.'

'*Merci, Jacques.*' In her excitement, without thinking, Daisy impulsively leant closer and kissed him on the cheek. She pulled back suddenly, realising what she had done. Overstepped the bounds of friendship they had created. 'Sorry,' she apologised with a twisted smile.

'Where have you been all my life?' Jack teased with a lazy wry smile.

Daisy panicked over the mixed message. 'Right here.'

'So, Charlie's present is arranged. What do you wish for Christmas, Daisy?' Jack asked softly.

She glanced at him, aware of her head and stomach reacting in an entirely unexpected way. 'A friend.'

'Then we can be a gift to each other.'

When he reached out and clasped her hand, the first intimate touch he had ever offered, Daisy stared at him in wonder.

'Perfect,' she smiled to cover her strange lingering sense of pleasure.

★   ★   ★

'Hey, Sis.'

Daisy noted her sibling's number and her immediate thought was how wonderful to be so fondly addressed. 'Maddie! What a super surprise.'

'Won't keep you long because if I remember Inlet Creek in the summer, you'll be run off your feet in the tearoom. But I just wanted to let you know that Dad, Tommy and I are coming to the beach house late tomorrow for a few days to swim and take a break from the heat before returning home for Christmas.'

'George, too? How did you manage that?'

'Well, actually, it wasn't too hard. Mother has already left for her Christmas in England. Once summer hits, she heads back to Upfield Hall.'

'You don't go with her to see your grandparents?'

'God, no. They're a stuffy lot. Only compensation over there is being able to ride horses so it's hardly worthwhile flying halfway across the world for something I can do at home.'

Daisy didn't ask about Aaron since he wasn't mentioned. She assumed he was busy. Always plenty to do on a sheep station, she imagined.

'Text me when you arrive and I'll come around after the tearoom is closed.'

'Great.' The usually chatty Maddie paused for a moment then said, 'One more thing. I know it's a long shot but Dad and I wondered if you want to come out here to Georgina for Christmas. Make it all about family this year.'

Daisy knew they had asked because of Ailie's recent passing, and she was touched. And with Elizabeth absent in England, too. Any other time she might have agreed to such a generous tantalising invitation. It would be so tempting to visit the homestead again after all these years and see how much she remembered from childhood.

'Oh Maddie, thank you so much for thinking of me but I'm afraid it's simply not feasible. I only get the one day off for Christmas Day then I'm open again all summer holidays. I'll be fine, really. There are a few local people here and friends who don't have family around either, so I was thinking of inviting them for lunch.'

Maddie sighed. 'Worth a shot. It's a long drive,' she chuckled, 'especially in the heat. So how's it going with the Charlie thing?'

It was so good to talk to another female, especially of a similar age. Daisy wondered if Maddie felt the same. She had never missed having a sibling. Until now. 'For me? Winding down.'

'Oh, Daise.' She heard her sister's genuine regret. 'You sounded like you shared an amazing relationship.'

'We did but it was more a physical attraction

than anything deeper and more lasting.'

'Yeah, you said you had concerns that day of our picnic in the orchard. I'm sorry.'

Although Daisy appreciated Maddie's understanding she realised now that since the decision was at least made mentally in her head, she was prepared for the actual final meeting with Charlie in person when he came into town again.

'*C'est La vie*,' Daisy smiled, finding since knowing Jack that she dropped a few French words into conversations now and then.

'That's French for, like, *whatever*, isn't it?'

'More or less.' Daisy laughed.

The sisters discussed details and food then, since it was her specialty, Daisy offered to bring desserts.

After they hung up, despite the short conversation, Daisy felt uplifted and lighter of heart, although touched by a pang of nostalgia. There would be no fabulous cook up with Granny, Mae and Ailie ever again for Christmas or any other celebration, with an abundance of fresh produce from the farm, followed by lazy days doing absolutely nothing together but talking, eating and drinking tea.

She had moved on now and was making new friends in Inlet Creek, feeling entirely settled in the seaside village even after only a few months. Which surprised her since being nomadic for a decade. Maddie, Tommy and George would always be in her life, Aaron and Elizabeth she suspected only on the perimeter. But that was okay. Some people, even family, weren't meant to be close.

That evening after the tearoom and bakery closed, Daisy sprinted across the main street to Jack.

'Can't stay. Family's coming to visit so I'll be flat out baking tonight to cover the next couple of nights when I might not be in. Could you manage something special for a pre-schooler, a tomboy stepsister and an outback father?'

Jack didn't question or object. His smile was so soft and indulgent, she could have kissed him. 'Done.'

'Thanks. Just add it to the invoice for the shop account. I can come pick it up, okay?'

He nodded and waved as she left.

Maddie sent a text late the following afternoon saying they had arrived, opened up the beach house and were fully stocked for a beach barbeque. *Come as soon as you can*, Maddie ended. Daisy replied with a thumbs up icon.

At day's end, she closed the tearoom and did the quickest clean up ever. Showered and changed into a floaty ankle length skirt and gypsy shirt with sandals on her feet, Daisy went to collect her treats for the family from Jack.

For once, he was still in the shop and his gaze slid over her with appreciation as she entered. Daisy felt heat rise all over. He had placed the pastries together in a box and covered it with a white sealed paper bag.

As he pushed it toward her across the counter, he said, 'Family is special. Enjoy your evening.'

'I will.' It occurred to Daisy how lost he looked in that moment and she was hesitant about what to say. 'Thanks for this but I can't see what you've made,' she mocked, trying to lighten the mood.

'*Exactement*. So it will be a surprise, no?' he teased back.

She loved his usual easy-going fun nature, hidden this evening, and she wondered if she would ever know the depths of him.

As she strode back across the street to the old ute parked in the rear parking space behind the shop, Daisy felt stupid. Of course! She was with family and gushing about it and his were half a world away. How could she be so dim? Ouch. She should have been more sensitive. He was sure to ask about her evening when next they met so she must remember not to blather on.

★ ★ ★

As Daisy arrived, the beach house looked alive and welcoming with its shutters and blinds thrown open, lights blazing from every window and the familiar dusty four wheel drive parked outside.

Presumably at the sound of her clapped out old farm ute's throaty engine, Maddie flew down the side steps wearing a tank top, denim shorts and bare feet, beaming, and wrapped her stepsister in a fierce hug. A toddler with a mop of dark hair like his mother followed and stared up at her with interest.

'Tommy this is your Aunt Daisy.'

'Hey Tommy. I have special treats for you.' She indicated her basket of goodies from Jack and a chocolate and berry dessert cake she had made especially late last night. When she lifted the lid so he could have a peek, his laughing dark eyes doubled.

'Where's George? Didn't he come?' Daisy asked Maddie as they climbed the few steps onto the veranda and went indoors.

'He's down on the beach. Seemed to need time on his own.'

Daisy wasn't surprised. For herself as well when she looked around, she was suddenly plunged into a revival of the happiest childhood memories filled with bittersweet images of times spent here as she grew older. It was years since she had set foot in the beach house, freshened up with new paint and décor, but still in the same familiar remembered shades of pale blue and beige and white.

An attempt at an Australian Christmas tree was a bunch of gum branches stuck in a tub filled with beach sand and decorated with strands of gold and silver tinsel.

Since Maddie seemed to have the food under control, Daisy said, 'I might go down onto the beach. Say hello to George.'

She crossed the front veranda and down the shallow wide steps onto the beach. With his back to her, George was looking across to the moonlit sea, watching white wave caps rolling in. To their right, the twinkling lights of nearby Inlet Creek faintly lit up the oncoming night.

Daisy cleared her throat to warn George of her approach. He turned but, for once, didn't flash his usual blazing smile that always let her know he cared, even if he didn't show it.

113

Because he looked so dismal, Daisy reached out to give him a kiss on the cheek and a quick hug. 'Happy early Christmas, George.'

He didn't return her warm greeting. In fact, he seemed surprised and embarrassed and she was shocked up close to see such a haggard tired man. Lines were etched deeper on his face and there was a sense of sadness about him now. And wearing jeans, boots and checked shirt was hardly beach attire. She gave a sad smile. Some people didn't change. He had begun the fire pit on the sand but the piled wood wasn't even lit yet for coals to cook the meat.

So Daisy said brightly, 'Let's get this barbeque happening.'

When she briefly darted indoors to find a match, she asked Maddie, 'Is George okay?

'Sure. He works too hard.' She shrugged. 'When mother's around, she's such a nag. She can be so rude and unbearable at times.'

From her own encounters with Elizabeth Sheldon, Daisy suspected the older woman's snippy behaviour was a permanent characteristic.

Later, with the fire lit and blazing, Tommy was enticed down onto the beach to watch the leaping flames burn bright then reduce to create perfect barbeque coals. Maddie seemed to do everything. She set up a table on the sand with all the food and they sat around the warming fire to chat while dinner cooked. Maddie drank white wine, George and Daisy swigged from small bottles of beer. The heavenly smell of onions frying, meat soon sizzling and cooked raised their appetites. Served with Maddie's tossed salad, they eventually settled to eat.

Letting the first course digest and with conversation companionably lazy, Daisy's thoughts and gaze drifted further north to the end of the rocky outcrop where Charlie always swam. She shook herself out of reflections and scrambled to her feet.

'Who's for dessert?'

Tommy squealed with delight. 'Absolutely,' Maddie declared, 'I don't know where I'll put it but I'll find room.'

George just remained seated in his beach chair, staring into the fire. Pretty much his posture all evening. When Daisy frowned with concern and caught Maddie's eye across the fire, her sister just shook her head.

Daisy sliced her huge berry chocolate dessert into small triangle slices but handed out the yummy individual desserts first. 'These are from Jack's boulangerie.'

'He's the guy in the French bakery?' Daisy nodded. 'About your age?'

'Yeah probably.'

'See him much?'

'Most days.' Seeing Maddie's smug sisterly glance, she explained, 'He's just a business supplier.'

In a rare moment of participation, George latched onto the drift of the conversation. 'You seeing someone, Daisy?'

That was a tough one to answer because technically she was, and technically she wasn't. 'Not really, George, no.'

Just then, Daisy was given a reprieve as Maddie

suggested to Tommy he helped his mother bring out armfuls of presents and they all swapped. There was much ripping of bows and paper, scattered on the beach before being tossed on the campfire later, all for the toddler's benefit.

Tommy chattered over the bucket and spade beach toys, overjoyed with his gift from Aunt Daisy. In turn, she presented Maddie and George with a hamper of her homemade biscuits and preserves. What she did best and always baked with love.

'Oh gorgeous and yummy,' Maddie enthused, leaning over to hug her sister.

In turn, Daisy received a soft fluffy toy sheep from George.

'Made from *Georgina Downs* wool,' he muttered.

'Really?' Daisy was delighted and surprised, considering his reflective mood at the moment. She appreciated his thoughtfulness for its simplicity and meaning. Expensive gifts embarrassed her and had been expressly forbidden in the humble Sheldon household.

Maddie's gift to her stepsister was a framed family portrait of George, Lilly, herself, Aaron and Tommy. Elizabeth noticeably missing. She was impressed by Maddie's dreamboat husband never having seen him before, making her realise how distant she had become from her only family.

When Tommy started yawning, Maddie scooped him up to put him in the bath and then to bed.

In her absence, George quietly opened up and Daisy wondered if this had been the direction of his thoughts all evening.

'Maddie probably mentioned Elizabeth always travels away for a traditional English Upfield family Christmas.'

Not with her own family. 'Selfish.' Daisy's honesty came from a daughterly compassion she failed to hide, seeing such a bleak personal life for her father. At least he had Maddie, Aaron and Tommy. The next generations.

'I have nothing to do with Elizabeth's family. Their estate and two storey Georgian country house is too formal for me. I prefer the outback life.'

'Really?' Daisy chuckled.

For the first time all night, a grin threatened the corners of George's mouth. 'Australia is home. I hate to leave it.'

'Travelling the world broadens your horizons and sure makes you appreciate what you have back home.'

Maddie returned and after a quick clean and pack up down on the beach, they all retired to seats on the front veranda, George and Maddie nursing strong coffee while Daisy sipped tea.

Voicing what was clearly on her mind, Maddie said, 'Aaron's car rally takes off in the New Year.'

'Summer in the desert will be hot.'

'That's part of the challenge. Much more sensible here by the beach. We should have made more use of this shack over the years, Dad.'

'Hardly a shack really, though, is it?' Daisy quipped. 'It's a rather beautiful house in a prime beachfront location.' It would be worth a fortune but the family would never contemplate its sale.

'Mother did redecorate it well.'

'It hasn't changed much.' The instant Daisy let the words escape, George checked her with a warning glare and they both waited.

Maddie instantly alert. 'You've been here before?'

Trying to rescue her unintentional error, she said, 'Um . . . yes.' She frowned, pretending to remember, when her memories were as clear as the aquamarine waters on their doorstep. 'You brought me here once or twice in childhood, didn't you, George?' She felt bad for tossing the ball across to him.

'I wanted you to know of its existence,' he muttered. 'It's a family house.'

Maddie bristled. 'I wasn't aware.'

'I didn't want to cause more disruption in the family than already existed,' George explained bluntly. 'But there's more. Maybe it's time you knew the truth.'

Daisy cringed. Surely not. One moment George seemed determined to withhold the truth, the next he was about to tell Maddie everything. Did she need to know? Wasn't it a bit tacky after all these years? And just before Christmas? But if his past secret was to be revealed, it was certainly George's place to do it.

'Is this what you two were discussing when I returned to the cottage the day of Ailie's funeral?' Maddie asked with suspicion.

George heaved a sigh of resignation, as though a weight was about to be lifted. Yet Daisy harboured grave concerns about the wisdom of revealing the truth at all.

'Yes.' He sounded defeated. 'This place holds

such wonderful memories.'

'But you were hardly ever here to have any.'

'I was actually.'

George and Maddie eyed each other like rivals.

'I'm not sure I want to hear this.' She sat forward in her seat. 'When?'

'With Daisy and her mother.'

'When you were first married?'

George shook his head. 'When you girls went to England in the summer with your mother.'

'What! You were playing happy families with your first wife while your second wife and daughters were away?'

'It wasn't like that, Maddie.'

'You've just said it was.' Maddie scoffed. 'You were living with that other woman while married to Mother? More than friends?'

'That *other woman* has a name and I expect you to use it,' George said with a fierce glare and narrowed mouth that Daisy noted shocked not only his second daughter but also herself. 'I had no issue with Ailie. I didn't want her to leave but she broke my heart when she did.' George looked off out to the sea in darkness. 'She was always very special to me.'

An understatement. Despite a divorce, Daisy knew George and Ailie's hearts had always belonged to each other.

'And mother wasn't,' came Maddie's simple bitter accusation.

'Elizabeth and Ailie were entirely different women,' their father vaguely explained.

'You say Ailie broke your heart. It never healed,

did it?' Maddie continued without hardly drawing breath or waiting for his response. 'So why did you marry mother then?' she hurled at him.

George didn't move a muscle or flinch. He was simply and honestly telling his daughter how it was. 'Many reasons. I needed a woman in my life and I wanted more children.'

'You mean sons,' Maddie said bitterly.

George's lined sun-leathered face settled on his second daughter. 'You're equal to any son, my dear. You're my ray of sunshine on the station. You're so at one with the land and content when you're on a horse, gender doesn't matter.'

'Maybe but this . . . news changes everything,' Maddie said in bleak distress.

'It shouldn't. Believe it or not I love you all equally.'

'Except mother,' Maddie shot back, brutally indignant, 'and don't even try to make me feel better,' she muttered.

George narrowed a fierce gaze at his daughter. 'I've lived my life as I see fit and answered to nobody. I work hard and earn my relaxation.'

'Relaxation?' Maddie scoffed, throwing her hands into the air. 'Is that what you call it? All those visits for years while you were married to mother?'

'Ailie was my wife.'

'Ex-wife.'

'You forget, your mother has also deserted me in recent years on a variety of excuses,' George continued quietly, excusing his adultery.

'Did Mother know?' Maddie asked with soft anger.

'I have no idea. We don't talk much anymore. Your mother lives her own life these days.'

'You don't love Mother anymore,' Maddie said in a horrified whisper.

Her father responded without words, just the slightest shake of his head.

Daisy witnessed Maddie's building fury and resentment, eyeing her stepsister warily with suspicion, as though tarnished by association, being a member of what appeared to be his father's favoured family. Regardless of Daisy's complete innocence in it all, she stiffened against a streak of hurt, afraid how this revelation would harm her new sisterly friendship.

This explosive truth would ruin the newly forged family ties. Damn.

Maddie hadn't yet succumbed to tears. She was still too rigid with anger, her fists clenched, her back ramrod straight in the beach chair usually meant for lounging.

After a pause, she asked quietly, 'Is that the only reason you agreed to come back here with Tommy and I?'

'It presented an opportunity.'

'Bloody hell, Dad,' Maddie lunged to her feet. 'You didn't really want to come with us, did you? You just wanted to get back here and wallow in memories. Well, you can do that somewhere else. Feel free to leave first thing in the morning,' she said in a low voice, trembling.

Daisy wondered how George was expected to accomplish that since they had all come in the same vehicle. Uncomfortable and aching for Maddie, the air thick with tension, she realised her cue to exit should be sooner rather than later but hesitated, waiting for the right moment.

'You should never have married mother,' Maddie flung at her father as she started to walk inside not sparing Daisy a glance which hurt her sister more than a physical slap on the face.

'Then I wouldn't have you and Lilly.' Maddie stopped to turn at the agony in her father's voice. 'You have no idea how much you mean to me. That's why I took you to Ailie's so you girls would all know each other and be a family when I'm gone. You won't have one with Elizabeth.'

Unconvinced, a shaken Maddie disappeared. Daisy rose to leave, filled with heartache, the promising family visit having turned into a nightmare.

Damn George. She tossed him an unkind glare of disappointment and frustration. Although she hoped he had approached his revelation with good intentions, in her father's grief for Ailie, still evident in the way he clung to his sorrow, he had obviously felt the need to confess. Which only served to hurt everyone all around and emerge harsher than Daisy felt necessary.

Fair enough, she and George were still grieving in the wake of Ailie's death but to blast it out and let it come to this? Hurting the people he claimed to love.

Flooded with annoyance and regret for George's outburst, Daisy said, 'Not looking like a happy Christmas for you, George.'

And who knew when she would ever see Maddie again herself. Maybe with time, when her stepsister had a chance to process the unwelcome news, she would be more open. At the moment, Daisy thought it best not to make the first move. The next one was up to Maddie.

Feeling the impact of an unpredictable situation, Daisy gathered up her presents and sadness, said, 'Goodnight George,' and walked out into the mild summer night.

He rose and followed her through the house. 'Think I'll head over to have a chat to Harry,' he muttered. 'Give Maddie time to think.'

'I hope you all recover from this,' Daisy said, feeling a gap of distance opening up between them. The last thing she felt like was giving him a hug. 'You realise out of loyalty, Maddie may tell Lilly and your wife.'

'I don't care.'

As she stood at the ute, Daisy watched a sad defeated George trudge away from the house in the dark through the bush toward the single distant light glowing in Harry's hut.

9

Daisy returned to her flat, devastated by the evening's events. At this time of night, she couldn't bother Jack. He would be asleep before his usual early morning start in the bakery.

Adding to her emotional woes in the run up to Christmas and the summer rush that would last well into autumn, Charlie phoned. At the sound of his voice, her thoughts still in a fog of distraction, Daisy almost felt like she had known him in another lifetime, their former connection broken. At least for her.

He brought both good and bad news.

'I won't be coming into town again for a while, I'm afraid. My sons and families are all coming home for Christmas so I'll be staying out here on the property.'

'Oh Charlie, that's wonderful. It's what you've always wanted since Miriam's gone,' she injected enthusiasm into his news.

Ironically, while her family was being torn apart, it seemed Charlie's was being reunited. At least for Christmas. But while Charlie was finally having the family life for which he yearned, it delayed Daisy's announcement which courtesy demanded must be done in person.

'If I invited you to *LowLands* to join us, how would you feel?'

He was reaching out, advancing their relationship even, when Daisy, now knowing about

Clare, sought release. 'Perhaps more to the point, how would your sons feel?'

Charlie's seconds of hesitation told her all she wanted to know. 'To be honest, I haven't mentioned you. Yet.'

'Probably wise.' She took a deep breath before dropping a hint in advance of a future meeting. 'It's been rather like a lovely summer romance between us, hasn't it?'

The pause at the other end suggested contemplation of her comment. 'I would really love to have you here. As a dear friend.'

'That's so sweet, Charlie, but you know what? If I came out it might raise more questions than we have answers. I would be intruding,' she said gently. 'It's a magical time for children, especially all your grandchildren, and for families to be together. How long are they staying?'

'A few days.'

'That all!'

'I'll miss you,' came quietly from his end of the phone.

'Charlie Richmond,' Daisy sighed with tenderness, 'you're too sentimental and I'll miss you, too, but enjoy your family while they're home. Promise?'

He chuckled. 'Yes, my dear.'

'Happy Christmas, Charlie,' she said softly.

With the looming demise of her exquisite brief affair and the conflict this evening at the beach house, Daisy almost broke into tears.

'You too, my love. I'll see you in the New Year.'

Oh dear. Daisy closed her eyes and cringed as she pressed the button on her mobile phone. Did

Charlie realise their stunning and passionate little affair must end but he wasn't admitting it to himself yet? When she had left *LowLands*, she felt sure there was an awareness between them that they were fated to separate. With Clare so deeply in Charlie's memory and heart, she doubted he could ever truly let another woman in.

When he returned, she would jump in first and give him his belated Christmas present. Then surely he would guess without having to tell him.

Moving on, Daisy decided not to wallow. There was stuff to do. The Sheldon women would expect her to embrace and enjoy the festive day. No matter what.

Those habitual tourists that came to Inlet Creek for Christmas without fail every year were already rolling into camp sites and settling into holiday houses and flats. The main crowds would hit between Christmas and New Year when families from all over the country travelled to their annual seaside holiday destination. The village swelled in numbers to embrace the busy influx who lived for its freedom over the summer.

Daisy's baking ready for Christmas both for the tearoom and her own planned lunch became therapy. It helped avert the emptiness. Missing Charles, just a bit, but with fondness not regret. For the first time in her life not having Ailie, Granny or Mae. And nagged by the rift that opened up with Maddie since George's declaration.

But she pushed through it all and, on Christmas Eve, felt compelled to attend the church service the locals had promoted for weeks. A nativity scene had been set up by the school children in front of the altar. The small brick church smelt of pine from the huge Christmas tree glowing with coloured lights, the altar and its surrounds abundant with native bush wildflowers.

Just as the organ sounded, Jack slipped into the pew beside her. Perhaps both of them without families sought company and a sense of the festive season and its true meaning here.

She glanced at him in surprise, not expecting to see him until their shared Christmas lunch tomorrow. He playfully flickered his eyebrows so she couldn't help but return his smile. She smelt his presence, that familiar male cologne. His warm deep voice enthusiastically sang carols, strong with that endearing accent, and the sleeve of his crisp white shirt brushed her bare arm.

After the service, parishioners and tourists alike spilled out into the warm summer evening, moonlight sheening the water, lazy waves swirling themselves up onto the beach on an incoming tide. With the smell of the sea all around them and everyone chatting and swapping seasonal greetings, Daisy's heart lifted with an impression of feeling at home.

'Shall we take a Christmas Eve drink together?' Jack asked casually.

With her emotions having gone through the wringer in recent days, Daisy's heart leapt in anticipation of his unexpected suggestion. 'If you like.'

He followed her back to her lovely seaside apartment still redolent with the aromas and spices of her Christmas baking. In typical Jack fashion, never empty-handed, he always brought food. Tonight it was smoked salmon toast *canapés* washed down with a rather lovely light red wine. After the first glass, to Daisy's surprise, she believed she might actually be growing to like the rich red stuff.

The front sitting room windows were wide open to admit the cooler night breeze. With their shoes kicked off, Daisy stretched out the length of her sofa with Jack backed up against it sitting on the floor, the bottle of wine and platter of food leftovers handy nearby. The relaxation of food and wine and release from their daily work prompted conversation and reminiscences for them both.

'What will your family be doing back in France tonight?'

Jack shrugged. 'In the past they shared the traditional *Réveillon*. A big family dinner after mass but nowadays we have drinks and presents on the Eve and the main meal tomorrow.'

'Do your family all come home?'

'Mostly. They don't live far. My brothers are Alain, René and Lucas, and the youngest is my sister Joëlle. *Grandpère* André began our boulangerie in the village a long time ago. It is *très magnifique.*' He flashed his appealing grin. 'I think you would love it, too. Low white cottages, blue shutters, rose-filled gardens and tiny pedestrian streets.'

'Sounds pretty.'

'The Landry's have always lived in the Dordogne. Inlet Creek is like the seaside where I grew up. I love it here also.' Fully relaxed now, he stretched and held up the wine bottle.

Daisy extended her glass to be refilled. 'It's incredible that life moves us perhaps where we are meant to be.'

'*Oui*. I believe it is fate that I needed to leave France. My fiancé, Juliette, was unfaithful with an older married man.'

While his words newly spoken still hovered in the air, Daisy's mind and body were momentarily checked as she finally grasped why Jack had held himself at a distance all spring. No wonder he was wary. It was the exact scenario with herself and Charlie. Jack had been hurt in a similar situation.

Daisy felt sure that her precious waning liaison with Charlie was meant for a purpose in her life, although it now seemed to have run its course. So she felt no need to feel accountable. Jack's statement said it all and she now fully understood his reaction.

His admission left the mood reflective, humming with unspoken thoughts. Until Jack idly mentioned the latest rumour.

'I heard from other fishermen that there is drug smuggling offshore.'

'Really? In little old Inlet Creek. Who knew? Maybe some tourist has brought in their holiday weed,' she chuckled.

Jack shrugged and yawned. 'I understand it is much more serious and the authorities are bringing in extra law enforcement to deal with it.'

By the time Daisy had unscrambled herself

from the sofa a short time later to go wash glasses and brew tea for herself and coffee for Jack, she returned to find he had stolen her comfortable place and fallen asleep. No surprise since he would have been up since the early hours of this morning in the bakery and it was now closing in on midnight.

Quietly observing the gentle rhythm of his breathing, she drew one of Granny's crocheted rugs gently across him, switched off the lights, pulled down the front sitting room window blind against the morning sun and crept from the room.

When she woke, showered, dressed and padded out barefoot next day, Jack was still sprawled on the sofa sleeping. It was still early and she considered walking on the beach at this magical time of day when living creatures were only just stirring and few people would be about. Elsewhere right now, adults were probably all being woken by children keen to unwrap presents.

Instead, as quietly as she could in the kitchen by hand mixing, Daisy prepared batter and began cooking crepes which she intended to fully load with summer tropical fruits bought from yesterday's market. Ripe juice-dripping mangoes, chunky sweet pineapple and luscious fat strawberries.

Because Jack dropped in more often lately, Daisy had bought ground coffee beans to make his favourite café au lait.

Engrossed in the kitchen, she didn't hear him wake until he came up behind her and murmured, '*Joyeux Nöel*, Daisy,' turning her around to be kissed on both cheeks, making her intensely aware of his nearness and warmth.

'Happy Christmas.'

He closed his eyes and inhaled, smiling. 'Smells wonderful. I will go home to shower and change then bring something to share for breakfast. Don't get attached to anyone else while I'm away, will you?'

He would only be across the street! Daisy had always been quietly charmed by his boyish honesty and very sexy French appeal. And she loved his romantic accent that only grew more endearing with every conversation.

Since Charlie had told her about the lost love of his life, she was already thinking of him as belonging to Clare, emotionally releasing him, even though she was yet to officially sever ties. So she discovered a space was slowly opening up in her heart for another.

Jack and Daisy had decided no presents. Today, as normal for both of them, it would be all about the food and they had agreed to share in its preparation.

He returned within half an hour with a cane basket. 'Genuine French croissants,' he pointed out.

'You made them while you were gone!'

Jack threw back his head and laughed. '*Non, non.* Last night before church.'

'What makes them genuine?' she was intrigued to know.

Jack's eyes gleamed with enthusiasm. 'Only the best flour with no additives, top quality butter and baked on the premises from which you buy. Flaky pastry crusty on the outside yet soft inside.'

He always spoke with such gusto about food, Daisy was entranced.

After a long leisurely indulgent breakfast, both more relaxed than either had been for months, Jack and Daisy moved on with Christmas Day lunch.

Because Bill and Marj's family lived in far north Queensland and overseas and would not meet up until after New Year, they were invited with gratitude and no objection to the traditional Australian-French Christmas lunch Jack and Daisy planned for them all.

Tara and Susie promised to call in at some point later in the day and, during the morning, florist Molly had already dropped in an amazing table creation of red and white flowers. Which now made a gorgeous Christmassy complement to the one big table made up of smaller tables Jack pushed together in the tearoom downstairs.

Small balls of watermelon, slices of lemon and orange, and chopped mint from Jack's garden floated among tinkling ice cubes in a large glass jug of punch, beaded droplets of moisture already gathering on its side.

Once the guests had arrived, Jack produced fresh oysters and a small terrine to serve with their pre-lunch drinks. When they all finally sat down at the table it was to taste his delicious garlic soup followed by a salad of peas, green beans, carrots and potatoes.

Then came the *pièce de résistance* of the day. Daisy's traditional roast turkey with vegetables and gravy.

After an interval of lively conversation and

sweet wine, dessert later encompassed Daisy's passionfruit pavlova, Jack's yule log, eclairs and profiteroles oozing with crème filling and glistening with chocolate glaze.

'Well, Bill, I don't know about you but I'm feeling like that turkey. A bit stuffed,' Marg declared.

As promised, the shop girls appeared later, fresh in denim shorts and tank tops over bathers after a dip in the sea.

'Loads of people down on the beach. You should all go for a swim.'

Everyone groaned.

'Don't think I could manage it just now, Tara,' Daisy laughed. 'I believe I'd sink.'

The girls left and Bill and Marj made movements too, offering profuse thanks to their hosts and cooks for the day. Daisy and Jack shared out the leftovers for everyone to take home and cleaned up.

It wasn't until the glowing gold and orange of the summer sunset that he suggested, 'A wander on the beach?'

Daisy nodded. Removing her shoes once they hit the warm white sand, with families and strolling couples still about making the most of their festive day, she and Jack joined them. He rolled up his canvas trousers and his silky white shirt flapped in the onshore twilight breeze.

Jack's fingers brushed hers and twined together. 'Today has been wonderful, Daisy. A Christmas to remember.'

'I agree,' she murmured, amazed at the warmth that engulfed her from his touch.

'I would like to know you better,' he said as

they paddled in the shallows, frothy spent waves washing over their feet.

Breathless that such feelings welled up inside her so soon after having Charlie so intensely in her life and unable to speak, Daisy nodded.

This gift of another person in her life who was growing to mean much, and deeply so, felt like the best Christmas present ever. A slow building burn of recognition stirred her heart. They ambled the long crescent length of the beach and then back again until it grew dark. Everywhere Christmas lights were flickering on in town.

'You don't need to walk me across the street,' Daisy grinned as they paused in front of the boulangerie.

As he leant forward, she held her breath. He kissed her with such an aching brief tenderness, it was almost as though their lips hadn't tasted each other at all. The first step beyond friendship. Afterward they just stared at each other in silence for a long time.

'If you could read my heart, Daisy, you would see a place for you there,' Jack whispered, as they stood close holding hands, in the shadows of the softly glowing French street lamp across the pavement.

An amazing confession which Daisy treasured. They had both travelled rough roads to emotional ease this past year. But before Daisy could make a similar pledge, she had one last thing to do.

'I know,' she murmured. 'Thank you.'

'*Bonsoir*,' they called out softly to each other as they parted.

★ ★ ★

Two days later when she heard footsteps on the back stairs up to her flat, Daisy assumed it was Jack. They saw each other now as often as possible with pleasure and kisses and deepening joy. She swung around with a ready smile to greet him.

'Charlie!'

She frowned, deeply sad to realise that, within weeks and the events of change in her life, he had become a stranger. A recognition, perhaps in her heart that their affair was over. His mood seemed distant, too, and after making a pot of tea, they sat together on the sofa, briefly asking each other about their respective Christmases.

'I have a present for you,' Daisy said lightly and disappeared to fetch it, grateful for a moment alone to regain her composure.

She handed a large envelope and separate card to Charlie, clenched her hands together and watched him carefully as he opened both to discover their contents. When he realised what it held, they stared at each other for a moment.

A confusion of pain filled his gaze until he said, 'You have found Clare for me?'

She nodded. 'With Jack's help. It wasn't hard. His knowledge of France and lots of Googling.'

Looking as if he was almost afraid to read the pages, Daisy rested a hand on his arm, 'You might want to take it away and absorb it at your leisure. But basically, we found her through an art gallery and, digging deeper, learned that she is single, never married and is available!'

'Daisy — '

She shook her head, close to tears but bravely smiling. 'This is your *happy ever after*, Charlie.'

His expression grew pained. 'What about yours?'

'I'm sure it's just around the corner.' Actually it was just across the street but she would never mention that.

He slid the papers aside, drew her up against him and they hugged long and tight with one final kiss goodbye between friends knowing it was the last time.

'Thank you for allowing me to love you, even for a short while. I will never forget you.'

'I needed you as much as you needed me. Now go and get Clare.' Daisy's eyes watered up.

'Will you be all right?' Still chivalrous to the end.

She nodded.

'You made me so happy, my darling Daisy. You gave me two wonderful unselfish gifts. Yourself and Clare.'

'You're welcome.'

★   ★   ★

Within days, Charlie sent her a text. *I have booked a flight to Paris.*

Let me know how it goes, she replied, excited and nervous for him.

Within a week, she heard from him again. *I have met Clare and all is well. It is as though we were never apart. My darling Daisy you have gifted me happiness beyond measure.*

Daisy sent Jack a text with the good news.

Maybe it was the emotional load the previous year had settled upon her life with Ailie's passing, her great joy and nostalgia in the wake of her affair with Charlie, and now the promise of a newfound happiness with Jack but Daisy suddenly crumbled into tears. She sank onto the rug in the centre of the sitting room, put her face in her hands and wept with relief and happiness.

Ironically as she sobbed, she became aware of the familiar sound of Jack's leaping steps on the outside stairs. Always sensitive to her possible needs and with a rampant ESP growing between them, he had obviously crossed the street on a hunch.

She was already a mess and didn't bother to hide her happy distress. 'I'm being silly,' she apologised, sniffling. 'I'm so happy for him. To have such a love . . . '

Jack sat cross-legged beside her and wrapped a big comforting arm around her shoulder. 'There is only one happiness in life. To love and be loved.' He kissed her hair. 'I think tonight we need pizza and beer.'

True to his prediction, that evening, hot freshly baked pizza sitting on top of dewy chilled bottles of beer in a small esky found their way onto a rug on the beach. Little conversation but much chemistry and unspoken harmony passed between them.

Only days later, fighting wind and a light shower of cool summer rain, Daisy had her head down dashing back to the tearoom after her usual early morning market trip. She collided with someone and glanced up to see who it was.

Jack.

Without a word they both simultaneously grinned, memories of their first night together rampantly fresh in both their minds. They laughed and stumbled around each other, moving on.

Daisy meant to keep going but something made her stop and give in to a silly urge to turn around so she did. Silly thing was, Jack had turned back, too, beaming. Daisy shrugged.

'*Bonjour*,' he called out, eyes twinkling, mouth edged into a devastatingly sexy grin, as if meeting her for the first time. And perhaps they really were. 'Do you live in town?' he asked, walking backwards away from her as she was from him.

She nodded, amused.

'Then perhaps I shall see you around?'

Daisy raised a hand and a smile, forcing herself to turn around and watch where she was walking, humming. Most definitely. Knowing the truth in her heart now, she acknowledged that Jack had always been her future. She just hadn't realised.

And because there was now most definitely a very attractive reason, it seemed highly likely that she just might stay in Inlet Creek.

* * *

Hot on the heels of the most utter and complete peace and happiness she had known in years, Daisy had just finished in the tearoom for another day. It had been an unusually quiet one because a misty drizzle was sweeping the coast with yet another cool late summer change and

138

patrons were scarce. Probably in their caravans and apartments playing cards or reading.

She ran upstairs to Jack, already preparing dinner. He smiled lazily as she greeted him and was lovingly kissed. When her mobile phone beeped, she answered, frowning with surprise at the caller. There had been no contact with him since that fateful evening in the beach house before Christmas.

'George?' It was a bit late but was he calling to wish her a Happy New Year?

As he started talking, Daisy went cold and dropped down onto the sofa. After the briefest conversation, she ended the call and glanced across to Jack, feeling a deep sickness in the base of her stomach.

'That was George. Horrible news.'

PART II — MADELEINE

10

Maddie Harwood-West sat stiff-backed and dry-eyed in the front pew of the small weatherboard church in town that serviced the surrounding sheep stations like *Georgina Downs* for hundreds of kilometres.

She made the difficult decision not to bring Tommy to his father's funeral. If Aaron had been determined to live a reckless life, then Maddie was equally furious and stubborn in not putting their three year old son through the trauma of a funeral service sitting feet away from his father in a coffin, and the burial later where he would see that same coffin being lowered deep into the dry hard-packed Australian dirt.

This past week, the boy had constantly asked after his father. Unable to cope with explanations until today's formalities were over, Maddie had simply told her son that *Daddy is still away* until she gathered the courage to tell him *Daddy is never coming back*. For now, Tommy was safely in Nanny's care in the homestead until they returned.

How dare Aaron put his wife and son through this?

Maddie stiffened with the same raging fury that had possessed her all week. Irony was, the very reason she had loved him was also the one that had taken him away. The flashing white teeth behind that wicked hearty laugh, the charm and banter that had captured the boss's daughter and attracted every other female in the district, the sex appeal oozing from every muscled pore of his stunning suntanned body.

All that now lay at rest, robbed of life. Apparently because of a bloody big hidden rock buried beneath thick red dust on the rally track that had hurled his rally vehicle into the air and rolled it countless times until it stopped upside down in a crushed mess, leaving one of its occupants dead. Aaron's navigator mate, Nobby, had somehow survived and was recovering in Broken Hill Base Hospital.

Maddie barely heard the voices up front or registered the hymns that were sung. Her mind stayed focused on being strong, enduring the day and getting back to the homestead and her now fatherless son.

The one redeeming spark in a horrifying week was her little sister, Lilly, who sat next to her. She had flown all the way home from London with their mother as soon as she heard the news of her brother-in-law's sudden tragic death. Dutiful as always and wearing a smart little black dress, Lilly had yielded to their mother's insistence that only sombre colours were acceptable for a Harwood family funeral.

Maddie had rebelled. She didn't care that people stared at her bright fitted summer dress and sweeping wide brimmed hat with its jauntily dipped brim. Normally indifferent to fashion, she had loved the outfit for the spring race meeting last year the instant she saw it in a Goulburn dress shop window. It was perfect for

144

today. Aaron had loved her in tight jeans but also in sexy dresses so she was giving him one last look.

Their parents sat stoically further along the pew, tolerating each other in public for dignified show. Mother in graceful grey and a small black and silver fascinator with just enough net to cover her forehead but not her eyes. Her father for once in a suit again. The last time had been only months ago at his first wife, Ailie's, funeral.

Just before Christmas, she had been shocked to learn of her father's past adultery. Secret meetings out at Ailie Sheldon's cottage and trysts in the Harwood family beach shack at Inlet Creek while Maddie, Lilly and their mother holidayed in England. And big sister Daisy had known, a part of the happy family trio.

Christmas had been a strained unbearable front. Aaron rabbiting on about the bloody outback rally that would kill him within weeks. Kirra cooking food that was barely touched. Except for Aaron and Tommy. Ignorant of the undercurrent, they had eaten everything in sight.

And to top it all off, as she walked into the church earlier, Maddie had noticed her stepsister Daisy and partner Jack seated in a pew toward the back of the church. Wise move. Out at the homestead countless times since news of Aaron's death numbed the station and homestead, Maddie's mother had already expressed her resentful opinion that Daisy was not welcome at Aaron's funeral. And raged that George had phoned *that girl* to tell her.

In no uncertain terms, her father had told his

wife *that girl* had a name and in future she would be advised to use it.

Maddie still wasn't sure what to feel about the recent rift with Daisy who had known about their father's ongoing affair. It was his culpability. No blame lay on his oldest daughter, an innocent child, but being from his first family, she associated them and, since Aaron's death, had pushed the unhealed wound to the back of her mind. To be dealt with another time.

So she resented feeling respect for Daisy coming all this way from Inlet Creek on an eight hour round trip to the funeral and dragging her Frenchman along.

When organ music struck up again, Maddie realised the service was over. *Georgina Downs* workmen and some of Aaron's mates from the rally carried the coffin as they walked from the church, others formed a guard of honour outside.

Maddie didn't feel like talking so, dragging Lilly with her, she escaped to the exclusive comfort of the shiny black stretch limousine her mother had hired for a show of Harwood presence. *So we can all be together as a family*, she had claimed. Happy days!

'Daisy's here.' Lilly's voice and eyebrows rose in surprise as they climbed in.

'I know!'

'Why are you so grumpy?'

'I've just lost a husband?' she snapped bitterly.

'Well I think it's admirable that she came all this way.'

'Don't know why she bothered. The favoured

146

daughter pushing her way into Dad's affections again.'

Lilly frowned. 'Daisy's not like that.'

'Honestly, Lilly, you're so innocent, it's annoying. Maybe neither of us knows her as well as we think.'

Lilly pushed out a gentle tolerant sigh. 'Is it because of what you told me about Father and his first wife?'

'Of course.' Maddie flashed her a scathing glance.

'You haven't spoken to him since I arrived. It's not your fault Father was unfaithful to Mother and that Aaron was killed.'

'Don't be so insensitive. He was my husband.'

Overwhelmed with everything happening and not wanting to cope with any of it, Maddie's eyes watered and she despised herself for showing weakness. She just wanted to disappear from view. The driver slid into the front seat and their parents joined them, facing them in the back.

Elizabeth constantly fanned herself even with the air conditioning pushing its icy chill into the vehicle interior. Misunderstanding her daughter's tears for grief, she said crisply, 'Don't waste any of those. I never thought he was good enough for you.'

'Elizabeth!' George growled.

Lilly handed her sister a lacy handkerchief. Maddie glared at her mother as she swiped at her wet cheeks.

'Well, I loved him,' she retorted from between thinned lips. She had at the beginning. What happened? She glanced between her parents. 'But you two wouldn't know about that, would you? Your marriage is a disaster.'

Maddie knew she was ranting and hurting her parents and meant to. Her mother snubbed her outburst and looked out the window. Her father stayed silent which was nothing new. They had hardly spoken since before Christmas and the blow up after the controversy at the beach house.

Compounding it all, she had been nothing but stinging and cruel to everyone since Aaron's death. Except Tommy, of course. Oh God, she just wanted this day to be over so she could snuggle up with her beautiful precious son in bed and forget the world.

The limousine moved off and slowly motored behind the hearse the short distance from town back to the family cemetery in the far corner of the station homestead paddock. In the blistering heat of high summer, the land was brown, dry and dusty with whirlwinds sweeping the property and choking the air.

Yes, it was desolate for a few months but Maddie still loved it. The silence, the vistas, even the danger of cold blooded snakes who emerged to coil and bask in the summer sun. By autumn, the heat would moderate, nights cool down and life grow more bearable again.

Once the first breaking rains came, Rambler's hooves would thunder beneath her on the first thick swathes of lush green pasture grasses that completely changed the landscape. Maybe she would feel better by then.

As the limousine slid to a stop, Maddie glanced out the window and froze. The driver opened the doors for them all and the others moved out but she hesitated. This would be the hard bit. When this was over she could return to Tommy and hugs, and numb her crushing life's reality with ice cold beer.

The family waited for her while she finally stepped out into the scorching sun. Thank God for sunglasses and a big hat.

At her father's insistence, the workmen on *Georgina* maintained the station cemetery in immaculate condition. As a child, she had accompanied him out here on his regular trips of inspection. The only one interested enough to do so. Mother kept to the homestead and Lilly was rarely adventurous. The entire burial area was surrounded by a smart mesh fence and central gate. Keeping the grass down was hardly a problem at this time of year. No rain, no growth.

Still in a mental daze, Maddie trailed behind her parents and Lilly along the neat gravelled central path by other family graves. Her Scottish grandfather, MacKenzie Harwood and his wife, Mairi. The sadness of their deceased babies and children, struck down by the harsh pioneering life or disease. Kenneth MacKenzie aged 3 months, Douglas MacKenzie aged seventeen months and Heather Mary age three. Maddie knew them all by heart. As far as she knew, only her father George had survived.

As well, although to one side, some early workmen including aboriginal station hands lay resting here, too.

Maddie distracted herself from the minister's droning monologue, the coffin waiting to descend and banks of dirt either side of the grave, with thoughts of the deep shade on green lawns back at the homestead to come. The tent pavilions erected for their guests, some open-sided for a cross breeze, would shelter mourners from the sun but not the heat. Chairs already arranged around the broad verandas not to mention the loads of food Kirra had prepared, ice filled troughs for chilled drinks and great glass bowls of punch.

And then, thankfully, it was done. Her husband was buried. Maddie's hands were clasped, cheeks kissed, shoulders grasped in hugs and kind words spoken. She appreciated it all but did not care, only offering murmured responses. Hardest part was the agony and hesitancy of Aaron's mates coming forward to embrace her, words impossible for any of the outback men to find. She just wanted to leave.

From beneath the brim of her huge hat as her disinterested gaze wandered, Maddie caught a brief exchange between George and Daisy, awkward beneath Elizabeth's piercing glare, her mother bitterly detesting the offspring of her husband's first marriage. The conversation seemed to be nothing more than a greeting and acknowledgement of each other's presence between her father and his oldest daughter. Then they parted.

The homestead cook, Kirra, approached Daisy too. Begrudging even such a tenuous connection, Maddie disapproved but Kirra would remember her from childhood and the few brief years Daisy and her mother, Ailie, lived on the station. Now they were hugging!

Kirra took Daisy's hands into her own and

spoke for a few moments. Daisy raised hands to her face and seemed upset; maybe it was surprise or happiness. Then she was nodding and smiling.

With a grudging hit of envy and feeling an uncharitable scorn, Maddie acknowledged Daisy's connection as part of the Harwood family by birth whether any of her father's second family liked it or not, and that Daisy had lived in the same homestead she herself and little sister Lilly also knew as home. The vision was a fresh sting of Daisy and her father's blood tie.

As mourners left the cemetery and climbed into cars for the short trip to the haven of the homestead and its surrounding gardens, kept verdant with bore water, Maddie noticed that Daisy and Jack drove away from the property back toward the main road in the French guy's noisy combi van. Ironically, Maddie sighed with a pang of resentment that they could escape so soon.

Daisy wisely knew her place. As long as Elizabeth Harwood was alive, her husband's oldest child would never be welcome here. Surprised to feel it, Maddie suffered a sense of discomfort at the heartless situation.

★ ★ ★

By early evening, the last vehicle finally departed from the homestead on the track back to the main road amid a cloud of lingering dust. The sting of the lowering orange sun was not quite so acute but although the household prepared for dinner, Maddie ignored her hunger. She had no appetite.

The whole of *Georgina Downs* grieved. Workmen and domestic staff alike. All Maddie could cope with while enduring the heavy agony in her chest was on shielding Tommy with mountains of love and hiding her private anger over her husband's useless death so young.

Ignoring her mother's whining protests, she changed into riding gear later as the hot day cooled and headed for the stables. As she saddled Rambler and set his nose along familiar trails toward the sluggish dwindling creek and billabong, Maddie agonized over how to tell Tommy the truth about his father. The ordeal would be crushing for both mother and son, especially since Tommy had been chattering all afternoon about Daddy missing the party.

Because of their rift since Christmas, her father remained distant. Worse, her mother was utterly useless. Telling staff to be quiet, fussing importantly about the house yet doing nothing. Still cross because she had been forced to come home from England's crisp snowy winter to the Australian outback summer heat. For Aaron of all people. She had never made a secret of her disapproval over the match. Maddie doubted Elizabeth would stay long and use any excuse to leave. The sooner the better, as far as Maddie was concerned.

Lilly was another matter. Maddie loved having her little sister home again. Only yesterday she had probed, 'If Mother goes back to England, will you stay on?'

'She and Father have been arguing about her flying back and all the travelling expenses.'

152

'Yes, I heard. It's why I asked.'

'I'll take as much leave as I need if you want me here.'

'If you can't manage much more time, that's okay. I know you must return eventually,' Maddie had said generously while in her heart wishing her sister could stay.

Lilly would cave if Elizabeth pressured for them to return to England together. If that happened, there would be just Maddie, her father and Tommy. A confronting thought, revealing the reality of her changed life situation now. It felt as though the homestead was slowly fading. At least Aaron had brought a measure of life to the house. But he wouldn't be here anymore.

Mother would leave, then Lilly. In the autumn, Elizabeth would return. That might prove even worse. Just her parents, herself and Tommy.

Bugger. Suddenly her life and world seemed to be a shrinking mess.

Maddie gently pulled up the proud bay horse she had trained from a two year old, dismounted, hooked the reins loosely over a low tree branch and sat on the creek bank. She kicked off her boots and let her feet dangle as she watched the lengthening light stripe golden beams across the sluggish water and overhanging gums cast reflections on its surface, her mind filled with contemplations of guilt.

She and Aaron had not been as blissfully happy as everyone thought. Even after marriage, he had continued to flirt with other women. Along with his killer smile and attitude, he thrived on winning and attention. Maddie had always wondered if she was merely another conquest, a prize to be won, a trophy like all his rally cups and previous women. If he had known, would he still have wanted her?

With the sun setting and Tommy's bedtime looming, Maddie pushed herself to stand and rode back to the homestead.

She encountered Lilly in the hallway. 'Kirra's kept some dinner for you.'

'I need to put Tommy to bed.'

'You should eat something.'

'Maybe later.'

In the end, perhaps because he was yet so small to fully understand, Maddie's explanation of Aaron's death seemed to fly over Tommy's head. She believed he still thought his father would be back one day.

So she told him, 'Whenever you feel like it, just spread your arms wide and say *Hi Daddy*. Talk to him. He'll be listening.'

How could she spread such a tale to her son? Maddie excused herself because he was still a child. Maybe she would explain better when he was older. For now, all they could do was take one day at a time.

Because he had always loved it, Maddie lay on top of the sheet with her arm lightly draped across him while Tommy backed up against her and soon fell asleep.

More relaxed and with relief in the aftermath of telling her son about Aaron, she must have dozed off for a while. Stirring, Maddie eased herself from his bed and room, to freshen up in her own suite. As she did every day, she avoided glancing at the last clothes Aaron had worn before leaving on the rally, carelessly tossed over his chair. She couldn't look at them and couldn't touch them. Maybe Lilly could help her. It seemed wrong to bother the house girls to help.

Everywhere reminders.

When she composed herself enough, she padded off down the tiled hallway, always lovely and cool on bare feet in summer, in search of food. Seated in her favourite chair by the closed side veranda window, Kirra looked up and smiled as she entered the kitchen.

'Hey Missy.' She nodded toward the massive double range. 'You know where to find it.'

'Thanks.' Maddie bent to take her plate out of the oven and found cutlery. She sniffed the curry and rice appreciatively. Even in summer, her father preferred hot meals and Kirra obliged by preparing them. 'Smells so good.'

Maddie pulled out a chair at the huge scrubbed timber table where Kirra prepared wonderful meals, and began to eat, her appetite improved since the distress with Tommy was over.

'I've taken tea into your Mother's suite. Miss Lilly and Mr. H are in the sitting room with cool drinks.'

'You should be in bed, Kirra. You've worked like an entire team of caterers all week.'

'I'd do anything for you, Missy. I'm just so damn mad that boy Aaron gone and got himself killed. But you gonna be okay. You got your Tommy and your home here on your own country.'

'Yes, I do.' Maddie paused. 'Go to bed, Kirra,' she pleaded softly.

'Now why would I be doin' that when I can sit and chat with you?'

'Sunrise is around five o'clock. I'll bet you've been up since then.'

'Don't you start nagging like your Mother,' Kirra muttered in a low voice.

Maddie glanced across at her and they burst out laughing, the cook's dark-skinned face gleaming, her chest heaving with mirth. They had shared countless similar private jokes as far back as Maddie could remember. She rose and poured herself a huge mug of tea from the kettle always simmering on the hob. Then crossed the kitchen and pressed a kiss on top of Kirra's curly black hair.

'Thanks for everything today. *Now* go to bed. Goodnight.'

She left the kitchen to the sound of Kirra chuckling.

In the sitting room, Maddie was pleased to see her father had apparently retreated to his study. He wouldn't be in bed. He rose at dawn and rarely retired before midnight.

Lilly looked up from reading a glossy country magazine at one end of the sofa. 'Tommy okay?'

Maddie nodded. 'I told him but not sure he really understands.'

'You've eaten?'

'Yes!'

A second before she was about to sit and wind herself comfortably into a leather armchair, she caught sight of her wedding photo where it had always been on the massive carved sideboard across the room. It had never bothered her before but, suddenly unable to bear looking at their smiling faces filled with love and hope only four years ago, she strode over and laid it face down.

Looking at Lilly's concerned frown as she returned and before her sister said anything, Maddie held up a hand and sipped her tea. 'I'm fine.'

'Anything you want to talk about?' Lilly laid her magazine aside.

'Not really. Just feel crap and restless about everything.' She stared into her tea and muttered, 'Sorry I was a bitch today.'

'A gorgeous bitch,' Lilly murmured, not a hint of a smile. 'Wearing that outfit today was brave and stunning.'

'Thanks. Think that's a compliment.'

Gentle Lilly eyed her shrewdly. 'Should feed local gossip for a few weeks.'

'I don't give a damn.'

'I know you don't. That's what I admire about you.'

'You care too much about everything. Cut yourself some slack.'

'I'm trying. It's not always easy.'

Sounded like her little sister was on a path to discovery. Maddie was pleased to hear it. 'Still love living in England even after five years?'

Lilly nodded. 'For now. I get to take holidays on the Continent and Oliver has amazing friends and parties.'

'So, this boyfriend, are you two serious?'

'He's so well connected. You won't believe who he knows.'

'So you're impressed by him but do you really *like* him? I mean, the whole person?' Maddie worried when Lilly grew uncomfortable and took a while to answer.

'Most of the time,' she said, not totally reassuring, 'but there's always an issue in any relationship, isn't there? I mean, we're all human. Nobody's perfect.'

Maddie couldn't disagree with that but it sounded like her sister making excuses. 'Sure. It's about give and take. So long as there's not more take than give, if you get my drift.'

She finished her tea and set down the mug, contemplating her own experience of marriage. Even on the day of his funeral and just being buried, Maddie acknowledged that Aaron had been a selfish prick at times. After the initial explosion of love and hot sex followed by a quick marriage, Maddie had suffered feelings of hovering behind in his shadow. It became all about his mates and drinking and pushing boundaries. And, she knew, also women. He worked hard but he also played hard.

But who was she to criticise a man who was no longer around to defend himself? To compensate and taking Tommy's schedule into account, she had turned to more station work, shouldering more of the load and being out on the property as much as possible. Going on musters and camp outs. Riding alongside her father at every opportunity.

In the last year as their son grew older, Maddie had taken to bringing Tommy along on single overnighters. Sitting him between her legs

158

backed up against her with Grampa and the workmen around a campfire. Eating stew and damper. Snuggling him into a sleeping bag beneath the stars on a mild clear night. She had only wished Aaron had been there with them more. But he often had an excuse to be somewhere else. Ruffled his son's head and said *Maybe next time.*

'Maddie?'

She grew aware of Lilly's voice. 'Sorry?'

'Just asking about Father. I haven't seen him for a year and he looks, oh, I don't know, so lost and miserable.'

'You noticed,' Maddie said.

'Do you think he's, like, still grieving for his first wife, Ailie?'

'Probably.' Maddie felt guilty on that front, knowing her father suffered and yet she had hardly acknowledged him in recent months. 'And with Aaron's death now.' Maddie shrugged. 'They worked close together. Not sure if Dad was grooming him to take over or at least manage the place alongside me one day, but it must be a lot for an older man to take in. He's emotionally beat for sure, but he's still as physically strong as ever. He'll pick up again.'

'Hope so. He looks miserable. You should turn in. It's been a long day.' Lilly sat forward on the sofa and stretched.

'Think I'll wait a while. I haven't been sleeping well.'

'Not surprising.'

As her sister left the room, Maddie stalled her by asking, 'You will give me some warning before you leave, won't you? Give me time to get used to not having you around again.'

'Sure. Oliver keeps asking me when I'm returning,' she wrinkled her brows in good-natured annoyance, 'but I'd love to stay longer.' She smiled.

Left alone with too many thoughts, Maddie's mood turned restless as it always did this time of night since Aaron's death. In its wake, the load of guilt over what she had never told him laid heavily on her mind. Plus reminders of her husband were everywhere in the homestead and especially in their bedroom suite.

Crazy, because she had always thought of *Georgina Downs* as home and never wanted to live anywhere else. But this wretched feeling of being haunted out here on the station by unwanted memories and poor decisions, made each new day an ordeal.

In the shadow of her husband's death, she should be embracing life. Instead, she could only wait and hope that the nagging burden of her secret would fade from her mind.

11

In the days following the funeral, passive Lilly, much to Maddie's surprise, proved to be her older sister's salvation and protector where their mother failed. The formerly docile Lilly had acquired a quiet strength. At times she still yielded, at others she chose small battles wisely while Elizabeth wilted in the heat. A fiction because the homestead hummed with the cool breezes of ducted air conditioning.

Many afternoons, as the summer sun beat down and reigned supreme outside, Maddie and Lilly lazed on cushioned cane veranda chairs, long glasses of iced drinks in hand, while Tommy went mad in his bathers and sunhat with a hose on the lawn. Squealing with delight, wickedly squirting anyone who dared come close. At those times, Maddie winced to reflect that her son was indeed exactly like his father.

But she grew all too aware that her time with Lilly was ending. The poor girl was receiving constant texts from her boyfriend back in England.

Plus their mother endlessly paced inside the homestead, doing nothing, anxious to escape again. She and Lilly had overheard more than one conversation where their parents argued in tense low tones. It seemed the more they were together, the unhappier they became.

Mainly on her father's behalf, above every

other churning emotion she was handling at the moment, Maddie felt the deepest pain. Her cold-hearted mother, unable to show or give any love was unlikely to ever receive much in return. At least from outspoken Maddie, very much her father's daughter. Lilly by nature was more compassionate and tolerant and prepared to excuse Elizabeth's imperious behaviour.

The morning Elizabeth dressed for display and made the long drive into Goulburn travel agency was the unspoken signal. Maddie knew she had pressured Lilly to return, too. Her sister, tumbling over herself with apologies, had reluctantly agreed to go. Between her pestering boyfriend and their domineering mother, pliant Lilly was never destined to win.

And so with cases, hand luggage for the flight, passports and tickets at the ready all packed on the veranda just outside the front door, Maddie found it shattering when the day arrived to say goodbye to her little sister. And finally appreciated just how much Lilly meant to her and how much she would be missed.

As the two sisters hugged, both fearful of letting go it seemed, Lilly made a whispered suggestion. 'Give yourself a few months and come visit me in the English summer.'

As they pulled apart, both with watery gazes, Maddie said, 'Maybe. I'll think about it.'

As for farewelling her mother, as always they simply air kissed. According to Elizabeth's rules, polite and acceptable enough.

George would drive his womenfolk into Goulburn to catch the train to Sydney before a night flight via Dubai back to London. For most of the next twenty-four hours they would be in the air. Maddie could only bravely smile and privately pray for safe travels as she madly waved, Tommy in her arms, while the four wheel drive moved away, growing ever smaller and leaving a familiar trail of swirling dust.

When her father returned for dinner, it would be just the two of them and Tommy in the homestead again. Maddie was surprised that he had offered to leave the station, usually only out of strict necessity. But he had mumbled something about an appointment so she assumed it was business, one of the few reasons he ever journeyed beyond *Georgina's* boundaries.

He wasn't so much a hermit as a victim of his own hardworking ethic and love of his land. The one time in his life he had ventured further away far beyond the station fences and Australia's borders, he had met and married the wrong person, suffering for it ever since. Perhaps the very cause of his growing solitary lifestyle.

Which only made Maddie all the more bitter that his second marriage and two offspring had been a huge mistake. And revived the core of their existing standoff. That George's first family had been the one real happiness in his life, only to be lost.

When Tommy went down for his short afternoon nap with Nanny keeping watch, Maddie saddled up Rambler again and cantered toward the creek, mindful not to push her horse in the heat. On its low reedy banks, she reflected

163

on the stalemate with her father. When they were alone together again in the homestead, it would be impossible unless they tackled the source of their disagreement. Amidst her raw and present grief, the confrontation filled her with fear that the opinion she held might be true.

Maddie hadn't long returned from her ride to find Tommy wide awake and ready to play when George returned from his day trip into town. From indoors where she played SNAP with Tommy in the front sitting room, she watched the four wheel drive rumble slowly past the homestead window and disappear into the nearby machinery shed where vehicles and equipment were parked.

Not five minutes later, her father's boots stomped across the timber veranda and into the long tiled hallway. Catching sight of his daughter and grandson through the open doorway, he dropped his big battered hat onto a side table and came straight in. Maddie sensed with a deep measure of caution.

She looked up but didn't speak. Tommy filled the gap by brightly bubbling, 'I'm winning, Grampa.'

'Good man,' he said warmly.

After a long and awkward silence, he finally faced Maddie. 'I know I'm not your favourite person right now but we should talk.'

So, they were on the same wave length, then. Maddie was amazed he would instigate a conversation but was relieved that he did. It meant she didn't need to raise it herself. 'Sure.' She glanced meaningfully toward Tommy. 'After dinner?'

The only words spoken between them for the

rest of the day and throughout the difficult meal. Only once Tommy was fed, bathed and eyelids drowsy with stories, did Maddie tiptoe from his room.

'He's out on the side veranda,' Kirra said softly, as Maddie entered the kitchen and took two beers from the drinks refrigerator.

She smiled weakly at the cook. There wasn't much the household missed. 'Wish us luck,' Maddie whispered, snapped off the bottle lids and left.

With no outside lights on against the swarms of annoying summer insects and bugs drawn to them, just a faint golden glow from indoor lamps filtering outdoors, the damp air off the mown lawn grasses kept the mild evening a few degrees cooler.

Maddie handed her father a beer and sat beside him in the fading dusk that would soon draw the cloak of darkness about them. He still wore his smart town clothes of jeans and a clean checked shirt. Unless she went riding, Maddie pretty much opted for her standard summer garb of denim shorts, a singlet tee shirt and bare feet.

Her father took a long swill of his drink before his low quiet words punctured the silence. 'I know I was unfaithful to your mother and that you don't respect me for it but a man can't change the way he feels and who he falls in love with.'

Nor a woman, Maddie reflected with irony, knowing all about being disloyal but not within marriage. Although there were plenty of men on the station with winks, sexy muscled bodies and a ready smile, she had never been tempted, but couldn't speak for Aaron and never dared to ask.

'Did you ever love mother?'

'I thought so.'

Maddie took a sip of her drink and let the amber bubbles slide down her throat. Love was a minefield for sure. She knew her father would never apologise and did she really expect it? He was merely pointing out the truth and expecting her to deal with it. Perhaps that was all it took and all she wanted for now. But there was a side issue.

'I need you to be honest, Dad.' She swallowed hard and hesitated. 'Were you disappointed when Lilly and I came along?'

'A bit. At first.'

She knew it! Emotion clogged Maddie's suddenly dry throat and tears threatened. She tossed back a long gulp of beer to dull the hit of pain to hear the truth. For which she had asked. And she sure got it.

He reached out and laid a hand on her arm. 'If it's any consolation, my disappointment didn't last long and I love you both dearly.'

Maddie quietly sobbed. Through gulping hiccups, she managed, 'How can you not fall in love with your child the moment you set eyes on her?' As she had done with Tommy, despite everything.

'I wasn't allowed near the nursery. You were bottle fed and your mother hired a nanny. She made it clear, raising children was other people's work. It was how Elizabeth was reared. I wasn't encouraged to be part of your lives when you were young.'

Maddie suspected that already but her father went on.

'I saw you as much as I could but I was out on the station and often away for days at a time. She dressed you like little princesses until you could walk and talk. Unlike Lilly you became fascinated with horses.'

They both reflected to themselves in the settled surrounding dark. Maddie didn't remember back that far but loved hearing her father speak of it. She just knew she had always loved riding and that much more fun and adventure beckoned outdoors. Only Lilly became her mother's possession.

'I'm sorry it was like that. I hated mother telling me what to do,' she admitted.

'You were a sweet rebel.'

Maddie sighed. 'I never meant to judge you. As we grew older, Lilly and I could see that you and mother weren't . . . close. And then you started taking us sometimes to visit Daisy and her mother.'

'It was twofold, Maddie. I resisted Ailie as long as I could,' George rasped out, 'but there was no denying what we still felt for each other. Probably always had. So I insisted to Elizabeth that you girls get to know your stepsister.' He paused and his voice lowered when he resumed. 'Which gave Ailie and I the excuse to be together.'

'Over the years,' he continued, more easily now, 'your mother started returning regularly to her family in England for the summer there. While her parents were still alive, she said. But it

167

was just an excuse to leave.'

Maddie was content to listen, sip her drink and feel the night breeze cool, softly brushing her skin. She digested his words, let them flow over her, finding it easier that way to accept them.

'So, one time, feeling pretty damn lonely, I must admit, I invited Ailie and Daisy to the beach house at Inlet Creek. It was winter and not too unpleasant. Always milder by the sea. So it became a habit each time your mother left and took you away for months at a time. I won't deny, Maddie that those times in the shack were when I most felt loved and part of a family. It didn't mean I didn't love you and your sister but the circumstances out here on the station just weren't the same.'

George finished his beer and set the empty stubbie bottle on the veranda at his feet, staring out across the shadowed garden. 'Now you and I are both grieving for loves lost.' He paused. 'Makes a body think ahead. Lilly's still under her mother's influence. With just you and Tommy here, it could be twenty years before we know if he's interested to take over *Georgina*. Unless you find yourself someone new. One day,' he hinted mildly.

'Cripes, Dad, Aaron's only been gone a few weeks. That thinking isn't even on my radar.'

'I know, Maddie, but love's a bit like the wind. We never know which direction it will come from.'

'Are you and Mother staying together?'

'I imagine we'll go on as we always do,' he said

with sad resignation, 'but I've been giving the future of the property some serious thought.'

'You thinking of retiring?'

'No, but my options are disappearing fast.'

In the quiet that followed, Maddie could hear his mind ticking over. It would be a tough decision. Grieving and confused with her own life right now, she didn't know what she felt about *Georgina* anymore.

'To be honest, Dad, I can't see myself running this place unless I had another partner who could share the load, a really strong dedicated man like you by my side. It's a huge business that I'd rather not face alone in the coming years waiting for Tommy to make a decision about it himself.'

'You've a good handle on station management, Maddie. I've tried to keep you informed on market information and decisions about breeding, buying and selling stock. You know that any money coming in depends on wool characteristics and prices. You know the stocking rates based on each paddock's carrying capacity.'

Maddie could hear from her father's urgent tone that he was sounding almost desperate. In her head space right now and with emotions hitting her on every side, she simply couldn't handle a deep and meaningful about the future of *Georgina Downs*. It was too much.

'Dad — '

'I know. You've got loads on your mind but would you promise me, as soon as you're ready, you'll think about it. If we're to survive as a family property, I need to talk about ewe and wether selection. It's so important for different breeding strategies for better fleece measurement and profits,' he said passionately.

It had been her father's and grandfather's lives but could it be hers?

While she mulled over the enormous decision and defaulted from participating in any further discussions, he continued pushing his point.

'We have all the rainfall, climate and long term weather patterns and outlooks on computer now. Just needs studying up a bit.'

Maddie knew there were bigger pastoral companies who might own a million hectares over 100 different properties, making them the nation's biggest landholders. Would George one day be forced to sell out to them? It would break his spirit and his heart.

With her mother virtually estranged from her father and station life now, and Lilly in England, Maddie could see why she had become George's focus.

'Would you not want to stay because of memories of Aaron?' he asked.

'Honestly, Dad, I don't know. I'm still numb and I have Tommy to watch out for. See how he misses his . . . father,' she stumbled over the words. 'I probably just need time. I love this country and the outback life but right now I simply can't promise anything.'

George shuffled forward in his chair, as if to leave, clasping his rough suntanned hands between his knees. 'I can see you're unsettled. Only natural. Just wish I could help you. Why not head across to the beach house on the coast and take a break?'

Maddie was shocked at the question. 'And leave you alone here?'

'I'll be all right,' he said roughly. 'It's cooler down there. Give you time and space to think. Tommy loves the sea.'

'Are you looking for some peace and quiet yourself,' she teased, 'without Tommy yelling and tramping all through the house?'

Her father slowly shook his head, his mouth even threatening to edge into a smile. 'He gives the homestead life. Besides, someone needs to stay here. Workmen to manage and stock to watch. And there's always the threat of fire this time of year.'

Maddie crossed her arms and tucked her long bare legs up beneath her. Crazily, his suggestion had given her food for thought. Her brain had been pretty much scattered lately.

But even while the idea took root, she knew if she was bound for Inlet Creek, she would no doubt run into Daisy and have to face her again. She had really enjoyed her stepsister's company and been uplifted by their brief renewed friendship late last year. Daisy was a warm and natural person, easy to like.

But despite the truthful revealing discussion with her father tonight that gave her a small measure of peace toward healing, it was still hard to swallow the fact that her stepsister was the child of his favourite wife. Until she could come to terms with it, her jealousy stung.

* * *

Within the week, Maddie had given her father's suggestion more thought. Only once the decision was firmly made in her mind, so as not to upset Tommy in case she changed it, did she tell her son. And was rewarded with screams of delight.

So today saw them both packed in the four wheel drive and ready to leave the sheep station. Maddie worried at leaving George. It seemed his whole family had deserted him in recent weeks. He cut a dejected figure of an otherwise resilient outback man standing on the veranda as Tommy dashed about with excitement.

Before they piled into the vehicle to start the trip to the coast, Maddie was moved to give her father a long and genuine hug. 'Take care, Dad. We'll be in touch.'

'Stay as long as you need.'

When Tommy clung to his legs, George hauled the boy up into his arms. Smaller arms wrapped around the older man's creased suntanned neck and Maddie wondered if she imagined a glint of moisture in her father's eyes.

'Come and stay with us, Grampa,' Tommy pleaded. 'It's the beach,' he beamed, as though that would be the clincher to seal a visit.

The pleasure of a child not equalled by a man who preferred wide open spaces and vast flocks of sheep to strolling idly along white sands.

'Yes, Dad, come visit,' Maddie urged to reinforce her son's plea. She ached to be leaving him out here alone. There would be household staff but no family. Not even a wife to stand by his side.

He grunted. 'I'll see. Always plenty to do out here.'

'Don't hide from life, Dad.' Maddie touched his arm. 'It does exist beyond this station, you know.'

'I didn't call her *Georgina* for nothing. She's my mistress.'

His rare and dry attempt at humour fell flat. Maybe that was the essence of her father's own problem, Maddie reflected. Why two wives had felt driven to forsake him.

As she drove away in the loaded four wheel drive, Maddie's only concern was that leaving the station and returning to Inlet Creek might be considered running away from the reality of her life right now. Aaron's recent death, the unfortunate homestead situation because of her parents' unhappy marriage, and her father's infidelity. Although Maddie was beginning to soften her opinion on that issue after talking to him.

And, buried deeper, the secret she wondered if she would always be able to keep. Or would it return to haunt her in the future?

'Is it the beach soon, Mummy?' Tommy frowned with concern, kicking his small feet in the car seat behind her.

'Not yet, sweetie.'

'There's *Rambo*,' Tommy pointed out with delight a short time later as Maddie turned off the Hume Highway for a lunch stop.

Maddie smiled at the name the locals had given it. He had seen the *Big Merino* often enough on their trips into Goulburn and knew it well. Fifteen tall metres of concrete named after a stud ram from a nearby property. The entire district, of which *Georgina Downs* was a part, ideally suited to sheep with a relatively mild climate and vast areas of natural grassland.

In town, Maddie stopped at Belmore Park to let Tommy escape and run around. Originally a market place, it was now a quaint landscaped city square and community space. A popular landmark for residents and visitors alike featuring a six sided ornate rotunda, glass conservatory, gardens and fountains.

Kirra had packed a finger food lunch that Maddie set up on a table in the cool deep shadows of a great old tree. Tommy kept returning to grab another handful of food in between racing around and playing, especially on the favourite bright red train he always loved to scramble over.

As she suspected, once they were on the road again, the weary boy dozed off in the car for the longer afternoon drive through small villages and winding through the national parks on the eastern escarpment of the Great Dividing Range between the outback and the coast.

Arriving in Inlet Creek about mid-afternoon raised recent memories of just before Christmas and that other unfortunate issue that had blown up in her face. The lovely promise at the beginning of the family evening, the food and wine, then the shocking revelation that followed, destroying Maddie's idealised vision of her father and casting blame on Daisy where she was generous enough now to concede it did not belong.

Since hearing her father's perspective, she understood all the factors that contributed to his affair with his first wife, and the undeniable call of love between them, but the distance with Daisy prevailed.

Finally reaching the Harwood beach house with the sparkling blue waters of the ocean beyond washing up to its front steps, Maddie released Tommy from his seatbelt to race between the shack and the sand while she unpacked the vehicle.

Her son knew he was forbidden to go near the water without her but she kept a keen eye on him anyway. Watching out for him, calling his name to which he would answer, 'I'm here, Mummy,' and she would be reassured he was alright.

Later, as Tommy played down on the sand, Maddie took her mobile, a bottle of beer and a book out onto the front veranda. As she settled into a deck lounger and pushed on sunglasses, she wondered what now?

12

Maddie's tumbling thoughts on her first lonely nights and days at the beach house evolved into the realisation that, with Aaron's untimely death, her life had permanently changed. She and Tommy were now flying solo together without the man who had been the centre of their lives. Even if there's had not always been a model family unit.

To be granted time away from the homestead and all that it meant was both a curse and a blessing. No matter where she was, grief battered Maddie's fragile emotions. Aaron had been so full of life, genuine heartbreaking sorrow and resentful fury rocked her world.

She indulged in sadness for the decline in true love on her behalf in the last years of their marriage, wishing she could have felt the same fiery spark of love that spun her world out of control when she and Aaron had first met. She could do nothing about the past but would she have changed anything? One glance at her son erased all regrets.

But she wondered if, one day, she might ever be allowed to experience that same gift of blazing passion again. Maybe next time it would last. But, even if a person desired it, how did one achieve that romantic ideal of lifetime love? Was it even attainable or worth it?

Had it been better that her father and Ailie

had parted, if unwillingly on both sides, but then amazingly gone on loving each other? Had their connection continued because of the excitement of not living together? Or been compelled by an absolute pull of obsessive desire? Maddie found it astonishing that her crusty old father had been capable of such passionate adoration. And probable that their affair might have withered and died had they remained together in disharmony under the homestead roof, Ailie the unhappy one, the conflict potentially destroying each other.

The Harwoods seemed hardly able to make a success of any marriage. Her parents a prime example. But was it wise to persist in a lifelong relationship that was destructive for one of the parties involved? Or better that one person had the courage to break free and allow their souls to independently flourish, perhaps find another mate? Did a person even need one? Nothing wrong with living single.

Within days, sick of obsessing over circumstances she could not change, Maddie was bursting with a stifled energy she would have ridden off on Rambler out at *Georgina*. She watched Tommy happily playing down on the beach sands, making channels for the incoming waves to flood. Upending buckets full of wet sand to make castles.

Some nights as she tucked him into bed and they snuggled up together reading stories and talking about their day, some little thing would trigger a memory and the boy would ask about his father. Maddie learned that keeping her answers simple was enough for a child his age.

There would be time enough for more thorough explanations and revelations when he was older.

'Tommy?' she shaded her eyes and called out to gain his attention. When he glanced in her direction, she added, 'Shall we go get ice creams?

His cheeky grin was her answer and his short little man legs carried him toward her at a toddler speed rate of knots.

Cleaned up and in the four wheel drive, for it was too far to walk into town on a hot day, they made the short run into Inlet Creek. It occurred to Maddie that she might encounter her stepsister but she planned on avoiding passing the tearoom anyway.

Licking their ice creams running down their waffle cones and strolling the main street, Tommy had run ahead before Maddie could call him back. They were getting way too close to *Daisy's* for comfort.

'Tommy?'

But it was too late. He had reached the shop. Worse, he stopped directly out the front, turning back to wait for his mother.

'Come back, sweetie,' she called out, hoping he would retrace his steps.

Tommy, ever his mother's son, stood his ground. 'I want to go to the park.'

Of course he did. It was on a broad corner allotment further down, the space covered by the dappled shade of big old gum trees across the next street. On the rare times they visited town, it was one of Tommy's favourite places. After the beach.

Maddie drew in a deep breath and went to

meet her son, trusting Daisy would be elsewhere in her shop and not notice her stepsister hurriedly walking past. But good fortune hadn't favoured her so far this year so why should it start now? Daisy was serving customers at a window table.

The moment the sisters' eyes met, they each knew a second of shock, like a kangaroo standing in the middle of an outback road stunned in vehicle headlights at night before bounding away back into the bush.

Maddie had stubbornly snubbed Daisy since she and George had argued in December over the discovery of her father's secret assignations with Ailie Sheldon.

Daisy reacted first with a surprised smile and wave. Maddie, her heart pounding with embarrassment, merely acknowledged her stepsister with a brief nod, then quickly pulled her gaze away and walked on, grabbing Tommy's hand and heading for the playground.

She almost expected Daisy to run from the shop and call out after her but there was only the sounds of the street, vehicles, pedestrians. The cry of sea gulls calling overhead and the distant thud of waves pounding up onto the beach nearby.

For which Maddie was grateful. A lucky escape. Mainly because she didn't know what she would do or say if Daisy ever approached her again. One thing was sure, it promised to be awkward. Even their distance at Aaron's funeral had been uncomfortable enough. A physical meeting would prove challenging.

After playtime in the park and holding Tommy's hand, Maddie crossed the main street to avoid *Daisy's* again. Thinking of the tearoom brought forward a sudden pang of memory when she and Daisy had spent a lazy afternoon late last year in the Sheldon farm orchard where they shared a picnic, beers and easy conversation together. Her stepsister had confided about her affair with the older man, Charles, and her reservations about it. Clearly they had broken up for whatever reason because Maddie had recognised the French baker, Jack someone, with Daisy at the funeral.

Her thoughts matched the moment they passed his boulangerie. Had they been on speaking terms, Maddie would have loved to ask her stepsister about this new boyfriend. For he surely must be if they had driven all the way outback to the station for Aaron's funeral in the man's rattly old van.

Maddie sighed. She missed Lilly and their chats.

Tommy skipped along beside her as they headed out along the pier. Fresh salt-laden summer breezes straight off the sea cooled the warm air. As they strolled, Maddie waved to the locals and fishermen she knew, some dangling a line fishing, others coming or going in boats of all sizes and descriptions.

An unfamiliar well-built blonde guy, perhaps here for the summer, just fitted beneath the canopy as he stood behind the wheel of a half cabin cruiser that chugged at low speed and edged toward the pier steps. The modest vessel was nothing fancy. The kind that blokes messed about with on the water but a stylish little blue and white number all the same.

Tommy stopped to watch him as he cut the motor and tied up.

When the man caught her son staring, Maddie smiled, shielded her eyes against the sun glinting off the sea and called out casually, 'Catch anything?' assuming like everyone else he had been fishing.

The guy shook his head and grinned as he stepped from the boat, leapt up the steps and onto the pier. His gaze settled on Maddie playing with her wedding ring.

'Nah, just took it out for a run. Not mine,' he nodded back toward the boat. 'A rental job.' He paused, frowning. 'I haven't seen you around.'

Really? Was he flirting? Confident types always did. 'Just down in our family beach house for a while. Live on a sheep station out west.'

He cleared his throat. 'Not trying to chat you up, ma'am, being a married woman.'

Maddie grew nervous and uncomfortable. She would encounter such comments from now on, she guessed. 'Oh I'm not,' she said hastily, but then found it confronting to voice the words she had not yet spoken to anyone. 'I'm widowed actually.' Her face clouded and a familiar nagging ache returned.

'Sorry to hear that, ma'am.' His voice gentled. Such softness from such a powerfully built physical man. Aaron had been muscular too.

'Thank you.'

'If you don't have your own boat, I'm happy to take the boy out for a run anytime,' he suggested casually, gently ruffling Tommy's mop of dark hair.

Maddie shrugged. 'No thank you. We're fine.'

She would want to know a lot more about this man before she trusted him with her son. But she sensed a kind heart behind his generous offer to a stranger. It didn't give the feeling of pity for a widow.

The big guy hesitated. 'Name's Josh Seymour.'

Maddie didn't introduce herself in return. Stunned by his forthright compelling attitude, she just stared him out. He didn't appear in the least bit bothered by her cool response.

'If you don't mind my asking since you're a local, I'm looking for work. Prepared to work long hours.'

For a big fit muscled man, Maddie was amused to see him appear embarrassed. A chink in the tough armour? Outback men didn't like to show it either. She stayed silent, observing him with interest as he continued.

'I don't suppose you know of any local fishermen taking on extra hands?'

'I've only just arrived from out west. Sorry.' She shrugged. 'You could try the pubs or the fishing co-op other side of the Point. Even any of the whale and dolphin tourist boats that tie up at the wharf around there, too.'

'Much obliged. I'll try them. You take care, now.'

With a nod of respect, Josh took off with lengthy strides back along the pier toward town.

Maddie knew because she turned to stare and watch him leave before she continued walking out to the end of pier barrier overlooking the sea.

Puzzled why she was still thinking about the man she had just met.

Maybe it was on account of her first impression that, underneath that confident exterior, he appeared as guarded as she had been. He was polite enough. Calling her ma'am. No one had ever done that before. The term sounded American but he didn't have the accent. That was pure Australian.

She might just ask around town about him.

★   ★   ★

That evening, with a happy and exhausted Tommy in bed, Maddie made an international phone call. 'Hey Lilly, it's me.'

'Maddie. How are you going?'

'Fine. I know its late morning over there and you're probably at work but I needed to hear your voice.'

'No problem but I can only talk for a minute.' She paused. 'Everything all right?'

'Sure,' she said automatically. Well, bearable. 'Dad suggested Tommy and I come to the beach house so I'm just phoning to let you know that's where we are. You can contact me here on my mobile for a while.'

'Dad's out at *Georgina* on his own?'

'His idea. He could probably use a call now and then from you, too.'

'Okay,' Lilly replied slowly.

'Have you seen mother?'

'Only once when she came down to London shopping. We had lunch. You know mother, it was an occasion at The Dorchester. White linen and embroidered napkins. Intimate and posh but exquisite food. She's mostly at Upfield Hall.'

The sisters chatted on briefly. Maddie noted Lilly didn't sound any more enthusiastic when she enquired about Oliver. At this time of night after a hot day she didn't have the energy to probe further as to why she persisted with the relationship. Clearly agreeable Lilly was struggling with it though for whatever reason.

Maddie yawned and ended the conversation, craving sleep, when there was a knock at the beach house front door. She started in surprise, her senses alert. Apart from the late hour, no one knew she was here except George. And Daisy.

Maddie uneasily uncurled herself from the sofa and padded barefoot to the door, hit with an edgy premonition. It couldn't be.

It was.

Daisy stood before her, hesitant, in all her wild blonde-haired glory, bright floaty trousers, a white sleeveless top and leather sandals. If nothing else, her stepsister sure had an individual boho style about her. No doubt inherited from her mother and freestyle upbringing on the farm. But then she had gone on to university and a successful overseas journalistic career. The girl was no slouch.

She had inherited a farm, sold it and opened tearooms in a busy coastal holiday village because apparently she loved to cook. Made Maddie curious to contemplate what else she didn't know about her stepsister.

When Maddie didn't speak because she was dumbly staring, Daisy said, 'Hey, Maddie. I just came to tell you in person that I was truly sorry to hear of Aaron's death. I didn't speak to you at the funeral because it wasn't the right time or place and I wasn't sure you would want me to, anyway.'

Maddie crossed her arms and glared. 'I got your sympathy card. No need for a visit. Or did you just come to see the sugar shack again,' she said bitterly.

Daisy winced at the verbal slap but instead of a retort, she seemed to take a moment to calm herself. 'Not at all. I just wanted to touch base and say hello. I know we're not speaking but we're still family and I'm here for you.' She hesitated and backed up a step. 'You have my number. Give me a call. If you want.'

And then her sister just turned and left. Coward, Maddie thought unkindly, as she closed the door and leaned back against it. But who exactly was the coward, she was unprepared to admit.

Maddie well remembered that idyllic afternoon in the Sheldon farm orchard again when they had simply been two stepsisters connecting. On that occasion, *she* had reached out to Daisy. Hard to imagine now. How had she let this happen?

This time, Daisy had been the one to make the first move. But Daisy was the favoured daughter, the child of her father's great love, Ailie. Full of fresh resentment, Maddie crossed the living

185

room to retrieve a bottle of wine and pour a glass to take out onto the front porch.

As she settled into a padded lounger, aware of her own inadequacy and blame in both cases, Maddie flooded with guilty grief over Aaron and reluctantly admitted that Daisy had been far less in her father's life than his second wife and daughters. What hurt the most was the fact that her father had unfaithfully and secretly met Ailie for years. Apparently preferred his first family to his second. That knowledge hurt and she couldn't let it go.

Maddie brooded, taking deep gulps of wine. Eventually, she phoned her father out on the station, knowing he would still be awake and working in his office.

After she established that he was all right, she said bleakly, 'Daisy called to see me.'

Her father heaved a deep sigh but said nothing. Maddie imagined what was in his thoughts so she didn't elaborate that it was a disaster. Of her own making.

Later, horrified but uncaring that she had emptied an entire bottle of wine, Maddie strolled down to just above the water's edge and incoming tide in the semi darkness. She sank onto the cool sand, dug in her toes and hugged her knees. Golden beams streamed from the house behind her. Street lights twinkled from Inlet Creek further along the beach and stars sparkled in the velvet night.

In the warm stillness, she heard the low chugging of night fishing trawlers heading out to sea, their navigation lights reflecting across the waters. And other smaller vessels she recognised as some of the locals by the outline and boat design. Not unusual for them to set off at night but they stayed in sheltered waters.

One caught her alcoholic gaze, causing her to look twice and concentrate. She believed it was the very one that belonged to the stranger, Josh, who had introduced himself on the pier this afternoon. He was keen, heading out again.

As he turned and steered about, other vessel lights sent enough of a glow over the small cruiser to define a single occupant. He was alone? Risky at night she would have thought. As he motored directly out from the beach in front of her, heading for the rocky point, she gained a better view. Yep. It was definitely him. Interesting.

Recalling his cautious manner at their meeting, Maddie couldn't help but be both intrigued and suspicious. You heard gossip locally of fishy business out at sea, and not of the seafood variety.

Too tired by now to give anything else much thought except the longing for her super soft big comfortable bed waiting inside, Maddie pushed herself to stand. Tomorrow was another day and she knew she was going to have to reach out.

Maddie had no real friends here. But she did have family. Could she be the bigger person and extend the hand of friendship again to Daisy? At least if they encountered each other in town while she and Tommy were staying, they could smile and be civil.

13

Next morning before Maddie changed her mind, she took a deep breath, grabbed her mobile phone and pressed Daisy's number. Damn. It rang out so she nervously left a brief message. Of course her stepsister would be hectic in the tearoom.

She paced, distracted, all morning with no response to her approach. Maybe Daisy had second thoughts after Maddie's rebuff last night? She had taken the trouble to make contact and extend an olive branch only to be snubbed. Something Elizabeth would do. Not usually a Maddie trait but she hadn't been the nicest person to be around in recent months. Damn again. She should have watched her tongue and shut her mouth.

She decided to face Daisy on her home ground so to speak and visit her in the tearoom. An afternoon cuppa to fit in around Tommy's schedule. See if they could heal the wound Maddie had so thoughtlessly created in their possibly new and definitely shaky friendship.

After lots of morning play for Tommy down on the beach while Maddie tried vainly to focus on reading a novel, and waiting while her son had his short afternoon nap, she dressed them both for a tearoom outing.

Passing *Daisy's* yesterday and managing a quick glance through the window, as well as her brief visit to the café two months ago seeking her stepsister before locating her out on the Sheldon farm and spending that magical afternoon in the orchard, Maddie knew the eatery was a fresh and beachy café with casual class. She wasn't into dressing up but wanted Daisy to see they had made an effort and respected the atmosphere she sought to achieve.

So with Tommy in his best pair of shorts and a smart blue checked shirt that reflected the colour of his eyes and the ocean on their doorstep, and Maddie actually wearing one of two sundresses she owned and had packed for their holiday break, even earrings and lipstick, they drove into town. Feeling just a mite stylish, Tommy excited, but Maddie nursing misgivings.

Taking that first step inside *Daisy's*, she learned, was like stepping into a paddock the first time for horse training. Uncertainty on both sides.

Her stepsister rarely missed much and noticed them right away. Maddie's hesitation clearly showed because in the split second of connection between them both, the moment their gazes met across the tearoom it was as though all noise around them stopped.

Daisy literally must have dropped what she was doing behind the counter because Maddie heard china clatter. Across the bustling space, her big sister beamed and immediately wove her way between tables to reach them. No words were spoken. Daisy just grabbed Maddie in a fierce and genuine hug, leant down and smiled *Hello* to Tommy, grinning up at his aunt.

She scanned the room for a free table and found one near the front window, a prime position with a perfect view of the ocean.

'I didn't mean to interrupt you,' Maddie apologised as they sat. 'When I didn't hear back from you I just came to check you got my message.'

'Oh I decided to let you stew for a while,' Daisy replied, straight-faced.

Maddie's face wrinkled in an *Ouch* moment. 'Fair enough.'

Then Daisy's expression broke into a grin and she chuckled. 'No, I'm just kidding. Its crazy busy here even with school holidays almost over and families leaving and February looming. Still heaps of travellers about until the weather breaks. I intended calling you tonight. I should have whipped you off a text but, honestly, I've hardly had a second to myself all day. Actually,' she paused, 'I thought maybe we could chat over a meal?'

Being honest with herself, the simple gesture of sisterhood that Maddie accepted from Daisy, who had been nothing but gracious and understanding and *available*, caused her to feel a rare depth of emotion that almost made her cry. She wasn't so alone after all. She had family here. Her stepsister. Maddie finally realised that in Daisy she had the gift of a burden eased, if not shared. She didn't always have to be the one always watching out for a younger sibling. Judging by her warm reception, Daisy was happily assuming that responsibility as a given.

Maddie shrugged. 'Come to the beach house.

I'll cook. You'll be raced off your feet all day and I'm lazing about on holiday.'

'You sure? Can I bring something?'

'Maybe one of your desserts?' Daisy nodded her agreement. 'We're spoilt having Kirra cook for us out on the station. My excuse for being hopeless in the kitchen but I can do a barbeque and salad.'

'Sounds perfect.'

'Tommy, would you like a milkshake and one of my cupcakes?'

He nodded madly.

'We had chocolate ice creams yesterday and I'm sure it will be chocolate on both counts today,' Maddie replied, raising her eyebrows and smiling toward her son for confirmation.

He nodded madly. Again.

'I have special ones with lots of sprinkles just for little boys,' Daisy bent down, leaning closer and speaking especially to Tommy.

The gesture opened Maddie's heart to her sister's natural consideration. She would be an awesome mother herself one day. Making Maddie an aunt. Wonderfully scary thought.

Looking down on him fondly, Daisy smoothed her hand over the back of Tommy's head. 'He is so much like his father, isn't he?' she said softly.

Caught off guard by the unexpected comment, Maddie hesitated. 'Yes, he is.' Which was true.

'So,' Daisy said to Tommy, 'what kind of tea does Mummy like to drink?'

'Really hot and very black,' he announced with certainty.

'He stands on a chair and chats to Kirra in the kitchen,' Maddie explained, grinning.

'Okay, then. How about a Turkish chai. It's just black leaf tea and hot water. It comes in a two piece teapot. So you pour the hot water from the bottom metal part into the porcelain teapot on top. It's served in a curved tea glass with a saucer of sugar cubes and a dish of nuts, fruits and dates.' Daisy shrugged. 'Unless you'd prefer something like a traditional Devonshire tea?'

Maddie shook her head. 'If you're bringing dessert for dinner I'll save up for that. The Turkish chai sounds lovely.'

In this weather and at this time of year she usually preferred a cold beer and a bag of crispy chips but, for once, she was embracing the girlie afternoon tea thing and enjoying the experience. And it was pleasant to dress like a lady. Not that she planned to make a habit of it or anything.

With brisk service, Daisy returned bearing Tommy's treats and Maddie's Turkish tea set out on a silver tray.

'Enjoy guys. It's on the house.'

'Can we come here every day, Mummy?' Tommy pleaded between big mouthfuls of chocolate shake, his lips smeared with chocolate icing from plunging his little face directly into the top of the cupcake.

Maddie heard her sister chortle as she walked away. As they ate and drank, she watched Daisy work tirelessly, clearing and resetting tables. Two younger girls helped and they all seemed to work together like a smooth team.

As she sipped her chai Maddie was impressed

and in awe that her sister had such purpose in life when she herself felt lost and drifting. She guessed, in time, the feelings would fade but never really leave her, and had to wonder where her own life would take her next.

Lately, the call from *Georgina Downs* didn't pull her as strongly as it had since her youth. Yet the weight of responsibility to stay and work beside her father was powerful. A dilemma she simply couldn't address right now. So she mentally pushed it aside, forcing herself, for Tommy's sake, to enjoy each day as much as possible.

A decision would come. It always did. To sway her in one direction or the other. Just exactly what *the other* might eventually be was anyone's guess.

Before leaving, Maddie used wet wipes on Tommy's face. 'There you are, hidden under chocolate,' she teased, pretending surprise to see his clean shiny skin again.

Seeing them stand, Daisy came over.

'About seven tonight at the beach house?' Maddie suggested.

'Perfect. Give me time to soak my tired feet in a long bath.' She hesitated. 'Jack sort of lives with me now.'

'Oh,' Maddie jumped in. 'Would you like him to come, too?'

'Actually,' Daisy wrinkled up her nose, 'do you mind if it's just us? Be nice to have some time alone together, yeah?'

Maddie nodded. 'Absolutely. But definitely another time with you both then, okay?'

'Sure. In my little flat. I'd love to show you my

place upstairs,' she pointed a finger toward the ceiling.'

'Deal. Look forward to it.'

Daisy settled her with a steady glance. 'Take care of you,' she said softly with meaning.

It was so unlike Maddie to be caught by surprise when she choked up with emotion again. For the second time this afternoon. So she just nodded, accepted Daisy's departing hug and grabbed Tommy's hand, dragging him away before she yielded to tears.

Life would go on but, despite all the more positive things happening for her lately, it was going to take a while. She just needed to be patient.

Through it all though, whatever happened, Maddie just knew with a certainty that could never be broken her older sister Daisy was in her life for good now and would always be there for her.

★ ★ ★

In a blur of misty eyes and still touched by Daisy's tenderness, Maddie hurtled off down the street head down toward the four wheel drive, Tommy trotting alongside trying to keep up with his mother, when they literally collided with someone on the footpath.

In horror, because she felt and therefore assumed she also looked, a mess, she saw it just had to be Josh, didn't it? Then despised herself, scowling. Why should she care what some stranger thought of her?

'Hey,' he grinned gently, gripping her arm in support as she stumbled.

Didn't look like he disapproved of her appearance after all. His gaze, not all that subtle, cruised over her with appreciation. His hold was warm and strong, his blonde hair gleaming in the sunlight. The teeth behind his smile absolutely perfect. She was almost glad she was wearing a dress.

Quickly collecting her wits, she acknowledged with a quick nod. 'Josh. Sorry, I — '

Releasing her arm and perhaps catching her edge of distress, he said smoothly, 'Nice to see you again, ma'am. Son.' He nodded down to Tommy.

As if to distract her, he continued, 'Good news. I bagged myself a job as crew on one of the big fishing trawler outfits.'

'You're staying around, then?' Maddie wasn't good at small talk and could have kicked herself for sounding so tongue-tied, and *interested*, as though it mattered to her where he lived and for how long.

'Seems like it.' As always, his response gave the impression of being deliberately vague.

To make up for her weakness, she confronted him with the intrigue nagging the back of her mind. Probably innocent enough but, for some reason, his actions just didn't add up.

'Saw you heading out in your boat at night recently.'

Instantly, all his shutters came down and he frowned. 'You did?'

Interesting response. Maddie shrugged. 'Our

family shack is right on the beach. I sit out on our front veranda sometimes. The peace helps me sleep. Recognised your vessel.'

Casually as you like and with a cheeky grin, he said, 'Flattered you're watching out for me.'

'Just wondering where you were going out alone in the dark? Big trawlers go out but they're commercial fishermen and have a full crew.'

'Boat's a hire job. Took it out for a run to get used to it.'

'At night?'

'I'm an experienced sailor.'

His calm explanation and steady gaze was almost a challenge that he knew what he was doing and she shouldn't interfere. And he hadn't really answered any of her questions. In fact he changed the subject.

'Won't keep you. Looked like you were in a hurry.'

Maddie pulled a tight smile. 'Yeah. We should get home.'

'You take care, now.'

He smiled at her for longer than was probably necessary before he began moving away. A familiar flicker of admiration that he slid over her each time they met, which didn't do her pride any harm.

Oh, why not? If he was going to be here a while longer. She couldn't have him calling her *ma'am* every time they met on the street.

'It's Maddie,' she called out. When he turned back, she draped an arm loosely about her son's shoulder. 'And this is Tommy.'

He planted his hands loosely on his hips and

smiled. 'Nice to meet you, Maddie.'

As they walked on, Tommy asked, 'That's the man from the pier, Mummy.'

'Yes. Mr. Seymour.'

'We're going to see more of him?' The boy misunderstood.

Maddie grinned. 'Not necessarily.'

The guy was unusually private and mysterious. All the same, she felt her spirits lift a notch as they drove home.

*   *   *

Josh Seymour strode back to his tough set of wheels, a rugged black Jeep. It needed enough power to get him out of a trouble without being conspicuous. The boys upstairs had chosen right.

His thoughts should have centred on the job at hand but, instead, his mind was crammed with images of the stunning woman he'd just bumped into again. Rewarding coincidence. His brain started ticking over and he allowed himself a satisfied grin.

Shapely legs beneath that pretty summer dress and, from what he remembered, had been pretty damned heart stopping in shorts the other day as well. Glossy brown hair that waved around her face and shoulders. He'd be willing to bet that, with such smooth honey-coloured skin, she was an outdoor type. Kid was kind of cute.

Maddie. He rolled the name around in his mind. Suited her. She had found it tough telling him her name and he had found it tough not being moved by that soft vulnerable side to her buried deep. But judging by her questions she was no fool. He respected that. In his profession you needed to read people fast. Not wising up could mean the difference between life and death.

With Michelle still in the background — but not for long — in his line of work, it probably wasn't wise to get too close. All the same, it might be handy finding out more about Maddie and striking up a friendship. That wary, sad edge about her might prove difficult to penetrate but, being a local, her knowledge could come in handy.

Idea was worth giving some thought except anyone close to him was always open to danger. And there was a child involved . . .

Damned annoying he couldn't forget that woman.

Meantime, he'd play it cool. See what the trawler job yielded. Work hard, keep his head down, not ask too many questions. Try to fit in like he always did but keep his eyes and ears open.

★ ★ ★

Situated on the eastern Australian coastline, Inlet Creek fell dark by six, even on summer nights. So Maddie had an hour before Daisy arrived. She bathed Tommy and put him in his short pyjamas so he would be ready for bed later.

He played with blocks while she bustled around the small beach house kitchen frying onions, chopping and tossing a mixed salad, boiling baby potatoes before folding them in a creamy dressing and sprinkling over chopped spring onions. Fat pork sausages and small tender cuts of fillet steak along with fresh fish fillets from the market were in the refrigerator ready to grill.

Maddie decided that from now on she would think of Daisy as her older sister. No longer stepsister. That old label seemed too far removed from the reality of their fresh closer relationship, as new as today.

When Daisy arrived she was like a breath of fresh summery air. The softly burnished pale skin of her face and arms glowed beside the simple white sleeveless dress overlaid with lace that draped her lithe figure, her toes slid into her usual leather sandals. Delicate blue dolphin earrings were just visible beneath her wild wavy hair that settled just above her shoulders. No wonder Jack was entranced.

'I bring gifts,' she announced brightly after they all hugged. 'This is from Jack.' She produced a chilled bottle of white wine. 'It's a Bordeaux Semillon sav blanc from his collection. He said it pairs beautifully with any summer fare.' She leaned closer and whispered, 'He usually drinks reds but he's sourcing some whites for me.'

'He didn't mind being left behind tonight?'

Daisy shook her head, her golden waves bouncing, and laughed. 'He was yawning as I left. His days start in the early hours. It's been a long busy summer.'

Then came the pièce de résistance. An

amazing creative dessert.

As she carefully removed it from her basket, Daisy said, 'I figured you had enough chocolate for one day so I brought a vanilla berry surprise. Granny Sheldon used to whip this up in late spring or early summer at the start of the berry season. Everything from the farm, of course.'

Tommy's gaze doubled at the sight of Aunt Daisy's treat.

'Thank you. This is magnificent.' Maddie placed it in the refrigerator for safe keeping until later.

Maddie had set the table for a casual meal indoors but flung the French doors wide to the front veranda, admitting the cool and salty evening air with the sound of breaking waves pounding onto the beach beyond.

Daisy noticed the bunch of large white daisies in a chubby glass vase in the centre of the table. The women exchanged a grin.

'In your honour,' Maddie said awkwardly.

Maddie poured the French wine as Daisy chattered about her day. Tommy wound himself between them determined to be part of their conversation. Sitting on the high kitchen stool across the counter while Maddie turned on the grill to cook their feast, Daisy hauled her nephew up onto her knee so they could share the bowl of crisps.

When the meat was done, the trio sat around the table set with meat and fish platters, salad and still warm potatoes.

'I've never had this,' Daisy glanced around the table as Maddie poured more wine and they held their glasses for a toast. 'A sense of wider family outside Ailie, Granny and Mae. At least George made sure we knew each other in childhood.' She reached out and squeezed Maddie's hand. 'Although it was the deaths of loved ones that brought us back together.'

Maddie nodded. 'That's when we need each other the most.'

'To family and the future.'

'Absolutely.'

They touched glasses in a toast, Tommy clinked them with his glass of water and the meal was on. The sombre moment soon passed as they each began serving themselves, Tommy managing well enough with his small hands awkwardly manipulating the big spoons. Maddie was determined that her little man should learn to be independent. Besides Grampa, without an immediate family male role model in his life now, she believed it was more important than ever.

'So I guess Lilly has returned to England?' Daisy asked.

Maddie nodded. 'She and mother went back together a few weeks after the funeral. Lilly stayed as long as she could. I loved being with her again. She was my absolute rock the whole time but I'm afraid she'll never want to return to Australia. She seems to love living in London and has this boyfriend, Oliver. Not sure how serious it is with him. Sounds like he's social elite but Lilly seemed unsure of their relationship. He phoned heaps while she was out here, probably just being protective. Maybe it's just a phase they're going through,' she managed a weak smile, 'and they'll live happily ever after. I worry that in the years to come, when Dad's gone, I'll be the only one left.'

'Give it time but there'll be someone else in the future for you. I know it,' Daisy said warmly, 'and trust me, you won't get rid of me again. I don't have any other family either.'

'Yeah, sorry. Feeling pathetic a lot lately. I should be more positive and grateful for what I *do* have.' She sent a meaningful glance across the table to her happy cheeky dark-haired son who, despite his significance, had brought her joy and solace, and gave her life meaning.

'We're growing morbid. We need more wine.' Daisy poured it. 'To sisters.'

Maddie needed to say something but had decided to leave it until later. 'To all three of us.'

Later when they ate it, Maddie groaned over her serving of Daisy's dessert — the lightest sponge she had ever tasted with just a hint of zingy lemon. It virtually dissolved in her mouth it was so soft, the whole concoction filled with whipped cream and layers of fresh berries in the middle. Daisy had finished it artfully with piped decoration and a piled tumble of berries dusted with icing sugar.

With Tommy drowsy, Maddie excused them, the little guy sleepily wrapped his arms around Daisy's neck in a hug goodnight, and he was whisked away to be tucked up into bed. When Maddie returned to the kitchen, Daisy had rinsed and stacked all the dishes with tea and coffee mugs set out on the counter.

'Wow, thanks.'

'Wasn't sure if you wanted a coffee or more wine.'

'I'll need the coffee to sober up.'

'Tell you what,' Daisy quipped, 'after one summer season in the tearoom I'm pretty damned efficient with boiling water and serving cuppas.'

When they poured their hot drinks, Maddie said, 'Let's take these out onto the porch,' and more humbly added, 'and this time I promise not to jump down your throat.'

Daisy pulled a wry understanding grin.

When they were settled into comfy chairs and the soft summer night embraced them, Maddie said, 'I am so sorry for being a bitch when we were here with Dad before Christmas and we had that . . . disagreement.' Daisy was about to protest but she held up a hand. 'Needs to be said. I won't deny it was a shock and I hated Dad for his betrayal. For a long time. But then I got real. Lilly and I knew our parents' marriage was superficial.' Maddie glanced up and held her sister's gaze. 'I know your mother was the first and the love of his life but it still hurts.'

'I get that. But I was a child at the time. A part of it purely by a circumstance of birth. If you have an issue, take it up with George.'

Daisy's blunt honesty was confronting but appreciated. 'I have. We dealt with it recently. We're in a better place now.'

A brief uneasy silence fell between them until Daisy asked, 'How are you coping since Aaron's death? Really.'

'Honestly?'

Daisy raised her eyebrows and nodded, hands wrapped around her tea mug, expecting the truth.

Maddie had never confided in anyone before, not even Lilly. It was a scary cathartic moment. She just needed to leap in and be true to her thoughts.

'Aaron West strode onto *Georgina Downs* looking for work. Dad gave him a job and I married him in a romantic whirl. He was so damned sexy. In dusty jeans and boots, hips swinging, with his shirt open and all that suntanned skin. Pile on a killer smile and he was impossible to resist. Every woman's dream, and nightmare,' she added with meaning, 'because every other woman idolised him, too.'

Maddie stared into her coffee mug and heaved out a long groaning sigh. 'I was cruel to everyone the day of Aaron's funeral because I felt the biggest hypocrite. People endlessly coming up to me at the cemetery and at the homestead later. How I had lost such a good man so young and Tommy losing his father, and every other version of sympathy along those lines.'

'Why did you feel a hypocrite?'

'Because I didn't love Aaron the same way anymore,' she confessed in a small voice. 'I looked at other men but I didn't touch. Aaron looked at other women and did. I heard rumours but refused to listen.' Maddie shrugged. 'I gave him plenty of rope.'

She glanced across at her older sister. 'Your parents were truly in love. My parents' lives are in a mess. How the hell are you supposed to know whether the man you fall in love with is forever? That you'll stay happy or it will all fall apart some day? What is a soul mate anyway? People talk about it but I sure never found it. At least, not with Aaron,' she said sadly.

14

'Sixty four thousand dollar question, huh?'

Daisy drained the last of her tea, held the empty mug in her lap and stared out into the darkness toward the beach, clearly reflecting on Maddie's question about soul mates.

'I can only tell you what I learned from my affair with Charlie last spring. I needed him at that time in my life. Ailie's death still haunts me with loneliness but I've been thinking about why some relationships last a few months or years, or even a lifetime.'

Maddie was all ears to hear her sister's theories.

'I've come to the conclusion that if any form of romantic partnership fails over a certain period of our lives, we're not necessarily meant to remain with that person. They might have served an important purpose, taught us something. Made us aware of something about ourselves that we hadn't realised before.

'Whether it's in a marriage or a relationship or there's a new love interest on the horizon, I believe we need to know what role that person will play in our life.' Daisy shrugged. 'All the brief relationships I had while I was travelling and constantly moving around overseas, were companions or best friends who filled a need for us both for a limited time.'

'Why did it end with Charlie?' Maddie asked softly.

'He already had a soul mate and didn't know it,' Daisy grinned, glancing back toward her sister. 'By then I already knew that his life and mine weren't compatible. He was accustomed to comfortable wealth and, well, look at me,' she spread out an arm. 'I prefer it as simple as I can get. We were attracted, we were both lonely, and we both genuinely adored and respected each other. But we were never meant to spend our lives together.'

'Who was Charlie's soul mate then?'

'He spoke about her once with such nostalgia and spark of life in his eyes that I knew right then and there, they were meant to be together. That was before Christmas so I enlisted Jack's help in tracing her. She is an artist in Paris, never married, so I mean it just seemed like fate that Charlie should have mentioned it and Clare,' Daisy smiled softly, 'was so easily found.'

She closed and opened her eyes again, and chuckled. 'And in finding Clare, I found Jack. He was there all along but working closely with him and spending more time together, I saw him in a completely fresh light. We were best friends first. I felt comfortable with him right from the start after I came to Inlet Creek to open up the tearoom. Whereas my connection with Charlie was forced at times. There was a reserve and stiffness to him that I wanted to tear open.' She shook her head. 'But he wasn't naturally like that, and it wasn't my place nor would it have been right of me to try and change him.'

'Wow, what a romantic ride.'

'Which is different for everyone,' Daisy

pointed out. 'Once Charlie was free to go to Clare and Jack opened up to me, I understood that he is exactly what I need now in my life. And,' she hesitated before continuing, 'I suspect, forever,' she ended, barely above a whisper with an expression of contented disbelief on her face.

'Oh, Daisy, I'm so happy for you.'

The sisters reached out across the space between their porch loungers and briefly clasped hands. A physical and emotional link of two hearts that hadn't given up on each other, shared their secrets and forgave their mistakes. On Maddie's part, it was so deeply brilliant to have this wise older person teach her lessons. Show her the way, in a manner that Elizabeth never could no matter how hard her mother tried.

Daisy's face glowed in the simple serenity of knowing she had met that right one. 'You know, one night I just asked myself *Is Jack the person to share my Life with*? On every level he ticked every box. He slid into my life so gently, without any fuss, no dramas. We share so much in common, have the same values and ideals. We're both delirious about food. You reach a certain stage in your life when you know what you want. The time is right. It's real and deep. Jack knew all along, apparently. So he told me later.' Daisy pulled a wry grin. 'Now I'm looking forward to spending a lifetime showing him that his patience was worth it.'

Maddie stretched and gathered up their drink mugs. 'Want another tea?'

Daisy shook her head. When her sister returned from the kitchen, she continued, 'It's been lovely to talk. I used to do this with Granny. We chatted about anything and everything. I miss her to bits. I'm the one feeling bad now because it's been non-stop busy in the tearoom and I haven't been out to the cemetery to visit my Sheldon women lately.'

'That's what I'm afraid of,' Maddie admitted. 'Going to Aaron's grave when I go back out to the station. I know I don't have to but I want to. There's stuff I need to say to him.'

'First time's the hardest. And going through their belongings. You want to keep stuff but you just know there's no point. That's tough.' After a moment's pause, she added, 'How's Tommy coping without his father?'

'He's been affected on two fronts, really. Not just because he's lost Aaron but now he's away from his Grampa, too. Dad idolises his only grandchild. Now he's getting bigger, he'll grab Tommy and take him off out on the property somewhere in the ute. Even introduced him a few times to the pony he bought for him. Tommy seems to be happy learning to ride. At barely four, I tended to be cautious but Dad reminded me I was on my Welsh pony, Bella, by that age, too.'

'From what you've said, Aaron was such a daredevil,' Daisy remarked. 'Tommy has probably inherited some adventure from his father. And you're an outdoor woman yourself.'

Maddie felt a wave of sickness to hear Daisy's comment but passed over it with a bleak smile. Aaron had never instinctively wanted to take Tommy out around the station so she judged it wiser to say nothing on that front.

'If there was ever a choice of going off with Grampa or staying around the homestead with me, Mother or Nanny, Tommy's answer was always Grampa.' She waited a moment in thought. 'I don't know if you noticed at Aaron's funeral when you were speaking to Dad but since your mother's death last year, he's really not the same. It's more than missing her and grieving. It's like he's beginning to give up on life.

'I used to hate his bellowing voice carrying all over the homestead when he was around. Especially when Tommy was a baby and I was trying to get him to sleep. Now he's withdrawn, hardly talks much anymore. The house is like a mausoleum. Mother doesn't care, even when she's home. I wish he was his old self.'

'He will be again,' Daisy said firmly. 'I don't know him as deeply as you do, of course, but he did seem a bit down. I thought perhaps because he had lost Ailie and now a son-in-law, the double whammy must have hit him hard.'

'Yeah, maybe that's all it is. I'd give anything to hear his loud voice giving out orders on the telephone in the office or yelling instructions to the workmen out on the station.'

'Even though it means being away from him, how's this beachside break working out for you? Do you have friends here in town from your childhood holidays or school days?'

'Actually Lilly and I went to private boarding school in Goulburn. Dad built this beach house when he married Mother. When we were little we came here every summer for the holidays. Elizabeth found it more bearable than out on the station but once we were older, straight after Christmas every year she went to England for pretty much the whole northern winter. Most years Lilly and I both went but from my teens I often stayed behind on the station with Dad.' Maddie wrinkled her nose. 'Upfield Hall isn't exactly my scene. So we didn't really get to know anyone here in the Creek. Met new and different kids each summer. Regulars usually camped together in the caravan park in town.

'Speaking of strangers in town,' Maddie continued, 'I met a guy out on the pier the other day and bumped into him again on the street this afternoon as we were leaving the tearoom. Tall, blonde. Apparently new in town. Said his name is Josh Seymour. He runs a small blue and white half cabin cruiser. Just been hired on a fishing trawler. Seen him around?'

Daisy frowned in thought. 'Think I know who you mean. Wow, you're well informed about him already,' she teased.

Maddie shrugged and felt a need to explain her interest. 'That's all I know.'

'Why the interest?'

'He seems . . . evasive.'

'Doesn't hurt that he's handsome and charming, huh?'

'It's not like that,' Maddie objected, scowling. 'I've just lost my husband.'

'Sorry. I know.' Daisy folded her arms. 'Don't know much more myself. You're right. Jack mentioned him the other day. We've seen him around Inlet Creek. Quiet bloke, seems nice enough but keeps to himself. Drives a big black blokey vehicle.'

'Didn't think he looked like a fisherman. They're usually on the rugged side. Josh gives the impression that he's street smart. Trained. Like a soldier or something.'

'I wouldn't be too bothered,' Daisy casually raised her shoulders. 'Sailors come and go, especially over summer when the big outfits are hiring for the season. Boats are coming and going in Jervis Bay all the time, and puttering up and down Inlet Creek. Dawn, dusk and night are prime times for fishing so his being out at night isn't all that unusual.'

'Well, the Jervis Bay has calm clear waters and the creek is sheltered but heading out to sea alone at night in a small vessel is risky,' Maddie disagreed. 'It can be dangerous enough in good weather and a big boat.'

'Yeah. A few weeks back when we had a storm with that summer cool change that blew up, the local marine rescue guys took a distress call. A fishing trawler was sinking in the waters off the Bay. It was making its way back to a bigger harbour for hull repairs but it started taking on water. Bilge pumps couldn't cope. Marine rescue boys used their emergency pump to bring down the water level low enough to do the repairs. Trawler anchored in the Bay overnight but it was okay to continue next morning.'

'Exactly my point.'

Daisy threw back her head with a lovely easy laugh. 'Oh, I'm all talked out for tonight. Think

I'll make tracks.' She yawned, stretched and rose from her lounger.

The sisters hugged.

'Thanks for everything,' Maddie said awkwardly. 'You know, putting up with me. Excusing my poor behaviour.'

'No need. I've never had a close sister before so I'm getting the vibes we can bitch and moan, drink wine, and then we're done.'

'I wish Lilly lived closer. Not sure as the older sister of two that I've been much of a role model in the past. I would so love her to know you better, too.' Maddie's eyes filled with tears. 'Your Sheldon women will be looking down on you with such pride.'

'Oh, stop it,' Daisy sniffed. 'They bent a few rules but their hearts were all pure gold. I'll get back to you about a night to come over to the flat for dinner with us, yeah?' she said as she left.

Maddie nodded, then her big sister drove away in her rattly old farm ute that was so basic Daisy, she simply smiled and shook her head. Because of that awesome woman in her life now reaching out in reconciliation, her own heart and soul were so very slowly coming to a place of peace.

⋆ ⋆ ⋆

A few days later, Maddie and Tommy lazed on the beach. It was one of those baking hot days of late summer when the heat pulsed over everything, the cloudless blue sky reflecting its cobalt colour onto the calm sea.

Sheltered beneath the brim of her huge floppy

sunhat, a hawk-eyed Maddie behind big sunglasses watched out for Tommy clad in a protective rashie top over his bathers. Living in the outback, with precious water often scarce and no swimming pools nearby, her son had not yet learned to swim.

They had already been in the sea, keeping cool, having fun while Maddie subtly taught her son to stroke out with his arms and kick madly with his strong little legs while trusting her in the water with her arms beneath him, keeping him afloat. She was using this summer break to grow his confidence in the water.

Now he was splashing and squealing among small waves in the shallows at the ocean's edge. Sometimes moving further away to play in the tidal rock pools, at low tide revealing small crabs, shells and sparkly stones. Which from time to time he brought up the beach to show her with such excitement.

Situated toward the end of the beach, their shack behind them enjoyed its own private stretch of sand, sheltered by the nearby rocky headland. On the other side was the estuary where the ocean met Inlet Creek and the tides created warm lagoon shallows surrounded by warm white sands, ideal for families with children.

Maddie's senses snapped to alert when Tommy suddenly yelled out, running toward her up the beach as fast as his small feet would carry him.

'It's the see more, Mummy.'

Maddie frowned, puzzled, until she realised

what he was trying to say the moment she recognised a tall and clearly lithe muscled person scrambling over the huge rocks. Not looking too shabby either in a black polo shirt with the collar up, beige cargos and deck shoes. Tommy almost fell backward grinning and staring up at the great height of the man.

Maddie's greeting was more reserved. 'This is unexpected.' How did he know where they lived? She hadn't told him.

His eyes, too, were hidden behind mirrored sunglasses so, in their lenses, she saw herself sitting on the sand. His pause before he spoke suggested he was studying her again.

'Hope I'm not intruding.'

'Not really,' Maddie was forced to admit, although found his presence confronting because she was fascinated by a man she had no right to, being recently widowed.

'Hey, Tommy.' Josh ruffled his wet hair and the boy beamed.

'My boat's anchored at the bridge just beyond the estuary shallows. Waiting for the tide to rise so I can bring it back around to the pier. Been out fishing longer than I planned.'

Recalling the day on the pier when he appeared empty handed, Maddie asked wryly, 'Catch anything this time?'

He chuckled. 'Bream and flathead. They're safe on ice in my esky on the boat. Mind if I join you?'

Feeling self-conscious, a rare emotion for Maddie, and knowing it would be rude to refuse, she nodded.

Josh sat down beside her, flipped off his shoes and nestled his feet into the warm sand, then raised his knees and casually draped his arms over them.

Impossible not to feel the vibes of his presence so close but she tried to ignore it and stared out to sea. 'How's your new job?'

'Settling in. Day off today. Going out again tomorrow night for a couple days. Trawling further out apparently.' Josh glanced toward Tommy who had moved away across the sand and lowered his voice. 'Listen, if you have time, I'm more than happy to take you and Tommy out in the boat today.'

'Oh,' Maddie said quickly, surprised by his unexpected suggestion.

This whole meeting and getting to know another man thing was happening too fast. She didn't want it. She wasn't ready.

'We could just go up the creek aways and explore.'

'I don't know.'

'Your call. Didn't want to say anything in front of your son.'

Maddie appreciated that small gesture of thoughtfulness but still had doubts on a whole bunch of different levels. 'Maybe not today.'

'Tommy will be quite safe.'

Ah but will I, Maddie wondered? If she said yes, her agreement became an opening that would probably be the start of something more. The man-woman chemistry thing was hard to ignore when it found you and she was sure feeling it with this guy.

Over her hedging thoughts, he murmured persuasively, 'Life jackets on board and calm water along the creek.'

Maddie still shook her head. 'No.' Because her words came out more sharply than she intended, she tempered it with a mumbled, 'Thanks anyway.'

'He'd love it.'

Did this man never give up? 'How do you know?'

'He's a boy. It's a given. And don't tell me a cool breeze out on the water isn't enticing on a day like this?'

She swung her glance sideways, totally charmed by that teasing grin. He sure knew how to influence a woman.

'How about we ask Tommy?' Before Maddie had time to object, Josh called out to her son.

The nerve of this sneaky guy. Obviously used to getting his own way. Of course Tommy would say yes. Maddie didn't fear for her son's safety and had no objection to heading out along the creek on such a sweltering day. It was her own jumbled feelings that gave her cause for concern.

While her distracted mind swirled in thought, Josh put his offer to her son so that Tommy was now tugging her hat brim, begging to go on the boat.

Who could refuse such cute pleading? And this could prove to be the worst decision she had made in a long while. She was being pushed and didn't like it.

Maddie sighed. 'All right.'

Tommy squealed, jumped up and down and

yelled out, 'We're having a boat ride.'

Apparently Josh had snacks and drinks on the boat. So Maddie grabbed her striped beach carryall, slipped on shoes and tied a white sarong about her waist over her bathers. She slid plastic Crocs onto Tommy's feet and they trailed Josh over the rocks to the other side.

He lifted Tommy and reached out for Maddie's hand, as necessary. Maddie reacted to his touch with a deep sense of awareness. It felt big and warm and secure. Basically everything it shouldn't.

As they walked, to everyone else they must have looked like a family. Maddie flooded with a heavy sense of guilt that she was betraying Aaron so soon after his death, attracted to another man. What kind of woman did that make her?

But since she had lost her husband, she was growing aware that she was very much alive and that life was fleeting and precious. She hadn't really given the future too much thought but she knew one thing in her heart. If she ever began a relationship again, after the withering of love for Aaron first time around and with Daisy's wise words still ringing in her ears, she wanted to get it right next time. Whatever form it took. Marriage or not. Any man in her life would need to be The Right One. For both herself and Tommy.

They had tramped in single file — Josh leading, Tommy trotting behind chattering, Maddie bringing up the rear — along the sandy creek edges the short distance past the estuary shallows and under the old timber bridge to

Josh's boat, moving gently at anchor on the other side.

Once aboard and wearing life jackets with the small cruiser's motor humming beneath them, and seeing the utter delight on her son's face, Maddie let out a long sigh of acceptance and decided to enjoy the trip.

★ ★ ★

It was a small boat and with three people crammed into the confined space, there wasn't a whole lot of room to move. Josh made it all about Tommy's enjoyment, the pair of them sitting up front in the two forward seats of the covered half cabin. At times, Josh let the boy sit in his lap and hold the wheel pretending to steer the boat. Maddie held back, reclining on the long padded seat across the rear. Distance was good.

For a modest vessel, the runabout was fun. As Josh predicted, it was more than pleasant with the breeze in her face, puttering at a leisurely speed of knots as they made their way inland along the creek.

Pelicans perched on old mooring posts. Willows draped their lacy foliage over the water. Flocks of seagulls soared above. With the scenery drifting by at such a rhythmic pace, Maddie found the tranquil expedition relaxing and her earlier tension eased.

She heard the obvious excitement and sense of adventure in Tommy's voice, expressed in endless observations and questions. Josh gave simple explanations and patient responses.

Later, Tommy toddled back to her and she held him firmly as he leaned over the side of the boat to trail his small hands in the cool waters rushing past.

They shared the creek occasionally with paddlers in kayaks and other small vessels. Half hidden holidays shacks were just visible, tucked away in the bush near the water's edge. At times, the shallows were so clear, it was possible to see rippled sand and grasses waving back and forth underneath the boat with the creek's gentle flow.

Maddie conceded that, surrounded and seduced by the beauty and tranquillity of the waterway, so removed from their life lived in the outback, this outing was indeed a rare and special treat.

Josh handed out snacks and ice cold drinks from an esky and proudly showed Maddie his catches for the day, as if to prove he could actually reel one in.

Impossible not to notice that Josh Seymour was everything a man for a woman and her son should be.

As shadows lengthened and the sun's sting weakened, Josh checked his watch. The tide had come in so he turned the boat about. They headed back down the creek again, and around the rocky headland, anchoring just out from the beach house.

Josh waded ashore carrying a sleepy Tommy up onto the sand. Maddie followed and took possession of her son.

'Thank you for this afternoon. It's been wonderful, especially for Tommy.'

'You, too, I hope.'

'Of course. Clearly a success,' she admitted. 'We've worn him out,' she said, kissing Tommy's forehead as he wrapped his arms about her neck.

Although resisting any close associations with another man in her life, Maddie was wise enough to see it's potential for herself and Tommy in the future to have that other person to make their family complete. For now, it was too soon. When it was time, as Daisy had said, she would know.

But today, aware of Josh's kindness in sharing his day off by offering the boat outing, Maddie couldn't let his generosity pass. Perhaps she would regret it but she opened her mouth and said the words. 'Would you like to stay for dinner?'

'Depends. I'm aware you and your son have lost a husband and father recently.' His deep voice softened. 'I like what I see, Maddie, but I'm prepared to keep it simple.'

He understood. 'Thank you. I enjoy your friendship,' she hesitated, 'so, if you don't mind scaling and grilling your fish then . . . ?'

His mouth spread into a lazy grin. 'Consider it done.'

15

As it turned out, dinner with Josh couldn't have been more informal. He made it so. Kept up simple conversation and was easy company. Maintaining physical distance, whether intentional or not on his part, definitely helped.

If he was being considerate, she appreciated it. She had only met the guy twice in town and there were a whole bunch of issues filling her mind about the sense in pursuing a friendship on such short acquaintance. But how else could you get to know someone unless you spent time with them?

Down on the beach, Josh built a fire, cleaned the fish and put them over the coals to grill. Meanwhile, Maddie slid a tray of chunky frozen chips into the oven and considered dinner sorted. She had no idea what Josh drank but hoped it was beer because, apart from sharing an occasional wine with Daisy, it was her personal choice and a six-pack was always chilling in the fridge.

When the food was done, they filled paper plates down on the beach, sat on the sand and ate it in their fingers. Josh gave off uncomplicated vibes, Tommy was rapt and Maddie was just thinking of how much washing she saved later.

She excused herself when it was time for Tommy to be in bed but when she returned, felt unsure how to approach Josh alone on the beach. His restrained air of biding time throughout the evening could have been because of Tommy. If so, what now? He had said *he Liked what he saw*, making his interest clear.

Standing on the top porch step, she rubbed her damp hands on her denim shorts and faced her apprehension. Her pull of attraction for another man tussling with a ridiculous sense of cheating. Crazy since she was no longer married. But the unexpected meeting and appeal for Josh had her believing it a weakness and thinking the worst of herself.

Josh glanced up at her approach and his warm steady gaze from those ocean blue eyes revealed that he wasn't going anywhere anytime soon. Right. So she adapted.

'Would you like another beer?'

'Best not.' He nodded toward the boat. 'Need to make it back sober.'

'Coffee?'

He nodded. 'Black. Straight up.' He sprang to his feet, bringing them face to face. Or more like nose to nose, in the shadows. 'Need any help?'

For safety, Maddie backed up a step and nervously laughed at herself. 'No thanks. I'm not much of a cook but I can boil water.'

Ten minutes later with both of them nursing big mugs, a few awkward moments passed as they both watched the almost-full moon and its path of rippled light across the sea. Nature could not have delivered a more romantic setting, emphasising their loaded situation. Maddie had no idea what Josh was feeling exactly but when she was around him, her spirits lifted and she filled with a crazy longing of hope and optimism.

Draining the last of her second beer and curious to know, she casually asked Josh, 'So, where's home for you, then?'

'Based in Sydney.'

'Family?'

'Four brothers. Our parents did it tough but they made sure us kids had every opportunity so we watch out for them.'

Maddie loved his fiercely protective sense of loyalty.

'I'm one of three sisters,' Maddie proudly announced, feeling liberated to include them all. 'I'm in the middle. My oldest sister runs *Daisy's* tearoom in the main street and my little sister, Lilly, lives in England at the moment.'

'I've walked by *Daisy's*,' Josh said, then continued, 'I guess you know most folks in town.'

'Not really. We live in the country and only come to the beach house for a few weeks each summer.'

'Know many of the local commercial fishermen?'

Maddie shrugged, thinking it an odd question when Josh had just learned she didn't spend much time in town.

'Only that I imagine most are lifelong residents of Inlet Creek. I believe some are family businesses. In an industry that is probably facing challenging times with environmental issues and sustainability, I guess it would be highly competitive. They would always be under threat of bigger players in the industry.' Maddie turned to him. 'Why do you ask?'

'No reason. But you're right. Since I started working on the trawler there's conflict on board and undertones of fierce rivalry.'

'It's a tough living but I guess it's in the blood. You don't give the impression of being a fisherman.'

'I'm not. Get work where I can.'

'So you're a drifter?' she voiced her speculation.

'In a way. I go where my work takes me.'

'You say that like it's something else apart from labouring or fishing. So what exactly is it?'

Josh grinned. 'I work for an . . . outfit.'

'If you're already employed why do you need a job on a trawler?' When he remained silent, she added, 'Want me to tell you what I think?'

'Sure. Why not?'

'You came here to ask questions and get information but I've ended up turning the tables on you.'

Josh chuckled low and deep. Most appealing. 'So what was it like growing up in the country? I'm a city boy myself but I get around.'

'Yeah. With that secret work of yours.'

Silence settled around them. Josh seemed comfortable enough with it but Maddie grew frustrated. The man either didn't trust people easily or it was some kind of secret business he was involved in. She would bet on that last one. To fill the quiet and because Josh's question started her reminiscing, she decided to respond, even if he was reluctant to share much of himself.

'In case you hadn't guessed, I was a tomboy and haven't changed much. I love the sheep station, riding, pretty much all of nature and the outback life. Caused a mess of trouble with my mother. She's English. My grandparents came from a grand country estate. Horses, polo, local gentry. My uncle, mother's oldest brother, inherited and lives there now with his family and a heap of cousins that I have absolutely nothing in common with and rarely see.

'When we visited and stayed, I hated it when all the womenfolk traipsed off to London to a posh hotel and shopping. High teas. Theatres. So boring. But Lilly loved and embraced it all. I think she still does to a certain extent.

'Mother has always expected me to be more of a lady. Sometimes I surrender to her wishes and frock up for a garden party to play hostess. Once I married Aaron and had Tommy, we lived in the homestead with my parents. It was logical to assume that eventually we would take over and run the station. Neither of my sisters is interested.'

Maddie discovered it helpful to unload but the implication of her recently changed circumstances suddenly hit home.

'To be honest, the way my life has turned out now, for the first time ever I'm not so sure where I want to be.'

Maddie pulled up from her ramblings with a sudden jolt. It had been so easy to start talking, regarding Josh as a friend. To be fair, he *had* asked in the first place but, really, perhaps her unusual chattering was beyond reasonable.

'Sorry. Probably too much information,' she muttered, realising she hadn't confided her private fears and doubts to anyone.

'Not at all. Sounds like you have some difficult decisions and adjustments to make now.'

In those first weeks after Aaron's funeral while Lilly was still home, it had been all about emotional recovery. Ever since her sister and mother returned to England, with just the three of them on the station, Maddie found that each day brought its own demons and examination of her future.

'Life seemed all planned out, you know? Aaron was a magnet for women so I felt like a princess when his gaze settled on me and never left. He put me on a pedestal. I guess from such a height, I couldn't help but fall into his arms, right?' She laughed self-consciously.

'But he was a wild soul and I clipped his wings when we married. By default, he became the station owner's right-hand man. I doubt father asked him. It was just expected. So Aaron took every opportunity to have adventures and get away from the station. He raced cars.' She faltered. 'Which is how he died,' she murmured. 'In a bush rally for charity.'

'If you don't want to talk about it — '

Maddie shook her head. 'No, it's fine. Sad part is, in the last two years, Aaron and I weren't as close anymore.' She shrugged. 'The fire died. We might have stayed together, worked it out. Who knows? That's a whole other issue I'm trying to deal with, too. The guilt . . . ' she released a heavy sigh.

Her eyes watered and her nose tingled with threatening tears but she swallowed hard and fought them off. She didn't want to make a spectacle of herself in front of a man she had just met and to who she was taking more than a passing shine.

Josh reached out then, clearly sensing her distress and vulnerability. And for the first time they touched. He shuffled closer on the sand and laid a casual arm about her shoulders. Maddie closed her eyes, absorbing the calm and comfort it conveyed.

'Worrying and blame won't help.'

'Yeah, I'm working on that.'

Feeling his bodily warmth against hers, the security from a virtual stranger who had set her heart and curiosity racing, and fudged her mind, caused both excitement and fear. Only weeks after tragedy made her a widow. That damned annoying sense of shame erupted inside her again that she should even look at another man.

Maddie admitted that, while Josh Seymour had his mystery, she was inclined to wager deep down he was a decent man. She hoped so because, responding to his touch, she was being tempted to continue and grow their friendship. Based on her initial attraction but mostly on today's revealing boat outing, if he used even the mildest persuasion, she would allow him more fully into their lives. With caution.

Josh had already established a connection with Tommy that was clearly not forced. Which was important because they came as a package deal. Any future male partner or role model in their lives would need to fit with both Maddie and her son.

As they sat in harmony on the sand, snuggled together, Maddie deep in her thoughts and Josh patiently beside her, he eventually asked softly, 'You okay?'

She nodded. 'Mmm.'

'Tide's lowering. I should probably move.'

He removed his arm, stood up and reached out for her hand. Pulling her up against him. Okay, so it was a warm summer night, the moon was out but more than nature, two bodies drifted toward each other like magnets for their first kiss. Like a test, as first kisses tended to be. See if there was any spark or reaction.

The way Maddie felt, it couldn't possibly fail. Her whole body came alive as though awakened from a deep slumber.

One of Josh's hands drifted up into Maddie's thick hair and cupped her head, the other wrapped around her waist. Because it worked the first time, the second kiss was inevitable, deeper and longer.

'Thank you for an amazing day,' Maddie said as they drew apart. 'Your Tommy's hero.'

'My pleasure.' He kept holding her. 'I'll be at sea for two days. I'd like to see you again when I get back.'

Maddie liked that he didn't ask, just put the offer out there. Responding to him as she did, she hardly intended to object. Okay, so he held stuff close to his chest but, outside that, finding a man who could potentially fit into their lives was exhilarating.

'Sure,' she said as they walked back up to the porch.

She was realistic enough about hurdles ahead. Both she and Josh were only temporarily at Inlet Creek. He would presumably return to Sydney and Maddie and Tommy would head back out to *Georgina Downs* again. Trouble was, her heart now tugged her in a completely different direction than the family sheep station that had always been her life. More than anything she had gone through in recent months that was the most confronting matter.

So Maddie was not only coping with the overpowering emotions of grief and loss, and the upheaval they caused. Added to that now was this fresh arrival of a potential and genuine romance in her life. She only risked opening herself to this development because of a sudden understanding after watching Josh's devotion to Tommy today.

Finally, with frightening clarity, she identified that Aaron had been a sex symbol in her life and to all the other women he attracted, but not a father. There had been no natural hugs and playing. Only distance. On her son's behalf, Maddie almost crumbled into tears of disappointment for him. Even though it no longer mattered.

As they stood on the top veranda step close together, Maddie murmured, 'Aren't you heading in the wrong direction?' She nodded to his boat gently bobbing at anchor inshore.

Josh shrugged and chuckled, drawing her into his arms again. 'Any excuse. I'll be in touch.'

Melting into another absorbing kiss, a husky female voice entered their awareness.

'Good. I found you.'

They broke apart and their combined gazes swung back toward the beach. Maddie heard Josh's constrained curse at the unbelievable interruption. A leggy blonde stared at them, a short tight dress skimming every lavish curve, a pair of sparkly strappy heels dangling from her fingers, a smile of amusement on her pouty red lips.

Maddie's first thought was that the woman obviously hadn't lasted long trying to walk in sand in that flimsy pair of footwear. And silently sighed over that enviable waterfall stream of wavy hair rustling about her shoulders and halfway down her back. The complete image exuded *player*.

'Maddie, excuse me,' Josh murmured.

Her attention snapped back to him. She finally connected that he knew their intruder.

Josh stepped away from her, as tense as a wild animal poised to pounce. He grabbed the woman by an arm and led her back down the steps toward the beach. Entranced as if hypnotized and feeling a rising fury, she wavered whether to rudely stay and watch or give them space. Plain as day they were more than friends.

Although his voice lowered to a growl, Maddie made out, 'Michelle, how the hell did you find me?'

'I have my ways.'

Maddie instantly disliked the tone of that sexy voice and her bristles rose. Not helped to learn by bombshell drop there was another woman in Josh's life and the cosy twosome she was beginning to imagine had suddenly become a triangle. Hovering on the veranda, consumed by a mixture of jealousy and disbelief, their voices floated up to her from the beach. She couldn't distinguish their conversation but Josh's rigid body language told her he was furious.

Shocked and upset by the whole sudden situation and this curvy city woman's appearance, Maddie recognised all too well the lure of dangerously sexy women for the muscled adventurous types. Like Aaron. And now, like Josh. The mystery man she has just met and who she wouldn't be seeing again.

She refused to watch anymore and retreated into the beach house.

★   ★   ★

Josh winced to see the agony of betrayal on Maddie's face as he left but he had this vixen Michelle to deal with and no choice. Best thing to do was get her as far away from here as fast as possible.

He wondered if Michelle's comment about *having her ways* implied what he thought. Possibly sleeping with yet another one of his mates to coax his whereabouts from an insignificant conquest. She'd sunk to a new low. Deep into this mission and having had this conversation before, Michelle's cheating was more than he was prepared to deal with at the moment. His selfish ex-girlfriend had deliberately arrived and put Maddie in the middle of an explosive situation.

'You know I'm working. You'll blow my cover.'

'Does she know what you do? Sucking face like that you looked way too friendly or was it part of your sting?' She ran her hands over his chest and pushed her body up against him. 'Baby, I don't care who you're with, so long as you come back to me.'

'Not happening and you know it. Wait here. I'll walk back to town with you.'

★ ★ ★

Maddie watched Josh leave the beach and his woman, striding across the beach and leaping the stairs which brought him indoors to her side. She shrank from his closeness, the smell of his cologne, and the outline of his strong profile against the porch light behind. She wondered if the pain across his face was real and equal to her own.

'I'll see Michelle to her accommodation.'

Seething, Maddie crossed her arms and couldn't help herself. 'If she found you, I'm sure she can find a room for the night. Or share yours.'

Josh ignored her retort. 'It's not like that.'

'You look pretty chummy together.'

'I'll be back in a while.'

'Don't bother. I understand.' Of course she didn't but while they were lying to each other . . . 'Really, she's obviously important to you. Go to her. She's come all this way,' Maddie drawled.

'Wait up,' he growled. 'I'll be back.'

Gobsmacked by his demand, Maddie was speechless. Any other time in her past green youth and even now with some life's experience to her credit, she may have revelled with excitement at that statement of promise. But seeing Josh grasp Michelle by the arm and walk away along the beach path back into town, she was furious with herself for letting down her guard and opening up emotionally to any man.

She considered turning off all the lights, locking the house tight, which she normally never bothered to do, and going to bed. She wouldn't sleep but it would clearly convey a message. Keep out. I'm protecting myself and my son. But that would be childish.

For her own sanity, Maddie desperately needed to hear Josh's explanation, his version of events. The extent of the relationship he clearly had with that gorgeous worldly woman who had swayed up the beach steps and invaded her privacy.

But most importantly, why the hell Josh couldn't be open about why he was in Inlet Creek. She guessed it involved the big fishing trawlers hereabouts as maybe a cover for something else since he'd been taken on as crew on one of them.

Exhausted from guessing and fed up with pacing the house as though she was the one at fault, Maddie fortified herself by opening another bottle of beer and took it out to sit on the porch steps, filled with dread. She watched the ebb and flow of the tidal incoming waves rush up and retreat across the sand waiting for Josh to return.

How could she have been so stupid? Exposing her son to a man who he clearly idolised and herself to a dreamboat who had the word *magnet* written across his forehead. All that wavy blonde hair and those dreamy blue eyes.

She should never have agreed to go out today. Kept her distance. This was a disaster waiting to happen. She had ignored all the warning bells clanging in her head and gone with her foolish heart the same way she had with Aaron. And look how that turned out.

Ironically, she noticed those bloody flashing lights out on the water again tonight. But Josh was ashore. Maybe she should mention it to him when he returned. If, as she suspected, all this night time activity was the reason he was down here, he had probably already seen them and knew.

Maddie finished her beer and sat a while longer. Josh was taking his time. Maybe he decided to ditch her in favour of the sexy newcomer. That would be embarrassing. She could be sitting here all night. But his boat was still bobbing offshore. He would have to come back for that. Maddie wished he would hurry up because if she kept drowning her worry with another beer, she might be too agreeable when he returned.

★   ★   ★

Josh alternately paced out in long strides and jogged back along the beach away from the direction of town on the wet hard-packed sand near the water, silence all around him except for the gentle wash of waves. He enjoyed the peace while it lasted.

Attempting to get rid of Michelle, not just tonight but out of his life forever, was like trying to detach a leech. In desperation and used to getting her own way, she had really outdone herself this time. He admired her guts but not her character. It hadn't taken him long to work that one out. He was no saint and had given in to her charms a few times but mostly tried to keep it casual with Michelle because of his job. He was away a lot so that helped. A valid excuse once he worked out her lack of scruples.

He always knew that, down the track, when he felt it was time or the right woman happened along, he may need to rethink his risky career. Michelle would never be that woman. Over recent weeks he knew he must end it and had a talk with her before he left Sydney. Clearly her stubborn nature resisted the break and his ultimatum.

If Michelle's appearance tonight put his new friendship with Maddie in jeopardy, he would not be a happy man. He was prepared for some hard and fast talking when he reached the beach house again. His success depended on how open Maddie was to listening.

★ ★ ★

At the sound of Josh's approaching feet pounding up the steps from the beach, Maddie rose and stiffened, preparing to face him. She padded indoors. When he appeared in the open

236

French doors, he looked exhausted. She softened with compassion, but only for a moment, before common sense and resentment kicked in and she hardened against his appeal.

He ran a hand through his thick unkempt hair, sheened by the indoor light, and planted his hands on his hips. 'She'll be gone in the morning.'

Deliberately contrary, Maddie didn't offer him a seat. Her mother would be horrified by her lack of hospitality and poor manners. Maddie wasn't too proud of herself either but she was annoyed to have let this man so easily and so soon seep into her life.

His explanation better be pretty damned good.

16

Josh took control of the situation, moved across the sitting room, grabbed a kitchen stool and sat on it backward, facing Maddie.

She should have felt bad. He had just walked two kilometres to town and back. In heavy sand. But she didn't. Instead, she retreated to the sofa and curled her body into a protective bundle. So far she hadn't spoken. Not because she was being stubborn but because she didn't know what to say to start the conversation.

Clearly not a problem for Josh because he launched straight into details. 'Michelle charmed some bloke at headquarters to find me. We had a brief friendship but no understanding. As you saw, she's needy and high maintenance.' He paused, then continued sounding deflated. 'And I suspect she's been unfaithful. Probably more than once,' he said with bitter honesty. 'I could never trust or be with such a woman. I have more self-respect than that.'

In the wake of Josh's statement, Maddie's resentment was overturned and instead she now shrivelled with guilt. Felt like the earth had opened up beneath her and swallowed her whole. The flame of hope that had flared into life after meeting Josh that she just might be worthy of an unexpected second chance in her life, for which she hadn't realised she yearned, instantly died. How could she have dared to believe she was good enough for this honourable man?

'Nothing to say?'

Maddie shrugged, feeling beyond inadequate, her mind and emotions a mess. 'Best if we call it quits,' she said quietly, aching as she said the words.

A shadow of concern crossed his face and Josh shook his head. 'I disagree. I'd love us to continue what we've started. I realise after tonight you'll need to give that some thought. So after I'm done with explaining, I'll leave it up to you to get in touch with me if you want. But, you should know what you're getting into.'

Did she have the right to let him continue? Should she stop him before he started? Stop this travesty before Josh wasted any more time on her?

But he had already begun.

'I'm part of a commando team working with Border Force off the south coast. At the moment undercover as a fisherman on a vessel of interest. After receiving a thread of information, it's been a two year investigation. We believe a local fishing company have bought the big super trawler to bring in drugs that originate in South America then across the South Pacific to Tahiti and Fiji. We've had the syndicate under surveillance for a long time and we're tracking them. We'll be out at sea. There's no danger to the locals.'

Maddie's thoughts were in overdrive. Josh's revelations were not far removed from her speculation. Irony was, she had just lost Aaron in a car accident where he would have pushed himself to the limit. Now she'd gone and let a

239

man into her heart who lived with danger every day. Only with Josh, he worked for his country to keep it safe. Aaron on the other hand, she had learned soon enough, had pretty much only lived for himself.

'Speak to me, Maddie,' Josh said softly.

She found her voice and said without emotion, 'So you claim Michelle's out of your life now and your work's risky. I get it. But I don't like the sound of it,' Maddie breathed in a small voice, revealing the fact that she still cared.

'We're all well trained. We have each other's back. Hundreds of hours of covert and physical surveillance goes into this. We don't jump until all our ducks are in a row and the highest levels give us the nod.' In support, he explained with such passion, Maddie was impressed. 'We could potentially stop a massive amount of cocaine hitting the streets. This next trip out to sea could be the catch. If it turns out the trawler is meeting the drug ship stationed out at sea, we'll raid and board it. A Navy frigate's ready offshore to assist and intercept.'

'Is this the overnighter you mentioned earlier?'

Josh nodded. 'It's only human to worry but try not to.'

'Easier said than done,' she scoffed, feeling more agreeable and informed, her sense of humour and spirit slowly returning. Against her will. It was proving so hard to resist this man's appeal. She uncurled herself and sat forward on the sofa. 'Why do you do it?'

Josh pushed himself from the stool but, instead of coming over to her as she might have expected, he walked over to the French windows, his back turned, hands pushed deep into his pockets. 'You remember earlier tonight I said I have four brothers?'

Maddie cringed inside and held her breath. 'Yes.'

'Our youngest brother, Bailey, died from an overdose five years ago. He was only twenty one.'

'Oh.'

Maddie let out a slow moan, compelled to unravel herself from the sofa, cross the room and hug Josh from behind. With her head pressed to his back she felt the vibrations when he spoke.

'After that I swore I'd fight the damned curse that has spread like a disease worldwide.' Josh turned around and she disappeared into his arms. 'Takes a lot to get over loss,' he murmured into her hair. 'Especially someone close and young, as you know. Like a kid brother.' He pulled back to gaze at her with meaning. 'So now he's the reason I get out of bed every day. Although I have to say you're starting to have the same effect,' he chuckled, grinning. 'Now where were we before our awesome evening was interrupted?'

Even as she gave into her desire and Josh kissed her like before, their passion re-ignited, their bodies crushed together, Maddie's thoughts wandered. It could never be the same again. There was an obstacle now. A cloud hanging over them. How could she continue to mislead this wonderful man?

If she told him she would lose him. But first she had to find the right moment and the courage. Which didn't feel like now. She was too loved up and mellow, her mind a haze of endorphins as a result of Josh's lips on hers and his hands doing their thing all over her body.

Later, Josh murmured, 'When this is all over — '

'I'll think about it.' Maddie pressed a finger over his lips to not only silence him but avoid considering the future.

'You're a lousy liar,' he growled, nibbling her ears and neck. 'You already have. Tell me I'll see you again,' he whispered urgently. 'Promise.'

He kissed her so deep and primal, his big hands cupped over her behind and pushing them together in the most suggestive way. They wanted and needed each other as if for survival like water in the outback. So Maddie excused her reasoning that there was still time. She didn't need to tell him just yet. Her confession could wait.

Intoxicated with desire, she forgot the world and caution, and nodded.

'Say it,' he drawled.

'Yes,' she laughed. 'I want to see you again.'

Which was true but heartache lingered behind her smile.

★ ★ ★

The following day Maddie's phone pinged with a text from Daisy, inviting her sister and nephew over to their flat for dinner that very evening. Curiosity was high to be meeting Jack for the first time. A perfect diversion to stop thinking and worrying for Josh.

At dusk, Maddie and Tommy drove into town. Handsome Frenchman Jack proved a warm and casually charming man with the added bonus of a romantic French accent. The manner in which he and Daisy related to each other, especially jostling in the tiny kitchen where it was clearly all about food between the two of them, made Maddie's heart brim with delight. Her big sister was so amazingly happy, a beautiful soul who had found her mate. And it showed in soft glances, teasing, shared smiles and laughter. The small touches and gestures for each other.

Maddie could only look on with aching envy that one day again she might be granted such a fulfilling romance. She had someone in mind, of course, but there remained a rather awful obstacle to overcome first. And the outcome would entirely depend on Josh.

Dinner was gobsmackingly yummy and a perfect distraction to Maddie's looming concern. Hot and tasty savoury nibbles started the meal which Tommy dipped in his own special bowl of tomato sauce.

The main course, ideal on this early autumn night nippy with a chill that warned of winter ahead, was a spicy bean and vegetable curry with rice.

All finished off with the creamiest mocha dessert served in small cute glasses and eaten with a long spoon to scoop out every last mouthful. Determined not to leave any, Tommy slid his little fingers around the insides as well.

Jack offered to wash the dishes so Daisy and

Maddie had time together. He stood Tommy on a sturdy chair beside him at the sink so the boy could play in the soap suds.

'He'll make a wonderful father,' Maddie whispered, leaning closer to Daisy on the sofa.

'We've actually already rolled that idea around. Maybe in a year or two. We want to travel together and Jack is keen for me to meet his family and see their village on the French Atlantic coast.'

'You're leaving Inlet Creek?' Maddie filled with disappointment. Having just reunited with Daisy she was about to lose her again?

'Only temporarily. We'll need to find suitable bakers and managers for our shops while we're away. Our core staff will stay on but, don't worry,' she laughed, clearly seeing Maddie's dismay, 'we're coming back. Over winter we'll be looking into what plans we can put in place so the new arrangements will be ready for next summer's tourist season.'

Jack brought tea for his Daisy and coffee for Maddie with a plate of French butter cookies. 'Don't worry,' he grinned, 'Tommy already has a handful of his own.'

'You two are spoiling my son tonight.'

'He's our only nephew,' Daisy protested with pleasure.

It was obvious to Maddie that children would be in their near future. 'Who is already yawning I see. I won't stay late. My little man needs bed soon and you two have early morning starts.'

Needing to share, Maddie updated her sister on her feelings for Josh while Jack and Tommy sat on the floor nearby complete with head-phones each, utterly fascinating the boy, so they could watch children's movies on the television.

Grateful for the privacy and without too much detail, Maddie repeated the blissful boat ride up the creek and that naturally they had kissed. 'Then of course came the famous interruption.' She went on to explain that fiasco and Josh's revelations later including what he did for a living.

Daisy's shapely eyebrows rose. 'Wow, you've really snagged a hero's interest.'

Maddie nodded. 'Cripes, Daisy, I can really pick them. Aaron lived on the edge and now I'm falling for a guy who's involved with guns and drugs. Legally, of course,' she said wryly.

Daisy was no fool. 'So, what's wrong?' she prompted.

Eventually Maddie admitted, 'I should be grieving for Aaron more. Now another man has entered my life and become important not only to me but he and Tommy so far have a lovely relationship.' She sighed. 'I won't see Josh for days. I don't know what the hell's happening out there at sea somewhere. He could be — '

'Don't even think it,' Daisy said, then threw her a lifeline. 'Jack goes out fishing.' She glanced across at her partner, caught his attention so that he removed his headphones and asked, 'You'll keep your eyes and ears open for Maddie about any news on this drug gossip that's circulating at the moment, *mon cher?*'

Jack shrugged. 'Of course, *cherie*.' He turned back to his movie with Tommy.

'Would you?' Maddie sank with relief. 'Promise you'll tell me as soon as you hear anything?' Daisy nodded. 'Even if it's bad? I want to know.'

'Josh will be fine but, sure.'

Maddie buried her fear down deep for Josh's safety. She had learned with Aaron that worry changed nothing and it wouldn't help Josh either. With Daisy and Jack on her side now, she would just hope and pray and wait.

Three days later, long after Maddie expected Josh to return to Inlet Creek, he still hadn't appeared. Knowing his line of work now, she grew anxious for news. The weather matched her mood, turning miserable, misty rain drifting inland across a calm sea. Soaking everything and restricting them indoors.

There was only so much television Maddie would allow her son to watch and the fun of repeatedly playing the same games soon faded.

Despite Maddie moving beyond impatient to alarm, she needed to maintain a bright face for Tommy. So they visited Aunt Daisy in her tearoom, read lots of books and drove along the coast just to leave the beach house. Pulled the vehicle into a lookout carpark, eating salty hot chips from their cardboard box as they overlooked the sea and watched huge heavy waves rolling in with the blustery change.

Another two long days later, Daisy arrived at the beach house in the early afternoon. She knocked on the door but breezed right in. Maddie loved that they were so open and comfortable with each other now. But when she saw the telling expression on her sister's face and realised that she should have been madly busy in the tearoom, she knew it had to be bad news.

'Where's Tommy?' Daisy asked.

'Playing in his room.'

In a low voice, Daisy jumped straight into particulars. 'Jack heard that the sting went down.'

'And?'

'Apparently it was a big operation and some guys were injured.'

'Shit.' Maddie pressed a hand to her forehead and frowned.

'Now, nothing's confirmed but I did some checking for you so I'd have more facts before I came to see you. Because I'm not immediate family, naturally the authorities wouldn't release any information. But they gave me a list of some phone numbers to call for more details.' Daisy tapped on her mobile. 'I've just sent the list to your phone.'

'I'm not family either. I won't learn much more than you did.'

'Tell them he's your boyfriend, partner, anything.' Daisy shrugged. 'A little white lie never hurt anybody. Anyway, Josh might not even be involved. They could be doing debriefing or whatever commandos do after a job. He just might not have had time to contact you yet. But you might at least find out enough to set your mind at rest.' Daisy regarded Maddie steadily and suggested, 'Maybe you should go home instead of sitting here worrying. You should be with family.'

'You *are* family.'

'Sorry.' She grinned. 'Still getting used to our new situation.'

Maddie planted her hands on her hips and paced. 'You might be right,' she said, not sounding entirely convinced, 'but what if Josh comes back looking for me here?'

Daisy chuckled. 'Trust me, from what you've told me, the guy will find you.'

'With Josh missing, it feels like my life is on hold, you know?' Maddie rubbed her arms. 'I want to be here but I probably should get back to the station. Dad's been on his own long enough.' She glanced across at her sister. 'I don't usually consider myself needy but I'd rather not travel alone with Tommy all the way home. He'll fall asleep for a while and my mind will be churning. I know you're busy full time in the tearoom but I don't suppose you could spare a day and come with me? Be nice to have someone to talk to on the trip back.'

'Okay,' Daisy said, frowning in thought. 'Leave it with me and I'll see what I can do. You want to leave like, today? Now?'

Maddie nodded. 'I'll call Dad and let him know I'm returning and then pack and I'm good to go.'

Daisy offered to take Tommy for a walk. She returned about half an hour later to find the four wheel drive packed, the house shuttered up again and Maddie ready to go.

'I just told Dad we were coming home. I didn't say why.'

'I phoned the tearoom while we were out walking,' Daisy said. 'Reliable Marj and Bill and the two girls will cover for me the rest of today. I phoned Jack, too. He'll come out to the station

248

and get me tonight. He can leave in an hour or two once business dies down and be out there by dark.'

'You can stay the night,' Maddie offered. 'Mother's still in England.'

Daisy smiled. 'Let's play it by ear, yeah?'

Maddie only made one stop on their drive inland and through the Southern Highlands to Goulburn, before the final leg out to the station. As predicted, Tommy slept for a time. The sisters' conversation was casual and random but Josh's unknown whereabouts, and the extent of his injury, still lay heavily on the back of Maddie's mind.

So it was with a huge sense of relief that, while it was still daylight, she finally turned the four wheel drive off the main road and onto the gravel track that led to the Harwood family station homestead.

They had only just pulled up when her father sauntered out onto the broad front veranda to greet them. With his wife beside him.

'Mother's home?' Maddie said in surprise.

'George didn't tell you over the phone?'

Maddie shook her head. 'Dad's not the best communicator. He still looks as sad as when I left a month ago.' And thought wickedly maybe because his discontented wife had returned.

The sisters piled out of the car and stretched. The moment Maddie released Tommy from his seatbelt, he scrambled to the ground and raced across the driveway.

'Grampa, we're back.' With sadness, Maddie noted he did not go to his grandmother.

249

George reached down to scoop him up as his adored grandson flew into his arms. Maddie endured a pang of regret for leaving her father and depriving him of his only grandchild. Disregarding the heavy load of recent events hanging over her, she was glad to be back. But for how long? The uncertainty brought its own wave of separate troubling emotion.

Her mother stood as rigid and unsmiling as any classic female Greek statue. Dutifully at her husband's side again, showing no excitement at seeing Tommy after being absent in England for months. The ice-cold glare she aimed in the direction of the recent arrivals was for Daisy alone.

In no mood for her mother's bitterness, Maddie leapt the steps and warmly hugged her father. 'Hi Dad. Mother.' She obliged her with the brief and expected dispassionate air kiss.

Meanwhile Daisy had approached and climbed the steps. Maddie noticed her father's face beam with pleasure.

'This is a surprise.' Father and oldest daughter warmly embraced.

'Mrs. Harwood.' Daisy acknowledged her with a polite restrained nod.

Elizabeth's response was a tight smile. Honestly? Maddie fumed. With all her supposed breeding, she couldn't be more hospitable? Staying close to the resentful woman she was sometimes ashamed to call her mother, Maddie hissed, 'Fake some feeling, mother. You do it all the time.'

Elizabeth didn't flinch at her daughter's slight. 'Is she staying?'

'We're sisters. We keep in touch.' Maddie deliberately avoided answering her mother's question. Let her stew. It was time for this ridiculous attitude to be addressed.

Standing so close, her father and Daisy couldn't help but be aware of the private undertones going on beside them. Maddie only hoped they had not overheard.

'Dad, can I talk to you in the office?' His face sharpened in surprise but he nodded. She turned to her sister. 'Daisy, you probably won't remember where the kitchen is but if you come with Dad and me, we'll point you in the right direction. Kirra will be beside herself to see you again. You'll have longer to catch up than you did at Aaron's funeral.'

No way would Maddie throw her sister at the mercy and into the company of the woman who hated Daisy so much. This statement of inclusion let her mother know in public and without any doubts that Daisy was part of their family. The admirable loving and generous woman Maddie was so proud to call her sister alongside Lilly had lived here in this homestead long before his second wife and daughters.

Finally, in her head and heart, Maddie felt she had got it right. The significance that, regardless of individual opinions, it was way past time that Daisy Sheldon was recognised and welcomed on *Georgina Downs* and into this house again.

As George left with his daughters, Elizabeth remained standing alone, abandoned on the veranda.

As Daisy peeled off to the kitchen, Maddie

said, 'We'll come and get you in a while or when Jack gets here.'

The sisters exchanged cunning smiles, knowing she would be safe and welcome with Kirra unless Elizabeth interfered. Not that the second Mrs. Harwood daunted Daisy in the least.

'Jack sent a text as we arrived. He'll be about another hour.'

'Perfect. See you in a bit.'

Maddie closed the office door behind them. She and her father took up seats on the worn and much-loved old leather sofa beneath the window.

'What's this all about?'

After a deep breath, Maddie launched into every detail about meeting Josh, his job, the recent mission at sea and the fact that he was now possibly injured. Being the wily successful land baron that he had become in his lifetime, she doubted he would miss the irony that it had been her father's suggestion for Maddie to take a break at the beach house. And enough clues had been subtly planted to cast her life and future on the station in doubt.

As she spoke, he had cast his gaze to the polished timber floor and quietly listened. When she finished, he glanced across at her, resignation clear on his lined face and an even deeper sadness in his eyes.

Yet, unruffled and a master of organisation and achievement, he simply said, 'Give me that list on your phone. I'll see if I can't call in some favours.'

Maddie knew these would be people of

influence and contacts in high places. While George phoned around, Maddie poured herself a splash of her father's best French cognac, the indulgence he kept here in his private domain for his own personal use, sipping it as she listened and paced.

Her anticipation rose as the intensity in his short responses and hastily written notes, when he paused to listen during the fourth phone call and exchange, sounded like he may have found answers.

He hung up, remained silent for a moment then slowly rose from his desk chair. 'Josh is in hospital in Sydney. Not sure of his exact injury but apparently he'll be fine.'

Usually made of stronger stuff, Maddie almost fainted with relief. And the agony of knowing when she saw Josh again, if she was honest about her past, it could be for the last time. No one, not even her father or her best friends, knew about that night.

'Go to him, my dear.' George handed her his scrawled piece of paper with the hospital address. 'Sometimes in life you have to let people go.' Impossible not to understand he meant his first wife, Ailie. 'But when they arrive in your life like a gift, you have to do something about it. Forget family loyalty,' he cringed. 'Comes a time in your life when it's all about letting go and moving on. Do what is in your heart.'

Maddie knew her father spoke from past experience and regrets. And was also referring to her recent loss of Aaron and a possible second chance at love.

'To be honest, I have no idea where I stand. What Josh thinks and feels about me. I'm only going to visit him out of respect and because I care, make sure he'll be all right. If it doesn't work out to be anything more, I'll be back.'

A ton of meaning lay behind those fateful words. Even though they hadn't known it at the time, their attraction had been strong from their first meeting on the Inlet Creek pier. The subsequent kisses had merely inflamed and confirmed that initial chemistry.

No, it wouldn't be easy, and what she had to say to Josh was right up there as the hardest thing she had done in her life so far. She might return to the station empty-handed but she would give it a damn good Harwood try.

17

By soon after dusk later that evening, Jack roared up to the homestead in his noisy but clearly reliable combi van to collect Daisy. Although the battered classic vehicle looked and sounded incapable, it had successfully made this trip twice in recent times.

Father, sisters, Jack and Tommy all hugged before Daisy's departure. Elizabeth was nowhere to be seen. Keen to return to Inlet Creek before it grew too late in the night, bearing in mind Jack had a super-early morning start each day in his French bakery, the pair piled into the van, waving madly as they left.

Maddie mouthed a silent *Thank you* to her sister who smiled and blew her a kiss in return. As they drove away, Maddie thought she had never seen a couple look so happy and right together.

⋆ ⋆ ⋆

Next morning, after one of Kirra's stellar roast lamb dinners last night — what else on a sheep station? — Maddie and Tommy appeared for breakfast in the dining room, its three long windows overlooking the garden at the side of the homestead. Her father sat alone looking solitary but brightened when his smiling family breezed in.

'Mother not up yet?' Maddie asked as she hugged him, a spontaneous gesture in which she didn't usually indulge but the weary hunched shoulders looked like he needed it.

'She's taking breakfast in her room.'

When she had no social obligations, it wasn't unusual for Elizabeth to lie in until late, emerging immaculately dressed. Her parents had not shared a bedroom for years.

Yet again, anxious on her father's behalf, Maddie imagined a desolate and unrewarding personal life for him ahead. At least while she was away, he would have the joy of Tommy's company. All the same, she still questioned her wisdom in chasing a man she barely knew who, in all probability, would reject her.

Maddie had already explained to her son that she must go away for a few days but that Grampa, Kirra and Nanny would be here for him. She hadn't mentioned Josh's name and why, in case it didn't work out. Amidst the upheaval in his small life lately, Tommy seemed able to cope so long as she explained happenings carefully, devoted plenty of time to her little man and remained as generous as ever with hugs.

To conceal her misgivings about leaving her father and seeking out Josh, Maddie piled two plates for herself and Tommy from Kirra's substantial spread on the sideboard, took a seat and asked, 'So what plans for today?'

'I thought Tommy and I would take the ute out around the sheep. It's been a long hot summer and with the good early rains recently, I want to check on how the grasslands are progressing.'

'Do you hear that, Tommy? You're going on a drive with Grampa in the ute.'

While her father and son grinned at each other, Maddie realised she was probably the only one who recognised and cared that, despite two marriages, three daughters and a sheep station to run, underneath it all George Harwood was a lonely man.

Once Tommy had gobbled down his breakfast and scampered off, no doubt to Kirra in the kitchen, leaving father and daughter privately alone, Maddie said sincerely, 'I feel like I'm forsaking you again.'

'Your mother and Tommy are here,' he said absently, lacking enthusiasm. 'You're a grown woman my dear. This new man in your life sounds damned decent. And, from what you say, he has accepted your son.' He paused and placed his cutlery across an empty plate. 'I could see that Aaron adored you to the point of obsession. Maybe it was the thrill of loving the boss's daughter. But one partner in each relationship always loves greater than the other.'

'I did care about him,' Maddie whispered.

'I know, but he was wild. Before you married, I made him swear never to mistreat or hurt you. I'm sorry he did that by being irresponsible for that one split second that took his life and left you and Tommy behind. But now, perhaps,' he shrugged with consideration, 'you need to move on.'

'Well,' Maddie hedged, knowing this was her father's way of giving his blessing, 'Josh and I did seem to have a connection. My visit to Sydney isn't a done deal, Dad. It's to see if he's okay, firstly, then if we both seek something more from our relationship.'

The gentle warning was to prepare herself as much as her father for failure. 'Tommy will have Nanny but will you keep an eye on him? Spend time with him?'

'Of course. Go,' he urged, eyeing her hard with affection yet also, Maddie suspected, the heartbreak of letting yet another woman he loved ease from his life. 'I know Josh's fisherman story was only a cover but don't let him be the one that got away.'

Unless he doesn't want me.

George Harwood had loved all the women in his life, two wives and three daughters, each in his own special way. Maddie knew that Tommy, at least in his Grampa's eyes, had been the family's little blessing and hope for securing the future of *Georgina Downs*. Maybe that dream wasn't meant to be but who knew what came next in life? Whatever happened, grandfather and grandson would always share a special bond.

★　★　★

After breakfast, when her father and Tommy had driven away in the ute, Maddie did her duty and knocked on her mother's bedroom door to tell her of the planned trip to Sydney. Of course she asked why. Maddie only divulged the barest information that she had met another man, he was a friend but injured and, out of courtesy, she felt obliged to visit.

'A new man?' Elizabeth sighed. 'Is Aaron forgotten already? You married one wild man after a swift relationship and now you're leaping straight into the arms of another. It's unrefined to chase after a man. If he's worthy, he'll find you. Really Madeleine, it doesn't look respectable.'

'Do I look like I care?' While her mother hovered with sour disapproval, thinning her bitter mouth, Maddie continued, 'You said Aaron was no good for me anyway. You never liked or approved of him. *Never thought he was good enough* for me. Weren't they your exact words in the limousine? On the day of his funeral no less!' Maddie made no effort to curb her anger. 'You of all people have no right to tell me what to do. I'll make my own decisions and mistakes. Just like you,' she tossed over her shoulder as she closed the door behind her.

It could all backfire and she could be returning to *Georgina Downs* in humiliation but she would face that hurdle if it happened.

Aaron had been handed to her as a gift.

Josh would be harder to win.

★   ★   ★

Before Maddie left *Georgina Downs* for the long drive up to Sydney, she gathered enough courage to saddle up Rambler and ride out to the family cemetery. She dismounted, looped the reins over the fence and strolled inside.

At Aaron's grave, still a dirt mound, Maddie realised she was yet to make a decision about his

259

headstone. She must organise that.

A soft cool breeze blew across the site as if whispering echoes of past conversations or secrets. Maddie knelt on the ground, folded her hands calmly before her and found it easy to begin.

'Oh Aaron,' she sighed. 'You burst into my life with such fire and magic, you were impossible to resist. Your past always remained a secret. None of your family attended our wedding but you refused to discuss why. It didn't really matter. We all embraced you.' Maddie smiled wryly. 'Except mother. But then she doesn't take to many people.

'And then little Thomas George was born bringing a whole new generation into the station homestead.' She paused, her hands growing restless. 'I was disappointed that you weren't interested in him much. He was such a beautiful boy, I never understood that. So I gave in to mother's insistence that we hire a nanny for him. To please you. Go out on the station with you, work alongside you. And we did. But I sensed you were always pulled in other directions.

'In the end, I realised I could no longer make you happy.' Tears pricked her eyes. 'Do you have the slightest idea how much that hurt? To see you laughing and happy with others but not with me. You were my gorgeous idol. The cowboy who stole my heart.

'But although we were growing apart, I would never have wished such a sudden death upon you. I had dreams, almost like premonitions, before that rally. As though something was preparing me for bad news. Do you remember how I hugged you and found it hard to let go before you left? And what I whispered to you. *Come home to us.* But you never did.'

Large tears began rolling down her face. 'I hated you for that. I was so angry on the day of your funeral. To think that any person with such a passion for life could be just gone, like that.' She snapped her fingers and swiped at her wet cheeks, managing a cheeky smile though watery eyes. 'Man you should have seen the dress I wore for you.

'Then father sent Tommy and me to Inlet Creek. Turns out it wasn't one of his worst ideas. I think you should know that I met another man there. I've only known him for the shortest time and he's probably everything you weren't, but it's like that magic is happening for me all over again and someone up there,' she glanced toward the clear blue morning sky, 'is giving me a second chance. I intend to take a risk. I'm going to tell him the secret I never told you. Might not work out so I'm praying and hoping someone out there is listening.'

Maddie slowly rose to her feet again, pushed her hands into her jeans and stood still in the country quiet for a while. The row of gum trees planted around the perimeter rustled as fingers of wind rushed through.

Maddie looked back over her shoulder as she gathered up the reins and prepared to remount Rambler.

'Sweet dreams,' she whispered, not only just for Aaron but everyone else who lay sleeping there.

Back at the homestead, Maddie wasted no time in loading her small carryall into the four wheel drive. With her mother's words of gloom and disapproval still ringing in her ears, and a measure of peace in her heart since visiting the cemetery, Maddie turned her sturdy vehicle down the track that led to the main country road toward Goulburn and eventually to the Hume Highway.

Wise of Grampa to divert Tommy's attention by taking him away out onto the station so mother and son were both spared a goodbye.

It would be a long four hour drive before she made it into the busy, noisy city. Maddie dreaded the urban surroundings to come and that next critical meeting with Josh. So she kept her mind positive with what she would say, listened to the radio and just drove.

George Harwood kept his grandson close out on the station as they drove around some of his prize Merino flocks. When it came time for lunch, they returned to the homestead, all three of them ate Kirra's tasty offering, before Nanny quietly appeared to put Tommy down for his afternoon nap.

A niggling hunch in his subconscious forced George's hand. Their grandson didn't sleep long anymore and he intended to use the window of opportunity when he and his wife were alone.

Elizabeth rose and hastily excused herself, no doubt intending to escape. George had other ideas. She had avoided him since her return from England. Before their disastrous marriage continued, they needed a conversation.

'We should talk,' he called after her across the impressive dining room.

She spun around to face him, wary alarm across her gracious face. She'd been a beauty when he met her and was aging slowly and well. Unlike himself. Some days lately, he felt weary and spent.

'I thought tea in the sitting room,' he suggested.

Her favourite room. It worked.

She hesitated only for a moment then said, 'As you wish. I'll tell Kirra.'

She pressed the button to summon staff, issuing her usual firmly spoken orders when cook dutifully appeared, then her footsteps faded down the hall. George followed.

Settled into beige diamond-buttoned fabric-covered Chesterfield sofas opposite one another, he offered, 'Would you care for a drink?'

Elizabeth shook her head. Knowing he would need something else stronger than tea, he poured himself a generous splash of his favourite French cognac. His expensive relaxing indulgence. He would need it. Neither spoke until after Kirra brought in a lavish tea tray with a plate of her freshly baked sweet treats.

'Thank you, Kirra,' he murmured, since Elizabeth never did. 'Please close the door on your way out and tell Nanny to entertain Tommy when he wakes. We're not to be disturbed.'

'Of course, sir.'

The quiet click of the latch sounded like a sonic boom echoing across the room. In its wake, the ticking of the antique mantel clock, one of the few pieces of any value bought by his father MacDonald Harwood decades before, punctured the silence. As Elizabeth served the tea, George cleared his throat, made himself comfortable and began.

'I would like to discuss our situation and the future.' No response, as expected, so he continued. 'I don't believe Maddie will stay on the station.'

Elizabeth scoffed. 'She's a country girl. She's meant to be here.'

'Only if it's her own wish and decision, not ours.'

His wife's cool expression blanched. 'Don't encourage her to leave,' she demanded crisply. 'She'll take our grandson.'

As he suspected, George finally saw the hint of fear she allowed to cross her expression. That she would be stranded out here alone with him and was clawing to keep family about her. Because she only did her barest social duty on the station, spent half her year in England and the rest of the time shared their bleak marriage, she had nothing else. Neither did he. But it didn't bother him as much because he lived where he belonged.

'You've never cared about children before, why start now? You hired nannies to raise our daughters instead of doing it yourself.' His retort shocked her but, determined to persist and resolve their marriage once and for all, George continued with the blunt truth of their current life situation and his own firm conviction. 'Children leave the nest, Elizabeth. Surely you didn't expect them to be out here forever? It is just you and me now.'

'No thanks to you,' she snapped. 'Maddie is demeaning herself chasing a new man but at least Lilly has my family in England and a respectable boyfriend.'

George took the slur against the Harwood name and reputation in his stride. He accepted he and his family were a hard lot but from nothing but honest labour they had built a prosperous pastoral empire.

'From what I overheard Lilly saying to Maddie at Christmas, it didn't sound like she was all that keen on this man Oliver in her life.'

'He comes from money.'

So important to Elizabeth. 'I suggest we start learning to get along.'

'I have no wish to stay imprisoned out here,' said quietly, steadily holding his gaze.

He had long since guessed that was his wife's wish. This discussion would be the catalyst allowing her the excuse to leave the sheep station for good.

'Goulburn is a thriving inland city on our doorstep. You have friends and a social life here.' Not many, he knew, but the enemy of isolation was the issue here and would not retain her.

Elizabeth couldn't look at him. She rose with poise and gracefully walked over to the window, gazing out, restlessly rubbing her arms. 'I'm leaving to live in England. Permanently.'

George had already prepared himself for this. 'You want a divorce?'

'Separation will be adequate so long as I'm financially supported.'

He knew exactly what his wife would expect. 'I'm not buying you an apartment in Mayfair.'

'That won't be necessary. Rental of a country house would suffice. I have old and dear friends I will want to come and visit.'

George didn't resist her decision to leave or beg her to stay. Living alone together they would both be miserable and verbally tear each other apart.

Over his silence, Elizabeth turned back to him, her voice a whip of venom and accusation, 'Have you nothing to say?'

'You're a grown woman. I've never forced you to do anything against your wishes. I won't start now.'

'You don't care that I have no desire to stay?'

His wife's leaving didn't bother him. They had been living as strangers for years. 'You've always done as you pleased, Elizabeth. Your decision disappoints me but it's your choice if it makes you happy.'

'How could I possibly compete with *her*? You always loved her best.'

'A wise observation.' Finally, to her face, George did not deny his wife's allegation. Elizabeth grew white and rigid with shock and fury at his confession. While she remained silent, her expression icy, he said, 'I'm sure you have a property in mind. Show me the papers so I can approve them before you go.'

With a heavy heart that another phase of his life was over, he pushed himself wearily to his feet, turned his back on his wife and walked out.

★   ★   ★

George sought the sanctuary of his office. Within minutes and without knocking on the door of his domain or a word spoken, Elizabeth breezed in with a set of papers which she handed over to him, then left. It revealed her choice for the lease of a fine but modest Georgian mansion house on a country estate. She had clearly done her research and prepared for this inevitable moment.

George scanned every page of the documents carefully and approved them.

With Elizabeth's imminent departure, he made phone calls to set up appointments in Goulburn with his accountant and lawyer for the following day. He intended to make damned sure his wife's spending was controlled by an allowance, although she would expect a live-in housekeeper and service.

Too sad that ice ran through her veins instead of blood.

The reality and thought of his girls all grown up and elsewhere, disinterested in helping run the station, pained his heart. But he had seen it coming. *Georgina* could have been a third and even fourth generation family property if Maddie and Tommy stayed.

It had been his deepest and most private wish

when he married Elizabeth that there would be sons to continue the tradition and inherit the legacy his father had begun and upon which he had built.

Maybe he hadn't tried hard enough emotionally to accommodate his wife's needs. The laughing carefree woman he knew and met in England that had ignited his first spark of attraction had changed with the years living on the edge of the outback, so different from the green and dampness of her home country. So that, over the years, their token affections for each other had slowly withered and died.

Ah Ailie, he pined with hopeless longing as he leant back in his well-worn and comfortable leather desk chair, closing his eyes to remember.

18

Maddie heaved a sigh of relief to be leaving the M5 and heading east around the Georges River toward Oyster Bay in southern Sydney. Grateful not to be fighting the even greater congestion of city traffic in the CBD.

Using her father's hastily written directions and the four wheel drive's GPS, she found the small private hospital. Somehow it didn't seem right to bring flowers or chocolates to a bloke so she decided to just bring herself and a ready smile. Sending up a plea that he even wanted to see her again. Even if he did, after what she needed to tell him, he might not want to keep her.

In the end it didn't matter because she didn't make it past the reception desk. Josh had already been released. Good news because that meant he couldn't be too ill, right?

How her father had dug out Josh's private address information, Maddie didn't know and certainly hadn't asked. She was just relieved to go and find him but daunted as to what lay ahead after that.

So it was only a short time later that she pulled up her big dusty country vehicle outside a modern duplex apartment building not too far away. She looked down at her jeans, white shirt and boots, combed fingers through her tangled brown hair and hoped she would do.

Her welcome was another matter. A wave of nausea lodged in the pit of her stomach as she walked to the door. Which was wide open. The glamorous and curvy high maintenance Michelle was just leaving, her blonde head turned, letting the man standing behind her inside have a piece of her mind. She couldn't see Josh because Michelle blocked her view.

'I hope I'm not interrupting.' Maddie spoke only to make them aware of her presence.

Michelle's attention whipped around. She glared for a moment before turning back to Josh to snarl, 'You threw me out for this wrinkled brown-skinned country bumpkin?' The outburst was accompanied by a string of following curses.

Maddie was used to hearing honest if cringe-worthy rough language from outback men so the attack from this piece of over-indulged skirt did not bother her at all, nor detract from her mission.

To fight for the man she was falling in love with. A gift even weeks ago she would never have imagined she might ever experience again.

Michelle brushed her roughly aside, dragging a wheeled suitcase along behind as she strutted off down the driveway teetering on scary heels to a small car parked on the street. She threw the case and then herself inside, fired up the engine and drove away at what Maddie considered a dangerous speed for a winding suburban roadway.

Left standing alone on the doorstep, the beaming sexy smile of mischief Josh flashed her and its accompanying cheeky wink set her heart racing with relief and flooded with love.

'Trust me, she won't be back,' he said, then waved an arm to indicate she should come inside. 'This is one hell of a surprise.'

Well, she had come this far. An apprehensive Maddie entered his apartment. Slowly moving further in, she caught sight of the magnificent water views beyond. Staring through the full length windows, she breathed, 'This is lovely.'

'I missed you,' he said softly behind her. His arms slid about her waist and she leaned back into him.

'Did you?' Oh, how lame. And this was going to be so hard. He was going to hate her and tell her to leave.

He sought her hand and, hobbling, led her over to a comfy sofa in the sitting area. 'Sorry I've not been able to get in touch. It's been mad since the sting and having an operation because of this shoulder,' he lightly shrugged and winced, 'rather held me up. Once they let me out of hospital and Michelle left, I was coming to get you.'

Maddie's heart lifted and broke at the same time so she delayed. 'The mission was a success?'

'Hell yeah. Never any doubt about that. We thought it might go down out at sea aboard the vessel but decided it better to track them into port in the early hours of the morning. When they offloaded into a van, we intercepted and arrested six people. One resisted. Thank God the guy was a poor shot. Injured my leg as I fell down but the team nailed them and we picked up a huge commercial quantity haul. Search warrants dug out a few more from residential properties around Sydney. That's why you've heard nothing. Had to keep information about the operation under wraps until we carried out the last arrests.'

'It all sounds scary and brave at the same time.'

'It's my job.' His steady gaze of surprise held hers. 'How the hell did you find me?'

'Daisy did some groundwork and Dad apparently has contacts.' She hesitated. 'It was his idea to come. I wasn't sure — '

'About what?' he teased softly.

She couldn't answer that but she was sure soppy love was written all over her face. 'Just wanted to see how you're doing.'

'Alive and walking. And all the better for seeing you,' he murmured.

Maddie didn't dare hope but the telling gleam in his eyes was reassuring. Sending out such heart-stopping positive signals.

'Maddie, I just want us to be together. How long can you stay?'

Damn. This was going to be hard but this time, before she embarked on another relation-ship, she had to tell him. 'Depends.'

'On what?'

'On what I have to tell you. You'll be disappointed in me.'

His forehead wrinkled into a frown. 'Tommy okay?'

She nodded. Not unusual that Josh's first thoughts should be for others. He was that kind of man. But oh so uncanny that his concern should be for her son.

'Take your time.' He took one of her hands and threaded their fingers together. 'Sounds like this won't be easy.'

Maddie thrilled to his touch but also felt as if she wanted to break away. And then because she was filled with the deepest fear of her life that she would lose this beautiful heroic man, she began to blurt it all out. She hung her head and once the words spilled, she couldn't stop.

'It was my hen's night out on the station down by the creek. A few local girlfriends, female station hands working seasonal. Lilly. We'd built a campfire for a barbeque. There was lots of beer. Night was getting on then a cowboy arrived. I thought it was odd that maybe he'd stumbled on our party by accident. Until I realised it was a dare. A conspiracy. The girls had set it up. In all innocence apparently but it kind of got out of hand.'

Maddie caught her breath, forced to pause. Josh was so still beside her and she wondered what he was thinking. Did he guess where her story was leading?

'By then I'd had way too much to drink. The girls started playing music and urged me on. I didn't see any harm in a bit of sexy dancing. Then someone stripped off and suddenly all the girls are wading into the creek naked. I grew concerned because even though the water wasn't that deep, we'd all been drinking, you know?

'The cowboy started leading me away from the water into the trees. I was laughing and stumbling and telling him I should go back. He said they'd all be fine. That they would watch out for each other. He pulled me close and danced, then started kissing me. I thought that was going too far but he was getting rough and . . . he pulled up my skirt,' she whispered, tears streaming down her face. 'He backed me up against one of the parked vehicles in the dark and I realised by then, even though I struggled, he was too strong and it was too late.'

'Jesus,' Josh growled.

Maddie crumbled then and began to sob. She didn't need to say anymore. He knew now. She could never have moved into a more serious relationship with a man this special without confiding her unknown truth. She was prepared to face the consequences. When she recovered enough, she would leave.

'It's no consolation . . . but I'll never . . . forgive myself. I was at fault, too. I was wearing a tight and very short denim skirt . . . that barely covered anything but I thought . . . we'd be just out in the bush with a bunch of girls. Having a harmless night of fun.'

'Oh Maddie.' Josh gathered her into his arms, love and agony in his voice. 'Did you ever report it?'

'Of course not. I was so ashamed.'

Five years of guilt and feeling dirty that had weighed her down in every way, finally erupted. She burst into a flood of tears and impossibly harsh crying. Reliving the horror of what she went through that night was confronting but also a relief to share. Even though it would only be for a while, she felt so safe and secure in Josh's arms.

As Maddie's shaking body slowly grew quieter, Josh said gently, 'Based on what you've just told me, what you suffered was not your fault. Have you ever believed that?'

She vigorously shook her head.

'Then start believing. That's the only way you can begin to heal. The reason I know that is from firsthand experience. So, while we're confessing . . . '

When she glanced up at him, red faced and tear stained, frowning, he brushed her wet cheeks with his thumb and said, 'My name's Josh and I'm an alcoholic.'

Maddie could only stare in surprise, her mind distracted, and speculate at his story and what could possibly have dragged him so low. She had an idea, of course, based on their past conversation at the beach house but she let him talk.

'After my brother Bailey lost his struggle with drugs, I kind of sank into drink to ease my own feelings of, you guessed it, guilt. I'm not proud of it but we two older brothers, Simon and myself, always watched out for the two younger ones. Bailey and Ben were twins. There was quite a few years between us. Our folks had been trying for a while to have more kids so it was a heap of excitement when it finally happened again.

'The night Bailey died, I was supposed to pick him up in the city but I was held up with traffic and late for our scheduled meeting time. When I arrived, it was to see paramedics giving Bailey CPR.'

Maddie softly groaned at the streak of anguish on Josh's face. 'Oh no. Don't.'

'You can't help it though, can you? It's all the *what ifs*. If I'd only done this or that. Taken another route. Phoned him to let him know. It might have made a difference.'

Or not. In that moment, Maddie knew. *This* crushing life's experience was the source of Josh's compassion for her own assault. Having gone through a private hell himself, too. Such an incredible coincidence which only showed that many people had a tragic story that impacted their lives.

In Josh's case it was his brother, Bailey's, lost struggle with drugs, then his own resultant descent into drink to overcome his blame demons. But, ultimately, he beat them and changed his life's direction to fight the criminals that created addiction in the first place.

'You know that you couldn't possibly have been to blame?' Maddie said kindly.

'I do now, yes. But it took years. What about you?' He sent a challenging glance her way. 'Are you ever going to forgive yourself and place the responsibility where it belongs? On the guy who pushed you too far?'

She shrugged and admitted humbly, 'You're the first person I've told. It's just so amazing that you believe me.'

He ignited her libido with a slow and soft decadently persuasive kiss. 'You're a beautiful person. I will want you,' he whispered. 'I'll always want you no matter what.'

After a moment, blown away by his tender

vow, she recovered enough to ask, 'Are you sure about taking on Tommy?'

'He's your son.' Josh gently placed a finger over her lips. 'That's what's important.'

'Thank you,' she whispered, tears pooling in her eyes again. 'I guess, like you, it's going to take time. Common sense tells me he took advantage and I was too trusting of a stranger.'

'All the same — '

'I know. I'll have to start thinking more positively.'

They held each other for a long time, buried in a mutual hug of support.

Later, Josh frowned, his voice genuinely surprised, 'You really thought I wouldn't want you?'

She nodded, looking sheepish.

★ ★ ★

He sighed. 'What am I going to do with you, Maddie West?'

'Keep having faith in me,' she pleaded softly.

'Done. How about we get out of here and grab a bite to eat? You're driving.'

'Sure, so long as you navigate. I hate cities. If there's more than one main street, I have no idea where I'm going.'

Josh grinned. 'I know a perfect little waterfront marina café nearby.'

After they had dined on fish and beer, feeling lazy, they sat replete together in harmony, gazing out over the calm blue water.

Josh pushed a hand through his thick sun

bleached hair, slowly shaking his head. 'This has to be the greatest day of my life. Fate that you came up here today.' He paused. 'I've just made a purchase. I'd love to show you. Want to see it?'

Intrigued, she said, 'Okay. Sounds interesting.'

Arm in arm, Maddie strolled and Josh limped to the marina below the café where they had eaten lunch. Leading her down a ramp and along the floating jetty, Josh halted toward the end where larger boats were moored.

'I kind of bought this.' He pointed to a gleaming white catamaran with the name *Ocean Blue* written in dashing lettering on its side. 'Just put my apartment on the market and cashed in all my leave. Need to give this beauty a trial run.'

Maddie clutched her throat and froze, her happiness dissolving, trying to sound excited for his planned adventure. 'You're taking off somewhere?'

He nodded, enthusiasm rife across his face. 'Up the east coast. Come aboard and take a look.' They stepped on deck. 'You can live off the sea, catch fish and crabs, trawl lines out the back of the boat. Find anchorage in a port some-where.'

With knowledge and eagerness, Josh pointed out the GPS for navigation. 'It's connected to an autopilot so it steers the boat as well. Mobile phone reception is generally good all along the coast. You can log into HF radio programmes to connect with fellow sailors and share informa-tion.'

Maddie had to admit the interior bunks, galley kitchen, seating and dining was all more than roomy and comfortable. The polished timber work gleamed. 'Like home away from home,' she murmured.

'That's what it's meant to be.'

She sank deep into disappointment believing she had interrupted his plans and hoping to hell he would be back soon. Rubbing her arms, she asked, 'How long will you be away?'

'See that's the thing. I'm thinking six months so I need a cook and crew. An irresistible sexy woman and, say, a boy deckhand about four years old.'

Maddie finally twigged and gasped, trying not to appear alarmed. 'You planning on taking this thing out into the open sea?'

'Not with precious cargo aboard, no.' His gaze held hers in complete understanding. 'We'll stick to the coastline.'

He stepped closer, slid his hands around her waist and in a soft murmured voice said, 'How about you drive back home, talk to your family and think about it. I'll sail down the coast and meet you and Tommy at Inlet Creek in a few days. If you decide to come along, we'll provision up and head back north up the coast. Keeping in sight of land all the time, okay?' he reinforced for her peace of mind. 'Over the southern winter we can escape to the warmer weather in the tropics. Then I thought maybe cruise out around the reefs and the Coral Sea.'

It was a lot to take in. A huge change of plans in her life at a moment's notice. Not that she had anything in mind for the immediate future. To his credit, Josh gave her space to process his offer and think. Holding hands, they sauntered the waterfront pathways and nearby parks, eating ice cream, chatting about idle stuff. He didn't mention the boat issue again.

Toward evening, when they returned to Josh's apartment, he asked, 'Can you stay awhile?'

'Is that an invitation?'

'Absolutely.'

'In that case I can stay as long as you want.'

He grinned, holding her gaze. 'We can eat and talk more. Later,' he emphasised. 'You on the same page?'

Maddie chuckled and nodded. 'After we're exhausted.'

'Might need help undressing though,' Josh drawled.

'Be my pleasure.'

And then it was definitely not about the talking, just lots of sexy moves and kisses and intimate touching. Josh made love to her with a fierceness that excited Maddie's heart and spoke of possession. Hell, if life with Josh was going to be like this, she would be walking around with a permanent smile on her face.

And there would be no problem conceiving more little Seymour commandos she had planned. When the time was right and they had talked about it. For now, they indulged themselves and enjoyed each other.

Loving, sleeping, dozing, kissing and nibbling each other was pretty much the deal for the rest of the night.

As dawn broke, sliding its first pale beams of the day in at the window's edges and they stirred amid their tangle of sheets, Josh pleasured Maddie soon after her sleepy eyelids fluttered open and she was barely awake.

Gasping with abandon, she moaned, 'Hell you're good. What a way to greet the morning but I'm done for now. I'm starving. For food,' she laughed when he raised his eyebrows in expectation.

Somehow they had completely missed dinner last night.

'You sure?' he growled.

She chuckled with delight when he determinedly followed her into the bathroom. Warm streams of water sluiced all over them and as Josh's hands worked their magic and she backed against the wall, he licked the water from her mouth and set about shooting her earlier statement to shreds.

'Talk about steamy sex,' she quipped as they towelled each other dry. 'You're rather agile for an injured commando.'

'I'm more fit and dangerous than you know.'

'Wonderful,' she breathed, standing on tiptoe to steal a kiss.

Dressed and tingling from loving, over breakfast on the balcony Josh asked, 'I know it's down the track aways but we'll need to think about where we want to live. What about the sheep station and your father?'

'If I'm with you, I can't be there. He understands that. We had that discussion before I left. He's my father and I love him and *Georgina* will always be my roots but you're my life now. Just don't go doing anything too crazy and scaring the jeepers out of me, okay?'

'Been looking into that while twiddling my thumbs in hospital. I'm leaving the Force. Thought I might train and work with coastal rescue.'

Maddie brightened, knowing Josh's adventurous nature could never settle for anything mundane. 'That sounds ideal.'

'Okay, so we could live maybe coastal hinterland someplace?'

She thought it sounded perfect. So long as it wasn't a city and Josh was with them, it didn't much matter. And they would still be a half day drive out to the sheep station.

She could bring Rambler and Tommy's pony to their new place.

★　★　★

Five days later that seemed way longer, at least for Maddie, after word finally arrived from Josh at sea, she drove herself, Tommy and Grampa to the coast. No way was she letting Josh go off on that boat alone.

Elizabeth remained at the homestead in the throes of packing for England. Her father had explained the separation so Maddie said her goodbyes before they left. Holding not only mixed feelings of her parents' unhappiness and dissolving marriage but also the added conflict that, because she and Tommy were leaving, George would now be completely without any family in the station homestead.

As they drove into Inlet Creek, at the first

sight of Josh's catamaran, Tommy grew delirious with excitement. Maddie had forgotten how beautiful it was, even anchored as it was a short distance away from the pier.

Josh was pacing stiff legged and swept Maddie off her feet while they kissed. George ambled behind holding Tommy's hand but not for long. The boy let go and raced to Josh who scooped him up. A measure of the trust and love the child had for this honourable man that a small boy's instinct sensed his worth.

George extended a hand. 'Pleased to meet you, son.'

'Sir,' Josh greeted him respectfully.

'George,' he grunted.

Maddie had already sent a text of the family's arrival from inland and Josh safely from the sea so it wasn't long before Daisy and Jack, having both happily deserted the tearoom and bakery, were striding down the jetty hand in hand, beaming.

Departure was set for the following morning but, tonight, they all retired to the beach house. A fire blazed its warmth against the creeping evening chill of autumn.

The sisters and Jack chattered in the kitchen, Josh lit the electric barbeque on the front veranda, braving the wind sweeping in off the sea the sound of breaking waves somewhere out in the dark behind them. With scudding cloud cover, the moon was hidden tonight.

Tommy hung about Josh and Grampa as meat and onions cooked, sending stomachs growling with hunger. Conversation deliberately avoided embarkation and tomorrow's departure. Maddie's glances and wrinkled forehead betrayed her thoughts that George would be driving back out to the homestead alone. He was no longer the strong man of her childhood and she worried for him.

Maddie thought she hid her concerns but Daisy must have noticed because she saw her sister sidle closer and slide an arm about her shoulder. 'He'll be fine. We'll keep in touch with him. Promise.'

'Thanks.'

Much later, as the family reunion came to its inevitable end, Daisy said, 'See you in the morning,' as she and Jack left, not intending to miss a moment of her sister's departure, whatever the early hour

George retired to the spare room, one of the few times he ever visited or stayed in his own beach house, which was becoming the hub of family gatherings.

With difficulty and alert with endless questions, Tommy eventually settled to sleep, while Maddie and Josh snuggled and dozed together in her room, neither really sleeping ahead of their new relationship and adventure ahead. Sometime during the night, Tommy crept into their bed, sprawling between them.

Disturbed by the boy's movements, Maddie mouthed at Josh, 'Are you sure about this?'

'Wouldn't have it any other way?'

'Damn, Seymour, you're one hell of a keeper.'

★ ★ ★

A succession of small boat loads conveyed their belongings and initial supplies from the pier out to the yacht next day. By mid-morning, they were done and parting could no longer be avoided.

Rugged up in warm clothes, Maddie cried more with happy tears than sad, although her feelings were jumbled as she hugged her father.

Then the trio was ferried out to the catamaran by a local fisherman, life jackets donned and sails rose majestically before the wind, the three intrepid sailors all madly waving, bittersweet smiles hiding the sadness of separation.

As did those on the pier, the mariners became specks out in the bay before disappearing around the Point lighthouse on the headland to sail between the coast and South Pacific Ocean for unknown but inspiring northern destinations.

For a long time, Daisy and Jack, arms around each other smiling, and George standing stoically beside them, remained on the pier, reluctant to leave.

Daisy broke away from Jack and tucked her arm into George's. 'They'll be back,' she said lightly.

PART III — LILLIANNE

19

Three months later, it was almost closing time in the tearoom when Daisy received the phone call at Inlet Creek. Fortunately, with custom tapering off for the day, she had taken a break and was upstairs in the flat. As her mobile buzzed in her smart tearoom apron pocket, she noted her father's station homestead number.

Daisy's hopes rose. Was George coming to the coast for a visit? With his wife now living apart from him in England and Lilly working in London, while Maddie and Tommy happily sailed north on *Ocean Blue* with Josh, perhaps her father was feeling the loneliness of an empty house and seeking the company of family.

Daisy eagerly answered the call, expecting her father's voice, so she was surprised to hear the housekeeper on the other end of the line.

'Kirra, lovely to speak to you.'

Daisy wondered why the station homestead cook would call. Perhaps she was passing on a message from her father? But, on the rare occasions he made contact, George usually called himself.

'How's everything out there?' she asked warily, suspicion already setting in.

'Miss Daisy, girl, I got bad news.'

Hearing the anguish in her voice, Daisy froze on the spot where she stood in the centre of the flat, closed her eyes and placed a hand over her mouth, preparing herself for some kind of accident.

'Miss Daisy, they sayin' it was his heart.'

No need for Kirra to explain who she meant. Being aboriginal, Daisy knew her community did not name a person who had passed away. Daisy's private fear mounted. Heart, she vaguely registered, her mind numb as Kirra continued talking. Daisy plumped down on the sofa and listened. This can't be happening. Not to a strong man like her father.

'The boss, he didn't come back to the homestead for lunch. I checked with the men in the worker's hut but none of them seen him either. I didn't start worryin' too much. That stubborn old man has always gone off around the property on his own but he always come back. He knew every mile of this place.'

Knew? Daisy picked up on Kirra speaking in the past tense. She could hardly breathe. Premonition pained her chest.

'By mid-afternoon, the big feller's dog, Bandit, he show up at the homestead here. He just sit at that back door barkin' his head off, tryin' to tell us somethin'. The workmen followed that dog back out onto the property right to where your father lyin'.'

Stunned with shock, Daisy just listened, speechless.

'It look like he fall from his horse,' Kirra continued. 'He weren't movin'. Them fellas they done first aid but the boss he already gone, Miss Daisy, before they found him.'

Daisy shook her head, hearing but disbelieving. Gone? George was dead? What kind of sick joke was fate playing that she should lose both her parents within six months of each other?

'Miss Daisy, you tell Miss Maddie and Miss Lilly?'

Daisy finally found her voice. 'Sure. I have Maddie's number. It might not be easy contacting them on the yacht up the far north coast but I'll try. Oh, Kirra, I can't believe this. And I'm so sorry. You've worked for George for a long time.'

'I surely have, Miss Daisy. Since before you was born. This house gonna be big and empty without him.'

Daisy heard the depth of Kirra's grief in her anguished tones and wished she was out there in the big homestead kitchen to give her a hug. They both needed it. And with the tragic news hung the sheep station's unknown future.

Pushing aside her grief for now to focus on reality, Daisy said, 'I'll be in touch again when I've contacted my sisters and let you know when they're expected back home.'

Never her favourite person, she certainly wouldn't be contacting Elizabeth Harwood, now living in England. That unfortunate duty would most likely fall to Lilly.

'You girls get out here to your country,' Kirra urged. 'This place needs you right now.'

Daisy's hands trembled as she set down her mobile and took a moment to try and process her father's death in her mind. George was gone. She clasped her hands together to stem their shaking and thought of sending a quick text to Jack. But no matter how much she desperately needed him at the moment, the urgent phone call to her sister must come first.

She could collapse later.

Even as Daisy pressed Maddie's mobile icon and listened to the dial tone, she wondered how on earth she was going to tell her. Based on her contact a few days ago, they were somewhere near Cooktown, planning to lazily sail out around the northern islands of the Great Barrier Reef. As the call rang out, Daisy crossed her fingers for good reception.

Sometimes prayers were answered, it seemed, because moments later Maddie picked up.

* * *

Maddie Harwood-West smiled to see Daisy's number come up on her phone. Her joy collapsed into shocked disbelief when her sister explained the tragic reason for the call. Her *boys*, as she fondly referred to them, were on deck so she motioned to Josh to take Tommy below while she talked freely to Daisy.

Seeing her distress, Josh hesitated but Maddie simply shook her head, waved him away and clung to the deck railing for support, clutching her lightweight sailing jacket tighter about her, utterly blind to the stunning approach of sunset.

'We're anchored in Cooktown. We should be able to get a charter flight down to Cairns and a domestic back to Sydney. Josh will need to rent a berth in a marina for the yacht somewhere.'

'Do you need me to drive to the airport and pick you all up?'

'No. Josh left his four wheel drive garaged with

a mate in Sydney so we can get back to *Georgina Downs* ourselves.'

'Can you let Kirra know when you'll arrive?' Daisy asked. 'She sounds so upset out there and just wants us all home.'

'Sure. Listen, I'll tell Josh to get our travel arrangements underway then try phoning Lilly in London. It will be early morning over there but she's likely stirring for work. If I can't get hold of her from out here in the middle of the Coral Sea, do you mind giving her a try?'

'No, of course not. I haven't had much to do with her in recent times though.'

'Don't worry.' Maddie eased her sister's concern. 'I've kept Lilly up to speed with everything happening back home. I'll text you her contact details, okay?'

'Thanks. Might be handy.'

'Oh, Daisy, this is all too unbelievable,' she choked up, bewildered, her mind cloudy. 'Oh! I'm so sorry. I'm forgetting, it's not only our father for you, is it? You lost Ailie last year, too.'

Numb from reality sinking in, Daisy preferred not to go there so she changed the subject. 'Yes, well, you lost Aaron. This must all feel like a nightmare for you, too. Hang in there and be strong. I look forward to seeing you both when you get home. If there's anything I can do, call, okay?'

'Of course.'

'One thing though, I would like to be told when you know the details and be allowed to attend George's funeral.'

'Allowed?' Maddie sounded appalled. 'What

do you mean? Why wouldn't you come?'

'Your mother . . . '

Maddie gasped. 'Daisy, you're our sister. He was our father. Of course you'll be there. Don't worry,' her voice tightened, 'we'll sort out mother when we're all home.'

As the sisters hung up, Josh appeared from below. 'I've put Tommy in his pyjamas and left him looking through a picture book in his bunk.'

After Maddie quietly stumbled through her explanation, he wrapped his big arms about her, allowing her to blubber into his chest.

When she recovered enough and let the evening breeze dry her wet cheeks, she whispered, 'I should have said more of a goodbye to him on the pier before we left Inlet Creek. And how on earth will I explain to Tommy that Grampa's gone now just like Daddy?' Before Josh could respond, Maddie continued, 'And what if it's my fault for leaving him all alone out there? I failed him.'

'Honey, you're not doing yourself any favours thinking like that. No one's to blame for George's sudden death. That's just plain old fate stepping in and nothing else.'

'I wonder if all the work and responsibility became too much for him? He was a work horse. He only thrived when he was out and about on the station. *Georgina Downs* was his whole life.'

'No consolation maybe just yet but at least he died out on the property doing what he loved so much.'

Finally, after Maddie had sobbed herself out, feeling empty, she dragged her composure under control enough to make the dreaded phone call to London. Now she knew exactly how Daisy must have felt getting the news from Kirra and having to pass it on.

In her own turn, Lilly would need to tell their mother that her husband was dead. Just like that. How that played out would prove enlightening.

★ ★ ★

Lilly Harwood was dozing in the huge and comfortable king sized bed of their Kensington apartment when her mobile buzzed on the bedside table. She scrambled for it, leaping out and closing the door behind her so as not to wake Oliver. Noting her sister's call, she brightened. Maddie didn't usually call this early though, she frowned.

'Hey Sis. You do know the time over here, right? It's not even six and barely daylight.'

Lilly's delight dissolved once Maddie began speaking and reality hit her with a blast. She gripped the phone, wishing at this very moment that she was in the same room as her sister and not on the other side of the world. Needing her closeness and comfort. She felt adrift lately living so far away from family and home. Not surprised by the truth of her thoughts that, despite living in England for years, *Georgina* Downs and Australia would always be home.

'But he can't be gone,' Lilly said. 'Aaron's just gone. Father can't be gone, too. This is not happening. Oh my God, Maddie, you must feel like shit.'

'More or less. My brain seems to be working but my body is missing. And stop always thinking of others. We've *both* just lost our father.'

'Oh bugger,' Lilly gasped. 'I'll have to tell mother, won't I?'

'It's like falling dominoes, isn't it? Telling first one, then the next . . . '

Lilly released a long slow sigh. 'I'll phone her now. This early, she won't even be awake yet which means she'll be super crabby.'

'Surely not when she learns the reason for your call.'

'God, our father has just died. Cripes, Maddie, it hurts to even think about it let alone say the words out aloud.'

'What about work? You'll need to take off weeks. Can you manage it? Will they mind?'

'If they don't like it, they can sod off and I'll resign.'

'Wow, don't normally hear you talking like that.'

'Yes, well, I'm a bit fed up with lots at the moment.'

'Well when you get home I promise you plenty of wine and talk, okay?'

'That thought alone will keep me going. Mother and I can rent a car from Sydney airport. Don't fancy being stuck with her for over four hours though. She'll be unbearable.'

After the sisters reluctantly hung up, Lilly listened. No sound that Oliver was stirring yet so she gathered fortitude and made the difficult call. She'd never needed to give anyone the sad

296

news of a death. Hard enough that it would be her mother on the loss of her husband. But even more so that the man was her own father as well.

Not surprisingly, it took ages before her mother answered. Even after her initial grumbles and Lilly's apology for the early hour followed by her tactful explanations of the reason, she wasn't sure Elizabeth understood the full impact.

There was a long silence. Where was the reaction, the grief? Even the slightest sign of anguish or tears, though she had never seen Elizabeth cry. 'Mother, did you hear?'

'Of course.'

'Are you all right?' Lilly ventured.

'I'm perfectly fine,' she snapped, then demanded, 'Why wasn't I told first?' The offence in her mother's tone was unmistakeable. Protocol mattered. At a time like this, Lilly couldn't have given a fig.

'Maddie phoned me and Daisy phoned her because — '

'*That girl* was told before me? Why?'

Lilly cringed to hear her oldest sister spoken of so unkindly. And by her mother. The supposed example of good breeding. Sometimes the cultivated manners she expected of others, simply did not shine through in her own behaviour.

'Because Kirra couldn't find any contact details for Maddie and us so she contacted Daisy instead.'

'What a ridiculous excuse. I'm sure we're listed in George's diary and address book. Kirra must have missed it.'

'Well it's done now. Daisy said Kirra was upset and phoned her because she was the closest person and the only one in the family she knew where to find.'

'Honestly, *that girl* continues to force her way into the family as though she's a part of it.'

'Daisy *is* a part of it, Mother.'

'Not as long as I'm in charge.'

Lilly disliked the tone of command in her mother's voice and attitude. Clearly she was wide awake now, thinking ahead and planning.

'She's our sister. I know you disapprove but, whether you like it or not, Daisy's a legitimate daughter from father's first marriage.' Lilly took a deep breath and pushed on. In the light of a comment Maddie made in their previous phone conversation, she even braved a rare dissent against her mother. 'Who will be attending his funeral.'

'She. Will. Not.'

Lilly faltered at her mother's violent words, clenched her free fist even as the other gripped the phone tighter and said, 'It's not your decision. You can't stop her.'

'I'll do my best.'

'Maddie and I want her there.'

'Lillianne Elizabeth, I do not appreciate your disrespectful attitude.'

Definitely confirmed then. When mother used either daughter's full name, she was officially angry.

As always, the whole world could be collapsing around her and Mother would remain stoic and proper. Lilly even wondered rather unkindly whether, in the light of her parents' recent separation and living apart in different countries, she really cared very much for her husband's death. She might play the part in public but, honestly? Lilly doubted she would ever really grieve over his loss from their family and the world.

She hadn't yet even asked the details of how he died. Elizabeth Harwood was only a people person when it was important or necessary for her own purpose. Lilly cringed to think she had once so idolised her Mother. In recent years, witnessing the real woman behind the façade, that admiration had dimmed.

'Well,' Elizabeth heaved a disgruntled sigh, 'I have to pack.'

And I don't? Lilly thought. And book tickets and handle Oliver.

'So you can book the first available flight. Business, of course,' she ordered.

'You'll need to pay the cost for your seat into my account, then,' Lilly said. 'I don't have enough money to cover it. I can only afford economy.'

Lilly heard her mother's huff of exasperation on the other end of the line. 'All right. At least we'll be on the same flight. Text me the details and I'll have my secretary arrange it.'

Her secretary?

'Then phone the homestead back in Australia and let the staff know when we will return. I've only just resettled here. It's an utter nuisance that I need to travel all that way back again. I can assure you it will only be until the formalities are dealt with then I shall be on the first flight home here as soon as possible. I don't need to remind you, Lilly, that these arrangements are urgent. This will all need to be done before you go to work.'

Lilly was appalled to hear the suggestion. 'Heavens, I won't be going into work, Mother. Father just died. There's heaps to do before we leave. I'll call my Sales Manager, Chelsea, to let her know what's happened and that I'm taking compassionate leave. It's usually just a few days for a death in the family but, since I have to go to Australia, I will be making it plain my absence will be longer.'

This was a sign. Her opportunity to leave England. For good. Lilly couldn't bear the thought of returning and having Oliver gleefully pounce and assume control of her life again. It wasn't the first time she had considered this option. After flying back to Australia for a few weeks to be with Maddie after Aaron's death, she hadn't realised the strong pull of her home country that lay dormant inside her.

With the morning's awful news, the same forceful feeling had returned even stronger. The catalyst of her father's death was the break she had been waiting for and her chance to escape. Yet Lilly ached, knowing the huge sacrifice of loss that lent her the courage and allowed her such freedom and life change.

When Lilly finally stopped weeping over a strong black coffee and tiptoed back into their bedroom, her partner, Oliver Remington, was still in bed. He usually expected her to be virtually fully groomed the moment she woke up. This morning, her dark hair, usually neat and framing her face, was tangled and her face red from crying but she simply didn't care.

Even as she watched him with the remnants of her affections swiftly eroding and a respectful amount of fear, her heart pounded while her head raced devising a plan.

'Ollie,' she whispered, 'are you asleep?'

'Hardly,' he muttered, 'with all your crashing about in the apartment and waffling on the phone.'

Lilly paused to calm herself. *Just agree with him*, she thought, *and get this over with*. 'Sorry. I grabbed my mobile the moment it rang so you wouldn't be disturbed.'

He rolled over, gorgeous blonde hair in stylish disarray and sat up. Despite everything and with a pang of nostalgia for more wonderful times past, Lilly still loved his daily choice of traditional pyjamas from one of the many top menswear retailers he favoured.

'So what's all the fuss about, then?' he yawned and stretched, leaning back against the velvet padded headboard of their sumptuous bed. All the furniture was his, of course. When he regularly pointed out the fact, it made Lilly feel like a tenant and not his girlfriend. 'Who was rude enough to wake us both up at this ungodly hour?'

'We'd both be up soon anyway.' Lilly gently sat on the edge of the bed feeling bleak and unsupported. She folded her arms across her chest and said quietly, 'My sister.'

'Horsey Madeleine from Australia?' he scoffed. 'What did she want, then?' He drilled her with a challenging glare.

What was it with everyone's nastiness and inhumanity this morning?

'Our father just died. Suddenly.' She paused and swallowed back a fresh flood of threatening tears, adding simply, 'Heart,' since it was all she could manage for the moment.

'Bloody hell, old girl. So sorry and all that.' He ruffled his hair and pulled a face. 'What a bore. You've just come back. Suppose you'll need to cross the bloody world again for the funeral.'

No kind words. No leaping across the bed to hold her. How she needed that right now.

'Of course.' She paused. 'I might need to be away for some time.'

'Chelsea and Edward won't appreciate that attitude,' he scoffed.

Knowing her employers, Lilly disagreed. 'Australia is hardly just up the road. I'm sure they'll understand. If they object, which I doubt, they can readvertise my position.'

'Steady on, old girl. I got you that job with perks. Top position and salary. Name on the door. Business wheels as needed. Free flights to Europe.'

Having learnt fashion at her mother's knee and under her influence over the years, Lilly loved her work as a senior retail buyer in Oliver's friend's exclusive fashion boutique. With no experience, but on his pushing and recommendation, she had applied for the job change and been given a trial. So she determined over the past two years of hard work to prove herself and

302

impress them on her own account. They now trusted her to source and suggest the ultimate garments for their rich clientele.

'I know, Oliver, but I didn't ask you to.'

He never liked hearing them but truths didn't hurt occasionally. Right now she ached inside, the sadness building and lending her the strength of honesty. And she was leaving. ASAP. So she wouldn't have to endure the usual fallout any time she disagreed with his opinion.

He had only bothered to suggest the more prestigious position anyway because he didn't consider the job in behind-the-counter sales she already had when they met was good enough for his girlfriend.

Lilly saw this trip back home as her salvation to reassess her life from a distance. She had used up all her annual leave returning home for Maddie after Aaron was killed. Although the trip had been for such a tragic reason, she had loved but forgotten how the familiar homestead and countryside still ran so deeply in her blood.

Except this time there was going to be a massive decision to make about the fate of the sheep station. With her mother now widowed and neither daughter interested in running the family property, would she keep it in the family? Engage a manager perhaps? Or the most horrible thought, sell it?

God it was all such a mess.

Larger than life big George Harwood was gone. She would never see her father again. Innocently, she had assumed he would live forever. Tough old bugger. Yet he was always their anchor, the tough grit that, despite his own personal emotional distance, ploughed along the difficult path of keeping their incompatible family together.

Oliver's hostile demanding tone filtered into Lilly's consciousness again, invading her personal thoughts of overwhelming despair and grief and imminent action.

'Rather than risking an important career for the sake of a few hours at a funeral, do you really need to bother, poppet?' Oliver challenged.

Lilly gaped. He was serious.

'I mean,' he casually drawled on, 'he's hardly going to know if you're not there, is he?' He gave a sarcastic chuckle.

Lilly scoffed with exasperation and disgust. 'Don't be crude,' she said with quiet fury. 'You would never entertain the notion of not attending your own father's funeral.'

'Well it's the done thing though, isn't it? One needs to be seen to be doing the right thing. Of course I would be obliged to attend.'

'Obliged! Is that all you think of your father?'

'It's the way of life, isn't it? One generation dies, the next inherits.'

Oliver's arrogance and heartless attitude left Lilly speechless. Despite being an intelligent Gen Z, with or without Oliver's assistance with a *better* job, she still blindly continued, after a two year relationship with her yuppie Englishman, to be appalled by his lack of compassion.

Was she a slow learner or what?

Feeling deserted in every way, and especially emotionally, her composure began to crumble as the substance of what had taken place in the past hour slowly sank in. Her father was dead. Impossible. Unbelievable. George Harwood, tough and hearty countryman, family patriarch and irreplaceable owner of *Georgina Downs* was suddenly snatched away forever.

While Oliver sauntered into the bathroom, Lilly took advantage of his absence and the peace to open up her laptop and start making the travel arrangements her mother demanded.

She could hardly get her head around the reality of this new unwelcome situation in her life let alone think what on earth to pack. Everything, she decided. Just in case. Even if she had to pay for extra baggage weight.

With their last minute flight booked, the homestead advised via an emotional phone call with Kirra, and her mother's secretary informed, Lilly focused on everything to be done before she left.

She made a list.

When he emerged later, Oliver didn't question the two large suitcases Lilly was packing as he left for his managerial position in his father's financial company.

'What time's your flight?'

'Overnighter,' she wrinkled her nose, pretending an echo of his usual boredom.

'Good. I'll be back before you leave.'

Didn't matter when he returned, she wouldn't be here. When she stood dutifully in the hall to see him off to work still wrapped in her silky robe, he lovingly kissed her. She hoped he didn't detect the eagerness for his departure floating above the underlying grief and heartache for her father.

But he said nothing, straightened the already perfect tie, checked himself yet again in the mirror, combed a hand through his thick sandy hair and said, 'See you tonight.'

After Oliver left, Lilly inhaled calming breaths of exhilaration then set about ticking off the items on her list. She felt too distracted to eat but sat still long enough to grab a piece of toast with a mug of tea.

Shivering with nerves that Ollie would somehow have a change of heart along with a radical change of personality and reappear, she showered, dressed and began cramming every possible piece of clothing into her bulging cases, then went out.

Lilly smiled as she shoved her gloved hands deep into her coat pockets and strode briskly along the Kensington High Street with a light jaunty step in the nippy early spring air. It would be autumn back home. At her bank, she paid off her credit card, closed her account and exchanged a wad of cash for Australian dollars.

Because a weak sun came out, she allowed herself the indulgence of lingering in her favourite café one last time.

Back at the apartment, she double checked her baggage and documents, taking one last sweeping glance around as she waited for her black cab out to Heathrow. She hadn't done the dishes and their bed remained unmade. Oliver would be ropable. Good.

She hauled her belongings down in the lift and

waited impatiently on the street. Her mother was being driven down from Suffolk so she had arranged to meet her at the airport. Even as the cab left the kerb and joined the stream of traffic heading west in a sudden burst of spring rain, Lilly wondered if there was anything she had forgotten and if she could have crammed in more.

Somehow, within three hours, once she and her mother were on board although parted for opposite ends of the plane, she settled into her economy seat at the rear, keeping her mind occupied for the endless flight across the world, grateful for every single mile passing beneath her tens of thousands of feet below. Because it meant Lilly Harwood was going home.

Ironic, yet such a gift, that yet another heart-rending death in the Harwood family should prove the gift prompting her return. Karma in her retreat from Oliver's increasing sense of entitlement to control everything in her life.

Despite the tragic reason, Lilly knew in her heart that being back with her family again would bring her nothing but her long lost peace.

★ ★ ★

Further forward on the same plane, Elizabeth Harwood sipped champagne in her indulgent business class seat and sighed, closing her eyes as she reflected.

After the initial shock of Lilly's phone call from London earlier today, she had slumped into her favourite chintz chair in the morning room, uplifted by the realisation that she would inherit *Georgina Downs*. That dreadful sheep station she had always despised.

She had then cast a satisfied glance out over the sweeping lawns surrounding her beautiful leased country house with its tended garden beds, in mid-spring now alive with the nodding golden heads of daffodils and the massed plantings of bluebells across the field among the trees in the adjoining wood.

Idly, she wondered how long it took to sell a sheep station and smiled, contemplating the comfortable lifestyle the proceeds would afford.

20

Lilly chewed her lip as she drove the rental car and swallowed hard upon her first view of *Georgina Downs* homestead from a distance as it gradually grew closer, calling her home.

The midday sun gleamed on the iron roof and filtered among the red and gold-brown leaves of late autumn still remaining on the deciduous trees in the garden, giving it a lush park-like setting, an unlikely oasis in this tough parched country. Her shoulders sagged with weariness after the long drive from Sydney and relief from the tedium of her mother's irritable company.

Lilly almost broke down anew to see Maddie waiting on the front veranda, her sister's equally dark but longer hair whipped about by the brisk southerly breeze.

Maddie was running toward the car before Lilly even had the door open. She stepped out and the sisters flew into each other's arms for a long tight hug.

'Saw your dust,' Maddie whispered into her sister's ear. Lilly felt her damp cheeks against her neck. 'Been waiting since you sent the text from Goulburn. We've only arrived a few hours ago ourselves.'

'He can't be gone,' Lilly gasped out. 'It's not possible.'

'I know. I know,' Maddie whispered in firm reassurance. 'You must be buggered.'

Lilly pulled back and swiped at her own tears. 'I managed to snag us an early afternoon flight out of London yesterday with a Singapore stopover before the second leg. We landed in Sydney early this morning. Lost a day somewhere in it all.' She half turned. 'I've rented the wheels for a week in case we need them. A courier driver will pick it up after that and return it to Goulburn.'

Both daughters became aware that their mother was now standing in silent expectation behind them.

'Mother.' Maddie stepped forward to give her a token embrace.

The girls retrieved the cases from the car and hauled them indoors, following Elizabeth, straight-backed and poised, looking as fresh in uncrushable black as the hour their flight took to the air over London thirty hours before. Lilly always admired and wondered how she did it. She shook her head. It was a gift.

Indoors in the dim hallway, Kirra waited, her dark-skinned face looking desolate. She respect-fully nodded to her mistress first. 'My sympathy, Miss Elizabeth.'

Their mother swiftly assumed the role of entitled heiress, barely acknowledging Kirra's presence. 'I'm utterly drained. I hope my suite is made up. I need a long bath.'

Elizabeth managed to convey the impression that she was the only human being to ever endure a flight halfway around the world. And not just one of many family and friends all having travelled long distances to get here and

310

sharing in their grief.

'Yes, Miss Elizabeth. Whole house been made ready for you all.'

'After I have recovered, I shall make an inspection that everything is in order.'

'Of course, Miss Elizabeth.'

Lingering behind Kirra, Josh and Tommy patiently waited. In silence, Josh and Lilly hugged then she scooped her nephew up into her arms. 'Do you remember me?'

He nodded. 'You're my Aunt Lilly.' His tiny round face turned sad. 'Grampa's not here no more.'

Lilly glanced understandingly at Maddie who nodded. So, he had been told then.

The child looked so unhappy that Lilly quickly went on, 'No he's not. And we'll all miss him, won't we?' She struggled to keep her emotions in check but forced herself to glance around all the family present and say brightly, 'But look at all the family that are here together now, hmm? Mummy, Josh, Grandma and me. And Kirra.'

Tommy grinned fondly at their homestead cook. Perhaps he remembered, as they all did, not only the unforgettable meals she served up in the dining room but those special dishes she made for children. The endless delicious baking for afternoon teas. Elizabeth's breakfast delivered on a tray every morning. All done without complaint. To Elizabeth Harwood, Kirra was a servant. To everyone else, the cheerful natured woman was another member of the family.

Elizabeth pulled a stiff smile and disappeared down the hall toward the south wing and her private suite. She offered no affection to anyone, remaining cool and detached, seeming to be, outwardly at least, unaffected by her husband's death. Or perhaps not allowing herself the luxury of showing emotion.

The younger generations lingered in the hall, hugging and murmuring disbelief and regrets. Josh began delivering the cases to bedroom suites, Tommy trotting alongside, believing he was helping.

Kirra announced lunch in the dining room when they were ready so, after freshening up, everyone ambled into the grand room, feeling lost, the mood sombre, all moving purely on instinct.

Appetites mostly returned at the sight of the wafer thin and tender slices of lamb, implicit on a sheep station, together with boats of rich gravy and platters of vegetables. A still-warm and familiar circle of crusty flour-dusted damper sat on its marble base waiting to be sliced.

Conversation was muted and general, mostly focused on the small insignificant details of the various family members' travels to get back home. Carefully avoiding the lingering matter that lay so heavily on everyone's mind.

Long after they were seated and half finished eating, Elizabeth belatedly stunned them all and appeared to join them. She placed a tiny portion of food on her plate and assumed George's seat at the head of the table which everyone had deliberately left empty out of respect.

Lilly and Maddie shared a disapproving glance across the table as if to say *That's father's chair*.

'That's Grandma.' Tommy's small voice was heard over the scraping of cutlery on plates.

Elizabeth's arrival sank the mood of the room's occupants into a hush of reflection, each person withdrawing into their own thoughts. Only Tommy's occasional comments awkwardly dropped into the silence.

Maddie was the first to make a move and stand. 'Well, I'm going to grab Dad's bottle of cognac from his office and then,' she faltered as tears began streaming down her cheeks, 'how about we all retire to the sitting room for a toast to a grand man and an awesome life fully lived?'

Lilly ached with mutual anguish and her heart went out to her sister but Josh reached out and squeezed her hand, springing up beside her, wrapping a comforting muscled arm about her shoulder, Tommy in his turn flinging his small arms about his mother's legs, confusion on his small innocent face.

'There are decisions I've made that need to be discussed,' Elizabeth quietly added before she rose and swept from the room, glaring at her oldest daughter as she passed as if in disapproval for any show of sentiment.

As they all dawdled down the hallway to the front room, Lilly wondered if they were all equally aware that an indefinable spirit, the essence of this fourth generation family home-stead, was now missing without their father. Despite his widow, children and grandchild being here, with staff reverently bustling about, the building had somehow lost its soul. George's presence had given the station its energy when his boots stamped its hallways and his big voice bellowed between rooms.

Now the house just seemed to be quietly awaiting its fate, as if haunted. For the coming unknown and possibly unwelcome decision on everyone's mind? Except for the grandfather clock in its special hallway alcove, its pendulum ticking in loud and solid rhythm as if in deliberate defiance. Grandfather Mac Harwood's hearty influence perhaps?

Once the family were settled in the sitting room and Tommy was settled down for his afternoon nap, Kirra brought in Elizabeth's requested tea tray. Their mother poured and politely sipped. Lilly on the other hand, in united company with Maddie and Josh, indulged in George's special French cognac, clinking glasses in a subdued toast, letting the fiery auburn liquid burn a trail of remembrance as it slid down.

Elizabeth took the lead, looking toward her oldest daughter. 'I imagine the property is still running somehow without George?'

'Yes,' Maddie replied. 'I've phoned Dusty, our station manager out at the workmen's hut and he's on top of things outside for now. I've briefly gone through Dad's bookwork in his office. It all seems up to date as usual.'

'I know nothing about the management of it all, Madeleine. Your father taught you so I leave you to handle all that,' she dismissed her involvement and interest. 'Later this afternoon the funeral director is coming out to make . . . arrangements,' she continued, suddenly changing topic to discuss what confronted them all. 'I imagine we all wish to get on with our lives so I shall organize it as soon as possible.'

Lilly closed her eyes and released a sigh of irritation over her mother's cringe-worthy heartless comment. When she opened them again, she stared directly across at her mother. 'I haven't booked a return flight as you know, mother, so I shall be staying as long as I need. Maddie?'

Her sister cast a consulting glance to Josh and he nodded. 'Us, too.'

'Well it should hardly come as a surprise to either of you but England is my home now. I was born there. I've wintered in Suffolk for years to avoid the nasty hot summers here and the isolation of living on the edge of the outback. You would hardly expect me to stay.'

'I have invited Daisy and Jack to stay,' Maddie intervened. 'They will be here for two nights. Before you say anything mother,' she stalled her open mouth and dark glare, 'they need to because father's lawyer in Goulburn phoned yesterday. He asked that, under the terms of father's will, we three daughters and you, mother, should be in attendance here in the homestead the day after the funeral for a legal meeting.'

Elizabeth's response. 'Why didn't you tell me when I arrived?'

'I just did.'

Clearly unimpressed, her mother said, 'I do not see why *that other girl* needs to stay in this house at all. Why can't she stay in Goulburn and drive out here as needs must? And why on earth is she entitled to be party to any private family legal discussions?'

Lilly saw Maddie stiffen. 'She's our father's daughter and we want her here with us.' They

315

glanced at each other in united confirmation.

'Half-sister,' Elizabeth corrected. 'Well I find her presence upsetting. Keep her away from me.'

Lilly didn't see that as a problem. Considering the strained family dynamics between some of its members, she imagined it would be the other way around. Daisy would willingly and gratefully avoid her father's second wife.

'One other thing, mother,' Maddie said. 'The lawyer asked if you could phone him before you make any funeral arrangements.'

'Why?'

Maddie shrugged. 'Have no idea but it sounded important.'

Shortly after, Elizabeth excused herself from the uncomfortable family gathering and was overheard by most within earshot on the homestead phone in the hall speaking, as instructed, to their father's lawyer. Within moments, her voice rose to shrill, the handset was slammed down and her footsteps faded into the distance.

No one thought anything of it when she did not reappear until Lilly and Maddie innocently waited in the sitting room for the funeral director's visit. Their mother strode in stiff-backed and unsmiling, seated herself opposite, knees and feet formally together, hands clenched in her lap, obviously claimed by a seething fury.

The sisters glanced meaningfully at each other, wondering what on earth had caused it, but the remembered disruptive telephone call from earlier came to mind. Whatever discussion had taken place with the lawyer was clearly not well received.

'Are you all right, Mother?' Lilly ventured innocently.

'I shall never forgive him,' she snapped. 'One. Final. Insult.'

'What is it?' Maddie dared to ask.

Their mother glared at them as though they were the enemy. 'Your father,' she spat out with venom, 'has left strict instructions that he wishes a private family burial. With Ailie Sheldon. Which I most certainly shall not attend.' With her daughters stunned into silence at the news, she continued, 'I am, however, permitted,' she sneered, 'to arrange a memorial service in our local country church.'

Lilly felt Maddie stiffen beside her and grasp her hand, both aware of the humming tension in the room. On the one hand, she felt empathy for their mother suffering this totally unexpected decision from their father. On the other hand, it was his right. Even though their mother may have tried to keep it secret, there wasn't a single person in the family and possibly in the wider surrounding district community who did not know that the Harwoods of *Georgina Downs* had separated.

Obviously George's feelings for his first wife, Ailie, reached beyond death so that he chose to shun the family cemetery plot on *Georgina Downs* to be buried elsewhere with her instead.

Bugger, Lilly thought. What a situation. The fallout would last forever. But right now, what did a daughter say to her mother in this situation? Since she had no idea, she decided to keep her mouth shut. Maddie beside her, equally silent and unsure, chose to do the same.

'When the funeral director arrives,' Elizabeth addressed her daughters, 'I will inform him of my instructions for the public memorial service. After that I shall leave this room and you girls can make whatever arrangements you wish for your father's burial. I want nothing to do with it.'

The remainder of the afternoon was a nightmare. Once the official service was scheduled for two days hence and their mother swiftly left, Lilly and Maddie consulted each other in murmurs.

'We need to get onto Daisy. Since father wants to be buried in Ailie's grave, she needs to be a part of the decision and give her permission. After all, it's her mother, not ours.'

They excused themselves from the undertaker and bolted to their father's office to phone their sister.

After the initial shock, Daisy gasped, 'Oh my God, your mother — '

'Is livid. Don't even ask,' Maddie said. 'The memorial is in the afternoon the day after tomorrow so you'll need to be out here tomorrow night for father's burial the following morning so we can arrange it prior. It's short notice but mother wants the funeral over as soon as possible so she can return to England. With you both managing businesses, is that doable for you and Jack?'

'Absolutely. Marj has offered to hold the fort here in the tearoom. Trade in the cooler months now is quieter. She assures me she and Bill can cope.' After a moment of hesitation, Daisy added, 'We don't wish to cause any more upset in the family so Jack and I are prepared to make a day trip of it.'

'Oh Lord no, we want you here longer than that,' Maddie objected. 'Besides, you need to be here.' She explained the legal reason. 'And we're going to need wine and girl time.'

Daisy sighed. 'Okay. One other thing. On instinct, I drove out to see old Harry. George always made a point of walking over to his hut on the adjoining property on those rare times he ever came to the beach shack or visited Inlet Creek.'

'Good thinking, Daisy,' Lilly said.

'Harry took it hard, actually. Understandable because they seemed to be great old mates for years.'

'We never did ask how they knew each other,' Maddie said.

'I told him I would let him know when I heard about the funeral. I hope you don't mind but he sounded keen to attend. Since Jack and I are coming out anyway, we offered to bring him with us. He seemed really grateful for the offer and mumbled that he would like to say goodbye.'

'Of course that will be fine. Generous of you to offer to give him a lift.'

'Good, but now you've told me I need to stay overnight, where can Harry stay out there?'

'Oh he can bunk down out in the men's quarters,' Maddie assured her. 'Now, I have a suggestion. I know father has been naughty throwing us all into upheaval but mother will no doubt be wearing black. How about we sisters defy tradition and stand out with a splash of

319

colour? Nothing too wicked. Just make a statement. Of course it will be a sad day but we all have each other for support. Dad was too full of life. He would never expect us to be drab at his send off.'

'Love it,' Daisy said. 'If Lilly agrees, too,'

'Absolutely.' Maddie glanced at her sister. 'She's nodding her head.'

'Sorted then. See you late tomorrow.'

'Oh, Daisy, it's going to be awesome having you here and we three sisters all together,' Maddie said.

Yet even as she heard her sister's words, in the back of Lilly's mind was the problem of how they intended to get their sibling through the front homestead door, past their mother and out of sight. Elizabeth would explode if she caught so much as a glimpse of their father's oldest daughter.

21

Next morning during breakfast in the dining room, Lilly heard Josh ask Maddie, 'Okay if I take Tommy out around the station?'

'Of course. Great idea.'

So man and boy headed out in a vehicle with one of the workmen onto the property to spend time away from the household upheaval.

Lilly admired the way Josh took her sister's son under his wing, spending time with him, distracting him, sharing the load of Maddie's bereavement and Tommy's confusion.

Elizabeth played lady of the manor, making it clear she preferred to receive all district visitors and personally take phone calls. Flowers began arriving and she took pleasure in fussing over where they should be displayed to advantage about the hall tables, the finest reserved for the sitting room. Her false outward poise no doubt concealing a deep wounded anguish while she informed callers about the memorial service, avoiding any mention of her husband's burial; discreetly telling people it would be a private family affair.

As Lilly moved about the homestead watching, she wondered where her mother's grief sat in all this. If she chose to stifle it, channel her efforts elsewhere. Whether sorrow would hit her later. Even if she felt any sadness at all. An uncharitable thought, Lilly knew, but it surfaced all the same, seeing her mother's focus on public image and pretension. At least outwardly so, seemingly devoid of emotion. Perhaps personal rage at her husband's burial preference was keeping her feelings hidden.

With strain in the homestead, Lilly and Maddie decided their most tactful position was to retreat into their father's office, both also needing reassurance from a tangible sense of his existence. Lilly by running her hands along the rows of books on shelves and family photographs along the fireplace mantelpiece while Maddie worked on the station computer and rummaged in drawers and filing cabinets.

'Damn,' Maddie rattled one huge wooden drawer in the bottom of her father's desk. 'Can't open this one. Must be a key somewhere. I'll try and find it later.'

Knowing their intentions, Kirra had lit a fire for them which now crackled its warmth out into the room against the morning chill.

'I never knew Dad had all this stuff.' Maddie dumped files and photo albums onto his desk, surprised and excited. 'Looks like he's kept everything about our family.' She paused. 'Except of Daisy and Ailie.'

'That sounds odd. Father loved them as much as us.' Lilly edged over beside her sister, both drawing immense comfort from each other, aware of the distance their mother's resentful behaviour created. The sisters finding peace in alliance.

'Ailie's gone now so I don't know why mother has such an ongoing issue with Daisy,' Maddie

322

said. 'If she knew her lovely generous personality, she would understand that our big sister is absolutely no threat. Everything she says about her is just ignorant hot air.'

'Actually,' Lilly reflected, 'I find mother's unkind words against Daisy personally hurtful. She has no regard for our feelings.'

'Not nice to be having such thoughts about our mother, is it?' Maddie murmured.

When Kirra brought in a morning tea tray, Lilly poured them each a cup while Maddie grabbed a warm freshly baked ginger biscuit.

Cook bustled over. 'You daughters been yarnin' all morning. What you found?' Then shook her head with nostalgia at the spread of decades of photographs, some old black and whites, some sepia. Kirra tapped one with a chubby brown finger. 'That big feller Mac, boss's father.'

'Our grandfather? You knew him?' Lilly asked.

'I left my mob when I was about eighteen I reckon. Just before Mr. Mac died and before the boss married Miss Ailie.' Kirra shook her head sadly. 'You sisters know it but the boss he was a one girl feller. He tried again with Miss Elizabeth but he wasn't never happy.'

'Father wants to be buried with Ailie,' Lilly said softly.

'That sound about right,' Kirra murmured, gave each sister a hug then thoughtfully slipped from the office, leaving the girls alone.

Still unsure how to take her father's burial decision, Lilly had been thinking overnight and more or less come to a conclusion. Understand-able that her mother should be so shocked and offended but, since her parents had separated, did it really matter?

Lilly wasn't sure how that left herself and Maddie, caught in the middle. Right now, amidst a quietly burning sorrow and the cavernous hole of her father's loss, she couldn't process the wider implications of her parents' troubles and indulge in resentment or even anger. As far as she could see, it served no purpose. Her father was gone. For the moment, that was all she could cope with emotionally. Maybe in time a broader more informed perspective for it all would come to light in her mind.

Lilly sighed. Daisy, Jack and Harry were due late tomorrow in time for the private and public formalities for the family to begin. It promised to be so hard saying goodbye to a man she believed would live forever.

And even more of a challenge keeping Daisy and her mother apart. No problem at the burial, for Elizabeth wouldn't be attending, but around the homestead?

For the first time in her life, Lilly identified a conflict of loyalty. She respected her mother for stoically enduring her father's infidelity while married. Elizabeth could have chosen divorce and challenged her right to half a prosperous sheep station. But community appearances and public opinion defeated the public shame and embarrassment of failure.

Yet Daisy was also wrapped up in Lilly's own childhood memories of pleasing memorable visits to the Sheldon farm. Maddie had always scampered off outdoors with their big half-sister while Lilly was more feminine and sedate, content to remain indoors.

Sometimes her father and Daisy's mother disappeared for a while, out walking, so Aunt Mae took her out into the garden picking flowers, full of interesting facts about plants and gardening, a gentle mother figure so approachable and unlike her own. Or Lilly happily watched Granny Sheldon working in the tiny cottage kitchen preparing delicious meals, her tanned wiry little arms easily mixing the batter for a special cake she always baked just for the other sisters' visit. Kirra used to let her do the same in the homestead kitchen when Mother shooed her away and Maddie was out riding with their father somewhere on the station.

Lilly remembered being in awe of her very different wild older sister who did not live with them in the homestead, discovering the true reason as she grew older. Was even a little envious of Maddie's closer friendship with Daisy but was always excitedly drawn into those rare times when the two oldest sisters played dress ups and rummaged in an old chest that apparently belonged to Daisy's granny, beckoning Lilly to join them.

That evening, still filled with conflict and nostalgia, Lilly joined the others in the sitting room. Their mother, as always, had retired to her suite. Maddie and Josh snuggled together with Tommy scrambling between them, open photograph albums on their laps. Lilly sat opposite, glass of wine in hand, watching the strong bond and interplay between them, wishing she had a partner or special person who respected and cared for her, too.

She didn't need the benefit of being half a world away to realise Oliver would never be that man.

★   ★   ★

Late the following day, Daisy and Jack arrived at the homestead rattling noisily up to the homestead in their Kombi van with old friend and passenger, Harry, on board. As they pulled up, the lowering autumn sun stretching long shadows across the homestead lawns.

As Maddie hugged their big sister first, Daisy said, 'This is just awful meeting together again in such circumstances.'

'Well, we're all here now and that's what matters.'

Then Daisy turned to Lilly, giving her an equally warm hug and her full attention. 'Your flight from England would have been a bummer. You must have felt so alone and miserable.'

Lilly nodded, touched that this girl she had always admired from a distance, should prove to be so worthy of her adoration and respect. The ideal role model as the eldest sibling, their father's daughter, too. In the family fold again where she belonged, no matter what their mother said or thought.

As the girls reunited, they heard Jack ask Harry, 'Have you ever been out here before?' The old man shook his head. 'It's a lovely place, isn't it?'

'For sure,' Harry agreed, quietly observant, casting his gaze over the large rambling house and surrounding leafy garden sanctuary.

Their father's old mate was not his usual scruffy self as they had usually seen him around the hut on his bush block at Inlet Creek behind the Harwood beach shack. The shabby beard was tamed and trimmed. Today, for the first time ever that Lilly could recall, he was smartly turned out in jeans and a checked shirt.

Perhaps because of this change, something about his presence drew her attention longer than normal. Then she was given no more time to dwell on her wayward thoughts as one of the station hands drove up to the homestead in a battered ute.

Maddie said, 'See you tomorrow, Harry,' before they all waved as he gathered up his overnight bag and was driven away to the workmen's quarters.

Daisy and Jack brought crates of food from Jack's boulangerie, all manner of luscious creamy pastries, and Daisy's own extra baking of beautiful cupcakes and biscuits from the tearoom, which they had done especially for tomorrow's afternoon tea following the funeral.

'I've already organised caterers,' Elizabeth snapped ungraciously with displeasure when told of their generosity later.

Lilly noted that her mother had allocated Daisy and Jack to the rarely used spare bedroom at the rear of the house in the oldest wing with a view over the courtyard and paddocks beyond. Sending a subtle message to the family, perhaps.

But Lilly smiled to herself at the pointless action because such pitiful spite simply didn't matter. She and her sisters shared a growing bond stronger than any attempts her mother might make to break it.

On the sisters' first night together now that everyone in the family had arrived home for the funeral the following day, Josh offered to put Tommy to bed, and Jack found his way into Kirra's kitchen, talking food.

Elizabeth, utterly remote since George's death and especially since his burial wish revelation, had once again sought the sanctuary of her own rooms.

So the sisters grabbed a bottle of white from the kitchen and gathered together in Maddie's suite, sprawled over the bed or nestled in comfy bedroom chairs.

With glasses filled and safely in hand, Daisy asked, 'How is your mother?'

'Don't ask,' Maddie scoffed. 'I'd rather not lie.'

Daisy frowned. 'No, really. Is she all right?'

'I know Dad wronged her and was unfaithful and, even in death, has pretty much twisted the knife wanting to be buried with Ailie, but, honestly? Mother hasn't shed a tear, yet. At least not in public. I doubt privacy would make much difference,' Maddie said bluntly.

'I gather their marriage wasn't perfect but they must have been happy for a while.' Daisy looked between her step-sisters. 'They had you two.'

'After Aaron died and we talked about marriage and families, Father did confide to me that he believed he loved mother. Once.' Maddie glanced at her little sister, adding, 'He admitted that when Lilly and I came along we were a disappointment to him.' Lilly gasped. 'Only at first,' Maddie hurriedly went on. 'Apparently mother wouldn't allow him near us. We were raised by nannies and Father was out working on the station all day so there was little chance. But as we grew older, he became more involved.'

'Well, that's an awful thing for a father to say,' Lilly said.

'I know,' Maddie agreed quietly, 'but, in a way, it was reasonable. We weren't sons and this sheep station is mostly man-country. Besides, it sounds like mother used huge influence to intentionally keep us apart from him.'

'Punishment because of Ailie.' Lilly reflected for a while. 'Makes you realise how little we really sit down and talk to our parents while they're alive, doesn't it? Mother completely unapproachable and Father always out on the station checking or supervising something.'

'If it's any consolation,' Daisy chipped in, 'it was the same for me. Ailie was a nomadic spirit. I presume I inherited my travel bug from her. She was often away working when I was growing up. She was a fabulous country cook. Catered for big shearing concerns in the outback, huge country functions. My Aunt Mae and Granny raised me, really. I grew accustomed to Ailie being away but it was always a wonderful special reunion when she returned.

'The first night she came back I was allowed to sleep in the big soft bed with her. That closeness and reassurance let me know I was unconditionally loved. It was all I ever needed, really. I never had a single doubt about that.'

'Well we were all raised in the country and that has to be better than the mad cities. No matter what our family situation, we survived,' Maddie said. 'I guess most children do. Tommy has been exposed to loss twice this year, too. He seems to be handling it okay for now but, for each of us, it will take time and be a different journey.'

A mood of contemplation settled over the room as the girls sipped wine and stared into the orange coals glowing in the open fireplace.

'Do you remember any of this homestead from your childhood?' Lilly eventually asked Daisy.

'I've not been back since we left when I was a toddler, I don't think. At least not that Ailie ever mentioned. Mostly it all seems totally strange yet, somehow, just walking through today, small fleeting memories slip into my mind and something seems familiar. Only vaguely though, you know?'

'It may not be home for any of us much longer.' Maddie pushed out a deep sigh, expressing Lilly's fears, too. 'Mother hates this place. She'll sell it.'

'Fact is though, how can she keep it?' Lilly put in sensibly. 'Other than this place being our home, none of us is invested enough to take it on. Except you, Maddie, and you have other priorities in your personal life now that will take you away from here, too. Once Father's will is read, Mother will list *Georgina Downs* on the market and return to England.'

'George would have known that,' Daisy said, 'so whatever choice he's made for the property, he did it with that understanding in mind.'

★ ★ ★

The service for George Harwood's burial took place on a damp autumn day, scattering soft life-giving rains over district sheep pastures.

Apart from immediate family, Harry and Kirra were the only outsiders to attend the burial. They left the homestead mostly crammed into Jack's Kombi van with Josh, Maddie and Tommy leading the way and driving in Grampa's ute to honour their father and grandfather.

As decided, the girls lent a splash of colour around the graveside.

Daisy in a multi-coloured mid-length skirt, denim jacket and vibrant draping scarf. Lilly noticed her composure weaken to be standing by her mother's grave of only six months before but Jack was immediately at her side, hugging her against him in comfort.

As she stepped from the ute in jeans, boots and a red woollen cowl necked jumper, Maddie tilted her umbrella aside, allowing the soft misty rain to dampen her face. God's gift to the earth, her father always called it.

Lilly joined her sisters, softly smart in a dusky pink coat with a beige and pink floral scarf over trousers. They linked arms beneath shared umbrellas and stood reverently together to farewell their father.

For Lilly, the ceremony was ghastly and the worst experience she had ever been through. She broke down halfway and never recovered. Her deep sense of crushing loss pushed through this quiet observance where, unlike the company of her sisters at the homestead in recent days, no other distractions intruded in this private moment, allowing her grief to surface. Her shoulders shook as she sobbed.

Standing beside her, Daisy edged away from Jack to link arms and rub Lilly's cold hand. The compassion when her oldest sister must be equally suffering only raised her regard for the alienated one of her father's daughters.

Lilly turned away from the gaping grave as soon as possible. Enough. She preferred to remember her father as a big capable man, perhaps only secondary in her life due to the influence of her mother, but as the powerful human being and irreplaceable anchor in their family.

Why must everything change?

As she slowly moved away and accepted the minister's sympathies, impatient to escape, she felt her mobile's vibration in her coat pocket. Blast. She had forgotten to silence her phone. Probably another text from bloody Oliver. The untimely interruption turned her sorrow into irritation.

She grappled for it in her pocket and turned it off. On today of all days, she could have expected words of empathy at least. But, no, instead he was no doubt continuing to harass her about how soon she expected to return.

Little did he know.

The only reason she had kept her old phone was to monitor Oliver's contact, so far only brief annoying texts claiming to miss her and call him.

Standing miserable and cold beneath her umbrella, Lilly waited by the Kombi van while the others said their private goodbyes then all walked pensively back to their vehicles.

Without words, Maddie hugged her tight. 'You okay?' she whispered.

'No,' she rasped out. 'We've just buried our father!' Then scrambled into the van, just wanting to be left alone.

Josh, Maddie and little Tommy, who appeared stunned and silent throughout the whole service, piled back into George's ute. The rest of them joined Lilly already in the Kombi, old Harry choosing as before to sit apart at the back.

'Although it caused difficulty and upset your mother, somehow it seems right that George and Ailie are here together,' Daisy said to Lilly as Jack drove them all back to the homestead.

On edge and obstinate from a combination of penetrating grief and Oliver's pestering, she immediately took offence on her father's behalf. 'That's a selfish thing to say. I disagree,' Lilly said loudly from behind. 'I understand his decision but I think he belongs on *Georgina*.'

Daisy turned around in concern and said tactfully, 'Lilly, I'm so sorry. I didn't mean to offend you. But, sweetie, what if the property is sold? It won't even be Harwood land anymore. The family cemetery will mean nothing to whoever comes after us all,' she pointed out.

'I know but it still seems . . . wrong. And we

have to go through all this again after lunch,' she muttered. 'In public.'

'Oh, Lilly — '

She crumbled again, tears rolling down her cheeks. Life as she knew it was dissolving. Yes, she had two amazing sisters but the day's soggy mood left her feeling bleak and unsettled. *Georgina* would never be a part of her world ever again. Life would move on for them all. As though all her father's hard work had been for nothing except to get a good sale price so their mother could live in luxury back home in England.

Hard enough trying to comprehend never seeing her father again but the enormity of *Georgina Downs'* fate was also profound. The reality came crashing into her emotions leaving her stunned.

Then, halfway home, she sensed Harry move from his seat at the rear to come and sit beside her. He took his big rough hand in her soft one and gave it a squeeze. Somehow that small gesture from a man who had only ever been casually in her life lent her comfort. Lilly inhaled deeply and grew calmer.

She thought to ask him how he knew her father but didn't have the strength for conversation. She must remember to ask him later.

★   ★   ★

Before a light lunch, everyone gathered their composure, hung up damp coats to dry then forced themselves to eat. Daisy and Jack joined them in the dining room since Elizabeth predictably remained in her suite. Lilly had recovered and Tommy seemed brighter, the little blessing among them all.

For the next stage of proceedings, all the family, including Elizabeth, plus all the station hands and everyone else in the district it seemed, judging by the rows and rows of cars, drove to fill the small community church. Since the light misty rain persisted, a marquee and additional chairs were hastily set up outside to cater for the spill over.

A worthy crowd to farewell a prominent and long-time district identity,

Georgina Downs stopped for the day, still and silent. Every employee, outdoor workman and member of the homestead staff, was in attendance. A marked tribute to their boss.

Lilly knew Daisy and Jack had driven well behind the line of Harwood vehicles and she saw them creep into the far end seats of their pew across the aisle, still correctly at the front near family but hidden from Elizabeth's line of vision.

Her mother sat stiffly in immaculate tailored black, a cocktail pillbox hat embellished with satin and a small veil perched elegantly on her head. With her pale complexion and no lipstick, her widowed image was stunning and classic.

Sitting on one side of her mother with Maddie, Josh and Tommy on the other, Lilly as always felt overshadowed and insignificant.

Speeches, accolades and humour signified George MacKenzie Harwood's memorial service of thanksgiving for a life fully lived. Trying to ignore her mother's air of superiority, Lilly felt inspired and positive throughout, pushing down any grief that threatened to surface.

Then it was over and all mourners trod the increasingly muddy ground, returning to their vehicles to head for drinks and a magnificent afternoon tea beautifully laid out on tables under the deep homestead verandas.

An unsmiling Elizabeth responded to everyone with lethargy and platitudes about missing *her dearest George* and that she couldn't possibly stay on *Georgina* because it would raise too many memories every day.

Lilly clenched her fists and wanted to cry out *Liar!* and begging this endless day to be over.

22

After the long funeral day was finally over and the last vehicle had driven away, Lilly felt a sense of deflation settle over everyone in the homestead. The resilient mood that had been holding them together simply vanished, leaving them all feeling only a hollow emptiness and lack of purpose.

Since being home again, both she and Maddie had made approaches to their mother to join them or chat and been politely rejected. Lilly wondered why Elizabeth sought her own company. Surely being alone at such a time must be worse than surrounded by family?

She was shocked to feel an urge to shake her mother and beg her to talk. What was she thinking, feeling? Could her daughters help in any way? The woman had just lost her husband. How had that affected her, even though their marriage was virtually over? Surely her father had accounted for some feelings in her mother's life, caused some sentiment on his death?

But Elizabeth had never been inclusive so her daughters expected her absence and were not surprised that their mother was missing again that night. Feeling disloyal, Lilly could only think that at least it made it easier for Daisy and Jack to be among them.

They all gathered as usual in the big comfortable sitting room, a vigorous fire ablaze warding off the late autumn chill and sending out its cosy warmth. Tommy was allowed to stay up late with the adults, everyone replete not only from the afternoon tea leftovers of hot savouries and finger food, but also the steaming tureen of pumpkin soup and fresh damper that Kirra produced.

Although she preferred beer, Maddie helped knowledgeable Jack raid the homestead wine cellar, raising glasses from George's collection of rich reds and pale golden white wines to a husband, father, grandfather and instinctive countryman.

Thoughts and talk edged around to the future and Maddie was the first to voice them.

'Daisy, with all that's been going on in recent days, we've hardly had a chance to talk. What's happening in your life now?'

'I've had an update from Charlie and Clare in France. They're still together and apparently very happily so.' Lilly noticed she glanced fondly toward her partner. 'Actually, Jack and I thought that perhaps over the coming European summer, we might take a few weeks and travel to see his village and family in France.

'And while we're away, a local builder is going ahead with extensions for my apartment above the tearoom. Jack might just rent out his apartment above the boulangerie and he's contacted a fellow baker who will run the business with potential to go into partnership and even expand later on.'

To Lilly, it sounded like her admired big sister had her future sorted and suppressed a degree of envy. Admittedly in the past, she had been influenced by her mother's advice with unsuccessful romantic choices. But that situation was about to change so maybe she would know better luck with a potential future partner of her own choosing.

'What about you, Maddie?' Daisy asked. 'Will you and Josh be returning to the yacht?'

'No.' She glanced at Josh and he sought to link their hands. 'As wonderful as our travels have been, our focus will be on settling for Tommy's sake. He starts school next year. So,' she brightened, 'once Josh completes his coastal rescue training, we'll be looking for an acreage property in the hinterland. With room for Rambler and Tommy's pony but close enough to the coast for Josh's work.'

Maddie turned to her sister. 'Lilly, what are your plans? Are you staying on?'

'Yes.'

'You don't need to get back?'

'No.'

'What about Oliver? You've been popular with him since you're home.' Maddie teased.

'It's only a casual relationship really,' she mumbled.

'Oh yeah, we've all heard that one before. He's been persistent.'

With ironic timing, the subject of their conversation made contact yet again when Lilly's mobile pinged with another text from him. Often she just ignored them or set her phone to silent. This time she quickly glanced at it, frustrated to read more insistence and pressure.

As the others chatted and pretended not to, Lilly felt their gazes upon her, watching. When she looked up, Maddie had that determined look on her face that said she expected more information and to know exactly what was happening in her little sister's life.

Lilly shrugged. 'Same old same old. He wants me to return ASAP.'

Maddie frowned. 'He knows we only just had the funeral, right?' she pointed out.

'He just wants me back,' she said, knowing she sounded weak.

'Well, I know this guy is your partner, Lilly, but I have to say his attitude sounds unreasonable to me,' Maddie muttered.

In the telling silence that followed, Daisy quietly entered the conversation. 'Is everything all right, Lilly?'

Dear observant Daisy. Where Maddie reacted with a blunt honesty that Lilly knew and appreciated, she noticed that their older sibling tended to just sit back, watch and listen. Had an endearing sense of vulnerability at times yet also produced a wiry strength underneath when needed.

Lilly didn't want to burden her family with her distressing personal problems, on today of all days when they had just buried their father. Daisy's appeal was so tempting but was it the right moment to share? Especially with Jack and Josh listening in. She felt as if she stood on shaky ground with the opportunity to finally reveal her situation. And no doubt gain some honest opinions in return.

She took a deep breath and admitted, 'Not really.'

First hurdle over. She glanced across at her sisters, both their expressions showing surprise and interest to know more. So Lilly obliged.

'Ollie and I were introduced at Upfield Hall when mother and I stayed there with family when we first arrived in England a few years ago. Uncle Randolph, mother's brother,' she quickly explained for Daisy's benefit, 'as tradition has it over there, being the oldest son, inherited the estate. Oliver was a mate to our Upfield cousin, Simon.

'Apparently I passed muster,' she said wryly, 'because Ollie asked me out. As a member of the broader Upfield family, I was considered part of their elite inner social circle and therefore *acceptable*.'

'So?' Maddie pressed.

'We dated and I became part of the Upfield and Remington social circle of young friends.' She paused. 'All went well for a while then Ollie started becoming possessive, demanding I guess, and preferring I did things his way.'

'I can imagine that didn't go down well,' Maddie said.

'No.' Although Lilly agreed she couldn't admit that she was so smitten with Oliver, in the beginning she had considered him like a mentor and tried to please him. 'But over time I grew frustrated that Ollie used his rich background and credentials to control me. Always thinking he knew best. How I should dress, where we went and what we did. He even organised what

341

he considered to be a more appropriate job because he didn't think the one I had was good enough.'

'So, where are your feelings in all this? Honestly,' Maddie insisted.

'That's the point. I don't feel anything anymore. Just smothered. In my mind we're over and Ollie is beginning to realise it but while I'm still compliant, he won't let go. I doubt he'd bother to jump on a plane and come down here to drag me back though.'

'Would you go?'

'No!'

'Then we're all here for you. You're obviously unhappy with the situation,' Daisy said.

'Yes.' The open admission was such a relief. 'I've decided I'm not returning to England but after being together for two years, it doesn't seem right to break up over the phone.'

'Well, considering what he's like, that wouldn't bother me. Just do it, Lilly. End it.' From Maddie.

'Don't nag. I know in my heart what I have to do but I've been putting it off. I know him. You can't possibly imagine how he will react. If you challenge a Remington, you take on the whole of his snobby clique. They stand together. It's prestigious to be part of the inner circle. I'll be blamed and badmouthed all over London.'

'If you're not going back, do you care? Does it matter?'

Maddie was so right. 'No, of course not, but they all protect each other and their grubby little secrets. I've heard whispers and been appalled what they think they can all get away with just because they're rich and can pay lawyers and buy off people. When you're on the inside, you don't step aside or leave unless you're pushed or banned.'

There was more but Lilly didn't have the courage — yet — to tell her sisters exactly what a sleaze Oliver actually was. When they were alone. In the light of what she had just learnt, she was still reeling with embarrassment to think that she ever had anything to do with him, let alone trust him and become his partner, allowing him to rule her life. She felt so weak and pathetic.

'I'll phone him. Soon,' she promised without conviction.

With an unconvinced expression on her face, Maddie went on, 'Well, I could spend a few more days here, but frankly I think we all need our space at the moment.' They all guessed she was referring to Elizabeth. 'I'll have a bit more of a rummage through Dad's office, make sure there's nothing I've missed, especially before the lawyer's visit tomorrow. But then I'm going down to the coast for a while. Even though the weather's closing in, Tommy loves the beach.' She shot a grin toward their big step-sister. 'And we'll be near Daisy and Jack. Lilly, do you want to stay on here with Mother until she leaves or come to Inlet Creek with us?'

'Mother expects I'll be returning to England with her but that's not happening. I'd rather be with you. It's been years since I stayed in the shack.'

The next morning, as arranged, the Harwood

lawyer, Webster Phillips, arrived punctually from Goulburn out to the homestead to read George's will.

An older man of average height dressed smartly in a dark grey pinstriped suit, his salt and pepper hair neatly styled, was so well-presented and looked like the kind of capable experienced professional man you could trust, Lilly and everyone else in the room could understand why he had been chosen to handle the vast estate's legal business.

Assembled necessarily in the sitting room because they had all been summoned, after the polite monotony of formalities and reassurance that George MacKenzie Harwood was of sound mind when he made his will, Mr. Phillips launched into the contents and beneficiaries.

Expectant widow, Elizabeth, straightened and almost leapt from her comfortable seat in a single sofa chair when it was announced that the massive property of *Georgina Downs* had been left equally, one quarter each, to George's wife, Elizabeth Harwood nee Upfield, and his three daughters, Harmony Sheldon known as Daisy, Madeleine Elizabeth Harwood-West and Lillianne Frances Harwood.

While it was a stunning surprise decision resulting in quiet gasps and expressions of amazement between them all, Lilly's only thought was that her father couldn't have been fairer to everyone but that her mother wouldn't like it. One quick side glimpse in her direction to see Elizabeth's thunderous face was proof enough. She was too incensed to faint.

Trouble loomed ahead.

All week her mother had been acting with an air of presumptive authority. They had all been way wide of the mark, Lilly thought. Their father's wish to be buried with his first wife Ailie and not in the Harwood family cemetery on *Georgina Downs* was not the final insult after all. This was.

While everyone remained in a shocked silence, Mr. Phillips next handed a large cream parchment envelope to Daisy.

'This contains a personal letter from your father and a key. His note explains its use.'

Lilly caught Maddie's equally triumphant gaze. The bottom drawer they couldn't open in their father's desk, their stares agreed. Which left them both wondering what was in it.

And then, although the next beneficiary in question was absent, Mr. Phillips finally announced that the bush acreage block behind the Harwood family beach house at Inlet Creek was bequeathed to his illegitimate half-brother Henry MacKenzie Harwood, son of their father MacKenzie Harwood and a former domestic servant Ellin Anderson, supported by a registered birth certificate.

If the family had been stunned by previous revelations in the will, this disclosure of a new identity in the family caused a verbal eruption.

'Harry is George's brother!' Daisy said, grinning.

Maddie was equally excited. 'That's why they used to see each other and chat. So he's our Uncle Henry, then?'

'I knew it!' Lilly crowed. 'When Harry arrived the day before yesterday he was almost recognisable but I couldn't think why. Now I know. Once he was all cleaned up, he reminded me of Father.'

The girls looked toward Elizabeth to ask if she knew about Harry but seeing the equal shock on her face and air of sick disgust revealed she was as ignorant as everyone else.

Once the remaining matters were dealt with and the front door closed on Mr. Phillips' exit, an unsmiling Elizabeth slowly rose.

'This is not what I expected,' she uttered viciously. 'George has committed the ultimate unforgiveable humiliation.'

She stalked out and a blanket of silence covered the room.

23

The heavy hush that descended over the sitting room lingered long after Elizabeth disappeared. Josh took Tommy out to play football on the lawn, kicking up wayward autumn leaves in the process.

Still reeling from the stunning disclosures in the will, the girls sprawled and stretched out over chairs and sofas. Kirra brought in tea but the general mindset was for something stronger.

'In the study,' Maddie said gently to a restless Daisy. 'The big bottom right-hand drawer.'

'Thanks. Jack?' He rose, took her hand and they left the room to read George's last words to his eldest daughter and discover the contents of the private drawer.

'Did you know Daisy's real name was Harmony?' Lilly asked.

'No. Just assumed it was Daisy. I love it!'

'Well Father's decision has changed everything and placed the responsibility for the fate of *Georgina* equally into all our hands.'

'Which was absolutely his intention.'

'It belongs to all of us so it must be a joint decision but Mother will want to sell.'

'Father was nobody's fool,' Maddie said. 'He knew mother would dispose of it quick sticks. This way at least we all have a say. It was no secret he would have loved a son but hoped at least one daughter would show interest.

'As I grew up I know he wanted it to be me. It's true I love the outdoors and riding and learning about how the station worked, doing the books in recent years to ease his load, especially on the computer, but I wasn't interested enough to take over management. My heart wasn't invested enough in *Georgina* to take on that role. Even when I met and married Aaron, and had Tommy,' she paused to glance at Josh, 'after Aaron's accident, Dad could see my heart and focus wasn't on the station any more. He didn't show it but I know he was disappointed.

'Apart from having wonderful memories of riding every day and camp outs and mustering with Father, I no longer felt the same interest and attachment. I have a new life with Josh now but we won't be far away.'

'It must have crushed his soul to watch each of us go off in other directions,' Lilly said sadly. 'Our futures were never going to be on the station, and Mother has never made any secret of her dislike for the challenging Australian countryside.'

'She played her role all their married life,' Maddie said, 'but that's why Father shared the property between all of us. He surely realised it wouldn't remain in the family but at least its future would be put to a democratic vote. This way, it allows the whole family to at least have a voice even if that decision is pretty much a foregone conclusion.'

'Maddie, we can't sell this place, can we?' Lilly anguished, her eyes glazed over with horror. 'It was Father and Grandfather's life's work.'

'Sweetie, as hard as that thought is to bear, it's inevitable. But I can tell you now, it won't be to just anyone,' Maddie added fiercely. 'I intend arranging a meeting to speak to all the workers. They all need to know the situation. Give them an opportunity to buy into it as a syndicate. The last thing I would want to see is some bloody great pastoral conglomerate buy it up and stick in a manager. It would be great to think *Georgina* could stay in family hands. This homestead was meant for it.'

'Well whoever wants it will need bags of money,' Lilly muttered, 'so our options will be limited. The choice might not be so simple.'

'The right buyer is out there,' Maddie said hopefully, 'but whoever comes after the Harwoods on *Georgina Downs*, we can set conditions on the sale that the station is a going concern and all the employees must stay and be part of a package deal. Dusty has been Father's manager for years now. He may be interested. He's dead keen on this place and loves it like his own. We have to at least do right by all current workmen, tell them the situation and give them a chance of refusal.'

Noble words, Lilly knew, trying to hide her distress and stop tears but her sister could hardly miss them.

'Don't worry,' Maddie said sensitively, giving a reassuring smile, 'we're not rushing into putting this property on the market yet. It's a prosperous sheep station. You can bet the local estate agents may well have potential buyers already circling. They all have their contacts. But, before any decision is made, the four of us have to agree.'

Lilly nodded. 'I know. Responsibility and duty are just hitting home.'

At that moment, Daisy and Jack returned from the study, their arms full of folders and a number of what looked like very fat albums. Their sister's eyes were red from crying, her face flushed, but a glow of happiness clearly put there by whatever they found.

'As if it wasn't enough being included in the sheep station,' Daisy said, 'George left all this.' She and Jack dumped their load on a side table.

'What is it?' Maddie asked.

'Heaps of what looks like all the family photos ever taken of George and Ailie and me while they were still married and I was young. Safely locked away against the possibility of anyone ever finding and destroying them.' The unspoken silence suggested they all knew who that might have been. 'And get this.' Their oldest sister opened one of the fat albums to a random page. 'Somehow George has gathered and collected virtually every single newspaper cutting of my travel articles ever written from all over the world! I'm speechless. This is beyond precious.'

'Wow,' Lilly sighed.

Lilly grew still, filled with a moment of hurt and embarrassment. Even their father didn't trust their mother. Opposite, she suspected Maddie's mind was ticking over with a similar thought. And the answer to the question in their mind as to why no records of their father's first family could be found.

While they clearly shared a sense of grudging

envy that George had taken such secret precautions and gone to such lengthy efforts to follow his oldest daughter's life and career, this was hardly a time for she and Maddie to entertain resentment. Daisy's innocent sharing and joy took priority over such a clearly loving gesture by their father to the other daughter but this was no time for feeling irritation. He had dealt sensibly with his life's situation and done what he thought best for each of them.

Her immediate knee jerk reaction was to examine what her father had done in equal measure for her, pushing aside any unfair judgement that Daisy always seemed the absent, yet favoured, daughter. Then logic kicked in and Lilly appreciated that simply wasn't so.

In a moment of clarity, in Lilly's mind it was as though a veil had been lifted and insight suddenly emerged. In his own way, their father had done the best he could under every circumstance for each of his daughters.

Daisy in following her career, as she had just revealed.

Maddie in cherishing her tomboy ways and sharing the station and its vast outdoors, perhaps George's dearest hope for the future of *Georgina Downs*.

And herself, Lilly finally grasped on reflection, in releasing her to go with her mother, acknowledging the attachment of her youth. Over time, allowing her to find her own way back to him and her roots, to become strong enough in her own right to fight for the independence she had always lacked. Had he known that was what she needed when Lilly had not even identified it herself?

And throughout, their father had strengthened the bonds between all three sisters by maintaining contact, fostering their blood link so that against potential disharmony, bad decisions and insecurities, they all accepted each other through that firm shared connection.

'Sorry, we've probably interrupted your discussions,' Daisy said, perhaps sensing the distracted mood in the room.

Maddie shook her head. 'Just mulling over the fate of this station actually.'

'Of course. Well, count me out of any decision. I have few memories about this place. Besides, since I've just sold the Sheldon farm, I don't want or need any more than I already have. As it is, I feel overwhelmed to have inherited such security for my future. And now, thanks to George, I have all these personal memories, too. So I'll go along with whatever you girls and your mother decide.'

Daisy turned to her partner. 'Jack and I feel we should make tracks. You'll want to discuss this morning's announcements with your mother. How do we let Harry know we're ready to leave?'

'I'll phone the workmen's hut and ask one of the men to drive him over here to the homestead,' Maddie said, already tapping numbers into her mobile.

When Harry arrived, a familiar cream parchment envelope was tucked under his arm that looked suspiciously like Harwood family business. So, everyone knew then, Lilly silently beamed at him and was rewarded with an emotional spark in the old man's eyes, making words unnecessary.

So although nothing was spoken, the goodbyes were especially sentimental and touching.

'See you at Inlet Creek, Uncle Harry,' Lilly heard Maddie whisper to him, their hug hesitant but warm before the three travellers all piled into the rumbling loaded Kombi van.

Maddie, Tommy, Josh and Lilly waved madly as half the family began their journey to Goulburn then on through the rolling hills and heritage towns of the Southern Highlands, winding their way back to the coast.

★   ★   ★

Because the lawyer's visit was early and the personal fallout astounding for everyone, it left each with a need to process the morning's events. So it was barely midday when the remaining family trooped back indoors, seeking warmth from the sharp winds that swirled the last autumn leaves about the garden.

With Daisy gone, it was no surprise that Elizabeth quietly reappeared to join them for Kirra's lunch of a huge vegetable and pasta bake with pumpkin damper, all gratefully appreciated.

Their mother wasted no time in voicing her wishes. 'We need to talk about this place. It will be sold of course. I have telephoned the local land agents and arranged for them to come out tomorrow and value it all. Have photographs taken, get the advertising campaign underway.'

'No, Mother,' Maddie objected with horror. 'You can cancel everything. How dare you do anything without our approval? Daisy has given us permission to act on her behalf so whatever we decide will be a joint agreement.'

'That's entirely unfair. We all know the outcome. You're merely causing a delay.'

'Not necessarily. We've all given it thought and are being realistic about our life situations now. Where we want to be in the future. But I believe we should take more time. There are other options and consideration first before we go public with the property sale.'

Which Lilly doubted Maddie would share with their mother. It would only cause even further disagreement.

'I want to leave as soon as possible.'

'You've made that quite plain, Mother, and we all know your wishes. I can assure you we know where your vote lies. But, honestly, we haven't even had time to get our heads around what's happened. It's too soon. I'm not rushing into anything.'

'Well I need the money to move on. Lilly,' she turned to her younger daughter, 'we should book our return flight back to London.'

'You'll need to arrange that yourself, Mother. I have no idea yet when I'm returning.'

Elizabeth huffed her surprise and disapproval. 'Well don't procrastinate. I can stay for a week at most. Meanwhile I'm instructing the household staff and going through every room as to exactly what I wish to keep and have sent to England.'

Lilly and Maddie exchanged a glance of

exasperation. Elizabeth simply didn't get it. The sisters would need to stick together.

'I tolerated my life here but I do not plan to stay a moment longer than necessary,' she continued, unaware of her daughters' frustration as she shuffled another tiny portion of food onto her fork.

'By all means, Mother,' Maddie sighed. 'Do what you must.'

All of which meant they weren't prepared to struggle against her anymore and would likely rarely see her again.

With lunch done and the family grateful to escape the undercurrent in the dining room, the sitting room once again became their haven for the afternoon. With Tommy down for his nap and only the adults gathered, Lilly witnessed Maddie's growing impatience and soon understood why.

Maddie inhaled a deep slow breath and asked their mother, 'Did you ever love Father?'

Elizabeth's return glare was glacial. She hesitated for a heartbeat, even softened ever so slightly before she admitted, 'I was quite smitten with him. Once. He was a dashing man.'

'That's not what I asked.'

'Lilly,' their mother announced, ignoring the question and Maddie's persistence, 'you'll need to be organised and ready when I want to leave. No later than this time next week.'

'I told you I'm undecided.'

'You're not staying in Australia surely?'

'Yes. It might be nice to spend time with my sisters. I've been away for years and I'm looking forward to reconnecting with them and letting Tommy get to know his aunt.'

'But what about Oliver?'

'Apparently he has other interests.'

Maddie raised her eyebrows and flashed a glance of surprise at Lilly across the room as if to say *You haven't told me.* Which was true. But she was reluctant to own up to her foolish naïve mistake just yet and admitting that a twenty-something still listened to her mother. Not anymore.

'A fine upstanding young man like him? Really, Lilly, I very much doubt it.'

'Not according to his friends, who know him well.'

Their mother rose stiffly. 'Don't be too hasty, Lillianne. You don't simply toss aside a Remington. I shall cancel the estate agent for tomorrow. As you have wished,' she tossed at Maddie as she left.

Maddie waited until their mother's footsteps could be heard echoing down the long homestead hallway to her suite. 'I wonder if she ever really cared for Father,' she muttered with sadness. 'But she's right you know. The fact is, we're going to have to sell.' Maddie rose and paced. 'Christ. Dad's still warm in his grave but he knew this would happen. He must have been gutted.' She turned to her sister and frowned. 'I wonder if that caused his heart attack.'

Lilly straightened on the sofa. 'Surely not. It would be dreadful to think that might have been the reason. This station was his whole life.'

The sisters exchanged significant glances.

'Give Mother the good news in the morning, then?'

'We could wait for a few days until we leave. Let her sweat a bit longer.'

'Tempting but best not. You're coming to the beach house with us?'

'You know I used to idolise Mother and I'll always respect her backbone and class. She was the image of the woman I wanted to grow up to be. I've been trying all my life to emulate and please her but failed.' Lilly shook her head. 'Mother is not who I want to be. I simply can't bear to be in this homestead alone with her when you and Josh and Tommy leave.' She paused. 'You don't mind, do you?

'No.' Maddie reached out and hugged her warmly. 'Just think. We'll all be together in the same place. We three sisters. That's never happened before. At least, not for a long time. You and I made day visits when Father took us to the Sheldon farm when we were growing up, remember? But, right now, we should take every advantage to get to know each other better as adults. You've been away in England for years and I've hardly seen you. And Daisy has never been a close part of our lives but I have to tell you, from what I see of her, I see a really good person. She's nothing like Mother claimed her to be.'

'Three sisters. Not just two. I like that.' Lilly started to feel a strength building inside her, a sense of power in union.

'And when we get down to Inlet Creek, we must go visit Uncle Harry.'

'Yeah. Make ourselves known to him. Invite him to the beach house?'

'Sure.' Maddie rose. 'But for now we need to get some sleep. I still have sorting to do in Father's office, pack up all our stuff and see if it will fit in the four wheel drive.'

'We'll make it fit,' Lilly chuckled as they linked arms and strolled down the long wide homestead hallway to their rooms.

24

Two days later, the rest of the family left Elizabeth alone in the homestead on *Georgina Downs* crating up the household goods and furniture she wanted shipped to England. After the long drive to the coast, they wearily pulled up outside the beach house at Inlet Creek.

Before their departure, Maddie had gone out to the workmen's quarters on the station putting forward the situation and her proposal, leaving them to consider her suggestions and any potential opportunity should they be able to take it up.

Meanwhile, Josh told Lilly that he had put his Oyster Bay apartment on the market and was already receiving offers, with the aim of pooling their resources in the pursuit of a family home together, his life now firmly committed to Maddie and her son.

But while the sisters settled in, Josh immediately heaved a rucksack into his four wheel drive and headed for his coastal rescue training at the Sydney base.

Next morning, Lilly and Maddie settled their curiosity and agreed to visit Harry.

'Where are we going?' Tommy asked, swinging a stick he found along the way.

'To see Uncle Henry.'

'Is he old?'

'Mmm,' Maddie said. 'About as old as Grampa.'

'He could be my Grampa now!' The boy's

innocent face appealed.

She shared a nostalgic glance with her sister. 'Maybe.'

Even before the trio reached the fence surrounding his property, they saw the huge rustic hand-painted For Sale sign.

'He's not staying?' Maddie gasped in surprise.

Lilly shook her head. 'I thought this was his home?'

Curious as to why he might be moving, the sisters trudged through the gum trees, the minty aroma from their leaves drifting to them on the chilly morning breeze, Tommy trailing behind, the bush block a small boy's exciting playground.

Even as they approached the simple timber hut with its corrugated iron roof and pole posts supporting a small front porch, looking totally comfortable in its native bushland, Lilly noticed a gleaming silver Rover parked around one side.

Familiar with the type used by the wealthy of country England, Lilly's prejudice instantly rose and she frowned. 'Harry has a visitor.'

'Could be the estate agent.'

Hearing male voices from inside, Lilly grew wary but stepped forward to knock on the door, almost breaking the skin on her knuckles against the rough timber. The voices stopped and she heard shuffling. Lilly cast an uncertain look behind to Maddie and shrugged.

When the door opened, Harry's brown eyes glazed over then wrinkled lines appeared at their corners as he beamed. Lilly's heart lifted at his positive reaction.

'Have we come at a bad time?' She peered over his shoulder.

'No, you're family,' he said quietly. 'You come right on in.'

In that moment, nothing else needed to be said and it was as if they had always belonged.

Inside the compact hut was like a pioneering time capsule. Simple furniture, tin mugs, open shelves crammed with a few pieces of mismatched crockery and tinned food. A dated wood stove, a healthy fire licking behind its glass door, sending out welcome warmth into the small space. A blackened kettle singing on its cast iron surface.

But while the fascinating interior invited attention and Lilly took in her surrounds in a five second sweep, so did Harry's other visitor, the owner of the posh vehicle parked outside. Impressive, Lilly thought, annoyingly unable to find fault. And knows it.

Gorgeously handsome, smooth tanned complexion, thick blonde hair drifting back from his forehead in perfect waves. Judging by the understated tasteful clothes, it wasn't obvious he was here on business. Smart and neat, not overdone. Blue jeans hugged him tight and the black tee shirt with sleeves pushed up to the elbows beneath a padded down vest like Oliver would wear gave the impression of a trustworthy country man. Clever move, she thought wryly. Underplaying any sense of pressure for an old man.

'This here is Mr. Sam Ballard,' Harry introduced him, turning to the man himself to add proudly, 'and these are my nieces Lilly and

361

Maddie. And that's little Tommy.' He looked down fondly upon the boy whose chattering had stopped, his eyes wide taking in everything around him.

'Ladies, pleased to meet you.' The voice was deep and warm as a big hand shot out in response and his liquid blue eyes steadily held Lilly's gaze.

Nice manners, at least, she thought. But then, in her experience, the entitled rich often produced them for show. Lilly took his grasp and discovered his skin rough even as she grew conscious of a quiet sense of power about him.

'Mr. Ballard,' she said stiffly.

Maddie stepped forward to do the same.

Then Sam lowered himself to greet Tommy. 'And how are you young man?'

Oh, really smooth, Lilly thought with irritation.

'Fine, thank you,' Tommy said politely, adding with childhood simplicity, 'Harry is going to be my new Grampa.'

Lilly swallowed back the threat of tears at Harry's look of surprise and heard Maddie's gasp beside her.

'Then you're a lucky young man indeed.' Sam rose to his full height again. 'Mr. Harwood, sir. Great to meet you but I won't take up any more of your time. You have my card and I'll be in touch.' Flashing a cheeky grin around the general assembly, he added, 'I'll see myself out.'

The sound of the closing door and receding boots had barely faded when Maddie squeaked, 'Do you know who that is?' At blank looks all round, she scoffed. 'That's only the son of Spencer Ballard. A wealthy land developer well known in the region for all the wrong reasons. Buying up beachfront land north and south along the coast and developing hinterland acreage into smaller subdivision lots for decades. Obviously sent his son to sweet talk an old man.'

'Well now, he was polite enough to me,' Harry objected.

'We saw the sign,' Lilly frowned. 'I guess we just assumed you would stay.'

Maddie shot to the point. 'How much did he offer?'

'Just shy of a million,' he muttered and Maddie softly whistled. 'Worth thinking about but it's my first offer.'

'Well they jumped right onto it then, didn't they? Hawk-eyed Ballard never misses a bargain if he can strike one. You've obviously only just put this block on the market and I can tell you now, that will only be a fraction of what the land is worth. Did the estate agent discuss this block's value and did you agree on a decent realistic price?'

Harry shuffled uncomfortably. 'Ain't got one.'

'What!'

'Now you girls, I might look like it but I ain't stupid,' he said firmly. 'George and I had chats over the years and, even though he was my younger brother by some years, I learnt a lot from him. I'm saving middle man fees and Mr. Phillips out in Goulburn, he recommended me a good lawyer hereabouts.'

His information and quiet common sense

went some way to reassurance.

'Well, sounds like you're on top of things for now,' Maddie said with reluctant respect, 'but don't you sell to anyone until you run it by us first, okay?'

Harry nodded, grinning.

'We always wondered about your friendship with our father,' Lilly said.

Harry indicated his wooden chairs and they all took a seat, Tommy's short legs swinging above the floor.

'After our father, old Mac died, George bought this whole block from here down to the sea in his own name. Built the beach house down the front and marked off this back bit for me to live on. I never expected it but he insisted. I weren't never interested in farming or living out on the station so I've always been grateful to have a home.

'When I were younger, I just did labourin', mostly further out in the central west on big farms and station properties. But I'm getting too old for all that now. Me bones ache and I can't do all I'd like. Got me eye on a small place in the new retirement village in town here. Put me name down for the one up the back, near the bush.'

'Are you sure?' Maddie asked as Tommy climbed onto her lap, like Lilly, both fascinated by the old man.

'I'll be near help if I need it and I can go fishin'.'

'Well, we can all keep an eye on you,' Lilly said. 'I've been living in England but I'm staying in the beach house for now with Maddie and

Tommy, so if you need anything, you come see us, okay?'

The old man seemed touched and nodded. 'Much obliged.'

When offered, Harry poured them all mugs of strong black tea and they chatted a while longer. Not wishing to overstay their first visit, the nieces and surrogate grandson left soon after.

No more than an hour later, a now-familiar silver Rover cruised into the beach house driveway. The sisters showed only passing interest at the sound of tyres on gravel but Tommy, always curious about visitors especially living most of his young life in the relative isolation of an outback homestead skipped out to investigate, running back to announce happily, 'It's the man from Grampa Harry's house.'

Ballard? In disbelief, Lilly went to the shutters and opened them to check. 'Tommy's right. And the guy is looking no less irresistible,' she said with reluctant admiration.

'But what on earth is he coming here for? We have nothing to sell,' Maddie quipped, then, realising what she had just said, suddenly latched onto a potential reason and gasped, 'Oh surely not!'

When she wrenched the door open, Lilly wished he wasn't so blasted appealing. He looked so harmless and *nice*. Stick him in bathers with a surfboard under his arm, standing beside a lifeguard tower and every bikini-clad beach babe would be begging for surf rescue.

Unsmiling, she crossed her arms. 'Forget something?'

'Lilly.' He said her name so softly with the

whisper of a smile twitching his lips, she was caught off guard, but only for a moment. When she recovered, he was saying, 'Actually I came to chat to you and your sister.'

'Why?'

'May I come in?'

'Depends. What do you want?'

'I have a proposition.'

Lilly fumed. 'First you try and get around an old man on the quiet, now I suppose you want us to convince him to sell.'

He paused before responding then said easily, 'Not at all. As you probably know by now, Harry doesn't have an estate agent. To save fees. Happy to do business that way. You don't make money by being reckless with it.'

Sounded logical enough, made sense, but she was really pushing it to believe a single word that came out of this guy's mouth.

'There is actually another matter I would like to discuss with you and your sister.'

Without a word, Lilly shrugged and swept one arm wide indicating he could enter.

'Thank you.'

How annoying. The guy was almost grinning, making fun of her! Yet rising above her embarrassed irritation was slight panic that padding around the beach house in socks, leggings and a sloppy jumper, she hardly looked her best. Well, damn, he had seen her earlier. Why did she feel this silly urge to impress? What did she care? She wasn't pleasing any man ever again.

'Mr. Ballard,' Maddie said calmly, approaching. 'Please take a seat.'

'Sam, please.'

When his large frame was settled into one of the comfortable single lounge chairs, she asked, 'Well, Sam, how can we help?'

Lilly glared in silence from across the room. The moody sky and sea outdoors, dumping large waves up onto the sand, matched her disposition at the moment. The wind had risen and rain was due again.

'It's not common knowledge yet since we've only just filed the application papers with the local council for land rezoning but, clearly, with Mr. Harwood's bush acreage for sale now behind this house block, this whole site would be ideal to expand our planned foreshore development.'

Clearly. Lilly was alarmed and speechless to hear what the greedy developers had in mind. She exchanged a horrified glance with her sister.

Maddie shrugged. 'We're not for sale. Sam. Nor are we ever likely to be.'

'Name your price,' he said softly.

Lilly loved it that he needed all the land for the project the Ballard conglomerate had in mind. The humble little Harwood beach house was absolute oceanfront. Desperate times called for desperate measures, it seemed, if they possessed an open cheque book.

Worse thought still, they could have a bland square concrete structure rearing up behind them if Uncle Harry sold out to them. Lilly felt like naming an outrageous figure to see his reaction.

'If you sell, we could set you up in the penthouse for a fair price,' Sam said smoothly

'Penthouse!' Maddie chuckled. 'How many stories is this *development* going to be?'

'A five star resort.'

'In little Inlet Creek?' Maddie chuckled. 'Good luck getting *that* passed by council. Many before have tried.'

Lilly could see her sister was amused more than bothered, both staggered and shaking their heads at the Ballard intentions and generous offered proposal. If they were interested. Which they most definitely were not. No way would anyone take away this precious family holiday home and gathering place. Its value went way beyond a heap of dollars with noughts behind them.

'If it's more than a single storey, it's too high,' Lilly muttered, appalled that he would have so much front to come here. The handsome son come to chat up the women this time.

Hardly able to ignore the sisters' resistance, Sam wisely uncurled himself and rose to stand before them. He offered his business card. When neither of them accepted it, he placed it on the kitchen counter.

'At least think about it.' He cast his blue-eyed gaze around their beachy retreat. 'You'd still have a seafront residence with every convenience right on your doorstep, so to speak. A top class restaurant, casual bistro, heated pool, gift shops, gym.'

Sensing strong vibes of opposition from her sister, Lilly knew they were both on the same page, horrified, not impressed. She immediately considered the adverse effect such a glitzy complex would have on small independent family businesses like Daisy's tearoom and Jack's specialist French bakery.

The door quietly clicked as Sam Ballard left and the purring of his luxury motor vehicle could be heard backing away.

The girls stared at each other, shook their heads and sighed.

'Some people just don't get it,' Lilly said, frustrated that the Ballard approach should make her not only feel sad but also angry. 'My goodness, that man reminds me of the smug boasting from Oliver about how you can legally and financially screw people over. It's disgusting. And that Sam guy is no different. *Old father sends sexy son to sweet talk a bunch of simpering women,* she mimicked.'

'You noticed,' Maddie teased.

'What?'

'That Sam Ballard is sexy.'

'Doesn't mean we'll be swayed. I'm not changing my mind and I'm sure you won't either. The Ballards are trouble.'

'Maybe not all of them,' Maddie said quietly, grinning.

'Oh, please. Don't start making excuses for a silver spoon with perfect teeth and a killer smile.'

25

Everyone knew that growing up in the country and small towns, news travelled and was welcomed. Inlet Creek was no exception. This time, gossip came from one of the Harwood's own as, next day, Daisy came hurtling across the sand and up the broad beach house steps.

Gasping as she leapt onto the front porch, she said, 'God, I'm puffing. I must be out of shape.'

'Run all the way?' Maddie grinned.

Her big sister nodded, bending over with her hands on her knees gathering her breath.

Maddie grinned and patted her on the shoulder. 'That's a good kilometre on sand. You're doing just fine.'

Lilly handed her a long glass of water which Daisy promptly sculled, wiped her mouth and said, 'You will never guess who just ambushed me in the tearooms?'

As she looked between both of her step-sisters, she received only blank stares in return. 'A Spencer Ballard.'

'The father! Mister Money Bags himself.'

'Well I guess he must be,' Daisy frowned, rambling on, missing the knowing glance exchanged between her two younger sisters. 'He's interested in buying this house. Boastfully pointed out that there was an application in place for rezoning. That once he buys the bush block behind — I mean, that's Harry's, isn't it?

— the development would dwarf this house. Ruin its privacy yada yada. Started talking a million dollars, if you please.'

Maddie turned to Lilly. 'The old dog. He's covering all his bases, huh sis?'

Daisy frowned. 'What do you mean?'

'He went to talk to you because he failed with us.'

Daisy threw her hands wide and settled them at her waist, still breathing heavily. 'He's been to see you, too?'

They both nodded.

'This very morning,' Lilly said, 'right after we rejected an offer from his son, Sam. News in that arrogant family sure travels fast. Old man Spencer couldn't wait to come and visit personally. He made it quite clear he wants to buy everything from the road that fronts the other end of Harry's block right down to *our* beach, and he expects us to sell. Man is he one determined SOB. No grass grows under his shiny shoes. Rocked up to the house in a big flash car with a driver who *opened the door for him.*' Lilly scoffed. 'I mean, how poncey is that?'

'You should have seen our little Lilly get fired up,' Maddie grinned.

'I'm not little Lilly anymore,' she objected.

'You surely aren't, sweetie. You're small but you're scary now.'

'Anyway, the old guy said the house would be worthless, only land value once his development gets underway,' Daisy said. 'His offer was a joke.'

'This house is priceless,' Lilly stated. 'I told our mate Spencer you can't put a price on memories. *Well now,*' Lilly strutted around the living room replaying the earlier scene in a deep male voice, '*because of your recent Loss I can extend my offer a few days.* Bloody vulture.'

'Then,' Maddie continued the story, 'when we told him we didn't need any more time, that we knew our decision and the answer was No, boy did he get mean. Didn't actually make a threat but hinted that we would be really wise to reconsider.'

'He was not smiling when he left,' Lilly said.

★ ★ ★

Josh phoned Maddie a few days later to say he already had a seven figure offer for his city waterfront apartment and was due a day off from training, so the excited pair decided to go off looking for a property.

Because it promised to be a long day, Lilly offered to mind Tommy at the beach house. She had grown deeply fond of her nephew and witnessed how precious he was to Maddie, equally embraced and loved by Josh who would be the new father figure in the boy's life.

Lilly reflected on Maddie's husband, daredevil but charming Aaron. The ultimate womaniser. Lilly wondered if Maddie knew the extent of his infidelity and flirtation with anything female. Had she been jealous? Maddie never showed any sign of it. So wonderful that Josh had entered her sister's life. If he had been anything less than the genuine man he turned out to be, Lilly would never have approved of the match.

After a busy morning of playing together and a wild and windy walk along the beach, Tommy announced he was too big for his afternoon nap and finally settled on the sofa snuggled up beside Lilly with picture books for a while.

As she sipped a mug of coffee and Tommy flicked over pages quietly alongside, Lilly's thoughts about Maddie set her thinking about her own choice of men in her life. Although she had never been close to her father or shared a connection like Maddie who was an outdoor person and loved riding about the station with him, Lilly saw his strength and stability, his hardworking ethic and tolerance of his wife who had never been an easy person to live with.

Lilly preferred dressing up, a habit fostered by Elizabeth so that, growing up, she willingly took part in garden parties and special charity functions alongside her mother.

Then there was England. That foreign place to which she had been drawn on leaving school. She harboured no desire for university and was happily drawn into her mother's side of the family with its social life and extensive country estates.

There had been frequent acceptable boyfriends, always part of the approved inner circle and by whom she was charmed and admired. All preparing her for finally meeting Oliver, adored at first sight, being overwhelmed and drowned by his gorgeousness. On reflection, a hasty decision and one she came to regret.

Over time, she discovered most of his particular set of friends were superficial, the girls confident in their place in the world, pursuing insignificant careers and a fashionable lifestyle until making a *good* marriage, while the boys were not always the true image of gentlemen they portrayed in public.

Lilly shook her head to think she could ever have been drawn into such an artificial web and that her mother had encouraged and supported it.

As if mocking her thoughts, Lilly's mobile beeped. Always suspicious these days and thinking it might be Oliver harassing her again, she checked the message in case it was from Maddie asking about Tommy.

It wasn't from either of them.

As she read it, she discovered some startling news about Oliver from Pippa, a mutual female friend she trusted back in England. Lilly didn't feel in the least upset. Instead, a burning fury rose within her and she boiled with loathing. Leaving Tommy happily reading inside for a moment, she went out onto the front porch braving the stiff onshore breeze for a gasp of chilly autumn sea air.

That was it, Lilly thought. She was definitely not going back to England. Ever. Oliver could rot.

But where was home for her now, then? Partners Daisy and Jack were extending the flat while Maddie and Josh right this minute were scouting for a home for their new life together. Lilly had always assumed that *Georgina Downs* and the homestead would be the base to which she could always return but with her father gone, the station up for sale soon and her mother returning to England any moment, she was effectively homeless and adrift.

This beach house belonged to all the family and she knew she could stay here as long as needed. But, strangely, since seeing the new-found growing love between Maddie and Josh with Tommy so attached and readily accepting a new male figure into his little life, she felt the need for a fresh start, a home and new life she could call her own.

Lilly was suddenly hit by a stronger sense of loneliness than she cared to admit. Her father's death had been the unfortunate catalyst that gave her time and space to rethink her life. And, based on what she had only just learnt, she no longer wanted it to be anywhere near Oliver Remington or England.

Her thoughts whirled as she stared out to sea. Although the ocean churned over itself as its waves crashed ashore, Lilly found peace in the rhythm of nature. So it only took moments for her to compare her time overseas to the simple family life she was leading now back home in small town coastal Australia.

She now knew where her heart was and where home would be, letting down her guard to weep with tears of relief and hope for the future.

Which is how Daisy found her as she suddenly appeared off the beach and walked up the steps to the house where her youngest sister stood looking as bleak as the weather.

Full of concern, Daisy was instantly by her side and wrapping a comforting arm around her shoulder. 'Is it father?'

Lilly shook her head. 'Oliver, actually. But I don't feel as bad as I look.'

'I thought you were breaking off with him.'

'I haven't yet,' she admitted in a small voice, smiling through watery eyes.

'Oh, Lilly, you're stretching it out. Just making life harder for yourself at the moment when we've all lost our father. You have enough to cope with. Life has thrown big changes at all of us this past year. At least sort out Oliver and do something about him.'

'I will,' she said firmly, 'because I now have background information that will give me the courage to do it.' Lilly handed Daisy her mobile phone. 'Read that.'

Daisy became absorbed then gasped, 'The bastard! While he's been texting you and begging you to return, he's been on with other women?'

'Yes. You noticed the plural?' she said dryly. 'Not just one, apparently. So, after what Pippa has told me, I'm definitely not calling Oliver to break up. I never want to hear his voice again. I'll send a short text then block him from my phone. I couldn't bear to hear his lies and smooth words when I know what's really been going on. He'll deny everything.'

Daisy shook her head, scanning over the message again before handing back the phone. 'I'm so sorry, Lilly.'

'Don't be. I'll be fine. The fact that other women seem to have gained Oliver's interest, doesn't bother me at all,' Lilly said honestly, confessing, 'It's actually a relief that the pressure

376

is gone for me to explain and justify myself over here when, within a few weeks, he's forgotten he even had a partner for two years. As far as I'm concerned, he's welcome to all of them.'

Lilly felt Daisy shuffle beside her and watched her produce a large envelope from inside her zipped windcheater.

'Lilly,' she paused, 'please don't be angry with me but I've done some research. Sorry, journalist instinct coming out, I'm afraid,' she grinned. 'And what I've found is some extra ammunition for you regarding Oliver. Believe me, I did it with the best intentions because I had no idea I would find anything. I just played a hunch. But I just couldn't stand to see you so unhappy. You deserve the whole truth.'

'What are these?' Lilly asked as Daisy opened the envelope flap and partly withdrew some printed pages of documents.

'Evidence. Probably best to read them when you're alone.' Daisy slid the papers back inside and glanced behind them. 'How about you go to your room and I'll get Tommy to help me in the kitchen? This calls for a healing dose of comfort food. I'm thinking pancakes with bananas, maple syrup and a big dollop of ice cream. You come out and join us when you're ready. What do you think?' She was grinning.

'You don't need to go back to the shop?'

Daisy madly shook her head. 'Absolutely not. I'm here until Maddie returns. And before you ask, Jack already knows I might be gone for a while.'

Lilly hugged her big sister tight and nodded,

frowning with curiosity, having no idea what this was all about, only suspecting it related to Oliver. At this stage, she knew a sense of dread but wouldn't be surprised by whatever it was Daisy had found. She was numb.

She swiped away the remaining moisture from her cheeks as the girls jointly rose together and turned back toward the beckoning warmth of indoors.

What Lilly read alone in her room was an ongoing tide of allegations from newspaper reports and other documents. Oliver Sebastian Remington, it eventuated, had been previously taken to court for abusing and assaulting women.

Without conviction, she noted, a cold chill stealing across her heart. She wondered how much the lawyer cost his father so that his wealthy family could keep it concealed.

And to think Daisy had used her journalistic skills and contacts, not to mention the time it must have taken for all this research, and done all this for her from love and concern. That she should go to such length was mind-blowing. All with the aim of getting proof to protectively place before her sister.

Lilly slowly and carefully read every word on every page, growing rigid with fury as she scanned the lines, feeling utterly detached from the world about her, sinking into the depth of the appalling hidden scandal Daisy had uncovered.

Women paid off to keep their silence. An underage pregnant girl. The list went on, Lilly growing sick to think such a repulsive man had ever touched her. And yet, knowing all this, none of Oliver's friends ever said anything. Everyone colluded to hide his secret sordid past. Lilly cringed with humiliation for not wising up to Oliver and being duped instead.

Lilly idly wondered if her mother knew. At the very least, being in that social circle, she must have heard rumours.

With this revealing scandal and cover-up, the chapter of Oliver Remington in Lilly's life was definitely firmly closed.

She sat on her bed in silence for ages, feeling nothing but an aching emptiness and regret. Unsure if she could ever bring herself to trust a man again. Especially not one of the silver spoon variety.

Instinct told Lilly she was right in her decision not to contact Oliver. Instead she would keep this precious information, sensing she may need it at some future time for leverage — otherwise known as blackmail — if her snobby bastard of a former boyfriend ever dared to challenge her or blacken her name.

26

It was unusual but not impossible for bushfires even in the current cold weather, so two days later in the afternoon, with Josh returned to Sydney to continue his training, Maddie and Lilly frowned at each other and almost at the same time said, 'Do you smell smoke?'

Since the cool change had passed and the blustery winds died down, they were sitting on the front porch watching Tommy play high up on the beach in the sand. They both rose and began checking around the beach house. As they moved around the back, both saw the answer to their instinct.

'It's Uncle Harry's place!'

Maddie grabbed Tommy and even as they let themselves through the makeshift gate in the fence and ran through the eucalyptus trees toward his hut, the first local brigade truck had already arrived on the scene from the main road at the other end of his property. Firefighters leapt down from the vehicle before it had hardly stopped, springing into action with hoses.

'I hope Harry's not home.' Lilly put a hand over her mouth as flames licked through the timber structure.

Maddie raced forward and yelled to one of the firemen, 'Our Uncle lives in there.'

'He's the one who called us, Ma'am. We're checking for him now.' He indicated one of the suited firemen with breathing gear pushing his way into the flimsy building.

'Oh God, surely he's not still in there. He won't have a hope. He must be outside,' Maddie frantically hunted around, aware to keep back, but even from a distance feeling the intense heat pushing out from the fire.

Lilly followed, scouting around too. 'I can't see him anywhere.'

'Will Grampa Harry be okay?' Tommy asked in a small voice.

'I'm sure he'll be just fine, sweetie,' Maddie said.

An agonising five minutes later, two firemen carried a familiar figure from the shack which by now because of its wooden construction was already well ablaze and half burnt to the ground.

An ambulance arrived soon after so the sisters stood back, holding their breath as to Harry's condition and the state of any injuries.

Moments later as the paramedics began tending to him, Lilly cried out, 'He's moving.'

'God I hope it's not serious.'

They moved forward. 'We're family. Will he be okay?' Maddie asked.

The young man glanced at them and nodded reassurance. 'He's a lucky man. He was trying to save some of his possessions. It's looking like superficial burns and minor injuries but they'll do a thorough check in hospital.'

The girls managed a quick word to Harry before the ambulance drove away, letting him know they would come visit him tomorrow.

As the firemen cleaned up, Maddie and Lilly

surveyed the destruction.

'The shack is destroyed.' Lilly sighed. 'Harry will be homeless.'

'Site's only good for demolition,' Maddie shook her head.

'He could come and live with us,' Tommy said brightly.

'That's a very good idea,' she replied but, frowning, asked, 'I wonder how on earth the fire started? Harry's a bushman. He would have taken every care.'

★　★　★

Next morning, Maddie stayed with Tommy at the beach house. Daisy had been informed of the fire and agreed to come by and collect Lilly so they could go visit Harry in hospital together.

When they poked their heads around the door of his room, apart from an IV drip and some bandages, Harry thankfully didn't seem too much the worse for his ordeal and cheerful enough, beaming at the sight of his nieces as they entered.

'Not too early for visitors?' Lilly smiled, producing chocolates and planting an affection-ate kiss on his wrinkled cheek.

'Would you believe you're not me first for the day?'

The girls were surprised to hear it. 'You're popular then,' Daisy said. 'Anyone we know?' not really expecting they would since they knew little enough about Harry's life and friends.

'Spencer Ballard.' The sisters stared, speech-less. 'All charm at first till he hissed out a threat.'

Lilly gasped. She and Daisy exchanged knowing glances, all the fire puzzle pieces falling into place.

'Don't worry. Soon as he left I got the nurse to phone the cops and they're going to pay him a visit. I've seen some nasty types in me time but none match that bag of scum. He's all piss and wind. Just trying to scare me off. Wouldn't do business with the likes of him anyway,' he muttered.

The girls shared amused grins, realising wiry Harry was a smart old codger, no one's fool, to be cherished and protected. But appalled to begin suspecting the destruction of their uncle's razed shack was deliberate.

'So,' Lilly asked slowly, 'any news about the cause of the fire?'

'Heard this morning arson squad's involved.'

'What a surprise,' Daisy said wryly. 'How long will they keep you in?'

'Few days. Bit of all right in here I can tell you. Plenty of attention and good meals. When I get out though I know a mate has a caravan I can use for a while. I can set that up on me block until it's sold and I get a placement in the retirement home. With Ballard out of the running, I can wait and bide me time until I get another offer.'

With winter setting in, Lilly was unhappy about the idea of an elderly man living in such humble accommodation. No doubt during his lifetime he had lived in far worse places and conditions but her heart tugged with affection for him and the private wish that, if she had any say and influence in the matter, Uncle Harry deserved to live his life in far more comfort.

The girls turned at the sound of footsteps in the doorway. Lilly was horrified to see Sam Ballard.

She strode across the room, grabbed his arm, ignoring the raised eyebrow look of surprise and that irritating grin of amusement, to lead him out into the wide hospital hallway.

'You have a nerve!' She planted her hands on her hips and gave him a blast. 'We don't want anything to do with the likes of you and your family. Threatening people and burning down their homes. Well I'm fed up with rich folk thinking they can buy out anyone just to get what they want and make more money. It's disgusting. I can tell you know, you will not bulldoze all those beautiful trees. Nature like that can't be replaced. I suppose,' she jabbed a finger in his chest, 'that even though it's the Southern Ocean out there just off the coast, a hop step and jump from Antarctica, you were going to plant bloody palm trees around your concrete resort!'

'Are you done?'

'Excuse me?' Lilly halted, stumped by his soft tone, pulling back the indignant fury that burned inside.

He raised both hands. 'I come in peace.'

'Not funny.'

'I was sorry to hear about your uncle.'

'I'll bet.'

'Lilly, please listen.'

There was that appealing calm voice again, all smooth talking rich guy. Having momentarily run out of steam, she heaved a sigh of annoyance, crossed her arms and decided to hear what he had to say.

'I've only just heard about the fire and that my old man is implicated. I've always known he's ruthless but he's never stooped this low. At least, not that I know about. I've just come from a confrontation with him where he admitted nothing but I imagine he lied. Lilly,' he shook his head and pushed a hand through his sandy waves, 'never in a million years would I have wished this to happen.

'Based on the assumption my father is covering up to save his arse, I've just told him I'm pulling out of being a part of any negotiations for his resort development and will be withdrawing my construction company out of the project. And I won't be tendering for anymore in the future.'

Fascinated, Lilly watched him talk, hit with a grudging admission that she half believed what he said. His attitude was actually quite chatty and friendly although with an undercurrent of hurt over his father's actions.

She rather liked his outfit. Lightweight blue sweater, simple round neck, sleeves pushed up to the elbows which rather seemed to be his style. Fitted black slacks hugging his hips and thighs. With her anger subsiding in the face of his honest enlightening conversation, she continued listening.

'I doubt the old man will have much time to pursue his business interests anyway at the moment because, if investigations prove it, he'll be fighting a charge of accessory to a crime.'

Lilly was actually stunned to hear Sam's admission, literally cutting himself off from his father and that he didn't appear to be cut from the same mould. She found the revelation confronting and was forced to consider the handsome honest man in front of her in a fresh light.

'Well,' she reluctantly conceded, 'that all sounds very regretful, I'm sure, but you're a bit late though, aren't you? Uncle Harry's been seriously injured and he's now homeless.'

'I can arrange for the accommodation of his choice when he leaves hospital.'

Oh, did this man have no end to his charm? 'We can look after our own family, thank you very much. We appreciate your visit but I doubt Harry will want to see you.'

'How about we ask him then?' Sam took the initiative and repeated her earlier move of placing a big hand at her elbow and steering her back into her uncle's hospital room.

While Daisy and Lilly looked on in surprise, Sam went straight up to Harry's bed and carefully squeezed his hand. 'Sorry you had to go through this, mate. I can assure you, the culprit will pay and I'll personally set things right.'

Perhaps growing accustomed to surprises lately and taking this new development in his stride, Harry just gave a slight nod and mumbled, ' 'ppreciate it.'

Sam turned aside to Lilly and produced a business card. 'In case you've *mislaid* the other one,' he grinned.

When she accepted it, she made sure their

fingers didn't touch. Lilly rather suspected she just might feel a jolt of something like lightning.

'Anything you need to help fix things for Harry, give me a call. Daisy. Harry,' Sam acknowledged the others, then left.

'Wow,' Daisy winked at Lilly, 'hard not to be impressed, huh?'

Lilly scoffed but Harry nodded sagely and said, 'Yep. Decent bloke.'

★ ★ ★

Following Harry's fire, within days matters moved fast. The offending arsonist was found lingering near Harry's hut on the night of the fire and under pressure when questioned, soon spilled the truth; that he had been paid by Spencer Ballard to light the fire and hung around to see his work.

Because arson was a felony due to the potential for injury and death, a conviction held a fifteen year sentence. Although the girls learned that one year was most common.

After a family discussion at the beach house, the sisters used this information to instruct their family lawyer Mr. Webster Phillips. Because Ballard was implicated, they negotiated, forcing him to withdraw his development plans from the local council and sign an agreement for compensation to Harry. As to the rest of his legal battles, everyone assumed a lawyer would do deals to reduce any sentence and cover up rumours on his behalf.

Meanwhile, since Jack and Daisy were now living together in her apartment above the teashop, the flat above the bakery was vacant and offered to Harry as temporary accommodation to stay as long as needed.

From the day he left hospital, the elderly man settled in, constantly besieged with visits from his nieces and their partners. A bonus that he was right at the entrance to the pier for fishing, living directly above tantalising bakery smells wafting up from below, across the main street from *Daisy's* with free food any time he chose to eat, and any number of family members in town just a sprint or phone call away.

Then, filled with excitement over a suggestion by Maddie, the seeds of an idea were sown, the sisters all agreed and they planned to inform their uncle to trust them regarding his bush block sale. Feeling rather pleased with themselves, they cracked open a bottle of bubbly one evening in the beach house to celebrate.

27

Having decided to stay in Australia and in particular Inlet Creek, Lilly began scouting for not only her own cottage or apartment but also vacant premises in town to open a modestly exclusive boutique. Being a coastal town and holidaymaker's hub, empty shops were rare so she put her name down on a waitlist at the real estate agent.

Meanwhile, she used her time helping in Daisy's tearoom, blown away by her sister's thriving trade of customers borne of her personal passion for baking, learnt from the Sheldon women in her life. Lilly eagerly absorbed and learnt from the benefit of her experience and advice on necessary planning prior to opening, intending to infuse her own business with the same love and enthusiasm for fashion.

With reservations as to their reaction, Lilly contacted Chelsea and Edward, her former employers in London to advise them of her plans, tender her resignation and let them know that she and Oliver were no longer together.

'Wise move. He has a *reputation*,' Chelsea announced carefully.

Lilly groaned. 'So I've learned.'

She could have wept with gratitude when Chelsea and Edward not only generously offered her specific industry help and advice but praised her talent and experience, convinced she would be a success.

Then Lilly slumped with surprised relief when, despite Oliver's claims, they made it quite clear they were not as friendly with her ex as he had led her to believe. A man of deception on many fronts it seemed. But her London business friends also promised to champion her against any untrue anti-Lilly gossip Oliver Remington might choose to generate and spread.

Because she was out and about daily, Lilly's heart skipped a beat on more than one occasion when she first began noticing Sam Ballard still around town. He was a regular patron of *Daisy's* so, one morning, taking a break from research and ordering in stock on her laptop at the beach house, who should come into the tearoom as she was leaving?

Lilly had quickly grabbed her keep mug of tea and a sandwich, although she was always equally tempted by the luscious display in Jack's boulangerie, often returning to Maddie and Tommy with treats.

This morning, she literally bumped into Sam as she turned from the counter and headed for the door. He placed a big hand on her arm to steady her following the gentle collision.

'Not returning to the big smoke?' she quipped.

'I'm finding the local attractions rather appealing. Fixing to stay a while.'

Lilly privately groaned. Smooth. She didn't hang around but passed him and could have kicked herself when, unable to resist another look, she glanced back only to find he was staring at her, too. Awkward.

★   ★   ★

'I heard Sam's opened up an office in Inlet Creek for his construction company,' Daisy said later. 'Marj's husband Bill said he's tendered for a big new holiday house around the Point.'

The sisters and Jack had gathered for dinner together at the beach house. Daisy brought soup and a casserole, and Jack some leftover pastries from the bakery. Comfort food against the blustery change pushing along the coast at the moment, bringing days of rain.

Lilly wondered if she should be so vain as to think Sam was staying because of her. Interesting. Pulling out of the city to lose himself in little old Inlet Creek? Quite a coincidence when Lilly herself had also decided to settle here. Well she only hoped he had no expectations in her direction because she was off the market and off men.

'Frankly I'm surprised he's sticking around after his family's scandal,' Lilly said.

'His father's the criminal, not Sam.' Her big sister looked uncomfortable before adding, 'Besides, I might have mentioned you were staying.'

'Daisy!'

'Doesn't hurt to lend Cupid a hand now and then,' she teased.

'I'm not remotely interested in the guy.'

'Yet. We girls aren't always the first to know. Take Jack and I — '

'Yeah, well, I'll hear that story another day.'

Lilly wasn't up to mushy romance at the

391

moment although with both her sisters it seemed to be all around her and a situation she couldn't escape. Daisy and Jack constantly made soppy eyes at each other, always touching and sharing private smiles. They were leaving soon and she would miss them over the winter while they were in France. Plus Maddie and Josh clearly had a heat wave going on between them whenever Josh was around and joined them in the beach house.

'Well I think Sam Ballard is one of the good ones,' Maddie said. 'Look what he did for you.'

'Standing up against his father? So he should. The old man's a tyrant.'

'Why do you think he did that?' Maddie challenged.

Lilly muttered, 'Conscience finally kicked in maybe?'

'Lilly Harwood you are so stubborn. You know he did it because it was the right and moral thing to do. And for you.'

'Me?' Lilly scoffed.

'Maybe downsize the attitude a bit, huh sis?' Maddie advised.

Lilly squirmed in her chair. Maddie was always so annoyingly on the mark. 'What do you mean?'

'Stop being prejudiced. Open your eyes and your heart. Not all men are fakes. If you don't, a good man might just slip away.'

'Who said I'm looking?' Lilly mumbled, uncomfortable with the honest direction of the conversation.

Sure, on the surface it seemed Sam had performed as expected but she wasn't leaping into another man's arms any time soon no matter how damned attractive he happened to be.

Leap. Fall. Run into. All pretty much unavoidable in the Creek. It was occurring rather often that one certain blonde dreamboat just happened to be in the same place as Lilly. She wondered if he'd planted GPS on her or something? Because she had found shop premises right on the main street with immediate occupancy, she worked from there every day now. On her laptop creating a website for online sales and buzz marketing before opening plus organising a buying trip to Sydney.

With her excitement off the scale, in the evenings at the beach house found her sprawled over a lounge chair with sketch pad in hand giving it a shot at her own design creating a line of trendy casual wear with a stylish edge.

But today, again, the good-looking eyeful who seemed to have an abnormal interest in her life these days, appeared at her shopfront door with plastic tubs of Asian takeaway. Lilly's stomach rumbled in anticipation.

'Are you stalking me?' she tried to sound annoyed.

'Absolutely.'

'Creepy.'

'Not really. I figured while I'm around I can keep an eye out for you.'

'In Inlet Creek?' Lilly scoffed. 'Don't bother. I have two sisters, their partners and a tiger cub nephew for that.'

'Maybe they won't need to forever,' he hinted.

'I don't need defending.'

'Well sometimes we don't know what we need, do we Lilly?' he drawled, winking.

What a charmer! Using that sexy voice he dialled back to just soft and deep enough so she felt like it was only for her.

He was saying all the right things but then so had Oliver. Then she felt bad for such mean thoughts. Sam Ballard was proving himself a man of character, had dumped all business dealings with his criminal father and seemed happy to reinvent himself in a small seaside town.

'You got lucky with your shop position.' He set the food on her new shop counter. 'Mind if I stay and eat with you?'

Did she have a choice? Lilly shrugged. 'Up to you.'

'I'm a Master Builder and looking for work. If you need anything structural done . . . '

'I'll keep you in mind.' Too late, that was already happening. Handsome and rugged Sam Ballard was proving tricky to ignore.

* * *

After discussions that went around in circles each time, always yielding the same answer, the sisters finally decided to sell *Georgina Downs* and it was reluctantly placed on the market.

On the phone call Maddie made to inform their mother out at the station, Elizabeth snapped, 'About time,' and then announced her flight back to England in two days. 'I shall come to stay in the beach house overnight before I leave.'

After Maddie hung up, the daughters discussed her imminent arrival.

'Well I'm unpacked and settled up in the loft,' Lilly said, 'and you and Tommy are in the two main bedrooms downstairs, so if mother is only here for the one night, she can have the small spare room at the back.'

'She won't be impressed,' Maddie warned.

'Do we care?'

★　★　★

Even for only a matter of hours, Elizabeth under the beach house roof cramped her daughters' lives. As was their nightly ritual, sometimes with Daisy as well who never needed an invitation, Maddie and Lilly poured wine, chatting and laughing together at the kitchen island preparing the evening meal.

Even for the one evening their mother was present, after refills all round she said critically, 'Haven't you girls drunk enough?'

'Goodness, Mother, we're just getting started,' Maddie chuckled. 'A rather nice red Jack recommended. Sure you won't join us?'

'I think not.' She stalked out to the front porch, unsociably braving the chill night air in her own company but leaving the door open.

The sisters watched her from inside, shaking their heads and grinning but they didn't smile for long. As if in slow motion and possibly hindered by their pleasant state of alcoholic relaxation, they were slow to register the impending disaster. Daisy was striding up from the beach, taking the shallow broad steps onto the porch.

Indoors, Maddie and Lilly jointly spluttered into their wine.

'We didn't warn Daisy that mother's here!' Maddie hissed. She slid from a stool but Lilly caught her arm, holding her back.

'Too late,' she said, adding in a small voice, 'Daisy can handle herself.'

Because Daisy had her head down against the wind, Elizabeth saw her first. To their sister's credit, they saw Daisy's shock of recognition but quick recovery.

'Good evening, Elizabeth,' they heard her say politely, intending to move past and step inside.

'How dare you speak to me!' Elizabeth snapped. 'A wild child born of a hussy who sniffed around my husband.'

Rudely accosted, Daisy remained but said quietly, 'My parents were married. After they divorced, George always approached Ailie. Not the other way around.'

'Liar. My husband was a respectable man. He did not chase women.'

'I didn't say he did but my parents were drawn to each other beyond what either of them could control. I'm inspired that my parents loved each other so deeply and truly sorry for the predicament that placed you in and the unhappiness it must have caused.'

Elizabeth scoffed. 'Miss High and Mighty, what would you know of such things?'

'I do actually. Only recently I helped a dear friend reunite with his long lost love. True love is a precious thing. Life's gift. It survives no matter what.'

Elizabeth uttered a low growl of rage. 'I will not stay here and be lectured by a snip of a child. You have no idea.'

When she rose and returned indoors, Maddie and Lilly scrambled from eavesdropping in the middle of the room, fussing with meal preparation again at the kitchen island bench.

Elizabeth strode past them and down the hallway. 'I'm taking a bath. I do not wish to be disturbed and I shall be leaving first thing in the morning.' They heard the small back bedroom door slam.

'She'll be starving by breakfast,' Lilly said.

Maddie sighed. 'I'll take her to the airport shuttle pick up point in town in the morning.'

A shaken Daisy sauntered into the living room. Maddie and Lilly each grabbed her for a hug then filled her a glass.

'We're so sorry,' Lilly mouthed silently.

Ignoring dinner, they followed Daisy back outside again. All three sat on the top beach step, huddled together, shoulder to shoulder, looking out on the restless moon-washed sea across the sand. For a long while no one spoke.

Eventually Lilly said, 'It's not my place to ever apologise for my mother, Daisy. After speaking to you so cruelly she should do that herself. But I'm so sorry you were exposed to that.'

Daisy linked her arm and sighed. 'It's the conversation we were always destined to have. It saddens me to think she's dwelling on Ailie and the past when she has just lost George. I've been going to bed every night and sobbing for him. Poor Jack,' she managed a watery grin, 'neither of us is getting much sleep. Maybe Elizabeth has been doing the same but she certainly doesn't give that impression.'

'Do you know what?' Lilly turned to Maddie on her other side, 'when mother goes back to England, I doubt I'll miss her.' She sniffed and tears began rolling down her cheeks. 'What a pitiful admission about the woman who gave birth to me.'

Maddie reached out and squeezed her hand. 'We'll weather this together. She's not an easy person to know.'

'And now none of us has father either. For all his faults, there was a bloody decent bloke.'

The nostalgic moment of unity brought tears through laughter, clinking of glasses and refills. Daisy decided not to stay for dinner after all, judging it best to disappear. But after bonding in the wake of the evening's mess, Lilly realised that although they had only intermittently been a part of each other's childhoods, they were a vital part of the present together and would be important in each other's future.

'Here's to sisters,' she made a final toast.

★ ★ ★

Next morning, a thin-mouthed tense Elizabeth appeared for breakfast, dragging her two oversized suitcases ready for departure.

'You should be coming with me,' she blasted Lilly.

'No, Mother. I'm not your responsibility anymore.' She had two sisters for support and guidance, not to mention a rather gorgeous man hovering in the wings. Which she would pursue when she felt ready. 'I'm going to pursue my own goals from now on. Make my own decisions and mistakes.'

'That young man you're flaunting in front of us all is surely one of them.'

Lilly frowned, her defences bristling. 'Sam Ballard?'

'He's just a tradesman and his father is a felon.'

'No, Mother, Oliver was my biggest mistake.' She paused in reflection and a naughty smile tugged the corners of her mouth. 'Sam Ballard on the other hand — '

'Forget that boy,' her mother scoffed, 'he'll always be penniless.'

'But love isn't about money, is it mother? You married father because you thought he was the Australian equivalent of landed gentry but that didn't make you happy, did it?'

'I had competition!' Elizabeth hissed bitterly.

'Only in your mind. That's the pity of it all. You made yourself miserable.'

'How dare you speak to me like that?'

'I'm only voicing the truth you've never wanted to hear.' While their mother stayed white-faced and silent in shock, Maddie stepped in to say firmly, 'You can't airbrush Daisy and Ailie from our lives. Whether you like it or not, they will always be a part of our family. Now if you're ready, I'll take you to the airport shuttle.'

28

Within months, *Georgina Downs* station was sold. The inevitability of passing from the Harwood family into other hands was mixed with more than a tinge of sadness. Daisy and Jack had returned from France so the girls spent one last nostalgic time together at the half empty homestead sorting through the remaining contents deciding what they each wanted as keepsakes and mementoes of their former home.

Everything else was auctioned. On that day, neighbours and family friends from far and wide in the district turned up to attend. A chance for the sisters to say their goodbyes and put on one last fantastic country spread for afternoon tea.

The tearful farewell to Kirra who was moving further west back to her mob was a jolt to their emotions. Cultural connection to the land was of great significance to aboriginal people which the girls respected but their station cook would always be in their hearts and was offered an open invitation any time she wanted to leave the country of her birth to visit them on the coast.

With the four wheel drive and hired trailer loaded, Maddie and Lilly, more so than Daisy, found it hard closing the massive big front door on the house for the last time and walking away.

'I feel like we're deserting Father and leaving him here,' Lilly choked up. Maddie hugged her and they both swiped at mutual tears.

Daisy joined them for a group hug. 'We'll go visit his grave together, yeah?'

When they recovered they all bundled into their vehicle and drove away, not looking back.

'Mother sent a one page note on embossed letterhead giving me her new address,' Lilly said indifferently as they headed toward the coast. 'We'll need to keep in touch with her.'

Maddie sighed. 'Yes.'

'You going to visit?'

'England? Not any time soon. You?'

'As if.'

'When the station settlement goes through, I can't wait to tell Uncle Harry our proposition,' Daisy grinned.

The one highlight in an otherwise sentimental time for all of them was knowing what they had unanimously agreed to do. Within the month, the momentous day came.

'Well girls,' Maddie beamed as they gathered in the beach house as arranged late one mild winter afternoon, each holding fat cheques, 'it's official. We're seriously cashed up. Now let's go do what Father would want and give some of it away.'

Daisy disappeared temporarily to fetch Harry from Jack's apartment. When they returned, a bottle of fizz was already chilled and opened.

'Champagne, huh? Never had the stuff. What are we celebratin'?'

'Our news.'

When everyone was comfortably seated around the blazing winter fire with fluted glasses filled and bubbling, Maddie began.

'Firstly as you know, we've sold the sheep station to a lovely big family who we are so pleased to know already consider our beautiful old house like home. There will be challenges as there always are on the land but I hope they know much happiness and the blessings of a country life.'

Everyone clinked glasses and toasted to that.

'Next,' Maddie beamed at Harry, 'my sisters and I believe we have a solution to your problem. Putting in equal shares of our inheritance,' she swept a smiling gaze between them, 'we would like to buy your bush block. This will enable you, at long last, to get your hands on your favourite cottage in the retirement complex here in the Creek that you've had your eye on.'

They all noticed a glint of moisture in Harry's eyes as he looked away. 'Well now,' he dragged his emotions in check and cleared his throat, 'that's mighty generous. But what are you three going to do with a ten acre bush block?'

'Oh, we're not keeping it,' Lilly jumped in, smiling with excitement. 'We're donating it right back to the local council to become part of the surrounding protected Bushland Reserve. Which, I might add, will never be open to any form of development.'

Harry shook his head. 'Well, I'll be damned.'

'So you can go wander over it whenever you like,' Maddie said. 'It's public land.'

'If it's okay with you, Uncle Harry, once you've named your price, we'll go sign the contract in the morning.'

'Suits me just fine.' He raised his glass and

took another hesitant sip of his bubbly wine. 'This stuff ain't so bad. Like soft drink but not as sweet.'

Amid the laughter that rolled in a wave around the room, three ruggedly handsome men and one small boy appeared from elsewhere in the beach house.

Lilly gasped in surprise to see Sam in the shack again and felt her face flush with embarrassment. He hadn't been invited here since that first significant confrontation months ago when he came calling to buy up all the Harwood land for his father's hideous development.

One wry glance at her sisters sharing an amused grin told her Maddie and Daisy had set this up.

Neither Josh nor Jack needed GPS to find their women, strolling over to claim them with a possessive arm and lingering kisses.

Lilly just wanted to stare at Sam but was afraid to look. They had met each other around town but Sam seemed to get her message, keep his distance and take it slow. He was building up his new construction company and Lilly had hit the ground running since opening her boutique, setting up online mail ordering and taking buying trips to Sydney.

Which tonight just left the two singles awkwardly hovering. Well, Lilly felt awkward. Sam seemed pleased with himself and in a stride or two was beside her.

'Lilly,' he drawled, 'always a pleasure to see you. Just want you to know I'm here for you. Be around if you need me.'

Okay so he was putting himself out there that he wasn't going anywhere and was available. For her. No pressure! And made it clear the next approach should come from her.

Lilly panicked. She was so attracted to this man, in every way, and so soon on the heels of Oliver. Scary. She had grown to believe in Sam Ballard and knew she just needed to trust again. He was different. Nothing like her ex so she just had to lower her guard. Maybe this guy deserved a chance after all.

'You're looking pale, Lilly,' Sam murmured. 'Can I get you another drink?'

It's not drink I need, it's you. 'No, thank you.'

'Anything else I can do for you right now?'

Now there was a loaded question so Lilly took her cue and blurted out with way less confidence than she felt, horrified to hear herself flirting, 'Maybe stick around?'

With a cheeky grinning thumbs up, he murmured, 'Done.'

What a smile did to Sam Ballard's face was out of this world. Those blue eyes lit up and positively sparkled, tiny lines creased the corners of his eyes and she just wanted to melt against that big chest and into his arms.

If he took one step closer she wouldn't be responsible for her actions.

He not only closed the gap between them but the cheeky beggar took the liberty of scooping an arm about her tiny waist and stealing a long slow kiss. Their first. Which blew her mind and made her long for more.

Lilly was vaguely aware that someone in the room cleared their throat and someone else gave a soft whistle. Self-conscious but lapping up Sam's undivided attention, she just cringed in silence. She didn't care about the others because Sam's lips were close to her ear and he was whispering sweet nothings that set her heart racing with promises.

Despite the usual miserable winter weather along the coast, the future in Inlet Creek was looking kind of sunny.

The champagne corks continued to pop, Tommy squealing with delight each time. Daisy and Maddie produced grazing food from somewhere while conversation ebbed and flowed. Uncle Harry contentedly in the centre of it all, one small boy drawn to his knee.

As Lilly's gaze wandered around the room, her heart burst with happiness.

Maddie and Josh had found their ideal rural retreat thirty minutes south of Inlet Creek, ideal for country life and riding horses. A great place for little Tommy to grow up and attend the local small country school. Their acreage still close enough for the aunts and uncles to come visit. Josh had qualified and joined the Marine Rescue, already rostered on call at all hours to work along the south coast.

The latest announcement only days before had been Daisy and Jack planning a wedding at Christmas while the family were all together.

'Simple, floral and on the beach in front of the shack,' the future bride had declared, 'with my sisters beside me.' Then she teased, 'Maddie, you and Josh set a date?'

'Not really but we both figure it should be soon because we're pregnant!'

Lilly had screamed with excitement. 'Another little Seymour commando.'

'Well this time I'm kind of hoping I get to buy pink,' Maddie admitted.

So that had been another excuse for a big family meet up in the beach shack and tonight they all found another reason to gather.

Later, Lilly stood with her sisters on the top step down to the beach, arms around each other, looking out to an endless horizon, overcome by a moment of wistful reflection and thinking that anything was possible.

Daisy sighed, glanced behind and admired the beach shack with its blue painted timber walls and porch railing gleaming in the moonlight. 'Well, we might not have a big old family homestead anymore but I just know George is looking down on all of us and we're going to make a whole bunch of new wonderful memories here.'

'Yeah,' Maddie nodded. 'I think Father would be pleased.'

'By blood we're all bound together.' Lilly said.

'Funny you should say that,' Daisy murmured. 'Granny Sheldon always said *Don't forget your sisters.* When I was small I didn't understand so I asked what she meant. She said I will love my husband and my children but I will always need sisters. All the women who will come into my life.'

'I'll drink to that,' Maddie agreed.

'Oh come on, girls,' Daisy chuckled, disengaging herself from her siblings and beginning to strip off. 'We have heaps to celebrate. Let's do it with a midnight swim.'

'Skinny dipping!' Lilly squealed. 'You're mad. It's freezing.'

'It will wake you up.'

Maddie only hesitated for a moment. 'Hell, why not?' and peeled off her warm gear.

Lilly was the slowest and the last. Sam hadn't seen her without clothes on. Yet. So she nervously shimmied out of them creating a heap on the powdery soft sand and raced across the beach before the guys saw them and realised what they were doing. She gasped at the shoreline as she plunged her feet into the waves, waded and dived in.

★ ★ ★

In the shack, three men soon realised the sisters were missing and why. A larrikin smile spread around the room among them.

'So we should make sure the girls are okay, non?' Jack suggested.

Sam nodded and rose, already unbuttoning his shirt. 'Inclined to agree. You and Daisy thinking about making babies of your own yet?'

Jack pulled a slow grin. 'We work on it.'

'Pleased to hear it, mate,' Josh drawled, pulling off his sweater and kicking off his boots.

Sam slapped the men who he hoped would become his brothers-in-law on their bare backs as they eagerly dragged off their gear, streaked

407

down to the water's edge and stepped God-like, shiny and naked into the surf to go play lifeguard for their women.

'Can we go in, Grampa Harry?' Tommy pleaded, looking longingly out through the porch window and into the darkness.

'Maybe next time, son,' the old man hid a grin. 'Tonight belongs to Mummy and her sisters.'

We do hope that you have enjoyed reading this large print book.

Did you know that all of our titles are available for purchase?

We publish a wide range of high quality large print books including:
Romances, Mysteries, Classics
General Fiction
Non Fiction and Westerns

Special interest titles available in large print are:
The Little Oxford Dictionary
Music Book
Song Book
Hymn Book
Service Book

Also available from us courtesy of Oxford University Press:
Young Readers' Dictionary
(large print edition)
Young Readers' Thesaurus
(large print edition)

For further information or a free brochure, please contact us at:
Ulverscroft Large Print Books Ltd.,
The Green, Bradgate Road, Anstey,
Leicester, LE7 7FU, England.
Tel: (00 44) 0116 236 4325
Fax: (00 44) 0116 234 0205

Other titles published by Ulverscroft:

MAGGIE'S GARDEN

Noelene Jenkinson

On the rebound from being dumped after ten years with the man she'd hoped would be the father of her children, Maggie Ellis buys a neglected cottage in Tingara on acreage to start her life over and fulfil her dream of owning a garden nursery. Divorced truck driver and single dad Nick Logan has his hands full enough raising three sons alone without getting distracted by his new neighbour. As determined as Maggie and Nick are to leave their pasts behind and forget about relationships for a while, however, they can't deny the chemistry between them. But Nick already has a family, and Maggie wants children of her own. Can the two of them overcome their difficulties and allow their love to grow?

HANNAH'S HOLIDAY

Noelene Jenkinson

Workaholic accountant Hannah Charles takes a leap of faith and a badly needed holiday in a house swap from the Cotswolds to converted St. Anne's church in Tingara, Australia. There she meets handsome architect-cum-artist Will Bennett, who lives an alternative lifestyle in the small country town, and an electric attraction ensues. But Hannah is haunted by the recent deaths of her parents, which drives her to want to help others with family problems of their own — including Will, who is estranged from his parents and is less than receptive to Hannah's efforts to reunite them. When she's warned by an ex-lover of his not to fall for the charms of a 'bad boy hippie', she begins to wonder if a holiday fling is worth the heartache. Can love grow despite the challenges?

OUTBACK TREASURE

Noelene Jenkinson

Wrongly disgraced and her career left in tatters, palaeontologist Darcy Manning embarks on a mission to expose the fossil smuggling syndicate responsible, to clear her name and reputation. But how will she resist alluring country boy and fellow fossil-hunter Mitch Beaumont, when he is such a crucial piece of the puzzle? Set at Matilda Station in outback Queensland, *Outback Treasure* is one woman's story of a search for truth and justice, even at the risk of her own heart.